For Cheryl -

I hope you'll stay with the
series with book 4!

Thanks again!

John Griffith

THE TIME OF

RECKONING

THE LION STRIKES

BY

JOHN HOFFERT

Copyright © 2004 by John Hoffert

ISBN 0-7414-2207-7

Published by:

INFINITY
PUBLISHING.COM

1094 New DeHaven Street, Suite 100
West Conshohocken, PA 19428-2713
Info@buybooksontheweb.com
www.buybooksontheweb.com
Toll-free (877) BUY BOOK
Local Phone (610) 941-9999
Fax (610) 941-9959

Printed in the United States of America

Printed on Recycled Paper

Published July 2005

ACKNOWLEDGEMENTS

I have to say, so far this has been the easiest of the series in all aspects: 6 months from start to finish, no cases of the dreaded writer's block- even the cover art concept came together abruptly! It's probably because this is the end of the first part of the series. I still have no idea how far I'll be able to take it, but I think at minimum there will be three more installments...

As for the 'thank you's, we have the usual suspects: Cyndi again was my chief sounding board. Again, I appreciate all your help, and beware- I'll be getting underway with book 4 in October, once I've recharged my batteries. Dr. and Mrs. Howell, thanks very much for your input; you really helped me improve upon a couple parts of the story during my visit- and thanks again for your hospitality! Same with you, Cindy! Thanks also to Dale for your input. Mark, I think we agree that this was our favorite of the three covers. Thank you for your effort and your time. Lastly, but definitely not leastly, a big 'thank you' to my family, my extended family (you know who you are!) and my friends for your continued encouragement and support. You all help keep the wheels spinning.

And, off we go! I hope you enjoy!

- John

P.S. This was a classic case of 'open mouth, insert foot'. I ended up having to do the edit from hell on this one, as I pushed it out too quickly. The edit took as long as the first draft! Well, lesson learned, and the book is better for it...

Prologue

March 12, 2003

"Gee, Harry, I don't know if I've ever seen you so focused. I'd think you were watching one of those porno flicks you tell your buddies about."

That shook Detective Lawson out of his concentration and he glanced at his spunky partner, who was twenty years his junior and very sharp. She was quite sexy, but not conventionally so. Most guys on the force considered her aloof, unattainable and possibly not interested in men. She dressed very conservatively as part of her effort to keep her colleagues focused on her abilities as a cop, which, as Harry would attest, were very impressive.

She was Daddy's girl through and through, and had followed his path; her father served with distinction on the Force for thirty-five years. Inexplicably, in late '97, he committed suicide. No one brought that up in Danni's presence out of respect for both of them. "Uh-huh, I figured you were listening in on some of those conversations. If you're so interested, you could watch one with me- might loosen you up a little. How long has it been since your last date, anyway? You should try doing something other than working and working out."

Detective Danielle Searles held up her hand. "No, thanks-I'll pass. Maybe you should try *doing* either or both of those things for a change- might make you a better detective."

Harry laughed. "You need to speak your mind, Danni; you hold way too much back!"

She smiled. "I will say this, though- I'm glad you and Spence are so familiar with the area. God only knows how long it would have taken us to find this spot if you two weren't with us, although Spence seems a bit sharper!"

"Yeah, yeah! I used to know this watershed area- and this stretch of it in particular- probably better than anybody did. Guess I got a bit rusty, huh? I'll tell you this much; I wish we had a better reason to be here at this hour. Fuckin' guy and his 'anonymous tip'-how do we know he's not some worthless, brain-dead crack-head havin' a bad trip? Callin' the station at four-thirty in the morning...you know, this has all the makings of some damned

i

wild goose chase. I was up way too late last night to deal with such bullshit since 7 AM."

The crew had been digging for an hour and so far, no body. Harry had suggested they pack it up a while ago, which was reasonable, no doubt, but Danni wanted to be sure. After all, they'd done this much already. "Well, they're about five feet down. If there is a body here, whoever buried it wanted to make sure it wasn't found easily. They might have gone the full six, or more..."

"Maybe, but I doubt it. I still think this is all a hoax. 'It's been there for some time'- what could he have meant? A few years? Decades? And why in the hell did he have to tell us this today, in a fucking cold rainstorm? Too bad his 'crisis of conscience' couldn't have come when it was a little nicer out. I'm tellin' you all, we need to pack this shit up."

"Has anyone ever told you that you bitch a lot, Harry?"

One of the guys in the hole piped up. "Yeah, especially when *you* ain't even doin' any diggin'!"

They all laughed and Harry retorted, "Hey- I'm only trying to look out for you guys."

"Yeah, right! Next you'll try ta sell me some-"

"Whoa- I think I've got something here."

Harry froze for a moment, then jumped down into the hole and looked at what one of the others pointed out. The digger had hit a wooden plank with his pickaxe.

"Gimme that shovel, Spence." Harry grabbed it and cleared away more earth.

It was what they suspected, and after several more minutes of digging, they were in position to pry the lid off.

"Stand back, you guys. Depending on how long this has been here, there's a chance what's inside might help reacquaint you with your breakfasts..."

"What do you mean, it's gone?! How could that have happened?! This had better not be some kind of joke."

"It isn't, John. The sample's gone." The semen sample from Josh Strauss, which was the only physical evidence of him on record, had been 'misplaced' at the FBI, according to the most senior official Tom had been able to reach. Tom decided that he should be the one to tell John. "I don't know what happened to it-your guess is as good as mine. No one can track it down; that's their story."

"Those people could fuck up a free lunch, then turn around and somehow make you pay for it. As much as we've been in contact with them about that sample, as many tests and checks that have been made and some incompetent idiot loses it..."

"I know. I'm not happy about it, either, nor is Doctor Hughes. Now we have nothing on him, and still, we have no idea where to look."

"*Dammit...*"

"We've been at a dead end since the beginning, anyway, and now this...we probably can expect that the investigation at the least will be curtailed further. It hasn't been a big priority for months. They might even drop it altogether; you only can bang your head against the wall for so long."

"*They* might drop it, but you can be sure that I won't."

"With nothing to go on, what can you do? I know how badly you want to-"

"No, you don't, Tom. You don't know how badly I want to get him," John said as his blood began to boil again. "I'm not gonna miss anything this time- count on that...

"...somehow, no matter how long it takes or what I have to do, I *will* get him."

"Well, hello there! How are you?"

Kim had walked into the convenience store, her mind set on an ice cream after the impromptu display she'd put on at the local ice skating rink. Even as cold as it was, which prompted her to add her mittens, scarf and wool hat to the ski jacket she wore over her leotard and tights, she had the urge nonetheless.

To her surprise she'd been able to land a double jump, which she was very happy with since she hadn't even attempted one in some time. She also did a few tough spins along with two airborne splits. Some people had gathered around to watch her, their curiosity piqued when they saw the cameraman, who was following John and her around, filming her. They were further intrigued when they realized who she was and they applauded her when she finished. After Kim curtsied to them, she and John greeted them and mingled while their bodyguards monitored everyone carefully. Before long they took off.

They were to go right to their bed and breakfast, but Kim's hankering for her favorite treat, which she allowed herself on occasion, delayed them in getting back there. The three customers in front of her delayed her a bit more, but that delay brought her face-to-face with the child, who stared at her.

"Oh, you're shy, aren't you?" Kim squatted down, now eye-level with her, and smiled. "My name is Kim. What's yours?"

Still no response. Kim looked up at the man with her, who held her hand with what looked to be a very firm grip, and faced forward. "What's her name?"

He didn't answer, and moved up to the counter when his turn came. He pushed his money toward the cashier before she even said anything and didn't acknowledge her greeting.

Kim frowned, and focused again on the little girl, who continued to look at her with the same expression. She began to worry about something she noticed in the child's doe-like eyes...

...then she sensed it and stood up. "Excuse-"

That was all Kim was able to say before the man turned and took a swing at her, but he was slow and clumsy, which the alcohol she smelled on his breath probably contributed to, and she was ready. She ducked and counterattacked, landing a shot to his solar plexus that staggered him just enough.

In the next instant, the man was on the floor and pinned, with Herb holding his wrist, having bent his arm up behind him in what surely was a painful position. Mel instructed the cashier to call the police, which she did quickly. Just like that, it was over.

When the little girl ran toward her, Kim knelt back down and took her into her arms. "It's all right, Honey- you're safe now," she soothed as she held the sobbing child.

"You were *great!*" The cashier gushed as she came around and stood next to Kim. "That was the most awesome thing I've ever seen! Where did you learn to fight like that?"

John rushed in with the other two bodyguards. "What happened?! Are you all right?"

"We're fine, John. That man over there had- oh, I still don't know your name, Sweetie." Kim brushed away her tears.

"My name is Rachel."

"I'm glad to meet you, Rachel. Do you have a Mommy and Daddy?"

"That's my Daddy," she said, pointing at the man subdued on the floor.

"Oh…well, we're going to get in touch with your Mommy and get you back to her, Ok? While we're doing that, Mister John, our nice friends and I will take care of you."

The police arrived quickly and took the man into custody after getting statements from everyone in the store. All present found out that the man indeed was wanted for suspicion of abducting Rachel- suspicions that obviously were well founded. Once they were finished, Kim took the girl's hand into hers and they walked to the car, flanked closely by the bodyguards.

It wasn't long before they reached Rachel's mother, who'd been watching the news when the story of the rescue came on. Her gratitude came through loud and clear over the phone and already she was on her way to be reunited with her daughter.

Rachel lay in Kim's lap as they rode to the place where she and John were staying. While she stroked the child's hair, Kim couldn't help but reflect once more on her inability to conceive that as yet no one understood. Feelings of desolation were hitting her hard.

It didn't help when she looked up at John, who stared straight ahead, deep in thought, distracted and moody. That was becoming a more common sight.

She was beginning to worry about him; more and more, she was convinced that he was slipping back into an old habit. *What are you keeping from me, John? And, after all we've been through, why? Why would you do that?*

Also upsetting her was that she needed him and he wasn't available…

Kim wasn't aware that she'd drifted. He brought her back when he kissed away a tear as it fell, then traced along her cheek, smiling tenderly at her while he did. He looked at Rachel, who had fallen asleep, then back at her.

"You're thinking about it again…"

Compounding her deteriorating spirits was the guilt that rushed in over her touch of anger toward him a moment ago. The high she'd been on was all but gone, and so suddenly.

Knowing it would fail, she gave up her effort to stop herself from crying and let John pull her close to him. "I'm sorry."

"Shhhh. It's all right. I know where you are; I saw it as soon as Rachel ran to you."

"We're never going to have-"

"Don't say it, Kim; don't think that way. It's not your fault. We're doing everything right and we have to keep it up. I hate what this is doing to you- how much it's tearing you up. We have to keep believing that our day will come, though. I know how much you want a baby. I do, too. I also know it's hard to try to stay positive, but can you do that, Honey?"

She sniffed, but managed a smile. "I'll try- I promise."

After they kissed, she sighed and relaxed against him. She glanced at Rachel, who hadn't even budged, then turned back to John. "Thank you; I needed that."

Kim fondly recalled his similar reaction just a couple weeks ago when a reporter asked her if or when she planned to have children. The reporter wasn't being malicious, but it hurt nonetheless. John's protectiveness toward her kicked right in; he ended the interview, got her out of there and back to the privacy of their room. Contrary to her knee-jerk reaction minutes earlier, virtually every time when she needed him to be, he was there for her...

...which made her want to do the same thing for him, if he would let her. "May I ask you something?"

"Sure."

"Lately I've noticed that-...well, there are times when you're preoccupied, and you get really quiet. I've seen you that way before; I know it's something other than the campaign that's troubling you. Would you tell me what it is?" She was disappointed when she saw the shroud fall over him again, and knew what his answer would be before he even said it.

"It's...a little complicated. I don't have much information on it right now, so there's not much to tell, anyway."

"But what is it? Maybe I can help somehow."

John looked into her upturned face and gave her a smooch. "You already are, just by being with me. You shouldn't worry- it's not a big deal. I can handle it."

Not wanting to pester him, she relented for the time being. However, she wasn't able to do what he said and not worry. It had been a long time since he'd held anything back from her, which was something she'd hoped he'd never do again.

All she could do now was hope he'd either tell her soon, resolve the problem, or both, because in spite of what he claimed, this preoccupation was starting to take away from his concentration on the campaign, and also their marriage- at least, certain aspects of it. Valentine's Day had been a very welcome exception, but the overall trend was downward. It wasn't a case of him ignoring her, but it was clear to her that he was focused on something other than the race.

Worse, she was pretty sure she knew the identity of a major contributor to his increasing tension and occasional anger: Joshua Strauss. Every time his name came up in the news, conversation or anywhere, John's fist would clench, or his eyes would narrow.

I guess I should have expected this...

"...and the latest stop on their lengthy campaign trail is Boston, Massachusetts, where the couple was received warmly. The turnouts at his forums seem to be increasing as time goes on, and markedly so since this past November 4th.

"I would say Mrs. Stratton has done her part to keep the trend of those turnouts on the upswing. This afternoon she took to the rink and showed that she's some kind of a dancer on the ice. There's no denying her talent and ability in that realm; I wasn't surprised to learn that when she was only twelve she was a rising star in the world of figure skating. She sure came alive when the music started to play; those who were there stood back and watched her go. She fell on her first attempt at a double jump, but did that stop her? Unh-uh! She got right up, brushed herself off and proceeded to nail that same jump on her second attempt. Will we see a parallel drawn between that and her husband's run for the White House? He came up short in his first run, but he picked himself up as well and is going for it again.

"However, there's at least one man out there who underestimated the woman who could become our First Lady-perhaps because of her looks and femininity. That brings me to the main reason why she made the headlines today. Mrs. Stratton played a vital role in the rescue of little Rachel Williamson from her non-custodial father, who had beaten his ex-wife- the girl's mother-, abducted the child and fled.

"The Amber Alert had just gone out when the rescue took place. With that heroic act by Mrs. Stratton, we see yet another dimension of this fascinating young woman. The cashier at the convenience store where this episode took place had nothing but praises for her. Needless to say, a very grateful little girl and her mother echo those praises. Indeed, Kimberly Stratton is quite a woman, but not everyone sees her in a positive light, as evidenced by this rant from religious leader Pat Elwell:"

"...we Christians must unite and stop the march of this Godless, socialistic menace to our great nation and his Jezebel, who dresses and acts like the harlot she is! That billboard of this most sinful temptress hanging up for all to see over the most sinful city in our nation is all the proof we need! You don't fool us, Kimberly Stratton, making us think you're cleaning up your act! We see right through you! We will not allow you to represent our country and glorify the negative example you set for our young women!"

"Mister Elwell's reference, of course, is to that famous promotional billboard, which was moved to the Las Vegas strip, depicting Mrs. Stratton in a very sexy and revealing outfit as she posed in front of a huge male tiger. Elwell's hellfire-and-brimstone tirade went on for several more minutes, but don't worry- I won't subject you to it. I will show you Governor Stratton's retort, though:"

"That guy personifies narrow-mindedness. He's fixated on Kim's past, which is just that- the past. She posed for that shot when she was nineteen, for crying out loud! Any normal person who sees how she dresses would not come to such conclusions. My wife dresses a bit on the flashy side because she's very confident in herself and proud of the result of her efforts to keep herself in shape. I'm every bit as proud to be with her and I appreciate her efforts, too.

"Back to Mr. Elwell, he seems to get worse as the years go on. Isn't forgiveness one of the cornerstones of religion? Obviously, tolerance isn't in his mantra, which gives him a common point with the fanatical Islam fundamentalists. I think his congregation had better be careful with their loyalty to him. You saw how such blind faith panned out in 1978 for over 900 followers of the zealot Jim Jones, and Elwell is sounding more and more like him as the years roll on. Religious fervor can be very dangerous, if not deadly."

The camera went back to the anchorman. "No argument here. Mr. Elwell is getting pretty extreme and now, in light of Mrs. Stratton's action today, it looks like he'll be dining on some crow for his remarks directed at her. Wonder if he prefers light meat or dark. Then again, it might be hard for him to eat anything with his foot so deeply embedded in his mouth! I know- I'm a baaaad boy.

"Anyway, Governor Stratton caused another- and a bigger-stir later in the same conference. It started when one reporter brought up an issue he had with a point of criticism the Governor leveled against the major party candidates during the 2000 election; he brought that up right after this succinct and poignant part of the Governor's speech:"

"...we need to simplify things in our country- our tax code, our election system, our health care system, our educational system, our legal system, our trade and immigration policies-everything. The way it is now, things are so complicated that you need to be Einstein to figure it all out! It's ridiculous and, contrary to what all these lawyers would have you believe, it doesn't have to be like that. Under my administration, it *won't* be like that. Speaking of lawyers, they wield entirely too much power. I think it's time we took some of it away from them. We need far less lawyers and plenty more teachers and doctors."

"Mister Governor, you said just before the last election that you wouldn't even need six months to get your message out. Several congressmen who are presidential hopefuls- and President Black himself- brought up the point that you've been on the trail for the '04 election, on and off, since June of last year. What made you do what you railed against?"

"Necessity. The democrats and republicans get virtually all the media coverage; their message is the one that reaches so far because it's what's heard. Since the other parties like mine are left with the scraps, I had to take this action. The only real way I have to reach as many people as possible all over the country is to do what I'm doing. It's better having a forum, anyway, because I can answer directly the questions the people have. Best of all, based on some very good points some of the participants brought up, I've improved upon a couple solutions for the many problems we face. Their voices are being heard, and heeded as well."

"Mister Governor, I'm very curious about the remark you made a moment ago about reigning in the lawyers. How do you propose we do that?"

"For starters, capping their fees and salaries, including allowing them to take no more than 20% in any civil case. Add to that the tort reforms I propose that make the bringers of frivolous lawsuits and their lawyers responsible for both sides' court costs. If lawyers don't have the financial incentive to defend high-profile criminals or to push these lawsuits in which they make ridiculous demands in terms of money, the frivolous lawsuits will drop off. It also will become more difficult for high-profile criminals to abuse the system like they do and get away with all they do. The lawyers' motivation to help them buy their way out of the crimes they commit will be reduced, which I see as a good thing.

"It's a step toward equal justice for all- a step toward taking away the different set of rules that applies to the wealthy and also eliminating the excess of senseless lawsuits.

"Many lawyers complain about the outrageous tuition for law school- that's one thing they *won't* have to deal with anymore. We need to dissuade lawyers from the practice of twisting laws to justify even the most reprehensible behavior simply so they can win cases and get themselves on TV. In my system, lawyers who genuinely care about the underdog and also the pursuit and administration of true justice will be encouraged to pursue their quest while the greedy, unconscionable egomaniacs won't have so much motivation.

"Also in regard to civil cases, we need to place a cap on the maximum amount in damages a plaintiff can sue for. I suggest $5 million across the board for any individual civil case, including malpractice. I think that's reasonable. As a result, insurance companies- including malpractice insurance providers- would lower their premiums in turn, so it would be better for everyone."

"Don't you think you're giving the insurance companies too much credit there?"

"Put it this way- they'd be given the opportunity to do the right thing and lower their premiums. If they didn't, we'd sick the consumer watchdog groups on them and they'd face stiff penalties along with plenty of governmental interference. Plus, there would be all the resulting negative press- not good for business! Finally, if all those measures fail, then we'll simply make 'em drop their rates by way of legislation. We also need to revamp their policies and make sure that when disaster strikes, instead of trying to weasel out of paying claims like they do so many times, the insurance companies will fulfill their obligations."

"But what about the massive medical bills a plaintiff could have incurred?"

"That won't be applicable with the new health service. Also, doctors will be held to the highest possible standards. They can't be perfect- that shouldn't be expected of them or anyone-, but incompetence would be very costly for them and not just monetarily. However, the practice of pushing for excessive damages in these lawsuits has to be stopped; that's counterproductive on many levels."

"Sir, how do you respond to the latest criticism the other parties have directed toward you that you're an anti-capitalist, that you advocate overthrowing the government and that your reforms will spell the end of our way of life and possibly lead to anarchy?"

John laughed derisively. "That's how I respond! My reforms will end *their* way of life, which is what's scaring them. Make no mistake- they *are* scared and they have reason to be. With our victories in the last election and the multitude of promising prospects we have for those in this year and next, they know that they and their system are in deep trouble. They'll throw every distortion, concoction and outright lie they can at me to see if something sticks.

"That's what I expect from them, though, because the other parties don't believe in candor- they don't believe in being up front with you. That worries me. When leaders can't come clean and tell you things as they are, including when they make mistakes, they're not leaders at all and definitely are not examples for anyone to follow. Yes, that includes Mister Black. Despite how he wants you to believe that he sees things in black and white, he's typical of the state of politics today and also the state our nation is coming to.

"Many people are afraid- or for a host of reasons, unwilling- to say what they feel, whether it's right or wrong. Then, they figure their leaders lie or mislead, so why shouldn't they? The truth isn't fashionable; you're told to blunt your message so you won't offend anybody. Is that how you want your country to be? The most powerful nation in the world, but one in which people can't or won't tell the truth for fear of repercussions? I tell you without hesitation that's not how I want America to be and I will not back away from what I say under any circumstances.

"As for the message of my competition, it's all smoke and mirrors; their platform is weak at best and broken at worst. In many of the recent elections you've seen people not so much voting *for* one candidate as they were voting *against* another- the lesser of two evils scenario. The problem with that is you still have an evil- in this case, stagnation. We get these people in office that do nothing but churn out watered-down legislation that benefits no one other than special interest groups and lawyers. No one takes a stand for anything; all anyone wants to do is compromise. Then, if you disagree with the major parties and their candidates, they want to throw every bad name they can at you because you've caught on to them and they don't like it. It's your duty to speak up if you disagree, yet they discourage that!

"The two parties see us Progressives with real solutions that will deliver a new and drastically improved country in virtually every way. They can't handle that- they know they're not fooling anyone with their crap anymore, yet they still want you to vote for them and keep their corporate fat-cat friends in power. Their charges don't warrant a response other than for me to call them what they are- groundless, ridiculous and acts of desperation.

"To answer the other parts of your question, I'll say this- capitalism as we know it *is* failing us, and badly. It's become a license for corporate robber barons to rip off stockholders and their country at large, and rewrite the rules to suit themselves.

"In light of that, certain aspects of socialism- a couple of which are part of my platform- don't seem so bad, do they? My platform can be called egalitarianism insofar as I want all Americans to be on the same starting line and have an equal chance to succeed regardless of socioeconomic background and race. That has not been the case at any point in our history, but it *can* be the case very soon. My platform also is utilitarian, in that I want to do the greatest good for the greatest number of us.

"I do advocate the overthrow of *this* government because it doesn't represent its constituents or what's best for them. It routinely deceives and misleads. However, I call for a non-violent removal of them from office by way of the democratic process of voting. As for what my competition has to say, I'll just watch them wear themselves out while they throw their babble at anyone who will listen. The thing is, less people *are* listening to them. We're not buying this recycled garbage they're trying to sell us again."

"Sir, there's a constitutional question about you curtailing spending on campaigns, even when the candidate spends his or her own money. Isn't that a violation of free speech?"

"Maybe so, if you look at it from a purely legalistic standpoint, which is typical of the powers-that-be who want to use the letter of the law in order to keep us all in the doldrums of stagnation. Unfortunately, the double-talk and bait-and-switch tactics they use aren't considered violations of free speech, although they do violate the principles of common sense.

"In response to my critics and their charge, the war chest of a candidate with way too much personal wealth constitutes an unfair advantage over one who lacks that luxury. What they see as free speech, I see as a way for the wealthy to beat the people back and keep their stranglehold on power. Messages are lost in the money that affluent candidates spread around to buy votes and with all the advertising they do that their opponents can't do.

"In sum, many more people hear what the wealthy have to say in comparison to the ones with considerably less means. We need to put a stop to that. The same applies to the cash-raising machines we call major political parties, which are a big part of the problem. I've never seen such hypocrisy as I see in them."

"How so, Sir?"

"Well, during the primaries the democratic and republican candidates just beat up on each other endlessly. They smear and rip each other to shreds- tell us all the reasons why we absolutely should not vote for the other candidates. When the primaries end, they fall all over themselves praising each other, which makes you wonder why they even ran against each other in the first place!

"It's all a show. They just kiss and make up and put on their happy faces for everyone. They pander and they compromise their beliefs and ideals just so their party can win. That plays a big part in why nothing gets done; they're only energized during the race. I'm sick of it- sick of this endless cycle.

"Then come the favors for their friends and allies- big business and special interest groups. With as many times as the democrats and republicans have been bought and sold, they should be listed as commodities on the stock exchange! Even when those big businesses do us real damage, like Exxon with the Valdez disaster in '89, our government lets them get away with not paying the $5 billion in damages. They do little for the rest of our citizens other than throw us an occasional bone. That's the way things have been for a long time and another big part of why we're in the predicament we're in. It's a national version of the Tammany Hall days in New York City. The media also hinders us by giving way too much airtime to two parties.

"So, in the final analysis, which is the real evil? Would you allow the current establishment to wield the Constitution as their sword to silence the voice of the people that cries out for reform? Would you keep their broken system in place and continue to drive this country into the ground, or would you opt for real, substantial change that would benefit virtually all Americans?"

"But surely the Supreme Court would step in and strike any such measure down; already they've indicated that they would. What you're laying out is a direct violation of-"

"I would hope that the Supreme Court would do what's right and side with the 99% of us who would benefit from that change, which would allow those with broader interests to run for office. I'd also hope they'd support making life in general much better for the vast majority of our citizens via the cap on individual wealth.

"One measure I plan to take is to call for a constitutional convention during my first term as President in order to put into law my system- make it so no regressive-minded lawyers and/or judges can argue it away. In one fell swoop I would move to make Amendments out of my proposed changes that would benefit all of us except the wealthy elite. In truth, those changes would benefit them as well by making their country stronger, for those who choose to see the big picture."

"What if the Supreme Court ruled against your programs and you couldn't garner enough support for a convention?"

"Well, I could put those measures into practice bilaterally, via myself and the Congress, or unilaterally, if it came to that."

"So you would defy the Court?! That is drastically overstepping your authority!"

"Perhaps, but if my options were to do that or allow the system as is to go on, as long as the people are with me I *would* defy the Court- no question about it. What is right outweighs what is legal. What we Progressives are laying out to you is the right course of action for all, whether or not the courts choose to see it that way. In the end, it's what the people decide is best for them that counts- not someone else's interpretation of it.

"Consider this: how do you think our founding fathers would feel if they could see how things are today? If they could see what happened to their noble experiment- how big business runs America and determines the direction of our country, or the lack thereof? Things are bad today, everyone.

"Contrary to what some think, I hate having to stand before you and tell you this but no one else will. They say we're in good shape when, in reality, we're foundering on the reef. We're living in a modern version of a feudalistic society; we have executives and other corporate officers and/or crooks robbing us blind, destroying our environment and keeping our country in a state of stagnation. All the power is in their greedy hands.

"As far as I'm concerned, those in our federal government are accomplices because they're letting it happen while getting and giving favors in the process. And here I thought prostitution was *against* the law! It's illegal for women to sell sexual favors, yet elected officials can sell political favors and nothing happens to them! We need to clean out that den of vipers, which we Progressives already have begun to do with our victories last year and will continue to do over the next two.

"It starts at the top. If we can't bring about the changes we need from within the system, then maybe we *do* need to go outside it. Maybe we need to create a new system, like our founders, who also experienced taxation without representation.

"That said, I vow to do my utmost to bring those changes about by way of the Constitution once I become President. If that doesn't work, then, with the blessing of the citizens of this nation, I will find another way, use it and make our country better."

The camera went back to the anchorman again. "*Wow*!! I have never heard such language in all my years of covering campaigns! That's a powerful call to arms; he does seem to be trying to incite a revolution! Already there are strong reactions to it coming in from all over the country- including, of course, the democrats and republicans. No one can accuse this man of not telling it like he sees it! We really could have a battle royale in the works if he's elected.

"The Governor is spending a good bit of his own money on this tour. From the outset he's adamantly refused to accept any special interest, corporate or union money and he's been as good as his word. He's not advertising on television and he doesn't have a huge staff around him. Just as he said he would, he's keeping it simple. In his own words, he knows the course he wants to take and doesn't need pollsters and politicos to tell him what his opinions should be. He is insistent that any contributors to his campaign adhere to his hundred dollar limit per individual, which is what he vows to make law- along with the other campaign reforms he's outlined- once he's elected.

"The political world continues to reel from the impact of this fledgling party that Governor Stratton officially formed early last year. The name 'Progressive' suits them well, since his programs certainly are that. He was smart enough to realize he needed help-

and a lot of it- to advance his platform, so he embarked upon his campaign to recruit like-minded Americans to run for office. Scores of them stepped up to the plate and a number of them won their races.

"The Massachusetts contingent came up short in the interim election, but all have said they will run again. Governor Stratton's prediction that we would experience bigger turnouts at the polls sure came true, too! His home state of Maryland, of course, is where the Progressives had their biggest victories in 2000 and '02. In addition to Mister Stratton's successor, Laura Collins, winning her race, Progressives from The Old Line State captured a Senate seat from a long-entrenched democrat and sent six Representatives down I-95 to Washington, D.C. to boot! Along with their compatriots from other states, those new members of Congress are making their presence known in this legislative session.

"Although Maryland has the strongest voter base for the new party that poses the biggest threat to the established order that any third party ever has, that base seems to be spreading rapidly across the country. Six Senators, one each from Arkansas, Delaware, Louisiana, Minnesota, Missouri and Oregon along with sixteen Representatives- four from California, three each from Illinois and Ohio, two each from Michigan and Louisiana and one each from Indiana and Iowa form the rest of the Progressive contingent.

"With the gubernatorial races this year in Louisiana, Kentucky and Mississippi, we could see that contingent grow. Governor Stratton is stumping for Progressive candidates in those states, which could become good prospects for the party to capture more Governors' mansions. Mister Stratton's rising influence will be pitted against that of President Black in what could be a preview of the presidential election next year. As for 2004, the Progressive leader says there will be plenty more victories to follow, which is a sentiment echoed by everyone in that young- but growing, determined and vocal- political movement."

"*Movement* my ass- this is a fucking *earthquake*!!" Philip Raines, majority owner and CEO of Tizer Pharmeuticals, bellowed at the TV. After that he turned to his man- the one he knew only as 'Ray'. Raines often wondered about his background, which no one seemed to have much knowledge of. "So, do you still think I'm 'dreaming'? You still think 'those guys are a fluke'?

That 'Stratton's a flash in the pan who will have faded into the woodwork by next election'? That 'any Progressive will become irrelevant almost immediately'?"

'Ray' shrugged. "Maybe I was wrong."

"*Maybe*?! To say the fucking least, you were wrong! You didn't only miss the bull's-eye, you missed the whole dartboard, not to mention the wall behind it! This fucking guy's banging the drums of a form of socialism and a lot of people are starting to dance to his rhythm! Do you have any idea what'll happen if he's elected?! Our way of life *will* disappear- that's what'll happen!

"We'll lose everything! All our hard-earned money will go toward educating a bunch of ignorant, lazy bastards from every fucked up race we have in this wonderful melting pot of ours- probably none of whom will do anything that'll make any kind of difference- not to mention this universal health care farce of his! That alone will destroy my industry!

"Who in the *fuck* does this asshole think he is, Robin Hood?!! Trying to take away my right to keep what's rightfully mine…without me, twenty-four thousand people wouldn't have jobs! Every businessman I've talked to feels the same way! We deserve all we have- in fact, we deserve more than what we have because *we* make it happen! Our toils keep this country growing and moving forward, and he wants to penalize us for it!!'"

After letting a lot of his steam out, he relaxed. "I'm sorry about that rant. I hoped you'd have ended up being right about this son of a bitch and his movement, but he's strong- even stronger than I thought he'd be. He's also dangerous- *too* dangerous to ignore. I doubt we can rely on the majority of the population voting the way we want 'em to and keeping our people in office. We might have to consider doing something about him…

"…we certainly know what his main vulnerability is."

"You mean his wife." When Raines smiled, Ray went on. "Bad idea. She should not be harmed, even by accident- especially considering what she just did in saving that little girl. The public perception of her is sure to be even more favorable now. After today, most people might even forget that she ever was a stripper."

"Nobody who saw her dance will forget. I know I won't."

"Let's not digress here, all right? In the big picture, if she were to die he'd fall apart or, more likely, become even more powerful and determined than he is. With the outpour of public sympathy for him, he'd be a shoo-in. You don't want that."

"I didn't mean we should kill her."

"What, then…kidnap her?"

"It could be a very effective way of controlling him; there's no doubt that would distract him, at the very least. We saw what it did to him the last time she was abducted…"

Ray stood and walked over to the large window that overlooked the harbor. "She was grabbed twice in 2000, though- before she had security around her, which she has now."

"Which means they might not think it could happen again."

"I don't know about that. It would be risky. Not necessarily impossible, but definitely risky, and potentially costly, too. I'm sure you're thinking about what happened today- the way that guy she helped bust for taking his own kid was close enough to take a swing at her. My answer is yes, we might be able to create a situation that would give us the opportunity we needed. I'm just telling you, in my opinion it would be a lot harder than you think."

After a moment of deliberation, Raines turned away. "I see your point. Let's keep that in mind as a last resort, maybe. We really need to deal with him directly- find some way to make him look bad or discredit him somehow. There must be a weakness he has other than his wife, although I have yet to find one. We sure as hell won't be able to tempt him with another woman- even Ginger, my secretary.

"The bottom line is we have to stop him from becoming President. We'll have to see how things go in the Governor's races this year- see if Black's boys can dust his ass. If they do, we're all right. If Stratton's people win and it looks like things'll get worse, we'll have to finish the job his former Chief of Staff started. John Stratton sure can't hurt us when he's dead and I bet if we kill him, we kill the movement. That's usually how it works. Also, time is on our side; we have over twenty months until Election Day…"

He turned and looked purposefully at Ray before finishing his statement. "…a lot can happen in twenty months."

Chapter 1

May 8

Lieutenant Ike Miller, the head of the Missing Persons division of the Baltimore County Police leaned back. Two of his detectives, Lawson and Searles, sat across from him. "So we're no closer to determining who this guy was?"

Danni spoke up. "No, Sir. Based on what we have from the medical examiner, all we know is he died- was killed, rather- somewhere in between the late '60s and mid '70s. He'd been buried in that field off Warren Road in the Loch Raven watershed area ever since, presumably right after he was killed. We have little to go on other than that. We've tried every angle, every lead, even every reach and nothing pans out."

Harry joined in, too, in his delicate way. "Whoever the poor bastard was got the living shit beaten out of him- that much we *do* know. His jaw was all but crushed and so many teeth were knocked out of his head that we don't have a prayer of matching any kind of dental records. His right orbital bone was broken, left one fractured, five ribs on his right side broken, one broken and three fractured on his left…the actual cause of death can't be determined because of all the decomposition, but it doesn't take a genius to figure out the probable cause- or the multitude of 'em. We know whoever doled out this ass-whuppin' was strong as an ox, left-handed and highly pissed off. Obviously he wasn't the kind of guy you wanted to be around while he was in that state. To think the killer did all that damage with his bare hands…there was no blunt-force trauma with any bats, pipes, sticks or anything else. What could have caused him to do that? What could have set him off?"

Ike shook his head. "That's the million dollar question, I suppose. They think this corpse has been there since the early '70s, and really, they can't even be sure about that, can they?"

"No, Sir- that's what the Chief Examiner said, too."

"I figured as much. Same story for the mysterious caller who told us where to find that skeleton- we're no closer to finding out who *he* was, either. Damn…there has to be some way- some little hint we've overlooked. Something to do with where he was buried, maybe…

"So there weren't any possibilities from the cold case files, Danni?"

"Well, yes, Sir. We have a number of them, actually. It seems there's a list of missing persons cases between 1970 and 1975 numbering in the double-digits that never were solved, but our inability so far to make a positive ID on this one has been a big thorn in our side."

"No doubt. I guess it's time to think about enlisting some outside help," he said as he picked up the phone. "Stand by, you two. You might be taking a little ride to see someone..."

All in all, it had been quite a run for Tom. In under four months' time he would turn the reigns of the Missing Persons unit over to recently promoted Captain, which was bittersweet, as transitions always were.

The good news was that already he was being considered for promotion to Major. All the feedback from the high brass regarding his job performance was positive- and very much so, at that. From his first day as department head, Tom had done all he could to familiarize himself with the active cases his detectives were looking into and be as much of an asset to his people as he was a leader. He always made sure he was well abreast of all the goings-on. Under his rule, many more cases were solved than weren't, including some dating back a few years that had been sources of aggravation for the department.

Lately, however, he'd begun to take more interest in the cold case files- in particular, the relative glut of them he noticed over a five-year period. What really piqued his curiosity was the fact that that period was from 1970 until the end of 1974, after which the number seemed to drop off sharply in comparison to that span. The very personal nature of one of those cases also aroused his interest, as it always had. It also raised another possibility he hadn't considered until now, after seeing all the other cases in that timeframe...

Just like it had when Tom saw it for the first time as a Homicide detective in Baltimore City, the summary file of his father's disappearance still drew Tom in, especially with the new angle he was considering. He found himself devoting more and more of his already very small amount of free time to analyzing every little shred of that file and the number of open files of those

2

who had disappeared during the same time frame. His analysis of those other files led to several questions Tom had written down and meant to discuss with his detectives when he and they got the chance.

There was, however, a problem. As she had before, Donna was taking note of his increased absence from home or his preoccupation while he was there. Again he was walking the line of trying to placate her while carving out enough time for his investigation.

Tom, Sr.'s file was in his hand when the phone rang. He reached for it, remembering his assistant had gone to lunch. "Captain Stratton."

"Good afternoon, Sir, this is Ike Miller."

Ike was Tom's counterpart in the Baltimore County Police Missing Persons unit. "Hi there, Ike; how have you been? And how are things in my father's old stomping grounds?"

"I'm very well, thanks, and it's funny you should put it like that. Recently, two of my detectives made a discovery you might be interested in, which you've probably heard about."

"You mean the body that was dug up by Loch Raven..."

"That's the one; we're still drawing blanks on the identity. I figured it was time we enlisted some help and you were the first person I thought of. If it's Ok, I'd like to send my detectives over to see you, along with their files and notes so you can have a look."

Tom checked his watch. It was 3:30, and there was nothing on his slate for the rest of the day. He and Donna would be having dinner that evening, but not until seven, which would give him plenty of time. "Yeah- send 'em down. I'll be glad to check out what they have. I also might pick their brains about a matter I'm looking into, which might be related."

"...and as you can see, Sir, from a factual standpoint we're at a dead end- no pun intended."

"None taken," Tom cracked as he looked over the report and listened to the summary from Detective Searles, who giggled at his response.

"I'll be damned- did I just hear you giggle, Danni? That's a first!" Seeing her reaction Harry added, "and I've *never* seen you blush! You think you know somebody..."

"If you don't shut up, the next thing you'll see is a *lot* of stars!"

"So much for respecting your elders, eh, Cap?" Harry said to Tom, who was nearly doubled over in laughter.

It took a moment before Tom was able to catch his breath and reply. "Well, there's no doubt you two are partners! I will say this much, totally off the subject- a good laugh is always welcome here, especially lately..."

He trailed off as he looked at Detective Searles; the sense of familiarity he'd felt when she walked into his office was coming back as his concentration was diverted from the case momentarily. When she looked away and shifted a bit in her chair, he realized two things- one being that he'd drifted.

I hope I wasn't staring..."Um, Danni, I hope this doesn't sound cliché, but I could swear I've seen you somewhere else, and recently. I just can't place-"

"Law school, Sir, at the University. We're in the same criminal law class."

"I thought that was you! Small world, eh?" Although he wondered why she didn't mention that she'd recognized him, he didn't bring that up. He didn't want to give Harry more ammunition for his needling even though it was good-natured, and since Tom didn't know her personally, he felt it would be out of line for him to rib her. Plus, he knew of her reputation as a top-notch detective, and she deserved his respect as such. "It must be pretty tough for you- juggling law classes with your schedule."

"Oh, it is, but the end result is well worth it. I'm sure you can relate, Sir. You have the added burden of a family besides your position- you must not have a free minute."

"Well, I'd hardly call my family a 'burden', but I will say my time is at a premium."

The red shade returned to her cheeks. "I'm sorry, Sir, I didn't mean to imply that-"

"It's all right, I know you didn't. Anyway, speaking of time being at a premium, I guess we should get back to the matter at hand." Before he turned back to the photos of the skeleton, he noticed Danni's lingering guilty look and figured she'd appreciate him changing the subject. "Damn...we really are talking some extensive physical damage here, aren't we? After I hung up with Lieutenant Miller, I looked through these cold files again and tried to narrow down some possibilities as to who this corpse might have been, given the timeframe and the height data.

"I didn't have much luck. I couldn't eliminate very many of those cases from '70 through '74, and I even had to consider a few more as far back as '68 and as recent as '76. It really hurts, not being able to peg the date of death any better. With so little to go on otherwise…there's a chance that this guy never was reported as missing or dead, but I doubt it. He's one of these cold cases; I'm willing to bet anything on that. If I'm wrong, we have absolutely nothing and we might never determine who he was."

"For what it's worth, I think you're right, Sir. I can't offer any proof, but I have that feeling, too."

Tom nodded. "How about you, Harry? What are your thoughts? In fact, you were just starting out on the force in that timeframe, right? Were you involved in any of those unsolved cases in any way?"

Harry shook his head. "I wasn't in Homicide or Missing Persons then. I heard a bit of shoptalk about 'em, but nothing of any significance. As for this one, I'm totally baffled. Whoever killed and buried this poor bastard was pretty damned thorough- that's about all I know. I guess all we can do is go through this list, eliminate each one and just hope we get lucky."

"Yeah. I think we also need to concentrate more on this anonymous caller. It sure would help to find out who he is, what he knows and how he came across that information. I know that's been another fruitless search so far, but we have to keep on it.

"Now, about these cold cases we'll have to wade through, I want to go over a few things I've come up with that might or might not have something to do with your John Doe- unless you both need to take off."

Danni indicated 'no', but Harry got up. "Actually, I do. I have to pick my kid up at five-thirty, and it'll take me about half an hour to get there," he said. "Sorry."

"It's all right- I understand that completely. I appreciate you coming by, Harry." Tom stood and shook his hand. "By the way, I hear you're retiring. When?"

"June, Sir, but that might change. I'm feelin' run down lately; thirty-one years of this is enough. And then, you factor in the abuse I take every day from this one," he winked at Danni, who undoubtedly had a retort forming. He preempted her. "Only kidding, Detective Searles! You'll bring me up to speed tomorrow?"

"Sure, Partner- catch you then," she said, and he took off.

"You're sure you don't have to be somewhere?"

"No, Sir- I just have to take my run this evening. Otherwise, I'm free."

"Ok, good." He picked up his notes and the files and moved over to where she was. He handed her four of the cold case files.

After a cursory examination, she said, "I'm familiar with these, Sir. I've looked through them a pretty good bit recently."

"So have I, but just like when you watch a movie numerous times and you start to notice things you missed in your previous viewings, I've noticed a few things about these four in particular that I didn't pick up on before. Even with what I found, I don't have much to go on, mind you- maybe nothing at all- but it's made me look at 'em in a different way, especially since I doubt anyone else has done anything with this. I have a feeling there's a common thread weaving a lot of these cases together and this may or may not be the start of it.

"First of all, you saw that these four were charged with Class A felonies, right?"

"Uh-huh."

"Then you also saw that they never made it to trial; they were granted bail and disappeared. I contacted the bail outfit involved with each case and was told the suspects in question jumped. They never heard from any of 'em again. The guy who ran the outfit during that time died recently of heart failure, so I got this all from his successor."

"Right. So they jumped bail, went somewhere else and started all over. It happens. Their families, girlfriends, or whoever either don't know or won't tell what happened. Sometimes the perps are caught and hauled back, sometimes they're killed in shootouts, and sometimes they get away, like these guys might have."

"I know- I considered that angle, too, and it makes perfect sense when you look at it that way. But, see, that's just it. It makes too *much* sense; somehow it's too easy, considering the crimes these men were charged with. All four were charged with murder, two of 'em were charged with multiple rapes as well and we're talking about one pretty small time span for those four- between late August and early October of '70. These were the only ones

6

out of all the people on the list that were charged with crimes, too; there was that sudden spike, then no more, although a number of the others were suspects.

"If a case is strong enough, it's tried in absentia. It looks like these cases were pretty strong since bail was high. I looked at the court records from the arraignments; the evidence against them obviously was good enough to hold 'em over for trial. As for whether or not they'd have been convicted, I don't know. That part might have been shaky, but if there's enough at least to go to trial, you'd think they'd have followed through, considering the nature of the crimes we're talking about. I'm still digging; as you can tell, I've only recently gotten into this. Like I said, I know it's not much to go on and it still doesn't make much sense, but right now it's all I've got."

"You're right, Sir- that really isn't much to go on, although the way you present it does make me a bit curious, too. You don't have any corroborating evidence? Or witnesses of some kind?"

"I'm working on that. I know the prosecutor who tried two of those cases."

"Who was it?"

"Jack Weldon, our Attorney General."

"Really? That might be a good thing; I know he and your family are close. I'm sure, given that, he'll help any way he can. Let's just hope he knows something that *could* help..."

"How do you know we're so close?"

"Oh- well, a lot of people around the station seem to know that. There also was the interview he gave about your brother for the political show during the 2000 presidential race. He talked a lot about your family as well."

"Good point. I guess it is general knowledge, eh? I'd forgotten about that interview." He leaned back and stretched, inadvertently looking up at the clock when he did. It read six-thirty. "Uh-oh, I have to get going. I'm sorry, Danni, I didn't realize it was this late. Let me walk you to your car."

"Sure, Sir- thank you."

They gathered their things and headed out after Tom locked up. "How far will you run tonight?" he asked as they left the building.

"The usual five or six miles, most likely. I do it four times a week and I love it. I take it you're a weightlifter?"

"Absolutely. No offense, but running never was my gig; I'm much better geared for the weights."

"I can see that! I enjoy working out with weights, too; it's good to do both, and my strength really has helped me improve my martial arts abilities."

"I've heard stories about your prowess in martial arts- definitely a good thing for a detective to know! What made you get into that?"

"I don't know…it's just something I wanted to do, I guess," she shrugged.

"No doubt it does wonders for your self-confidence."

"Mm-hmm. So, how is your brief for our class going, Sir?"

Tom was just about to ask what her discipline was when she cut him off with her question. *That was a quick change of direction...*"Well, too slowly, unfortunately, but I'll get it done. You were right about this much- it's tough squeezing the time in, even for one class. Once my successor here takes over, that'll free up some more, though. I should be able to stay on track for graduation next fall or winter. It looks like the big challenge will be getting through this term."

"Sounds like it. You know, I'm pretty much done my brief. To make up for my remark about your family, would you like to meet one evening this week? Maybe I could help you with that behemoth over a working dinner."

"You don't have to do that. Really, it's Ok; I know it was an off-the-cuff remark."

"If you'd rather not, I understand, but I'll be at the library tomorrow evening to finish it if you happen to be free and in the area."

"Actually, that might work. I planned on getting the lion's share of that done tomorrow, anyway, and the professor did encourage teamwork on this one…all right, let's do that. Meet you at the library at seven, then?"

"Sounds good, Sir; I'll see you then. I'll also look at those cases again and see if I can come up with anything that might help you while the investigation on my John Doe goes on. Maybe we can talk more about those files. I'd like to hear what comes of your chat with the Attorney-General."

"Ok, thanks, Danni. Have a good night and enjoy your workout!"

"Sounds like she's doing well," John commented as Kim hung up with Rachel Williamson, the little girl Kim had played the vital role in rescuing three months earlier. Along with her mother Linda, Rachel kept in touch regularly with 'the pretty lady', which she referred to her savior as.

"She's the sweetest thing; just as friendly and upbeat as she can be. I'm so glad she and her mother are doing better now, but they really don't have anyone else. Linda has a hard road ahead of her; it's difficult enough when you have assistance and even worse when you have to go it alone. I worry about them and I hope she'll ask for help if she needs it, which I've encouraged her to do. Oh, I finally talked with Jenny today, too."

"It's been a while since you've heard from her, hasn't it? How is she?"

"She seems to be much happier since she met that new boyfriend last summer."

"What's she doing for work now? Or did she decide to go back to college?"

"She plans to enter the bikini contests again, which I'm not happy about. I thought she was done with them, but I guess not."

John and Kim rode along in rural Illinois, enjoying the peace and the wide-open space after their town hall meeting in Dubuque, Iowa, which had concluded an hour earlier and would be their last stop for a while. They were headed for Baltimore.

They'd been on the trail for some time without any real break. They were becoming so popular that families, such as the two John had mentioned at the end of the forum, were inviting them into their homes. The more receptive people in general became to his message- and the more they seemed to agree with it-, the more John's fervor to spread that message grew.

Even so, Kim knew there was something else on his mind.

She was glad that John finally agreed that they could use a breather. However, it took some convincing on her part, which culminated with her raising her voice to him- and that was putting it lightly. She could see the signs of his fatigue that others couldn't. The red streaks in his eyes from his irregular and sometimes abbreviated sleep were only visible from up close. Lately he'd even started to stumble on occasion when conveying points to his audience, which was very abnormal since that and debating always had been strengths for him.

Tonight, fortunately, he'd reverted to his true form- that of precision, conviction and persuasion-, but it still bothered her that he wouldn't tell her what was distracting him from time to time.

Maybe this hiatus will relax him and help loosen his tongue...

"I remember you saying how down in the dumps she was for a while and how suddenly her attitude changed. There's a better than average chance he could be some smooth-talking slime that saw a beautiful, wide-eyed young girl, said all the right lines and took her in. Don't get me wrong; I know Jenny's almost twenty-three and she's terrific, but she's also-...impressionable. She always was, no thanks to her father, I'm sure. I can't believe she hasn't heard from that man in three years. It's like he vanished."

Kim nodded. "I know. Mr. Jacobson's life did fall apart, from all indications, which probably has a lot to do with why he's been such a horrible father. Still, she's his daughter, though. A lot of parents in *worse* predicaments manage to do a good job of raising their children."

"That they do. I'd love to know where he ran off to. As for this guy Jenny's seeing, I wonder if he's the one who talked her into doing the bikini contests again."

"I have a feeling he did. I'm still really surprised that she entered any of them. That's not like her at all; Jenny said so herself after the first round, even though she did so well. Obviously, she has the looks, but otherwise I couldn't agree with you more. Unfortunately, it's quite possible this guy, whoever he is, has too strong of a hold on her- especially since Jenny's never really had a good relationship. I don't like how...well, *distant* she sounded with me while we talked."

"Then again, you know what happens to a lot of people when they fall in love. Primary loyalties can change pretty easily under those circumstances, depending on who you are and how hard you fall, and certain people have that tendency to clam up about certain things." He didn't answer that- there was no question he knew she wasn't referring to Jenny with her last remark.

Undeterred by his silence and with her frustration reaching a boiling point from his evasiveness, she pressed on. "Even though they know how much tension it causes to keep things hidden, they still choose to do that. It just doesn't make sense, especially when they know that by way of experience. Do you know what I mean?"

"Kim, don't start with-"

"Don't *start*? We're well beyond the 'start' phase here; this has been going on for some time now. I'm not the one who's holding something back and letting it affect everything I do, including the quest for the most important job there is other than parenting. Besides, *you* started this. I gave you lots of time and hoped you would come to me, but you didn't. Then, I've tried several times to get you to tell me what's eating at you. Same result. I feel like I'm beating my head against a wall."

"Honey, I've told you, I-"

"Don't have all the facts- yeah, I know what you've told me, which amounts to nothing but the same tap-dancing for which you criticize your political opponents. Dammit, John, you're doing exactly what you did before, and-"

"All right! Enough! I'll tell you, if it makes you happy!"

"If it makes me *happy*?! Do you think *any* of this makes me happy?! My husband keeping something from me and getting all defensive when I'm only trying to help, then trivializing my concern like you just did?! How *dare* you say that to me!! I'm not looking to be pacified, John. I want to help you solve whatever has been nagging at you- that's what wives who love their husbands do, but if you don't want my help, then fine. Keep doing what you're doing. Let it keep distracting you and making you angry- just go on withdrawing and doing nothing about it. I thought we were past all this, but apparently we're not." She turned and faced out the window.

Even if her anger hadn't come through loud and clear by way of what she said and how she said it, that emotion certainly was plain in the set of her face and its shade of red. "I didn't mean it like that, Kim," he said as he touched her hand. "I'm sorry. The last thing I want is for you to worry."

"But you know how much it upsets me when you keep things from me!"

"Take it easy- just calm down." She didn't resist when he pulled her close. "You're right, I shouldn't have held this back from you. What makes it worse is that it isn't the first time he's come between us. I have a feeling you've known for some time who I'm talking about."

"I thought it was him, but *why*? Why are you letting him get to you so much? He wins if you do that. Don't let him. It's over. He's not here and probably not anywhere even close to us. I don't think he'll bother us anymore. We haven't heard anything from him in almost three years; every day we get beyond that I feel better."

"You think he won't bother us, huh? Well, it's not exactly true that we haven't heard from him in that long."

"What are you talking about? He hasn't-"

"He sent us a copy of the video he made of you the last night he had you." Kim's mouth fell open, but she didn't say a word. "That's another reason why I didn't want to get into this with you. I knew what it would do to you if you found that out."

"When did he send that?"

"On our first wedding anniversary. It came when you were packing." John felt a torrent of anger rushing through her.

"That filthy *bastard*!! I cannot believe-...what am I saying? Of course I believe it."

"Exactly. I'm surprised that you of all people would suggest he'd leave us alone, given all he did because of his fixation on you. It's a textbook case of obsession and we came damned close to losing you, Jenny and all the other women forever."

She stared straight ahead for a moment; he could see the indignation in her eyes and in her tensed jaw, but he also knew she was in the process of claming herself down. Her version of taking a deep breath and counting to ten was almost totally internal- most of the time, anyway.

When she was ready, she broke her silence. "Ok, then...so it's been about a year since he's sent that. Has he done anything else in the meantime?"

"No, not yet."

"Well, maybe that was a last gasp or something. It doesn't necessarily mean he's planning some sort of scheme for revenge. Look what he's done already with that damned video; the authorities don't even know how many copies he sold, so I'm betting he made a big pile of cash. He is smart, so maybe..."

"You're looking at this from the most positive standpoint possible. Think about the guy's composition and his motivations and, again, think about all that history I just laid out."

"I know. Trust me, I haven't forgotten, but he knows we have security around us now. Remember that he got burned- and badly-, which had never happened to him. Don't you think it's even possible that that would make him stop? I mean, sending the tape is nothing more than a little poke at us."

He backed away a little and looked her in the eyes. "I don't believe for a second that he'll stop and deep down, in spite of your words, I can't imagine you do, either. I think he's biding his time, waiting for his opportunity. Our team can't keep us safe every minute of every day and he knows that. I do not accept that after all he went through to get you, he'd just give up. Add in his hatred and jealousy of me...I've seen such hatred before. It doesn't simply go away and it tends to take over every aspect of whoever feels it. It dictates almost every move the person makes."

"Well, you should know. You saw it in your former chief of staff, who tried to kill us three years ago."

"No, it was even deeper than what Daniels felt, as scary as that may sound. Look at all the money Strauss lost because of us...of course, even that was a small victory at best."

"Why do you say-...oh, right. It's because he really didn't even lose most of it."

"You've got it. $85 million still sits in those offshore accounts. As much as we tried to get the banks to turn it over, they won't until he's caught and convicted. Even then they might just decide to seize it for themselves."

"Really? How could they do that?"

"After five years of inactivity in the accounts, it becomes the property of the banks, so he has two years and two months to claim it. We can't touch it, but he knows we're watching, so it's likely he won't touch it, either."

"Unfortunately, Strauss has another source of income, though," Kim said as a dark expression crossed her face.

"That he does. It comes at your expense with that videotape. It still burns me up that he got away with that, too. All this technology we have and he kept finding ways to stay a step ahead of us. So, he disappeared- again- and we have no idea where he could be- again. He might have started another string of abductions- who knows? I do know this: he *has* to be nailed; I can't let him get away with all he's done. Plus, there's another part to his story that you don't know- that *none* of us know."

"But...Baby, what can you do? You just said you have no idea where to look and we're right in the middle of your campaign run. Don't you think this is more important? Besides, getting into the White House would give you plenty more resources available to get him. Why not just concentrate on getting elected? Maybe your influence would get the FBI back on the job and looking harder."

"Yeah, the same agency that lost the damned sample," John snorted.

"What sample? And what did you mean when you said there's more to this?" Kim asked as she looked up at him.

"They took a sperm sample from Josh out of Lisa Meyers' body when they did the autopsy. If I hadn't brought up the possibility of that genetic fingerprint of his being inside her and if Tom hadn't kicked that info up to the right people, they would have done a routine autopsy and probably wouldn't have given it any thought. That sample led to a strong possibility I've been going over and over..."

"Which is?"

He looked straight ahead. "That the scum we know as Joshua Strauss might not *be* Joshua Strauss."

"*What*?! How do-"

"Sorry to interrupt, Sir, Ma'am," Herb said as he lowered the partition. "I just got a call from a Dubuque Police detective. You won't like what he had to tell me..."

"Are you going to eat that steak or just stare at it?"

Tom looked up, then away, knowing he'd done it again. He expected another tongue-lashing, but it didn't come.

What Donna did instead was worse. With a sigh, she settled back into her chair.

"Don't worry, I'm not going to yell at you. I know what's going on. You can't let go. It's the same thing as before- you don't have to tell me. Once more you've become a stranger in our house. Even when you're there, you're not there. I also know you'll have to let this thing run its course, just like before. I don't like this at all, but there's nothing I can do about it. I'm not going to beat my head against the wall again."

"I'm sorry, Honey. I just-..."

"Yeah. Let's just finish our dinner, then you can get back to what you're doing."

* * *

"I guess those guys don't see this as a hoax?" John asked as he stared at the faxed copy of the note:

To John Stratton,
You have a beatiful wife. It would be a shame for me to have to kill her. I will kill her if you stay in the campain for President. Then I will kill you.

"No. They feel the same way I do, Sir; we can't afford to take that chance, same as with all the rest of 'em," Herb replied.

John nodded as he held Kim; she'd insisted upon reading it and was shaken by what she saw. It was the latest in the series of threats they'd received, the number of which had risen in recent months along with John's popularity and momentum. "It'll be all right, Kim. We can't let these crackpots shake us."

"I'm trying not to, but I'm still afraid. I can't help it."

"I know this is hard on you, which is what gets to me most about it. We're dealing with cowards that have to sneak notes and make anonymous threats; they don't have the guts to bring up their problems with me in any way that's honorable. I hate most of all that a number of them are so nasty to you, including religious zealots who sure don't practice what they preach. Then we have the freaks in the hate groups that want my head because I'm with a woman of mixed blood, let alone how they feel about my position on equal education for all. It's really unbelievable.

"The majority of these threats probably come from those who stand to lose the most, though; you raised that point before, too. Then, we get idiots like this that can't even spell," he scoffed as he crumpled the letter and threw it to the floor.

Herb entered the conversation. "I'm getting worried too, Sir. My team is so small, and with the increasing size of the crowds at your events…"

"Yeah. I guess it's good in more ways than one that we won't be on the road for a spell. We have to take a time-out and do some thinking about the security situation…"

* * *

"…Yes, Sir, I'm due to rotate out on June 1st."

Tom was engaged in some small talk with Attorney General Weldon. Normally, Tom was able to get to the point relatively quickly, but the primary reason he had for calling the Attorney

15

General was far from a normal one. He found himself more and more reluctant to even broach the subject.

I know Donna wants me to stop...maybe she has good reason. I'm really reaching here and I'm even on the verge of getting Mister Jack, Dad's closest friend, involved in this...

"...Tom? Did you hear me?"

"Oh- sorry, I didn't hear all of it, Mister Jack."

"Are you all right?"

"Yeah, I'm just a little tired, I guess. And now, on top of everything else, I'm looking into this case about the skeleton the County people unearthed in March."

"I had a feeling you might be interested in that. Sounds like something you should assign a detective to, though, especially with everything else on your plate. You're spreading yourself too thin, Tom; no wonder you're so tired."

"I know. You're probably right, but...well, with the medical examiner thinking that the John Doe in question was killed and buried sometime between '68 and '76, I guess I'm curious- more so because of all the cold cases during the span. The first thing I thought of was that relative glut of 'em from '70 'til '74. With all those possibilities, it could be that skeleton is one of 'em, but as we know there's no guarantee. It's also possible this one never was reported, or is from another state entirely- who knows?"

"Could be."

Here it was- the crux of the matter. Even more hesitant about it now, Tom tried to think of how he could present his next question without making it sound like an accusation, which it most definitely wasn't. All he was looking for was information...

...but this is really out there. Maybe I am *going nuts. I probably shouldn't even-*

"Tom? Is there something else?"

He realized he'd drifted again, but before he could simply say 'no' and go to another subject, it slipped out. "Actually, yes- there is something else. I, um, couldn't help but notice your name in those cases. You're listed as-"

"The prosecuting attorney. The defendants in those proceedings were granted bail and then jumped it, right?"

"Uh...yeah- I mean, yes, Sir."

"I remember those cases well and I've had access to the files a lot longer than you have, not to mention the fact that I was the

16

lead prosecutor then. I'm sure you saw your father's name on them, too- as the arresting officer.

"He was the best, most hands-on Sheriff I ever saw. He and I worked very closely together, along with Judge Cal Tippett, who those cases were brought before, and Tom's deputies, Henry Steele and Ben Jacobson. Ben was a damned good cop before he went down a different path. He and your father were really tight, and then...well, I won't go into that...

"You're quiet again, Tommy. You're thinking about your Dad, aren't you? I bet you have his file in your hand."

"Yes, Sir."

"That tells me where your thoughts are tonight. It still must tear you up every time you look at that damned thing, and I also know you can't stop yourself nonetheless. Maybe in a way you were even hoping that the remains the County detectives found were those of Tom, Sr., if for nothing else to give you, your brother and the rest of your family some closure. Christ, I hate what that must do to all of you. They just don't make 'em like him anymore...

"You know, on occasion I reflect on when we were in high school together. I never told you this- especially around your mother- but I used to write notes from our parents excusing us from school when we played hooky. I was so good at it and we did it so infrequently that no one ever knew the difference.

"Your Dad was a hoot, I tell you- always fun to be around in addition to how great a friend he was. I miss him, too. I'm so glad he left the world with such exemplary young men as his legacy. It does my heart good to see you moving up through the ranks like you are; it won't surprise me a bit to see you as our State Police Superintendent one of these days, just like your Dad was to have been. Hell, with you going for that law degree, you might even take my job someday! I can't tell you how proud I am of you."

"Thanks, Mister Jack."

"I hope you won't let yourself get carried away again with trying to put together theories about what happened to him. I don't say this lightly and I hope you don't think I do. I remember very well how close you and your father always were, but...try not to get so caught up in searching for the answers that just aren't there. It won't bring him back, and trust me- it only will cause you more heartache. You've been going too hard as it is, and you know how much of a strain it put on your marriage the last time."

"I know."

"Was there anything else you wanted to talk about?"

"Well...I was just wondering if you could give any details about those people in the cold case files you were connected with-something that might shed light on them and maybe give us some help in figuring out who this skeleton was. Nothing else has panned out so far and we could use all the help we can get."

He was silent for a moment. "I see you're not going to take my advice, eh?" He sighed. "I have to say, you're a chip off the ol' block as far as that goes. Your father was a bulldog, too- once he sank his teeth into something, he didn't let go, no matter what..."

"I've heard that once or twice."

"None of your other measures are turning up anything?"

"Not so far- every roll of the dice comes up craps."

"Well, I don't know how much assistance I'll be able to give you. When would you like to meet?"

"How soon can you?"

"Let me check...I'm open at ten in the morning on Thursday, but not for long. I'll help as best I can."

"Sounds good. Thanks again, Mister Jack- see you then."

He seemed pretty reluctant at the end...

...of course he was reluctant- that wasn't the best period of his *life, either...*

Already, Tom was beginning to regret having asked his old friend those questions, but on the other hand, once his curiosity was aroused, there was no stopping him.

He especially started to wonder about Jacobson and what it was the man had done when the phone rang. "Hello?"

"Hey, Brother- it's me. I just wanted to tell you Kim and I are on our way home."

"That's good news; it'll be great to see you two. How long will you be around?"

"Don't know yet- we have to work out a few things that have come up...will you and Donna be free for dinner tomorrow evening?"

"Not tomorrow. I have to work on a project for my law class. Maybe Thursday?"

"That probably would be better. I'm giving an interview to a reporter for News 11, anyway, but Thursday's totally open. So, how is everything? The family's well, I hope?"

"We're fine. I don't mean to cut you off, John, but I need to hit it. I have a lot of stuff piling up that needs my attention. Sorry."

"It's all right; I'm in need of a nap myself. I just wanted to give you a heads-up. See you Thursday."

"You bet. Catch you then."

Chapter 2

"Are you sure, Harry? You want to do this now- right in the middle of the biggest case we've gotten?"

"Yep. I've been ready for a while and I figure there's no sense putting it off any longer. Hey, don't look so surprised. Like I said to Captain Stratton yesterday- this job can wear you out, especially after three decades plus. I'm tired. Besides, you'll do fine without me."

Even though he'd been hinting at it since their discovery at the Loch Raven watershed area six weeks ago, Harry's retirement announcement still caught Danni off guard- mainly, the timing of it. Harry was the kind of guy who wanted to be in on the high-profile stuff...

...*which gives me more reason to believe the man was right.* She wouldn't like what was next, but..."I-...yeah, I can see your point. Well, congratulations, Partner," she said as she hugged him. "Enjoy yourself and relax; you have been looking rough over the past few weeks."

"Thanks. That's a big reason why I'm getting out. I'm in need of a very long vacation." He picked up the bag of his personal things- he'd come in early and cleaned out his desk. "Time to go make it official," he said. Just before he started toward Lieutenant Miller's office, he couldn't resist one last zinger. "You know, I do have one regret."

"What's that?"

"Never seeing you in a skirt." He gave her his trademark smile and wink.

Danni laughed. "Consistent 'til the end, aren't you? Well, if it makes you feel better, I doubt *anyone* here ever will!"

John was going over his notes when Kim took them out of his hands and plopped into his lap, kissed him, then lay her head onto his shoulder. With a contented sigh and a resplendent smile, she relaxed against him.

Kim was clad only in the sheer, stretchy, clingy full length black nightgown patterned irregularly with jade colored dragons- the nightgown he'd recently bought for her. She was fresh out of her bath, as evidenced by the intoxicating floral fragrance emanating from her and the additional softness and warmth of her otherwise tan-shaded skin, which now had a slightly pinkish hue.

"Well, hello yourself!" he quipped as he gave her a smooch in reply. "I take it you enjoyed your bath?"

"Always! I wanted to give you a little preview of what you have to look forward to this evening."

"No doubt this will be quite an evening, then. In the meantime, what are your plans for today while I'm doing my interview?" John had promised a local reporter an in-depth talk about his proposed national education program.

"I'm going to have lunch at Mom's with her and Sue while I'm there to pick the cats up, and pay Donna a visit since she's off today. I want for you and me to have a nice, peaceful time later on- not *too* peaceful, of course- and a good dinner, so I'll go food shopping, too. I haven't cooked in a while and I don't want to get too rusty!" Then she was quiet for a moment. "We never did finish our conversation about Josh, you know."

He put his pen down and removed his glasses. "Yeah, we had that little interruption."

"Since you have almost two hours before you meet the reporter, I'd say that gives us some time. How did you figure out that he could be someone else?"

"The blood type from the sample and the one listed on his birth certificate didn't match and I already had seen a couple other inconsistencies in the file we have on him, including his birthday. We thought it was October 29th, but it turns out the real Joshua Strauss was born on October 2nd, 1962, so I did some more digging. When we were in Pennsylvania last year I had the local police track down some people who went to high school with him.

"I got to talk with three of them and the picture they painted of him didn't jibe with what I knew about him. His former friends described him as quiet, but friendly, which the Strauss we came to know definitely was not. They said he was artistic- loved to write poetry, song lyrics and the like, and he even played guitar, none of which apply to our boy, unless you saw evidence to the contrary."

"Are you kidding? Not unless you consider kidnapping women an art form."

"I didn't think so. Apparently, Josh Strauss had no interest whatsoever in attending college, let alone law school. He never even broached the subject of becoming a lawyer to anyone he knew; he hated that whole system, anyway, according to his former friends. He wanted to become a musician, but not long after his parents were killed in 1981, which was the year after he graduated from high school, there came a point when he suddenly withdrew from everyone. It wasn't long before he was gone literally. None of them ever saw or heard from him again.

"They said he was torn up over his parents' murders; they figured he just took his inheritance and left, which makes sense. He was the only child of well-off parents who had no surviving siblings themselves. They left Josh a couple million.

"Josh himself, or whoever became him, gave me further suspicion that something was wrong when he had you and me on Suicide Ridge 3 years ago and was about to kill me. For whatever reason, he wanted to kill me at dawn, so I used the time in between to try to figure some things out. Among others, I asked him how he became so screwed up and if he blamed Eric and Hilda. He had a totally blank expression on his face when I said that.

"From the looks of it, he didn't recognize the names of his own parents. In fact, even when I pointed out that those *were* the names of his parents, there still was no trace of recognition for a moment. Then, the backpedaling he did made me even more suspicious. He babbled something about his father barely acknowledging him, then he corrected himself and said 'I meant, *they* didn't'. He just fell all over his words- like he had no idea what I was talking about and was trying to make something up. Another thing his high school friends told me was how close Josh and his parents were- another contradiction, from the impression that shitbird gave me the last time we saw him.

"With that list of inconsistencies you can't help but come to the conclusion I've reached. I'm convinced he's not Strauss. The problem is, I don't have clue one as to who he could be, where to look or how to get started. He's gone. He's been out of sight for almost three years now, he's probably made millions more from the video he made of you and there's no telling what he's doing with himself these days. Now you know what I know, which isn't very much and which is why I get so damned frustrated and distant sometimes. It pisses me off to no end whenever I think of him sitting somewhere, holed up and laughing at us because he got away with all he did...

"...and there's not a damned thing I can do about it."

Kim tried to digest all he told her. "I can see how that would make you so angry," she mused as she embraced him, "and I agree with your conclusion; there's no way he's Joshua Strauss. It sounds like he pulled an identity theft somehow, probably by murdering the poor guy, knowing that bastard like we do. Do you think whoever it was that took his place might have at least looked like him? Is there a picture of the real Joshua? Also, I wouldn't be the least bit surprised if the imposter killed his parents. Do you know how they died?"

"They were murdered. Somebody broke into their home and stabbed them to death the night of July 22nd, 1981. Josh wasn't there when the intruder killed his parents, but he did come home after a party and the guy still was inside. Apparently he spooked the killer, who took off out the back door. So, you can see why he was traumatized and would want to move away from there, which he did in mid-August. Good opportunity for a switch, isn't it? He didn't have any other relatives, which would have made him a perfect target for identity theft.

"Just like he did with his accomplices in the big heist, it's entirely possible that our boy used these innocent people to get him started by getting his hands on their money. He stashed Josh's body someplace where it never would be found, then 'died' himself in the summer of '89. The police never found the parents' killer, then the son, who long ago was ruled out as their killer anyway, dies in the Louisiana swamps and his body's never found. The case on the whole family is closed. Slick son of a bitch, he is…and yes- there are a few pictures of Josh in the file."

"I want to see them, but later. With all you've told me, that sounds like a perfect opportunity for him; I wouldn't be a bit surprised if he killed the whole family. There's no doubt in my mind that he has the requisite intelligence and viciousness to pull something like that off." She shuddered at the thought. "And this all happened in the summer of '81…obviously, that was a momentous period for more people than me."

"What happened to- oh, that was the summer of the treehouse incident, wasn't it?"

"Mm-hmm." Right on the heels of that, and all of a sudden, the digging that went on that day came back to her.

"Yeah, that was quite a season, apparently…you OK?"

"Hmm?"

"You drifted there a little."

"Oh, I was just thinking of that day and how I saw- and then heard- all the digging going on, I guess from Mister Weldon and his nephew. I don't know why, but that just popped into my head...maybe because of all those murders that apparently happened around the same timeframe."

"I can see how that-...hold on: you say, his nephew. I meant to ask you about that after the wedding, but needless to say, it got lost in more important matters. I don't know if he *had* a nephew; are you sure that's what Mister Jack said that day?"

"I'm pretty sure he did, yes."

"We'll have to ask him about that. Maybe he had one, but I don't think so...anyway, on the subject of who it is that became Joshua Strauss, I was thinking-...I never wanted to ask you because I don't want to reopen that chapter of your life, but-...never mind, it's not worth-"

"You want to know if, during all the time he inflicted himself on me, I ever picked up on anything he might have said that could help us find out who he really is, or maybe put us on the right track, at least." She pulled back. "That's the main reason why you were reluctant to tell me, isn't it?" When he looked away, she was a little miffed and was about to let him know it, but then she stopped herself because she knew why he'd held back.

Add to that how I reacted when he tried to persuade me to talk about what Daniels did- and almost *did- to me when he had me in that motel room after shooting John. I practically bit his head off...*

That dispelled her anger completely. She caressed his cheek and smiled at him when he looked up, chiding him only mildly. "You don't have to be so protective of me, Baby; in this case there's no need for the kid gloves, but I do understand why you used them. If it helps in any way to get him, I will be more than happy to tell you what I saw or heard. I'll have to think about it, though; it's been a while since I've done that, needless to say. I hope my memories of then haven't faded so much that they won't be useful."

"I can't imagine they have. You always did have an excellent memory, but don't think about that now. I don't want you to ruin your day because of him. Maybe later on after dinner we can see what you remember."

"Unh-uh, not tonight, either! We'll deal with that another time. There will be no diversions- especially any talk about him.

24

On this night, Mister Stratton, I will require every bit of your attention. Get it?"

"Got it," he said with a grin.

"Good!"

He chuckled, but after that took on a serious mien. "I've been absent a little too often lately, haven't I?"

"It's all right."

"I disagree; it's not all right."

"I know you didn't do that on purpose. Really, John, I understand why. You have so much on your mind with the campaign, and then I've been such a downer for you because, in spite of our best efforts, I can't become pregnant. On top of that, add in the stress from these death threats we've been getting, which I know is taking its toll on both of us. I've sure had more than my share of needy and impatient moments lately.

"No," she held up her hand when he started to object, "I know that's the case and I also know you were just about to defend me, even against myself, which is yet another reason why I love you so much. So, later tonight your high-maintenance wife will do some making up in the form of a scrumptious meal I'll put together for us and also with my, um, *dessert*, shall we say. I think you'll be happy to know that I'm feeling *very* creative, too!

"As for now, you should get back to your preparation and I need to be going. Mom's expecting- oh-...mmmm..." She'd started up out of his lap, but quickly found herself back in it with her arms pulled behind her and her wrists held together firmly.

He'd cut her off with a very welcome kiss that smoldered with the promise of what would follow. He also was demonstrating assertiveness, which always was a plus...

However, he temporarily put the brakes on. "You don't have to apologize to me for being yourself. I knew what I was getting into when we were married- both times, mind you- and I haven't forgotten. To correct one thing you said, I wouldn't call you 'high-maintenance' at all. I see you as sensuous, passionate, affectionate, loving and caring, which are not bad qualities by a long shot. I also know you're hurting, Kitten, and I don't want you to feel like you have to make up to me for that, because you don't. I still love you every bit as much as I ever have- that never will change."

Kim lowered her head as she knew the emotions welling up inside her weren't far from overwhelming her.

She didn't have to say what she was feeling for him to realize what it was, but when he saw her lips starting to quiver, he took the brakes off and began to steer her in a different direction-one that flowed naturally from the current they already were in. With his free hand he caressed her breast, then moved down along her body, enjoying the feel of the diaphanous gown that clung to her so tightly from her shoulders to her hips. He also savored the heat emanating from her body as his hand continued downward to her bare and exposed legs, which became his focus.

She began to wriggle as he continued to stroke her. Gradually she looked back up at him, smiling tenderly, but when she tried to pull her hands free to embrace him, he continued to hold them securely. A curious expression diluted her smile a bit.

John decided it was time to open up the throttle.

He smiled back at her, but his conveyed something else, which he could tell she picked up on right away. "Now, my lovely wife, I'd like for you to explain to me how you would give me such a preview and expect me to wait until tonight for the rest of the show. Can't do it, can you? I didn't think you could! So, as a modification to your last full sentence, for the time being you're staying right where you are so *I* can give *you* a preview of something I have in store for you tonight. Do *you* get it?"

She nodded eagerly and he loved seeing that sparkle in her eyes, which got him going even more. Already she was squirming in anticipation. He untied the sash around her waist and undid the four strategically placed buttons, which were all that held her flimsy gown closed, then eased the garment back. She gasped as he ran the tips of his fingers along the underside of her breast.

Then he cupped it and teased her nipple, his smile becoming more wanton as his other hand still imprisoned both of hers, although keeping her subdued was becoming more difficult.

I do believe it's time, he thought, eager to see what undoubtedly would be her reaction.

Kim's ever-increasing state of arousal led to his next move, which further increased the already high probability that both would be late for their appointments that day. She knew that move also would lead to another very pleasurable experience...

"And just what will you do with that?" she inquired with a saucy edge to her voice when he pulled the sash from around her waist and held it up. Well aware of his intention, she only asked that to egg him on, especially with the way she asked it.

Sure enough, with a dastardly snigger, he went to work. She felt the soft, smooth fabric being wound around her wrists, then cinched and tied off.

Next, John eased his willing and virtually nude captive back onto the couch and made her comfortable before he gave her a deep, titillating kiss. Then, much to her delight, his hands, lips and tongue coursed ever-so-slowly southward along her body; he quickly had her temperature soaring even higher. Her hands twisted in their binding.

Oh, yes, she mused just before her now-ravenous sexual appetite took over completely, *we most definitely will be late today...*

Things were good- there was no doubt about it.

No one had the first clue, and he had so little reason to go into town anyway that the probability was high that he would remain virtually invisible if he wanted to. All the necessities were taken care of, and she did a good job of it. He found himself incredulous at times over how things had turned out with her; he couldn't have gotten a better replacement. Soon she'd be his completely- and she wouldn't run away like Kim had; he would make sure of that.

Once more, life was as he wanted it to be...almost.

It sure would be nice to get my hands on the bulk of my money again. It just sat there in the accounts in the Bahamian bank, untouchable and gaining interest, which had been the case for two years and ten months.

The amount in those accounts now totaled $85,538,918.46.

All that money- *his* money- and he couldn't touch it or else it was certain he'd be caught. So many times he'd tried to formulate a plan to get it out of there and every time he'd failed. On the other hand, the government couldn't seize it either, due to Bahamian law. The money only could be withdrawn by the account holder- him, but he couldn't touch it.

This was the definition of a vicious circle.

As it was, he had close to six million dollars in cash and on hand. For the hour-plus footage of Kim, he'd charged a hundred dollars per copy. Even with that high price tag, they'd sold at a pace so frantic that he had trouble meeting demand. Staying ahead of the law enforcement agencies trying to track him down had added significantly to the difficulty level, and was something others who'd attempted to sell copies they'd acquired through other means had failed to do. In a couple cases, the offenders had ended up being corrupt police officers and clerks who had access to evidence rooms, thus enabling them to steal some videotapes and duplicate them.

All told, 'Josh' had sold over sixty thousand copies, most of them by way of downloadable DVD-quality video clips on various internet sites he'd set up and abandoned, which was his preferred method. There was no question in his mind that he easily could have sold twenty times that amount, and his method of protecting the content from being copied by anyone else had worked for the most part.

Finally, by late last year, he'd had to stop. He'd milked it for all he felt he could take without being caught and he was tired of constantly being on edge. For good measure, there also was the little phone call he'd made that had a good chunk of Maryland's law enforcement community buzzing. Even though he really didn't need the smokescreen, since there was little if any chance they would find him, it was about time the dirty secret that call would lead to was unearthed. It was time to make *him* sweat.

'Josh' had won. Again. In spite of his numerous urges to the contrary, he needed to remain invisible and to stick with what he was good at. It also helped that he was back in familiar surroundings, in a house that hadn't been compromised.

He was confident this was the last place anyone would think to look for him, partly because, in a way, it was so obvious. It certainly hadn't been his first choice and it had required some work, but after a couple months of toil it was up to par. Better yet, its owner had all but forgotten about it, which figured in to the richest irony of all. Although this wasn't nearly as nice and spacious as his place in Philly, which obviously never would be an option again, this one held some fond memories as well.

His thoughts again drifted to the young woman who'd filled the void and already had helped create more good memories in this place. He looked forward to the day when she wouldn't leave, which wasn't far off; initially that would be her choice, and the steps he'd take would preempt her from changing her mind later.

This time, he would not screw it up. She would be his.

There was no doubt- things had changed for the better...

...ah, why not? It sure couldn't hurt to let her know how much she's appreciated, not to mention anticipated, he thought, nearly salivating as he picked up the phone to place his order.

Kim sighed deeply when he finally finished. Not long afterwards, she smiled at him. "Now it's your turn," she purred. She struggled up, then tried to position herself, which was somewhat difficult since her hands still were tied behind her.

When John saw what she was doing he stopped her. "You don't have to do that."

"But I want to. You always do this for me and you're so great at it! I just-"

"No, Kim. It should be clear to you by now that I don't want you to do that. We've been through this enough times already."

"But-"

"I said, no- now, drop it!" He moved away and stood up. "I have to be going, anyway, and so do you."

Kim was stunned. She lay where she was and watched him finish dressing, then quickly gather his things and walk toward the door. He was about to open it when she realized he'd forgotten something very important. "John, wait, you-"

"I don't want to talk about this; I have to-"

"*John!!*" That got his attention. "You need to do one of two things. First, you can untie my hands so I can get dressed and meet my mother and Sue for lunch. Or, if you really want to punish me, you could just take me into our bedroom, finish tying me up, then gag me and leave me there. Make me suffer for daring to try to please you and for not being able to read your mind and figure out why me giving you oral sex is so repulsive. I mean, God forbid you actually tell me why, right?!"

Once her anger reared its head, there was no way for her to hold it back. "I suppose yet again we'll have to go through months of your mood souring, then you jumping all over me when I ask you what's wrong, won't we?! It seems there always will be something you can't handle that comes between us to some extent because you just can't be open with me, can you?!"

His face was as red as red could be. He glared at her for a moment, then turned and walked out of the study.

"Where do you think you're going?!! Don't you *dare* walk away from me!!" She got up and stalked after him into the bedroom. "This conversation is nowhere near finished!! We're just getting started, and-"

He whirled around almost instantaneously. *"BACK OFF!!! Dammit,* you *never* know when to-..."

Kim retreated from him, afraid of what she saw on his face. Not aware of where in the room she was, she inadvertently backed into the bed and fell onto it. She lay still and looked up at him fearfully as he just stood there, awash in fury the likes of which she'd never seen in him...

...but it wasn't long before his disposition changed. She saw another equally potent emotion emerging quickly...

When he saw Kim's fear, John's anger disappeared.

As it did, he realized that her anger was completely justified. Even though his nemesis, the real target of his wrath, was nowhere to be found, he still was wreaking havoc as evidenced by John's outburst...

...and the last person in the world he would take aim at had caught the brunt of it.

Compounding his rapidly rising guilt, that outburst happened where his archenemy held Kim captive and subjected her to all her worst fears and memories during the last of those eighteen horrible days in the summer of 2000.

All that time he had no idea whether he ever would see her again...

...and now...

Lying on their bed was the love of his life, nearly naked, confused and very upset, and with her hands bound behind her.

She whimpered softly, and seeing her eyes overflowing with sorrow and remorse made him feel sick.

She's worried about me. Even after I shook her up so badly, she's still thinking about me...

Disgusted with himself, he rushed over to her and took her into his arms. His eyes also were brimming. "I'm sorry," he kept saying as he held her. "I'm sorry..."

"I'm sorry, too," she replied in a choked voice.

Hearing that from her served to shake him out of his stupor. "You don't owe me an apology, Kitten- not at all. God, I didn't mean to yell at you and scare you like that. I just-...it's so hard for-..."

He trailed off as that horrible moment so long ago entered his mind again, but it wasn't so much when it happened. The real hurt and self-loathing had hit him hard a few years afterwards when he became painfully aware of the significance of that act.

Periodically, it still affected him in the way of causing him to try to make up for it somehow- offset what had been done…

…like it started to do at this moment.

He looked at Kim differently now, taking in her soulful eyes, her quivering lips, her full breasts, her tiny waist, her rounded hips, and her ever-so-sexy legs. He slowly ran his hand over them- all her curves, her contours. He also savored her helplessness and how much it aroused him to see her that way…

…he let her femininity wash over him and take control of him once more. He loved how she still affected him in the way she did; her spell was as powerful as ever. He needed that now- needed to know she did and always would. His hunger to dominate her was drastically on the rise. His urge to feel her giving the power to him so willingly, to see her so submissive, surrendering completely to him became stronger and stronger…

"Don't worry about that now…" She'd temporarily forgotten about getting him to untie her hands, but she was reminded of that again when she wanted to hold him and obviously was unable to.

That prompted her to cut off his apology just as much as her desire to impress upon him that it wasn't all his fault.

Then, there was his hand coursing back and forth over her legs, which triggered another reaction from her. That feeling was heightened exponentially since she was tied up…

…and the longer she remained that way…

"…it's all right, just-…please untie me, Baby- and hurry," she begged as she squirmed and looked up at him in supplication.

At that moment she recognized another emotion in his eyes- a very familiar one, which her plea combined with the state of bondage she was in served to magnify.

Now a bit bewildered, she regarded him as he took her in, but her surprise didn't last long at all. She'd seen him like this on other occasions and she remembered well what followed, which also without fail got her wheels turning.

When in this state, once he started there was no stopping him. It seemed like he was venting in some way and he would take her almost forcibly. Kim never objected; even though his intensity frightened her a little, it excited her a lot. He practically would transform into a primitive state and so would she.

She paid no mind to the fact that many women probably would consider that a criminal act, although she couldn't help but wonder on those other occasions what stirred him into such a frenzy and drove him to that point of near-violence against her.

This time, however, she saw something she hadn't noticed before- most likely because she only had sex on her mind the other times she saw that look on his face.

I could be wrong, but...it looks like...

...shame.

She didn't have but a matter of seconds before the other emotion she saw burning in his eyes took him over. She felt every bit of it in the way he took hold of and kneaded her breast more roughly than usual, and also in the kiss he laid on her...

...as Kim returned the kiss, she had another thought before her imminent surrender.

Something happened to you...

Of that, her conviction was growing quickly.

...what could it have been?

As she briefly contemplated the possible answers, she didn't like what she came up with. That made her more determined to persuade him to open up...

...but the matter went to the backburner, sent there by what he was doing to her, which never failed to ensnare her. Additionally, bound as she was, it normally wasn't long before that method of foreplay took her self-control away completely.

Her state of excitement would come through clearly in the way she struggled, which it certainly had to be now. Being so helpless while in the hands of the man she loved hadn't lost its appeal to her in the least, and obviously, seeing her that way and having her at his mercy still got John going every bit as much as before...

...and they'd just had a heated argument. Emotions were running high, which in itself was a potentially volatile situation in more ways than one. Already it was escalating within her, too.

She had no intention or desire to fight it off. It would be impossible for her to win that fight, anyway.

When she surrendered, the effect was instantaneous, as she knew it would be.

Kim released a primal wail as she elevated her struggling while they kissed. She twisted and writhed, pulling desperately at the sash that still bound her wrists, but escape was the last thing on her mind. As they pulled back from the kiss, she knew he could tell.

Combined with everything else, the hunger he saw in her was all the impetus he needed. He couldn't have held back if he tried; he practically was foaming at the mouth while he pushed her back onto the bed, with Kim entreating him further all the while...

Tom was taking care of some of his backlog of paperwork when his secretary buzzed him. "Sir, I have Detective Searles for you on line one."

"Got it- thanks...Hi, Danni."

"Hi there, Sir. Um, I'm sorry to change the plan on you, but I won't be able to make the library tonight. I forgot I was meeting someone at eight o'clock this evening and going downtown would be inconvenient. I was wondering if you could come to my place instead. I have all the materials we need for the project, anyway, and we still should be able to make plenty of progress- even more so, really, since we won't be doing so much driving. Actually, it'll be easier this way for you, too; I live in Owings Mills, a matter of minutes from your headquarters. Is that all right with you?"

"Uh...sure, I don't see why not, as long as it's all right with you. I definitely need to get that brief done and I appreciate you helping me out. I'm leaving here around four."

"Sounds good- I'm taking off early myself. That should put you here at 4:20 or so. Here are the directions..."

Kim lay on her stomach, feeling pretty spent.

He'd untied her and was massaging her, which she needed. John had a few kinks to work out of her shoulders, so she lay still for a while and let him do that...

...but it wasn't long before she went back to what had brought that whole episode on.

Once she did, she began to feel some anger seeping back in. That slowly but surely re-energized her. She was peeved with herself for losing control again, and thus losing her focus.

However, the main target of her ire was rubbing her down.

Eventually she stopped him, sat up and swung her legs over the side of the bed. She pushed his hand away when he started to stroke her, then stood and faced him. "I think we've had enough for now, don't you?"

"Never thought I'd hear you say that." His little jest was met by a very icy glare, which told him in no uncertain terms that this was not the time for wisecracks. He immediately shut up and let her go on.

"That only was a temporary diversion, anyway. Once again, we have unfinished business. How many times does this make? Is it three, or four? I'll tell you this: you don't get any more. I have had enough. This has to stop, and right now."

He looked away. "This is different, Kim. It has to do with-…it's just different. This was…personal. Very personal, and-"

"You know what? You can give me every excuse you can think of, but you're not changing my mind and you're not leaving this house until you tell me."

"Dammit, will you be reasonable here?! I'm trying-"

"Well, you're not trying hard enough. And, *I* am being reasonable; you're the one who's being bull-headed!" She stopped herself and took a breath. "Look, we're not going down that road again. We're going to have a talk and I'll tell you why. I'm not only worried because you're my husband; I'm also concerned because I'm a citizen of this country and I see something troubling the man who probably will become my President- something no one else sees or knows about."

"You've got to be kidding me! You mean to tell me you think it's a big deal that I don't want a blowjob?! That I find them repulsive?! So I'm different from most guys in that- so what? You're really reaching here, Kim. This is absolutely ridiculous and has no bearing at all. I'm not going to-"

"Is it so ridiculous? Look how you're reacting- again!" She tried to hide her growing irritation, seeing that he was moving in that same direction. She wanted to do all she could to keep the emotional level down. "I've come to know you pretty well. I remember how you used to react when I asked you about your parents, especially when your mother died.

"You would get so angry because it hurt you so much and you couldn't face what had happened, then you'd withdraw or change the subject, like you're doing this time. I know this is a deeper matter than you simply being repulsed by a blowjob because you're reacting in the same defensive, argumentative way. There's a reason why you feel so strongly about that, isn't there?"

"I feel strongly about a lot of things. If you know me so well, you know that, too!"

"Yes, I do know that, but like you just told me, this is personal- evidently, very personal. All right, John, I'll offer you an out. If I *am* reaching with this, convince me I am and I'll drop it. And knock that off!" she added petulantly, reminded of her nudity when on several occasions she caught him focusing on everything but her eyes. "The least you could do is have the decency to look me in the eye when I'm trying to talk with you! Now, am I wrong about what I said or not?!"

He turned away and, as she expected, said nothing.

"That's what I thought. Baby, don't you see? You have to have your mind clear of such obstacles and the only way you can do that is by purging it. The direction- and possibly the survival- of our country depends on you. Obviously this *is* a big deal to you and I want to help you through it in any way I can. What if it eats away at you so much that you have some sort of breakdown? Worse yet, what if it causes you to make a bad, knee-jerk decision at a crucial moment? Remember how you got near the end of your tenure as Governor?"

"Wait a minute; I don't let personal problems influence decisions I make when I'm doing my job- I *never* have! Even though some of my critics felt differently during my last year as Governor, my vision regarding what needs to be done is clear. That especially will be the case once I'm President!"

"Fine. So you haven't before, but how do you know this problem *won't* affect your decision-making? In fact, how do you know your troubles in the past didn't? And why would you want to let this matter continue to bother you? Haven't you had enough of-...John Stratton, you stop it right now! Don't try to change the subject!"

She held up her hand, seeing his expression and knowing what he was about to do. "And don't try to sweet-talk me, either; it won't work!" His attempts to create a smokescreen made her angry again, and the more she thought about the distinct possibility that her efforts would be for nothing, the more that anger boiled up...and then over. "*Damn you*!! Why are you fighting me?!! Don't you know I'm-"

Kim's ire dissipated and she found that she had to sit down.

Now, in addition to John, she was battling the forces of fatigue and frustration, both of which were very determined opponents. Their combined siege was draining her quickly. All the energy she'd expended earlier in a much more pleasurable way also figured in.

Despair was mounting as well.

How long can I keep doing this? How many more times will he hold back from me? How long until-

She looked up when he started talking.

"Hi, Sherry, it's Governor Stratton...well, that's why I'm calling. I, um, need to reschedule...no, no- we're fine. I just can't make it today, but I'll make it up to you- that's a promise. I also won't keep you waiting too long...thanks- I appreciate you bearing with me. I'll see you soon." He hung up and walked over to the window.

Kim didn't say anything or make a move toward him. She just sat still and watched him, waiting...

...and hoping.

"I'm sorry, Kim. You're right...there is more- a lot more. I didn't mean to-..."

For some time that was all he said, but as far as Kim was concerned it was a good start.

Unfortunately, however, just then she noticed that in addition to the other detractors, a nasty headache was coming on.

John noticed it, too. As he turned to face her, she touched her forehead and closed her eyes. "Migraine?"

"I think so."

"You've been getting more of those than usual, haven't you?" *Our argument sure could be part of the reason for this one,* he thought as he looked away. "I'll be right back with your medicine."

He disappeared into the bathroom and returned with a pill and a cup of water for her. "Take this and lie down, Honey." Once she did, he drew the comforter up over her.

After he called Diane, Sue and Donna and explained why Kim wouldn't be able to make it, he made sure Herb and the team knew not to disturb them. Finally, he drew the curtains to block out the light and joined Kim in bed. Fortunately it was a cloudy day, anyway, so there wasn't as much light to block out. "I'm staying here with you."

"You don't have to do that. I'll be fine after I rest."

"I want to; the interview can wait. Besides, I'm feeling pretty drained myself. A nap would be good for me, too."

She moved over and snuggled against him. "We'll talk later, right?"

"I promise we will."

"I'll hold you to that, you know."

"I know."

She kissed him. "I love you, John."

He traced her cheek and smiled at her. "I love you, too. Now, get some rest, Ok?"

"Ok."

It wasn't long before both fell asleep.

"All right, guys, let's break it down."

The stage crew in News 11's studio got to work striking the small set that was to have been used for Sherry Gardner's interview with Governor Stratton, which apparently was not to be today. Fortunately, there wasn't all that much to take down, so it looked to be a short day of work for those involved.

A new guy grabbed the chairs the Governor and the reporter would have used.

When he did, he noticed that one was heavier than the other, even though both chairs were exactly the same.

"Dammit..."

The stagehand was right on the verge of finding the explosive.

He'd counted on the setup being left as it was so he could slip back in and get his two pieces of equipment out of there. After a couple hours of observation, it looked like he'd be able to do that tonight when there would be less people around.

Obviously, the crew chief had a different idea. Ray's last hope that his stuff would go unnoticed was a faint one.

I guess you are leading a charmed life, Mister Stratton...

It wasn't supposed to turn out like this. There didn't seem to be any reason why the interview would be cancelled, yet it *was* cancelled. This seemed like a great opportunity when he found out about it, and a totally unexpected one. Generally, such opportunities, when dropped into one's lap, are signs that the person is taking the right course of action and often are indicators that success will follow. With that in mind he'd decided to take a shot.

Unfortunately, fate didn't appear to be on his side today, either- same as with the forum in Dubuque. Failure seemed imminent.

Worse, a screw-up in this venture could mean tighter security for the ex-Governor and possibly future President as a result...

...sure enough, the young guy turned the chair over. When he saw what was there, he dropped the chair and ran away, yelling at his co-workers to get back.

Ray flipped the first switch, then the second immediately after that, destroying the evidence.

Chapter 3

"Hi there, come on in."

Tom walked into Danni's apartment. When he saw the décor, it really threw him; since Danni seemed to be such a 'no-nonsense' person, he figured he'd see very simple and basic furnishings. Instead, her place was totally feminine, from the lace-edged pillows on the sofa and the pink telephone to the painting of a ballerina and the vase full of flowers, which accounted for the pleasant fragrance throughout the place.

However, her pad was very tidy, which did not surprise him.

"Not at all what you expected, is it?" Danni said with a grin, enjoying his reaction. She laughed when he looked away in embarrassment. "Oh, don't worry. I'm not offended. There's not a single cop who's had any contact with me who would have reacted differently than you just did. I love surprising people."

"Well, congratulations- you sure did that to me! I'm glad you didn't take offense; I certainly didn't intend any."

"I know. It's not something you'd do."

He turned back to her. "You know that?"

"Mm-hmm. I'm a quick study when it comes to people and a very good judge of character. I know when someone has substance and when he doesn't. It's not just in words and actions past and present; I also see it in mannerisms..."

This time, she was the one who looked away. "Um, we should get started; I know you didn't come here to chitchat. Are you thirsty? Or hungry?"

"I'm all right for now, thanks."

"Ok, come sit down. I have my notes and all ready, so we might as well get started right away..."

"No matter how many times you do it, I'll always love your way of waking me up."

Kim quit her nibbling, kissing and caressing and smiled at him as he faced her.

"Now, where in that did you hear even an insinuation that you should stop?" That made her giggle and he grinned in reply. "I see you're feeling better. The headache's gone?"

"Completely. That medicine does wonders, along with peace, darkness and sleep. Having you here with me helped a lot, too. I'm glad you stayed."

"So am I. What do you say we get something to eat? And no, I haven't forgotten about our talk; it's long overdue. We just don't need to be distracted by empty stomachs. I figure I'm not the only one in this bed who's hungry."

"You're right about that. I am famished!"

Both got up, dressed and quickly were on their way down the staircase when Herb walked toward them.

"Hi, Herb. Thanks for the privacy; we-" John stopped cold when he saw the grim look on the big man's face. He drew Kim against him; she also was worried about their bodyguard's demeanor.

"What happened?"

"...so, that's my interpretation of it. What are your thoughts?" When he didn't respond, Danni looked over at Tom and saw that he was staring, totally focused on something other than the criminal law class assignment. "Sir? I mean, Tom- what's wrong?"

He slowly turned to her. "I just thought of something...I wonder if any other bodies are buried in that same location."

"I had a feeling your mind was somewhere in that vicinity," she said as she put her notes down and stretched. "What makes you think there might be more of them?"

"All those cases in the same timeframe...that caller knew exactly how to direct you and your crew to find the skeleton you uncovered; he led you right to it. Who's to say that spot wasn't used to hide more of them? It's certainly a good location for that purpose. You and I are on the same page about this caller being directly involved somehow in the murder, either as a trigger man, or *the* trigger man, or maybe someone who helped bury the body once the killing was done. He could be a murderer or accomplice having an attack of conscience late in life, or maybe wanting to point the finger of blame toward someone else involved for some sort of absolution, or just to lead the dogs away from himself...

"...but then again, why would he do that? Thirty years or more have passed since this killing and no one had the first clue as to what happened. We still don't even know who the victim was, so these guys were in the clear. That part makes no sense...

"It's possible our caller is someone who overheard the story, but I don't buy it because that's a big area with an awful lot of trees. He had detailed, precise knowledge of where to find it- firsthand knowledge, I bet. Otherwise, how in the hell would he have known which one was the marker? Besides, that's a fairly remote section of the watershed area. I remember it a little; my Dad would take me fishing out there from time to time. As for locating a grave there, talk about having to find a needle in a haystack..."

"I know. If Harry hadn't been with us, we still would have had a hard time finding the burial spot- *if* we found it at all." He was quiet for a moment, his brow furrowed in contemplation. Danni was curious, but didn't interrupt him.

"I haven't been to that site yet." He turned to her again and asked, "would you be able to take me there tomorrow?"

"Hmmm...would early afternoon be all right? My morning is pretty full."

"That would be fine. I have an appointment tomorrow morning, too."

"All right, that's settled. Oh- look at the time; I'd better get ready. I've already showered, so I only have to get dressed. I won't be long, and we can finish up with the brief when I come back, Ok?"

"I won't be in the way? I could leave if-"

"No, you won't be in the way at all. Besides, it's our final project and it's due in a couple days; you know as well as I do how important it is, so we're going to finish it. Help yourself to something to drink if you like and I'll be right out." She disappeared into her bedroom.

He walked over to the refrigerator. He opened it and jumped a bit when she called out "try my iced tea. It's very good, if I do say so myself."

"That's some damned good hearing you have," he said under his breath. He poured some tea for himself. "Would you like a glass?"

"Sure, thanks."

Instead of going back to the law school assignment, he yet again contemplated the case he and Danni were involved with. There was no question it was sucking him in like quicksand.

41

Already he was wondering what other secrets the burial site might reveal...

However, that line of thought was halted abruptly when she walked back into the room.

"So, what do you think? Will he be impressed?"

Tom was totally awestruck; it seemed as though another Danni Searles faced him. He had to look twice to make sure it really was her.

The long legs emerging from the tiny and tight black skirt were very sexy. They were solid and muscular- probably overly so to many guys, but not to him. Her nylons made them shine- another plus-, and they were perched atop some high-heeled pumps, which kept her calves flexed, making those legs look better still. It seemed as though Kim had signed on as her fashion consultant and waved her magic wand.

As Danni turned slowly for him, he couldn't help but notice that her abbreviated skirt also called attention to a great ass that looked so solid that he was sure it would break the hand of anyone who dared to slap it. He also could see that her waist was small in diameter, and well defined. Her tight and nearly transparent blouse also revealed breasts that weren't large but were nicely shaped, in part because of the black bra she wore. She was very fit and toned, but in Tom's eyes still every bit a woman.

Danni's look was a radical change from what he was used to when he saw her in class, which was the same as what she wore when she came to his office with her partner the other day. Her glasses were gone and her long, dark, shiny hair lay over one shoulder, freed from the tight bun. She even wore a bit of makeup. All restraint and concealment was gone- every last bit of her sex appeal was unleashed, and there was plenty of it.

She was something else. The funny thing was, she wasn't striking- or even beautiful, really-, yet she still was sexy, alluring and above all, confident and quite comfortable in her own skin, plenty of which was on display. Her inner self was coming through. That sense of ease was what really gave her look its legitimacy; this was no façade at all.

With him, she seemed to open a door just behind her eyes and show him a part of her that very few other men saw- if any had- although apparently there would be at least one more besides him added to that count very soon. Suddenly it seemed utterly ludicrous that a woman whose deep, dusky eyes were drawing him in like tractor beams could be one who was largely ignored and discounted by so many and called asexual, of all things!

I'd better stop this right now, he thought, pretty sure that he'd been looking at her for a bit too long. "You sure weren't kidding when you said you like to surprise people! To say the least, your date will be very impressed- unless he's not attracted to women."

She giggled as her modesty surfaced again. "Thanks. Actually, from what I understand about him, he likes women very much…Well, what do you say we finish up now? It should only take a few more minutes; you just about have it nailed down."

"Uh, sure, let's do it." He sat down again and placed the drinks on the table.

Danni picked hers up and took a draw from it. She licked her full, ruby-red lips, then smiled at Tom as she put the glass back on its coaster.

He realized he'd been staring- again. "Um…I guess the last thing I need to make sure of is that I'm familiar enough with all the supporting cases, which I think I can…"

She swept her hair back and leaned in closer to take a look at his summary, crossing her legs as she did…

…just when he noticed how much he liked her perfume, his cell phone rang.

Thank God, he thought as he picked it up. "Hello?"

"Sir, it's Bill Rogers. Unfortunately this isn't a social call."

Tom sat up straight. "What happened?"

"A couple hours ago two bombs exploded in a studio inside the News 11 complex. Several people are in the hospital because of their wounds, fortunately none too serious."

"Two bombs in-…Jesus. But, why are you calling-" He froze when it hit him.

John was giving an interview there today.

"Tell me he wasn't-"

"No, Tom, the Governor wasn't there at all but we're sure he was the target. I wanted you to hear this from me first, and for you to pass it along to him and his security team. Something will have to be done one way or another, or it's very possible that-…well, you know what I'm getting at."

"Yeah. I appreciate you calling me, Bill- thanks."

Danni touched his hand as he hung up. "Oh, my God- someone tried to kill your brother?"

Staring for a moment, clearly stunned by what he'd just learned, Tom nodded. "I have to go. He might know about this already." He turned to her. "Thank you for all your help, Danni; you've been terrific. So, I'll see you tomorrow, then?"

"Yes. I'll come by your headquarters at one?"

"Sounds good." He collected his notes and headed for the door.

Danni followed him. When he turned back to her, obviously upset, she moved a little closer to him. "Will you be Ok to drive? I could drop you off at home, or take you where you need to go."

"No, I don't want to mess up your plans."

"Hmm? Oh- don't worry about that. I'll just reschedule. Two people already have tried to kill the Governor, so I have no doubt you're worried sick. I'd rather you didn't drive in that condition- not when you don't have to. Wait here for a moment while I call him."

"Really, you don't have to-"

"Well, I am, and that's final. I'll be right with you."

While she grabbed her purse and went over to her phone, Tom picked his up and called Donna. "Hey. What are you up to?"

"I'm at Kay's right now, but I'm about to head home. What's up with you?"

"I need to go see John and I was wondering if you wanted to come with me."

"Well, as you should know, Jess is coming home for the summer and she's due in this evening, so I'll need to do some straightening up. Aren't we going to John's tomorrow? Besides, he called earlier and told me Kim had a migraine, which is why she couldn't make it up here today. They were going to rest."

"I'm sure they're up now. A studio in Channel 11's building was bombed- the one where John was supposed to give an interview."

"Oh, no...that's the one they just talked about on the news report..."

"Yeah. So, do you want to come with me? The house looked fine when I left this morning; you don't need to clean it again."

"I would, but I don't want Jess to come back to an empty house, not to mention a filthy one- and no, it *isn't* clean. Why don't we wait until tomorrow to see them? They probably need some time to themselves, anyway; they've been on the road for all those months. Maybe a night with each other and without distractions would be better for them, especially considering how they are together. John hasn't called you, has he?"

"No, but I'm going to call him. Donna, my brother could have been killed today. See if Jess can visit with one of her friends for awhile and let's go down there. What he needs- what they both need- is for their family to be with them, so if you want to stay-"

"Listen to yourself, Tom; it doesn't sound like you should be driving in the first place. Just come home, Ok?"

"I won't be driving. One of my detectives is taking me."

"What, all the way to John's?"

"You make it sound like he lives on the other side of the world! It's not that far, for God's sake!" He turned to Danni, who regarded him sympathetically. "Look, I need to get going, and this conversation's headed in the wrong direction. I'll see you later." He took in and released a deep breath. "Don't you want to change?"

"No, I'm fine like I am. I'll just grab a coat. Besides, I figure you want to get going." She opened her closet, picked out a long black leather jacket and put it on. "So, it's off to your brother's then?"

"You don't mind?"

She shook her head in reply.

"I really appreciate this, Danni."

"I'm glad I can help." She smiled warmly in return as they walked out and she locked her door. "My car's this way…"

Every time Kim thought about what came very close to happening, she started to feel sick, angry and afraid simultaneously, which happened plenty of times since Herb broke the news to them. She did her best to concentrate on the fact that, thankfully, it *didn't* happen. "Even though I figured it would come to this, as I'm sure you did, there's really no way you can prepare yourself for it or lessen your fear when the threats become real and are acted upon. I certainly know how it feels to be in the spotlight and to be hunted. I have lots of experience with both."

"That you do, Honey."

"In a way, that makes it worse because I do know the feeling, and now that at least one of these elements has taken the next step…"

"I know. I've said it before: the hardest part for me is that you have to go through this, too. I knew it would happen eventually so I was as prepared as I could have been, but I can't stand seeing what it's doing to you..."

"I *hate* this, John; I hate all the trouble it's causing us..." She cuddled closer to him as his embrace tightened and he kissed her. "I take it we're not getting federal protection?"

"No. Technically, it's not campaign season yet and I haven't gotten ten percent of any primary votes, which obviously won't happen anyway since there won't be a primary for our party. That's the deal breaker, I'm afraid. Plus, we're not getting the media coverage that the majors get- not yet, anyway-, so I don't see federal protection happening at all.

"Furthermore, don't think the current occupant of the White House will bend the rules for us, especially since Mister Black and I aren't on the best of terms. I'm sure he'd like nothing more than to see me spend all my money on security for more reasons than the obvious one. He's probably waiting for the day when I run out of funds, hoping I'll drop out. I'd say he and I are pretty well beyond the 'philosophical differences' stage."

"That's putting it lightly. You certainly have more than your fair share of enemies."

"Yeah." He wasn't sure that the last thing she said was a subtle nudge- a reminder of the promise he made to her a few hours ago-, but it was a good possibility that was the case. All the same, she wasn't pressing him and she gave no indication that she would.

Whatever the case, he knew it was time. This had caused enough trouble in their marriage and it had affected him for far too long, causing him to erupt at Kim when she only was trying to help him. His attempts to forget about it were not working anymore.

He turned to her and simply started to tell her. "When I was a kid, there was this older guy I used to hang out with for a year or so named Christopher Hedges; he lived in my neighborhood.

"He was fifteen and he didn't seem to mind that I was so much younger. He was...I don't know- different, which I was able to relate to, being a misfit myself. We got along really well because of that. At least, that's how *I* saw it. We'd have these long conversations- generally they were pretty deep- about heavy topics like death and spirituality, and sometimes they were about nothing, more or less. I just liked to hang out with him since I didn't get along so well with most kids my age.

"Early one morning in the spring of '72 we were just shooting the breeze when all of a sudden he told me to go up on top of his garage with him. I did, without thinking anything of it. It was a flat-top garage with yellow siding that was butted up against the house and I remember the big tree next to it that shielded it from view…

"He…unzipped his fly and-…"

Kim closed her eyes; John confirmed what she'd suspected. "Oh, no…"

"I was seven years old. I had no idea what I was doing or what he was doing to me. I looked up to him- thought he was such a cool guy. I never would have thought he'd take advantage of me like he did. I was confused and I never told my parents or anybody else about it. I knew something was different, though, because the next time I saw him, he laughed at me and walked away.

"That really puzzled me; I was even more mixed up at that point because, just like that, he changed. Everything changed. Whenever I saw him after that, which wasn't nearly as often as before, he'd do something similar- either laugh at me again, or smile in a really twisted way."

"Baby, that's horrible! I absolutely *despise* anyone who would do such a thing to a child! I'm so sorry…" A few tears fell as she tried to stay composed, not wanting to upset him.

Fortunately, it wasn't long before her perspective changed with her next thought. She looked into his eyes, feeling the need to tell him what was on her mind. "I want you to know this doesn't diminish you - not in any way. You have nothing to prove to me that you haven't already proven with all you've done and all you are. I love you so much."

John just smiled at her for a moment. "I love you, too, Kim." He emphasized that with a kiss. "That's not the end of it, though. He ended up getting his in more ways than one, although I wasn't the one who gave it to him."

"What do you mean? What happened?"

"One night he spied on my mother while she was changing. He had a habit of doing that and not only to my mother. It turned out that he was a neighborhood Peeping Tom. Well, on this particular night Mom saw him and called out to my father, who took off after him. He got away then, but his luck didn't last. A

47

couple days later my Dad was outside and saw him throwing a rock at our cat. This time when he chased him, he caught him. Dad took hold of him and shook him like a rag doll, telling Hedges in no uncertain terms that if he ever caught him on or near our property again he'd beat him to a pulp. Hedges was terrified. He pissed himself right there. I saw that and pointed it out; I ended up laughing at him. You should have seen his reaction when I did…at the time I was glad Dad was there.

"Next, my father backhanded him hard across the face and sent him flying. Before then I would have been angry with Dad, given how cool I thought the guy was, but I saw him throwing the rock, too. Any feelings of friendship I had for that son of a bitch were gone, especially given how much I loved our cat. I backed Dad up- told Hedges that he got what he had coming. I've never seen such hate as I saw in him as he cried, then ran away screaming that we would pay for that someday. It wouldn't happen by his hand, though. The fall of that same year, Hedges was killed. That happened in October of '72.

"I have to say, his death had a strange story surrounding it. He and his mother apparently were shot but their bodies never were found. They were pretty unpopular in our community, to say the least. She was a drunk who sat in front of the TV all the time. She was a gossip as well; she'd go off and make wild accusations against some of the neighbors.

"Their house normally was a dump, so I guess it was no surprise when the police came that night and it was trashed. There was blood all over and evidence that they were dragged off, which was the assumption since they never found the bodies. That made sense, given all the other indicators they had. There were plenty of people who didn't mind a bit to see both of them gone, either, so the police didn't spend much time investigating. It seemed to be a case of goodbye and good riddance. It sure was for me, anyway, especially when it came to him.

"I was glad he was dead. As I matured and it finally sank in, what he'd done to me…it's haunted me ever since. I just suppressed it. Eventually I didn't think about it so often, but it still was there…"

Laura Collins looked at the screen, shaking her head as the breaking news was reported. There was no question in her mind, given the timing and location of the blast, that another assassination attempt against her predecessor had taken place.

Any remaining doubt as to what she needed to do was gone.

She hit the intercom button. "Adam? I take it you're watching this, too?…I thought you would be. I need you in here; we're going to take that measure for John that I told you about. It helps that the Assembly's still in session…"

Kim eventually broke the silence that had ensued after John finished. "That would explain why you reacted the way you did when I wanted to-…well, you know what I mean. Also, that tells me why you became so aggressive with me after I'd try. You tried to compensate for that."

"Yeah, I think that's exactly what I did. It probably contributed to all the problems I had for so long with girls and relationships, too, but it doesn't excuse how I treated you. I had no right to frighten you and I swear I never will again. I'm sorry."

"It's all right, Baby. You did scare me a couple times, especially earlier, but I know you'd never hurt me. Then again, your flare-up was partly my fault, too. I pushed you, which, as you know better than anyone, is something I do too much of on occasion. As for this episode and those of the past, now I understand what was behind them." She kissed him and smiled to reinforce her statement. "I'm glad you told me. You know I'll do anything I can to help you heal."

"I know," he said, smiling at her. "I'm glad I told you, too. I hated keeping it from you, but it was humiliating to the extreme. I've never felt so ashamed about anything else- not by a long shot- and so much so that I couldn't even tell you about it. Other than whoever it is that became Joshua Strauss, I never came to hate anyone as much as I hated him for what he did- and also for laughing about it."

"You have every right to feel that way. I've never seen such fury in you; that more than anything is what frightened me."

"I imagine so. Then, when my current nemesis got away after all *he'd* done, that left another black mark. He rubbed my face in it, too, with every bit as much glee as Hedges. The crowning touch was when he sent the video. He even added a little note in the case; it said 'I hope you enjoy this as much as I did', that fucker. He put it to me but good- to you, too- and got away."

49

"He sure did. Sometimes when I think about that...we almost were killed because I was weak and he took advantage."

"No, you weren't weak, Kitten. You never were. You may have a weakness, like everyone else, but you are far from weak."

That earned him another kiss, which Kim quickly bestowed upon him. "There you go again, making me feel better about myself like you always do, but we're focusing on you right now and how to go about erasing this mark. Unfortunately there's nothing you can do about this Hedges character..." She trailed off as the impulse hit her.

As ridiculous a theory as it seemed...

"...unless he pulled the same stunt the other one did and made everyone believe he was dead..."

That feeling had manifested itself again: what she'd just said did not come to her by way of happenstance. After listening to all John revealed, she couldn't help but see the similarities and although she had no proof of the possibility that was forming very rapidly, her intuition was buzzing because of it. "Baby, you might think I'm coming from left field with this, but-..."

John's wheels also began to turn when she put that phrase out in the open. It was so far-fetched, yet... "The phony Joshua Strauss assumed the identity of his namesake, probably in '81 after killing the guy. In '89, he faked his own death, in part to pull off that heist...so, who's to say he didn't fake it one more time- in October 1972?"

He paused for a moment as he searched his memory for any clues that might support that. "I don't know...given the deep-seated hatred and cruelty those two shared, in that respect I'd buy it, but...damn, that's a reach. While we're on the subject, though, I guess this would be a good opportunity for you to tell me anything you can remember during the time you spent with him that might make the connection. Or, if that's not the case, maybe you can provide some hint as to who he could be otherwise."

Kim fell silent for a bit as she concentrated. "I hope I can help shed some light on it...now, where to start...needless to say, most of what he did and said was intended to break me. Part of it was attacks on you. A lot of time has passed, so I need to think...there were certain things he said that stuck out in my mind, but I was so focused on trying to escape, too...

"Wait- there was something, and it was about you...I'm trying to remember exactly what he said. I *know* it stood out, now what was it?!...This much is for certain: there were moments when his enmity for you came through loud and-"

Kim covered her mouth and her eyes grew wide as saucers when what he'd uttered in anger while he had her in the tub jumped out at her:

'You wouldn't think he was such a he-man if you saw what he did when he was sev-'

Oh, my God...could he have meant to say, 'way back when John was seven*'?*

Right on the heels of that she remembered the other cryptic slip-up he made as he bound her and gagged her after she laid into him in the subterranean gym room. She cringed when she saw his face so clearly, awash in a rage as he yelled at her- a rage very similar to that which she'd just seen in John:

'You think you know everything about that self-righteous asshole, don't you?!! Huh?!! If you think what I've done to you is bad, you should have seen what I did to-...'

Any doubt she had was whisked away; those two heated outbursts together were all the evidence she needed. She looked up at John when she realized he was shaking her.

"...Kim? Honey, what's wrong?!"

"It was him...oh, John, it was *him*!! The phony Joshua Strauss is this Christopher Hedges; I'm sure of it!!"

When she told him those two phrases from 'Josh' that came back to her, his face blanched at first...

...but then, the red began to seep in. His jaw clenched and he began to shake. Before it got too bad he moved- and faced- away from Kim. "That *fucking* piece of SHIT!!!" In his irrational haze he picked up the closest object to him and hurled it full-force into the floor.

She was right. Deep down, even though he had no other corroborating evidence just yet, he knew she was right...

That venting helped. Also mindful once more that Kim was in the room with him and that he'd already upset her once, he calmed himself down rather quickly, although his anger was far from gone.

As his mind cleared John began to focus on the task at hand, which was coming up with more supporting evidence that also might help track the focal point of his loathing down. He faced Kim once more. "It does make sense...I guess it only stands to reason that there had to be more to his hatred of me than jealousy

51

because I was a better debater. He's twisted, evil almost beyond belief, yet he's casual about it. I do remember on a few occasions thinking he said and did things that were similar to what Hedges would have done. It wasn't possible, though- there's no way anyone could have seen that back then...

"...or maybe I just didn't want to consider that it really was him- that all along he was plotting revenge against the one who made him piss in his pants and the one who laughed at him when he did, which was *his* biggest humiliation then and quite possibly still is- aside from when you turned the tables on him three years ago. He never got over it. Given his mentality, he couldn't, and he devoted his life to getting me since he couldn't get my father...or could he?"

Kim looked up. "He disappeared two years before your father did; as far as we can tell, he didn't resurface until 1981. God only knows what he did during all that time. No one would suspect a corpse and based on what you've told me, he certainly had a strong motive."

"Mm-hmm. This does raise a possibility..." His thoughts drifted back to the conversation on Suicide Ridge that night in July 2000 when Strauss/Hedges was about to kill him- one exchange in particular. "...and you remember what he said about knowing who's responsible for killing Dad. Maybe in that case he wasn't full of shit after all. It's looking more and more possible that he either did it himself, played a part in it, or at the very least he knows who did..."

Once they started, the recollections of Suicide Ridge kept coming back to him. "Ok...remember when I told you I asked him about his parents while we were on the Ridge? When, after he gave me that blank stare, he said 'he never even acknowledged me'- *he*, meaning his father. He couldn't have meant anyone else.

"That fits, too; Hedges lived with his mother and-...that's right- he had a stepbrother, or half-brother, who was a few years older. I forgot about him, probably because I never met him. His name escapes me at the moment. I know it was something really goofy-sounding, though; I'd probably remember it if I heard it. Anyway, he took off in '69 or '70- somewhere in that timeframe. For all anyone knew, he just picked up and left...

"Anyway, there's also the question of Hedges' father; no one ever knew who he was."

"If there's a Satan, I'd lay my money on him."

John laughed. "I don't know if you meant it to be one, but if you did that was a well-timed wisecrack, Honey. I hear you, though; it wouldn't surprise me a bit, either. On the positive side, we do have a starting point...even so, if this is true- and I sure as hell believe it is- I wonder where he kept himself hidden for nine years? He had to have money to get by on and a place to stay. His mother was dirt-poor, as far as I knew, but that's another thing we'll need to look into, I suppose. We'll tell Tom; he could help us out with all this. He probably has access to any files we'd need to see that have any bearing on Hedges and the rock he crawled from under. Most importantly of all, we need to find out who's responsible for inflicting that piece of shit on the world..."

"Definitely. Maybe we can start looking into his paternity tomorrow, since we won't be on the campaign trail for a bit, although having to look over our shoulders because we have someone acting on these death threats won't help."

He sighed as that reality came back to the fore. "I know. I just-"

Suddenly the phone rang, making them jump as it did.

They exchanged an uneasy look. If either of them had any lingering doubts that the danger they faced was tangible and ever-present, their reaction to that ring dispelled them immediately. John's anger arose once more as he had to acknowledge that fact. He picked up the receiver on the third ring. "Hello?"

"John? It's me. I just heard a little while ago. How are you and Kim holding up?"

"Hi, Tom. As you can imagine, this isn't the best evening for us. What are you up to?"

"I'm on my way there, if it's all right with you two. I figured you might want a little company."

John looked at Kim, who was close enough so she could hear Tom. She looked up at him and nodded. "That sounds good, Brother. Is Donna with you?"

"Actually, no- a detective who happens to be a classmate of mine as well is giving me a lift."

"Oh, Ok...so there will be-"

Kim interjected. "Damn- I never got a chance to do my food shopping today! We don't have anything to eat..."

"I heard her, John. Tell you what, go ahead and call the place near you that makes the great fried chicken. Order enough for the four of us and your security team; Danni and I will pick it up."

53

"Where are you now?"

"We're on 695, probably 5 minutes away from the 97 split."

"So that puts you about 45 minutes from Holly's, which should be plenty of time for them to get all that together. Ok, we'll see you when you get here...and thanks."

"I hope you'll tell me that bombing wasn't your doing."

There was no 'hi', 'how goes it?' or any normal greeting from Raines- not that Ray expected one. "In this case, your hope is in vain."

"Great- just fucking *great*! I *knew* it!! Well, now you've done it, and you're even joking about it! The whole-"

"Just shut the hell up and listen!" Very few times did Ray lose his temper. When he did, it usually had everything to do with the pain in the ass he was talking to, who was trying to stare him down. Ray found that laughable. *It's a good thing you pay well...*

It also was good that he'd agreed to this meeting place, which was off US 50 just across the Bay Bridge, not far from where Ray needed to be shortly. "The opportunity presented itself, so I took it. That's what I do and why I get the job done. Sometimes I'm successful, sometimes I'm not. As with anything else, if the chance I take works I'm a tactical genius. If it doesn't...well, I look for the next one, which might be harder to come across in this case, but it'll come. That's not for you to worry about, anyway. You just take care of things on your end and keep my tab paid- that's all you need to concern yourself with. I'll take care of everything else. Is that clear?"

Raines was the one who looked away, of course. "Yeah. Since I *am* paying you well and there's plenty for you to hire some help, don't you think it's about time you did that?"

"Maybe. Look, I doubt that I need to remind you what's at stake. By employing me to carry out your wishes, you're insuring your future and that of your children, your wife and your harem. Although they won't come out and say it, you'll have the tacit approval of everyone like you who holds the reigns of power right now. Once I've accomplished my mission, you can rest assured things will remain as they should be and your America will be safe again. Another reformer will have gotten what was coming to him, or he'll have been derailed. I'm going to see which way works best- maybe he'll reach critical mass and become so unnerved by constantly being harassed that he'll forget about all this and find a safer occupation. Someone's tried to kill him already, and like you said, he has a wife to think about now. It might work, but if it doesn't, I go to plan B.

"On the other hand, if Stratton wins, you can-"

"Kiss it all goodbye. I know that, and no- I *don't* need a reminder."

"Good enough. Now, if you'll excuse me, I have a little follow-up to take care of." After a momentary pause he added, "Mister Raines, don't ever question my tactics again."

Ray didn't need to say any more. The man nodded and walked away rather quickly.

Philip Raines also was doing exactly what he'd been told not to do. He took out his cell phone and dialed another number he knew.

"Did you think of anything else today that might be relevant to our case?" Danni put that question to Tom as they headed south on I-97 and closed in on US 50. He'd loosened up and was more amenable to conversation now, and she decided to get back to that topic he'd brought up in the middle of their law school project. *It might help to take his mind further away from that bombing; might make him even more comfortable...*

...then, maybe we can get to the other matter...

He shook his head. "Not really. I got some crime stats I'd requested from around that time period, but I haven't had a chance yet to look 'em over."

"Why did you ask for them?"

"I wanted to take a look at the violent crime trends for Baltimore and the surrounding counties- see if the numbers I found told any stories. The more roadblocks we come across in our investigation of that corpse, the more curious it's making me. There's some kind of an undercurrent here; too many questions can't be answered, or they just lead to more questions. It's like a black hole, or a Bermuda Triangle or something- possibly some big mystery that was swept under the rug. Even though I can't figure out what it is, I can't let it go, either. I feel the need to keep digging but I don't know what I'm looking for."

"I hear you. No one's come forward to try to identify our John Doe, which raises more questions still...you'd think this guy never even existed."

"Sure seems that way, doesn't it? This has been frustrating- for everyone involved, obviously. It's taken its toll, too, in more ways than one."

"What do you mean?"

He needed to tell someone, and he didn't want to burden John or Kim when he saw them- not with all they had going on. Danni seemed like a good choice... "Well, I guess you saw how my conversation with my wife went."

"Yes, I did- I figured that was what you were getting at."

"This hasn't been a good few months, and that skeleton you and your crew unearthed has just made the situation that much more complicated. Those other old cases were sucking me in on their own merits as things were. The timing of yours on top of all that...it just seems weird somehow...

"Anyway, this isn't the first time I've become so preoccupied with the goings-on of that timeframe."

"Your father..."

"Yeah. When I first got into Homicide I looked into his case and got carried away. For months I used what spare time I had to investigate and try to come up with some sort of answer. Needless to say, I failed in that. My marriage suffered, too, which is what's happening now."

"In a way, I understand where she's coming from, but... we're talking about your father. I mean, if *my* father vanished like yours did, I'd leave no stone unturned in my search for answers."

"I guess what happened with your Dad was tough enough on you, huh?"

"Yeah, but at least I knew what happened to him. That was very hard, but *not* knowing must be hell...so your wife's giving you a hard time about it?"

"She's remembering what happened before and seeing the same thing now. She has a point, it's just-...I don't know, Danni, I feel like I'm in No Man's Land right now. I know I'm putting a strain on my family again but I want to *know*! I *have* to know what happened to my father! Why can't she understand that?!" Danni remained silent. "Sorry- I don't mean to dump on you."

"Don't worry about it- sounds like you needed to dump on somebody. What you're saying makes perfect sense to me, which

56

gives me another reason why we should keep cooperating on this- keep digging. Sooner or later we just might ask the right question or pull the one string that will unravel this thing that has us both- hey, isn't that Holly's on the left?"

"Yeah, we have to pass it and go back, with the way the exits are set up. Take this one, then turn left when you hit the junction at the end of the off-ramp..."

"It sure was considerate of Tom to give us plenty of notice before he came. That's one thing I'll thank him for when he gets here," Kim said as she nonchalantly looked through her wardrobe trying to pick something out.

As a result of his 'heads-up' they'd had enough time to take a bath together, and even enough to relax in the tub for a while before getting ready. Given the revelation he made to her, which led to the shocking series of possible answers to decades-old mysteries- including what happened to John's father-, they needed the time alone. "This is a very welcome change of pace."

"You can say that again." John was buttoning his shirt when the doorbell rang. "Ah- there they are. I'll go down and greet them, unless you need some help."

"I'll be fine once you zip me." She emerged from the closet with a little white silk dress she liked and slipped into it, then turned so he could take care of his part. He did that and kissed her on the back of her neck when he finished. "Thank you, Baby; it shouldn't take me but a few minutes..."

John headed downstairs just as Herb was letting Tom inside. "Hey, Brother, how-" The rest of his greeting never made it out of his mouth when he saw the attractive woman follow Tom through the door, which also made him wonder why Tom had her with him. John's suspicions about him and Vanessa surfaced for a moment...

...but he shook the thought off just as quickly. *That's not my business, anyway.*

Then he sensed the strength exuding from this woman. She had a certain air about her that said 'don't screw with me, or else'...

"Hi, John." Tom chuckled upon seeing his reaction.

"Hey, Tom. When you said 'Danni' I thought you meant-
...well, '*Danny*'!" He turned to her. "Anyway, welcome to our
home, and I hope you'll forgive me."

Danni also laughed. "Of course, Mister Governor. I'm
honored to meet you." She detected a fragrance coming from him
that most definitely was not masculine...

"Thank you. Kim's upstairs- she'll be right down."

"Still primping, is she?" Tom said with a grin.

"Hey- I never complain about the results, although along
those lines at least one religious leader is certain she's a demon, in
part because she's a bit flashy." John's levity disappeared when he
went on. "In all seriousness, though, we're both glad to slow down
a bit. We need some relaxation; a little privacy will be a good
thing, too. What better place to enjoy both than here, in our little
haven, not to mention close to our family?" he said as he hugged
Tom.

"I couldn't agree more. It's great to have you back." Tom
clapped him on the back a couple times. When they backed away,
his disposition also became serious. He also lowered his voice so
there was no chance Kim would hear what he was about to say. "I
never thought a migraine would be a lifesaver." He didn't say any
more- the hint he gave at what could have happened at the news
studio was more than enough.

"Yeah. I'd have gone through with the interview if Kim
hadn't come down with it." John looked away. "I don't have to tell
you how upset she was, and still is. This situation is getting
worse..."

"Tom, if you'd like, I could take off, and-"

John shelved his anxiety for the moment and interjected,
cutting Danni off. "No, absolutely not. I didn't mean for you to see
that. You came all the way down here, and at the very least you're
going to eat some of the best fried chicken you'll ever taste.
Uh...you *do* like fried chicken, I hope?"

She smiled. "It's not a staple of mine, but yes, I enjoy it
when I have it."

"Excellent. You won't be disappointed in the least; I guar-
awn-tee it!" His jest lightened everyone up, which he was glad to
see. He walked to the base of the stairs. "Honey? Are you ready?"

John frowned when she didn't answer right away. "Kim?"

* * *

"Hello, Kimberly. Looking terrific in white..."

The woman's life, literally, was in his hands.

With the slightest pull, he could end it...

...but there was no way he would. There was, however, the alternative he had in mind. Combined with what he'd already done on this same day, the timing seemed perfect. His added surprise really could serve to shake them- badly.

Maybe badly enough...

On a couple occasions he'd scouted the immediate area around their home, looking for a good shooting position and he'd come across the one where he was. It provided a good line of fire into the kitchen, and he was enjoying the added bonus of the view into the bedroom as he continued to watch her prepare.

Some things never change, do they?

On instinct, he ducked when she turned suddenly and looked right at him.

Kim had had such a strong feeling that she was being watched once before; it happened only minutes before she was abducted by Walter Daniels and Clyde Davis in April of 2000. She looked out into the darkness and saw just that, along with the lights and outlines of the neighbors' homes.

Even though it was highly unlikely that someone would break the window, rush in and take her this time since she wasn't on the ground floor, that unlikelihood didn't dismiss the apprehensive feeling she had. As her heart raced she thought about all the threats against her and John that still hung in the air like a super-cell cloud over their heads- ominous, threatening, capable of unleashing catastrophe that lurked within and perhaps only waiting for the right moment.

That cloud had followed them everywhere, and had become even more daunting over recent weeks...

...and earlier today, someone tried to kill John...

Just then, John's call from the first floor shook her out of that nerve-wracking train of thought. "Yes- I'm sorry!" Kim called back. "I'm finishing up now..."

What the hell is wrong with me? She can't possibly see me...

...or, can she?

Even as he almost laughed at himself for thinking she could spot him when he was five hundred yards away, it was nighttime and there was no moon, a notion that popped up made him look at the situation differently.

Women's intuition can be pretty accurate- sometimes right on the mark...

...and with all she's been through, hers could be very keen...

He set up again and sighted her in the scope...

...when she walked out of the room.

Catch you later, Gorgeous...

While he waited for his opportunity, he began to wonder about the woman who'd entered the house moments ago with Captain Tom Stratton. In the failing light he didn't get a good look at her.

Nonetheless, there was something familiar about her...

Whoa...

...now I see what all the fuss is about.

That was Danni's reaction upon seeing the famous femme fatale in person for the first time. The photos and video clips of her, as good as they were, still didn't quite do her justice.

Kimberly Stratton was clad in a short and rather tight white dress that was very chic and racy, but not sleazy. In a manner that was tasteful- also tantalizing- it outlined what it didn't reveal, clinging tightly to her from shoulders to waist, then flaring out at her hips. It was difficult not to become engrossed, not to mention jealous, especially given the highly coveted symbols of femininity she was blessed with- the 'nice cans', as her ex-partner would have put it. Of course, that was far from all she had.

Along with her slender but firm-looking arms, her often raved-about legs were bare and much of them was visible. They were further complimented by a sexy, strappy pair of white sandals with the lofty stiletto heels that seemed to be a mainstay with her. She descended the staircase very gracefully and took her husband's arm when she reached him at the bottom.

This woman sure can make an entrance...

...normally I'd hate someone like you.

Even though they were married for over two years, with their shared expression as well as the vibes and body language coming from them it almost looked like this was their wedding day, which made her white ensemble appropriate. The smooch they gave each other was the cherry on top.

First, she greeted her brother-in-law. "It's so good to see you, Tom; I've missed you," she said, greeting him with a warm hug and a kiss on the cheek.

"Right back at you, Sis. I've missed you, too." When Kim turned to her second guest, Tom made the introduction. "Mrs. Kimberly Stratton, I'd like you to meet Detective Danielle Searles of the Baltimore County Police Missing Persons Unit."

"Call me Danni," she said as she took Kim's proffered hand. As she suspected she would, Danni caught more than a hint of the same fragrance emanating from Kim as the one she'd noticed from her husband. *Some quality time spent together in the tub, no doubt...*"It's nice to meet you, Ma'am."

"It's very nice to meet you, too, Danni, and please- call me Kim. Wow! I love the uniforms they give detectives these days!" Kim said with a playful smile as she backed away a bit and appraised her guest. "And if I may say so, you wear it well!"

"Why, thank you! I don't know, though- I kinda like the one you wore better. It was a bit smaller, if I'm not mistaken," Danni countered, smiling in return as Kim looked at her blankly for a moment, then blushed and lowered her head. "Sorry- I couldn't resist. I heard and read about your little stint with us. That was very impressive police work, I must say- not to mention gutsy, since you really weren't trained for it and you were far from seasoned."

"Thanks. It was pretty scary, too- not something I'd want to do again, if you know what I mean."

"I can imagine." *It's definitely not your style, the incident in Boston notwithstanding.*

Tom stepped in. "In regards to what Danni's wearing, she had a date tonight but cancelled it so she could help me out by driving me here. I was on edge, to say the least, when I found out what happened at the studio. She noticed that and did me a big favor."

Kim turned to her. "How thoughtful of you! I always did admire that about police officers- how you look out for each other in addition to what you do. Besides Tom, a couple other very dear friends of mine are in the department. Well, I'm sure your date will understand. At least, he'd better!"

"Uh...oh- yeah, I'm sure he will." *Damn- that's the second time I slipped...*

...and I think she noticed, Danni mused as she noted the very slight change in Kim's expression. Fortunately, even if she did, her hostess moved on.

Hmmm... "Anyway, welcome to our home. The table is all set for dinner. Here- let me take your coats."

Danni was about to remove her jacket, but she stopped just in time. "I'll keep mine on, actually. It's not as heavy as it looks." She'd almost forgotten that she was in a see-through blouse. *That would have gone over well!*

"Ok," Kim said as she took Tom's. "I'll meet you all in the dining room, then."

Chapter 4

"…that's where we are and what we know, which so far isn't very much."

Tom leaned back and stretched after letting John and Kim in on the current case. The conversation gradually had turned to that, which wasn't a big surprise since it was so pervasive in Tom's thoughts.

John spoke up after he'd finished. "First of all, it goes without saying that Kim and I will keep this to ourselves. I know your investigation is ongoing and we won't do anything to compromise it. Is there any way we can help?"

"I'd have thought your hands would be full about now."

"Actually, we're taking a bit of a break while we figure out how we're going to handle our security situation. Herb's even edgy about it now and he has a very good reason; it's hard to protect Kim and me when there are only four on his team and we seem to have so many enemies.

"We need to figure out something soon because there still are a lot of places I need to campaign in, including- and especially- Kentucky, Louisiana and Mississippi starting next month. The Governors' elections there are critical; we have a very good chance of winning one of 'em and a pretty good chance of taking another. Nothing would please me more this year than to make one or two big scores in those campaigns- make Black eat a couple shitburgers. He and all his people would be shaking in their boots in addition to looking over their shoulders, but if our security situation stays the same or gets worse…"

Tom nodded, and watched with a pang of anger as Kim cuddled against him and lay her head onto his shoulder, her high state of worry apparent in her expression.

John sensed her anxiety as well and planted a kiss on her forehead. "We'll figure something out. In a way, this is a good sign; if the establishment's scared enough to threaten me so much, I must be more legitimate a threat than they're letting on."

A good sign?! Kim had to resist her urge to say what she felt about that remark and she needed a moment to herself. "Um, I should clear the table. I'll be right back." She went to get up, but he stopped her. Not wanting to cause a little scene, she stayed, but she was sure he knew that she wasn't happy with him.

John felt her bristling. When he thought about what had just come out of his mouth, he knew why. *Nice...I'm sure* that *made her feel better,* he thought, berating himself for making such a cavalier statement about their precarious situation when she was so edgy about it. "You don't need to do that; the dishes can wait. Just sit with me and relax, Ok?" He stroked her cheek.

Kim saw his implied apology, which made her feel bad for overreacting. *What's wrong with me? He didn't say that to upset me; he's just as concerned about the danger we're in as I am...*

...dammit, I hate this...

She started to lower her head, but he touched her chin and made her raise it back up, then kissed her tenderly. When they pulled back from the kiss, he mouthed 'I love you'. That brought her smile back and she snuggled against him once more.

"Do you two need some space? Danni and I could-"

John and Kim turned back to them, and it was Kim who spoke up. "No, we don't want you to go. We're so glad you're here; we want you both to stay for a while. I didn't mean to subject you to that. I just-...well..."

"You don't have to explain yourself to me, Kim. I worry about both of you, too. It would be great if we could jump ahead to November 2nd of next year and get you into the White House."

"Amen," John chimed in. "So you're going to see Mister Jack tomorrow?"

"Yeah, at ten o'clock."

"You don't seem to be looking forward to that."

"I'm not. Frankly, I don't even know why I asked him. The more I think about it, the more I can see how he might think I'm accusing him of something, which I'm not doing by any means. Most of all, I don't like the fact that I'm making him relive part of his life that I'm sure he'd rather forget, but on the other hand, talking with me about it might make him remember something that could help me break this all open."

John nodded. "I see the dilemma. Although it's part of your job, I can't imagine that makes it any more palatable for you or him."

"Honestly, I don't like the taste of any of this. It's like the fates are throwing out little teases here and there. They do that every so often, usually when the effects of their last one have worn off. They pique me just enough to get me on the trail, which never seems to lead anywhere, and there's the added bonus of throwing more turmoil into my life for nothing. The problem is, it always feels like there's something to it- like now. I know it's possible that the stiff Danni's team found is a completely isolated case but my instincts tell me it isn't. All the same, I can't find anything to substantiate my suspicions, so as a result, those suspicions are all I have. Again. This could add up to nothing, yet I can't let it go."

"This is the same conversation we had a couple months ago when the FBI lab lost the sample from our boy."

"That's true. The difference is, you actually have a live body you're trying to trace, only we still have no idea where to start looking for Strauss. Similar story there, only-"

"If you're searching for Joshua Strauss, you're not searching for a live body."

Tom looked back at him with a blank expression. "Huh?"

"Hold on to your seat, Brother; you probably won't believe what I'm about to tell you. Danni, this might be of interest to you, too. Now, you have to-…ah, screw it, I might as well just come right out and say it. The guy we think is Joshua Strauss, in all probability, is none other than Christopher Hedges."

"Christopher Hedges? Who's-…hold on, you don't mean-"

"You've got it."

"John, that's impossible! He's been dead since the early '70s, for Christ's sake!"

"Just like the supposed Mister Strauss was dead since '89? The same one who kidnapped Kim- again- three years ago?"

Tom didn't answer for a moment. He looked at Danni, who was silent, but observing the exchange.

John went on. "Think about it; we know his 'death' in '89 was a hoax- and a damned good one. He fooled everybody. Why did it work so well? Because he'd done it before."

"But…Hedges was a teenager! How could he possibly have pulled that off?"

"You've just voiced the question of the day. I don't know how he did it. Maybe he had help. You know about my research into the Strauss family history; Kim and I agree that our boy killed all three of them, assumed Josh's identity, then made off with the inheritance."

"I have another question: what led you to the conclusion that Hedges is behind all this? What evidence do you have?"

"Kim's memory played a big part. As for the rest…well, that's a little complex- and personal. It'll have to wait until later. Sorry, Danni."

"I understand, Mister Governor."

"Let's just say it's very convincing. You'll agree as soon as you hear it." John went back to an earlier subject. "Hey, do you think it might help if Kim and I come along tomorrow when you go to see Mister Jack? Not that we'd be there the whole time- meaning, for the official part, of course-, but having us there might lighten him up a little. Might help lighten you up, too." He turned to Kim. "Is that all right with you, Honey?"

"I was thinking the same thing. He always smiles when he sees me- having me there might show him that we're not accusing him of anything, which I know you're not, Tom. I'd love to go. Afterwards we can see Mom, Sue, Donna and Leslie- make up for today."

"Sounds good."

"Ok, now that we've settled that, I'm going to clear the table." Kim said as she stood.

Danni spoke up as Kim started to walk away. "Do you have any more of this tea? It's good stuff!"

"Oh, we have plenty left. I'll get more for you."

"I can wait until we clear the table; I'll give you a hand."

"Thank you."

"Lieutenant Miller…*what*?!! That can't be- he was just here a few hours ago!…When did she find him?…Ok, is she with you?…All right- I'll be right there."

After almost two months, you'd think they'd have known who their skeleton was by now, the 'anonymous tipster' thought as he picked up the phone and dialed the number again.

"Apparently, they'll need another nudge…"

"Jesus Christ…that motherfucker. That mother*fucker*!! I'd like to break every bone in his-" Tom had to take a breath, and it felt like he'd been punched in the gut. "I'm sorry, John. I had no idea…"

After the women went into the dining room, John filled Tom in on the history between him and Christopher Hedges. He went on to explain how he and Kim put the pieces together based on that and what he'd inadvertently spilled to Kim while he held her captive. "Now you understand why I can't let him fade back into the woodwork- not after all he's done. I want his ass nailed even more than before; I want him to burn."

"I'm with you. Unfortunately, even having Kim identify him doesn't tell us where to look for him."

"Yeah. I've been wracking my brain, trying to think of every little thing I can and I come up empty every time. For obvious reasons I didn't want to bring Kim in on this, but she knows a lot more about him than I do. She had more contact, needless to say…in spite of all he put her through, she's remembering a lot. I guess in a way it's therapeutic for her to be able to talk about those ordeals, although I don't want for her to dwell on them too much. You know I'll do whatever I can to protect her- and yeah, I know I overdo it sometimes. Kim reminded me of that, but considering all that's happened, plus the fact that he's still out there…"

"I understand, John, and I'm sure Kim does, too."

He nodded. "I have to say, in one respect I'm glad I did tell her and that it doesn't seem to bother her so much to discuss it. It wasn't long at all before those fragments she remembered answered the question of who he is.

"Shortly after she said that, I was convinced it was him. We'll go further into what she recalls about him- things he said to her, things she might have overheard, things that might come to her about where he was before and where he might be now. She's the best chance we have at possibly coming up with an answer. I still don't like having her revisit all this, but otherwise I have no idea how and where to start looking. Since no law enforcement agency has a thing on him, either, which also would be the case with Hedges, we don't have much of a choice…who knows, we-"

His head snapped around at what he heard next, from the kitchen.

How many times is this phone gonna ring tonight?!
"Lieutenant Miller."

"Sir, we just got another anonymous call. Same guy as before, I think; once more he didn't leave his name."

"What did he tell you?"

"The name of the murder victim your people dug up two months ago. He said 'it's taking you all too long to figure it out so I'll help you along'. He also said 'now that I've given you his name, you'll know that of his partner. There are more. You'll find them if you really want to. Follow the trail. Where it leads will surprise you'. Then he repeated the name."

"Talkative, wasn't he? So, what was the name?"

"That's funny..." Kim said as she looked out the kitchen window.

"What?"

"The neighbor's dog; he sure is barking his head off, isn't he? That's by far the most noise he's ever made..."

Danni frowned and walked over to Kim. Both women looked over toward the house next door. "So he's usually quiet?"

"Mm-hmm, very much so. I wonder if-"

In the same instant when Danni saw the flash, her instincts kicked right in. She grabbed Kim, who shrieked in surprise, and took her down as she heard the 'POP' when the bullet struck the window. As they fell, Danni rolled her body under Kim's to break her fall.

"What are you doing?!"

"Just stay down- it'll be all right." Danni drew her gun, looked up at the window and saw a pretty big indentation. She also felt Kim beginning to shake.

She might be going into shock, Danni surmised as she covered the frightened woman with her own body. Confirmation of that came with her brief look into Kim's eyes, which were unfocused and glazing over as she surely realized what had just happened.

"Danni?!" Tom rushed in with John right behind. When he saw the two women on the floor, he also dropped down and pulled John with him. "What was that-" He stopped when saw the pit in the window. There was no question as to what had just happened, and what very well could have happened if the original window had not been changed...

Danni was covering Kim, whose face almost was as white as her dress. John saw that, too; he immediately crawled over to her and pulled her close as Danni let go of her.

Herb was right on it. In seconds the whole team was assembled and awaiting his instructions. "Dawn, Derek, you stay here and protect Governor and Mrs. Stratton. Keep the radio clear unless you have good reason." He looked at Tom and Danni next. "Sir, Detective, I take it you won't mind helping 'em out? If there is somebody out there, it might be more than one person and a possible diversion for some sort of attack. Given what almost happened today, Mel and I need to check this out, but I'm sure your first priority's the same as mine."

There was no question his implication was that John and Kim's safety came first. "Definitely. Do your thing, Herb. Danni's shoes weren't made for walking far, anyway, let alone running. She and I'll stay here, and I'm calling this in to the State Police Barracks nearby. Looks like we could use the backup."

Herb nodded and turned to Mel. "Let's go." They took off toward the garage.

Dawn moved over to the couple. "Sir, Ma'am, let's get you to the safe room. Follow me…"

Ray already was gone and at that moment was making his way back to where he'd left his car. The dog had put a little wrinkle into his plan and the bulletproof glass was something he didn't know about. *Somebody was thinking- that's for sure…*

Unfortunately, that measure had cost him an unexpected chance to solve a nagging problem- one that nearly had proven fatal to him. Even so, the night wasn't a total loss. He had no doubt his mission was accomplished; surely he'd conjured up some fear.

Time to see what's next…

"Thank you all for bearing with me; I know it's been a long day and you have loved ones you want to get home to. I promise I'll only keep you a few minutes longer. This is a very important matter to me and I believe all of you will feel the same way."

With that statement, Governor Collins prepared Maryland's General Assembly for her proposal, which she launched right into. "I'm sure every one of you is aware that my predecessor and mentor was the target of yet another assassination attempt today. Recently, Governor and Mrs. Stratton have received numerous tangible death threats, one of which was acted upon in the form of the bombs planted in the news studio in which Governor Stratton was to have been interviewed this afternoon. I'm very thankful that he ended up canceling that interview. Otherwise-...well, I really don't need to elaborate, do I?

"For months John has tried to get federal protection, but to no avail; the government will not provide any. The excuses they use amount to loopholes in the campaign and candidacy rules. It seems obvious to me that President Black is worried about losing his job and a lot of his family's excess wealth, not to mention that of all his friends, and thus he cares nothing about our former Governor's safety. John and Kim have only four bodyguards, whom they pay out of their own pockets, which brings me to the reason why I've asked you all to stay a bit longer this evening.

"The man has done so much for our state and he'll do even more for the whole country once he's elected President, which I'm convinced he will be. He has to get there first, though, and we, the General Assembly of John's home state, can help make that happen. I think it's time we repay the services he performed for us.

"I propose to you a measure that will triple the Strattons' security contingent at a cost of one million dollars; this will ensure their protection until January 20th, 2005- Inauguration Day, when the Secret Service won't have any choice but to protect them.

"Time is of the essence. Considering what happened today, I doubt I need to emphasize that point any further. I ask for your immediate consideration and as quick a vote as you can make.

"Well, we have another long day tomorrow, but the session's just about over, so I don't want to hear any complaints!" Amid a chorus of chuckles and 'thank God's, she ended the evening for all of them. "Thank you for your time. Sleep well, everyone."

Not surprisingly, John had to carry Kim into the room Herb had designated as the 'safe room'- the one where it would be easiest to protect them. The whole security team had hoped it wouldn't come down to that but they knew in all probability that what happened while Kim and Danni were in the kitchen, or something along those lines, was inevitable. That sense of inevitability also had prompted Herb to oversee the replacement of every window of the house with the highest quality bulletproof glass.

Herb's foresight had saved Kim's life. There was no doubt in her mind of that as she slowly began to regain control of herself. As she did, the first emotion to assert itself was not exactly the one she expected to, and it quickly become stronger as the ramifications of this unknown assailant's action settled in.

It wasn't long at all before her anger took over.

"That *bastard*!! This is our *home*- our place of escape and now one person has *ruined* it!! How can we feel safe here anymore?!! Why is this happening, John?!! *Why*?!!"

He didn't answer. He knew she was venting, which she certainly needed to do. He drew her closer once she'd finished, and she lay her head onto his shoulder and wept.

"I don't know how much more of this I can take..."

John looked her in the eyes. "Honey, listen to me. Now is when I need you the most. I know we're in a bad way; there are some people out there who are trying to make us quit. That's what this is all about- you know it, too. I'm not trying to make light of it or rationalize it. I'm telling it like it is right now, but things have to get better for us sometime. I refuse to believe our situation always will be this way. They won't scare me out of this race. I'm not quitting." He turned to the window. "*You hear me?!! I'm not quitting!!!*"

Kim touched his face and he looked back at her. Not wanting to say it, she kissed him instead and settled back against him once more. She was certain he saw it in her expression, though.

Instead, John said it. "I know. I'm scared, too..."

As Danni sat with the others, gun at the ready, watching- and more importantly listening-, she reflected on the shot.

She looked over at Kim, who, after her outburst, appeared to be calmer- at least, for the moment. How long until she started to think about it again, though?

How could she *not* think about it?

Actually, I feel pretty lucky the glass stopped that bullet, too, because it just as easily could have been meant for me...

Danni jumped when her cell phone rang. She took it out of her pocket, looked at the screen and frowned when she saw Lieutenant Miller's number on it. "Sir? What's up?"

"Danni, there's...no easy way to tell you this. About an hour ago, Harry Lawson was found shot to death in his apartment."

"Huh?"

"You heard me right; I'm just leaving there now. He didn't suffer, which is the only positive I can see in this. Single shot to the head...sorry to lay such a shocker on you, but I didn't want you to hear that over the wire."

"I appreciate that, Sir."

"Look, I know that's a lot to digest, but there's another reason why I'm calling you. Our anonymous caller phoned in again. Seems he was a little impatient- he gave some cryptic information, but he also gave the operator a name. He repeated it and made sure she got it, then hung up. We had it checked out and, lo and behold, it comes up as the name of someone who's been missing since 1970. He said it's the identity of our John Doe."

"Really? What's the name?"

"Ronald Novak. His height/weight data from the time he disappeared definitely falls into the neighborhood of that of your stiff when he was alive. There's something else, too, which to me is the clincher. Novak broke his right fibula when he was a teenager; so did the man you uncovered."

"Sounds like that could be the break we've been looking for...I wonder why he's in such a hurry to help us along?"

"Beats me. He hinted that there are more victims to be found and he wants us to 'follow the trail'; he says we'll be surprised where it leads, whatever that means. I guess you'll be seeing Captain Stratton again soon. Would you like to pass that on to him?"

"Uh, sure, I'll let him know, Sir."

"Where are you now, anyway? I called your home first."

"Funny you should ask. Captain Stratton and I are at Governor and Mrs. Stratton's place on the Eastern Shore."

"*Governor* Stratton's place? What are you doing there?"

"Well, it's sort of a long story." She looked around at the sound of the approaching sirens. "I'll fill you in later, Sir- gotta go..."

"...look, you said you wanted me to put a scare into him, which is what I did." Ray heard the sigh on the other end, then came something that didn't happen often.

"You're right. It was a good opportunity and so was the studio attempt," Raines said.

"I'm glad you agree. I take it you know that Maryland's General Assembly will vote on a measure to triple his security, so you also know what that means."

"Yeah. It means we're at a decision point: take him out now before they pass that vote, which they will, or risk an attempt when he has a bigger security element. We also could cease and desist and see if he'll shoot himself in the foot somehow, or if his campaign will run out of steam…"

"Your thoughts?"

"I figured it only was a matter of time before he boosted his security, or someone or some group did that for him. He's gotta be scared- of that I'm sure- but is he scared enough?" After a pause, Raines added, "I don't know that you'll get another opportunity to take him out over the next few days, or even the next few weeks, whether it's before or after Stratton's security is beefed up. As far as I'm concerned, maybe you should go into passive mode and just wait for a mistake. What do you say the next move should be?"

"Infiltrate the security detail somehow. That would be the way to go."

"Do you think you could?"

"I don't know yet. It depends on where they select their prospects from and who's in charge of that. If we can find out both, it's possible. We just have to keep our eyes and ears open. If we're not successful in that…well, like you said, we'll probably have to switch to passive mode for the time being- just watch and wait."

"Right…watch them both…"

"What?"

"I was thinking, maybe it's time we shifted focus a little- go with something we discussed in March."

When Ray briefly thought back to their conversation, it came back. "You mean, his wife? As in taking her?"

"Yeah, if the opportunity presents itself. With her in our hands, he might snap somehow…I'm sure we could come up with some way to use her to our advantage."

"I'd say that's even less of a possibility now than before. Frankly, I don't see it happening."

"Well, it was a good thought, anyway. You can't blame a guy for trying. In more ways than one it would have been nice to have her, but I suppose you're right. I'll talk to you later."

That conversation made Raines' decision for him.

He had to do it, so he dialed the number. When the man answered, all Philip said was, "it's a go."

Ray hit the button to complete the latest installment on his insurance policy. He was especially glad now that he'd decided upon this course of action from the beginning of this venture with Raines. The man had a short temper, was self-centered and impatient. He placed little value on human life. There was a chance he'd just taken some sort of turn, given how calm he was. Ray expected to be screamed at after this gaffe.

I've already been a fall guy- for something that wasn't even my fault. That will not happen again, especially for somebody like Philip Raines...

"...thanks again, Laura. We really appreciate you doing this and for putting your proposal to the Assembly. Your timing couldn't have been better. Now, get some sleep, huh? If I know you, by now your eyes show more red than white...you, too. Good night."

All was quiet, more or less, as John hung up with his successor. Some of the multitude of State Police officers who had responded to Tom's call remained at the house by order of Governor Collins to supplement John and Kim's security detail for the night. Feeling safer, and with his adrenaline level back to normal, John found himself beginning to tire quickly. He glanced at Kim as she yawned- no doubt she was worn out as well. "You ready to go up, Kitten?" he inquired so only she could hear.

She looked up at him and nodded. He kissed her and caressed her cheek, then looked over at Tom and Danni. "I'm really glad you two were here tonight...although now you're probably thinking about what a lousy host I am. On top of what happened a while ago, you even had to bring your own food."

"That's my brother for you- always finding humor somehow," Tom said as he turned to Danni, who was laughing along with him. However, he became serious again when the gravity of both nerve-wracking events that day settled back in.

Kim voiced her appreciation. "I'm glad you both were here, too. You were right on top of things, Danni. Gosh, I can't believe how quickly you pulled me down!" she gushed. "I never even saw the shot before I was on the floor! I sure wouldn't mind having you on our security team, in case you're looking for a change of venue. Thank you so much."

"You're welcome. I'm glad I could help. As for a change of venue, I doubt my boss would like losing two of his detectives in one day, although in this case it would be for a good cause..."

"What do you mean, two?" Tom asked. "Speaking of Lieutenant Miller, wasn't that him who called you earlier?"

"Yes, it was him, but...as for what he told me, I'll tell you on the way back, Ok?"

"Ok, and good point; we do need to get going."

"But it's so late," Kim protested. "You should stay here tonight. We have plenty of room for both of you, and I can see that you and Danni are tired, like the rest of us."

"I think you're right," John added in concurrence with his wife before turning back to Tom. "In fact, I insist you stay. We'll help set you up; it won't take long at all."

"Well...it's up to you, Danni, since you drove."

After a moment she turned to Tom, who'd just asked the question, and nodded. "I am feeling pretty tired, actually- and, the Governor did insist."

"Indeed I did!" John replied. "All right, Tom, you can take the guest room down here. I'll come with you and make sure you have all you need."

"If you'll follow me upstairs, Danni, I'll show you where the other guestroom is," Kim said as she walked over to the staircase.

"Sounds good to me. Lead on." She went up behind Kim, eyes drawn magnetically to that body of hers- the envy of so many, and understandably so- as she climbed the stairs.

I wonder if there's anyone on this planet who could avoid *looking at her,* she thought as she took in Kim's amazing legs.

They reached the top and, after a very short walk down the hallway, turned into one of the most welcoming bedrooms she'd seen. "Wow! Very nice!"

"Thank you! I love this motif; it just makes you want to go right to sleep, which definitely fits. As you can see, everything's ready. The bathroom's just down the hallway to your left. Is there anything I can get for you? More tea?"

"No, thanks- I'm fine."

"Ok. Sleep well, and I'll fix us all a good, hot breakfast in the morning."

"I like the sound of that! 'Night, Kim."

"Good night."

A few minutes later, in Kim's favorite room, John unzipped her dress. She worked it down and stepped out of it. Clad only in her thong, she rested against him and looked up at him as he embraced her from behind.

There was only one thing on their minds, and there would be no waiting.

In his wife's eyes John saw love and something that came with it, and also from it. Intermingled with those potent emotions- and undoubtedly serving to fuel them- he saw her lingering fear from what almost happened that day to both of them, her desire to comfort him, and her need to be comforted by him.

As he had so many times before, John thought of the expression 'bedroom eyes' while he looked into Kim's. It seemed that whoever came up with that little saying had her in mind, especially in situations like this one.

Whenever she gave him the look, it never failed to work its magic on him- magic that always was so welcome...

...and very much so now. He gently gathered her into his arms and she kissed him as he carried her to bed...

...about forty miles to the northwest, the man gave up trying to figure out a way to patch the foundering ship, as another hole had been punched through its hull with this latest phone call. He'd stressed over it for hours and had come up with nothing.

The more he thought about it, the more it began to look inevitable. It wasn't like before, when there was plenty of help. Would he be able to stop it now, or hide it?

The caller didn't want him to stop it and he knew who the caller was.

It couldn't be anyone else; it had to be him.

Apparently, I'm not forgiven, even though all I ever did was help you...

...then again, I doubt very much that you're forgiven, either, he thought as he reached for the ringing phone.

Chapter 5

"I think your efforts to turn me into a morning person are starting to pay off."

Kim laughed as she lay against him. "As far as I'm concerned, there's no better way to wake up, with which you seem to agree. This is our time together, John, and I always want to make the most of it. Now is when there's no one else but you and me, same as it is when we settle in for the night. I love waking up in your arms, even more than I ever thought I would, and nothing gives me more pleasure than showing you how much I do."

"Well put, Kitten. I feel the same way," he said with a smile, then kissed her. "I don't hear anyone else moving around yet. Let's just lie here for a while longer."

"You know I won't argue." She cuddled closer and sighed...

...but it wasn't long before she began to think about what they discussed yesterday- that being Christopher Hedges. Kim also thought about John's determination to get him and her own desire to permanently eradicate that cancer from their life. In light of that, she went back to her periods of captivity, intent on remembering as much as she could of what he said to her and of what she'd overheard by way of phone calls he'd made...

"Kim? Is something wrong?"

"Hmm? Oh, I'm just-..."

He saw the same degree of concentration on her face the day before and knew where she was. He completed her sentence. "...thinking about Hedges and trying to come up with a lead or two he might have given you by accident."

She nodded. "I'm sorry. I didn't mean to break up our moment like that, but I know how important it is to you to find him. It's important to me, too- more so after you shared with me what he did to you."

"I know, and it's all right." He smoothed away a lock of hair that had fallen over her eye, then stroked her mane as something came to him. "Your hair's the same shade of chestnut brown as it was the day we met; I've been meaning to tell you that. It's another reminder to me of how happy I am that you walked up to me that day and changed my life forever. So many things were different afterwards- most of all, the decisions I made regarding what to do with my life. I started to feel this sense of purpose and direction ever since that day. Although I still felt it when you and I weren't together, it seemed stronger when we were, and it feels especially strong now." He smiled as he looked into her glistening eyes. "I wonder sometimes what would have happened otherwise; how things would have turned out for both of us if I hadn't been held back a grade..."

"Mmm- I've wondered about that a couple times, too. Even though I made a ton of money dancing, I still would have stopped when I did. It was time. I'm equally certain that I would have become a counselor. I might have kept doing the bikini contests for a few more years, though, and I'm sure I'd have stayed with cheerleading for a while longer; I really did enjoy that. I might have ended up going into show business after all- who knows? That is, provided our mutual acquaintance didn't happen across me on the night of my twentieth birthday and turn my life upside down like he did. Of course, he might have ended up somewhere else as well- maybe inside an incinerator!"

"Not a bad thought there!" he said as he chuckled. "How much did you make on an average night of dancing? I always was curious about that."

"I never walked away from a night at the Palace with less than a thousand dollars, and that was on a slow night, or in my first few months. When I became better known I averaged between two and three- closer to three in '90, my final year. On a few nights, the fetish nights in particular, I made five or more and my best was just over twenty."

"*Damn*!! Twenty thousand dollars in *one night*?!!"

"Mm-hmm. It was my last performance. Word about it had spread really quickly, and far! We had a bunch of professional athletes, some famous actors and plenty of businessmen- including a few oil sheiks- in there to see me off, along with all our regulars. We were sure the fire marshal would come in at some point and close us down because the place was so crowded. Then again, he might have been part of the audience that night, too!"

"I bet! Well, see you off they did, to say the least...*wow*!!"

"I was blown away, too, but enough of that. Do you think you'd have taken the same path you're on? I bet you would have."

"Most likely, yeah. I just don't know how everything would have turned out- whether or not I'd be in the position I'm in. I know the night on Suicide Ridge probably wouldn't have

78

happened. I might not have ended up in the U.S. Attorney's office- any number of things might have come out differently, or not happened at all because you and I didn't meet. I also know for certain that I would have been a hell of a lot less happy than I am now- if I'd have been happy at all," he added as he looked into his wife's smiling face.

"I'm definitely with you there."

"You know, it's funny how failing fifth grade turned out to be such a good thing."

"I won't argue with that, either. We might never have met if you'd passed. Just promise me you won't include that in your educational message, Ok?"

John laughed heartily. "Yeah, that sure could send the wrong signal, couldn't it? We might inspire a bunch of kids to fail deliberately in hopes of finding love. Well, don't worry- that won't be part of my message. Back to my topic, that wasn't all that factored in to our meeting. It almost did seem pre-destined, didn't it? If I'd been on time for school that day, or if you'd been on time…why *were* you late that day, Kim?"

She reflected for a moment. "Well, I remember waking up late that morning, or-…that's right- I went back to sleep after Mom left. She had to be at school early that day. I missed the bus that would have gotten me there on time and had to catch the next one. How about you? What made *you* tardy that day, Mister?"

He chuckled, but turned serious again when the recollection that started him on this topic took the forefront once more. "This'll really throw you for a loop. I haven't thought about it in years and all of a sudden it came right back just a couple minutes ago when I brushed the lock of hair away from your eye.

"I overslept that morning, too, in part because I had this dream about my Dad. It was the strangest thing…it started out with me walking through a patch of trees. I looked around and there he was, plain as day, standing right in front of me. He smiled at me and told me to keep going- that everything would be all right. I asked him how he knew and he said it again: 'Keep going, Son. All your questions will be answered'. He winked at me, then he was gone."

"Baby, you never told me that!" she exclaimed as she embraced him tightly. "What a wonderful dream!"

"It sure was. It's also strange how I forgot about it somehow. You'd think that one would have stuck out ever since. Maybe I just didn't see the significance of it back then, and of course, I didn't see our first meeting as a good thing in the early stage. Those first few months were torture. Then, things turned around for a while, then they got bad again…I suppose it got lost in all the turmoil and transition that year."

"That's so strange…you had the dream that very morning, yet, for the most part, you forgot about it until now."

"Yeah. Better yet, it all came back a couple minutes ago when I noticed the color of your hair, which made me think of the day we met and how important it was. Just like that, there was my Dad in the dream. At that moment, for some reason, that memory was a trigger. It acted like a time machine, taking me back to September 1st, 1982 and making me see what happened that day even more clearly than when I actually lived it. All from that one little detail."

"Wow…that gives you more reason to believe in fate, and intuition. I'm glad I read so much on the subject and talked with a few knowledgeable people about it. After my experience with those dreams and visions about our nemesis- at least, that's what he's been up to this point- I wanted to learn as much about those premonitions as I could. I hoped that if any such phenomena ever happened again to me or anyone I know, I might be able to decipher them and figure out what they meant. As for what just happened with you, I'm really curious as to why it came to you just now…"

"I don't know. Your guess is as good as mine, maybe better."

"In a way it's similar to yesterday, with me remembering those details about Josh- I mean, Hedges, when he had me. You're right, those little details really do matter, which is why I'm trying to remember more of them…is that why you said that?"

"Yeah, that's one reason. I guess another thing I'm trying to do is help make you feel as comfortable as possible about delving into that without getting on your nerves too much with my over-protectiveness. Who knows, maybe that played a part in me remembering the dream about my father- the coincidence, or karma, of that happening on the day we met. He's on my mind a lot lately- more so since Tom's looking into those old, unsolved cases."

"First of all, you're not getting on my nerves." She kissed him again, then pondered what he said after that part. "Hmmm…

seems to me it's more karma than coincidence, or maybe even some sort of insight. That could explain why your father is in your thoughts so much of late. It could be some sort of a sign."

"Could be. If that's the case, the obvious question is, what's the significance?"

"Right…it seems a lot easier to determine why you had your dream about him- or your vision, whichever it was- that morning we bumped into each other at school. That had to be foreshadowing." She giggled, unable to resist sharing with him what just came to her. "Maybe he was telling you, 'watch out, Buster- this one you're about to meet is a handful!'"

He cracked up, then came back with, "or, two!"

That remark earned him a little jab to the gut, but Kim laughed with him. "I sure opened myself up for that one, didn't I?"

"No comment."

"Good answer! Anyway, as for why you're thinking about your Dad now, the only reason that comes to me is the one you mentioned a moment ago, which is the investigation into those unsolved cases that took place around the time your father vanished. I wonder if that could be it- some sort of indication that the investigators, including Tom, are close to an answer as to what happened to him…"

John nodded. "Interesting…and a possibility. I've learned to not rule anything out, which goes double for female intuition and triple for *your* intuition. That's the other reason why I'm telling you all this."

"I figured it was. I've learned not to discount anything, too. I'm just glad I was able to get out of the mess that resulted from me ignoring all the signs that came to me."

"So am I, Kitten."

"Those nightmares I had; they were so vivid and frightening. All of them led to him, but it didn't make any sense because he was dead- so we all thought. That's why I discounted it as fallout from when Daniels abducted me. On that note, you shouldn't be quick to rule out what appears to be impossible, because depending on the conditions and the history…"

He nodded, picking up where she left off as he recalled a position paper he'd written years ago when he'd made such an argument as well. "…it might be that what you're taking into account isn't so ridiculous, or even unlikely. When you remove the cloak of perceived irrationality by considering situations in which the impossible becomes possible, you just might find your answer underneath. No matter how superficially nonsensical the scenario seems- or how unlikely the suspect- in a vacuum of tangible evidence, everything should be considered." He turned to find her looking at him with a curious glint in her eyes. "What's your take on all this, Kim?"

"I don't have anything concrete, but the more we talk about this, the more it's making me think back to all those subliminal warnings I got that I was in imminent danger of being kidnapped by you-know-who. In retrospect I saw the significance and relevance of those warnings. I know you've thought about your father lately, but have you dreamed about him, too?"

"No. I haven't dreamt about him since the day we first met."

"Well, I know I won't forget about that one anytime soon. That really is amazing! And who knows- maybe there was even more to it than the obvious implication...

"Anyway, given what you've told me, I don't know if it means you're close to finding out what happened to him, but all the same, it's possible. Maybe it means we should look through everything you have of his- everything connected to him even remotely- and see if there's some clue you might have overlooked. It also could mean that something relevant to his disappearance has been discovered recently- *un*covered, maybe."

He nodded. "Like Tom was speculating when he told us about all he and Danni knew concerning their investigation of that body the County guys dug up, and their theories surrounding it. As soon as I heard the report and the initial findings, especially the approximate timeframe of the death and burial, I started to wonder about that just like Tom did. I know it's also possible we're running around in circles, but..."

"I hear you. I suppose, one way or another, we'll find our answer- or not." With that, she pulled away from him and got out of bed. "For now, I guess we should get moving. I'm sure I'm not the only one in this house who's starving!"

Tom was not happy with himself.

As he lay awake and stared at the ceiling, he reflected on one of the events of yesterday- how he'd put himself in a situation that could have led to him cheating on his wife for the second time. That was exactly what he'd done by agreeing to go to Danni's place, knowing that at minimum there was some degree of mutual attraction. It was a dangerous and stupid thing to do, all in the lame guise of the assignment for the law school class, which he could have handled by himself.

It also was a heartless thing to do, given the underlying reason why he did it. Worse was the timing, with things being as they were between Donna and him…

A tap on his door snapped him out of his haze of guilt, but Danni's voice put him right back into it.

"Tom? Are you up?"

"Uh, yeah, I'm getting there. Are John and Kim awake?"

"I haven't seen or heard 'em yet. I wanted to tell you what Lieutenant Miller told me last night. May I come in?"

"No," he said a little too quickly and loudly. "I mean, I'm not dressed yet. Have a seat in the living room; I'll be right out."

"Ok."

Tom let out a deep breath as he heard her walking away. It was a bad situation that he felt had gone too far, even though nothing really had happened as yet. He had to draw the line, and quickly. As professional as Danni was, she'd understand.

At least, I hope she does…

On the other hand, there always was the chance that he was making too much of the situation, and that she'd laugh when he gave her his take on it.

If that's the case, no one will be happier than I am, he thought as he got up, dressed quickly and went out into the living room where Danni sat.

He took a chair across from her. "How did you sleep?"

"I was out like a light. That bed's as comfortable as mine, if not a little more! Your brother and sister-in-law sure know how to take care of their guests."

"That they do."

"I needed it, too. How about you? Did you sleep well?" Her eyes narrowed as she took him in. "It doesn't look like you did."

"I guess it doesn't. I have a lot on my mind. I slept sporadically, at best."

"That's understandable…"

Amid the silence that followed that exchange, Tom tried to formulate the best, but also the most delicate, approach for what he needed to say to her. More and more, he found himself hoping this was a big misunderstanding on his part.

However, before he could come up with the right words and the right way, Danni spoke up. "I suppose I'd better give you the bad news first. Frankly, I'm surprised I was able to sleep at all."

"What happened?"

"Harry Lawson's dead. He was found in his apartment late yesterday afternoon."

His mouth fell open. *"What*?!"

"I know. I saw him yesterday morning; he came in to give his resignation to Lieutenant Miller. He decided it was time."

"Christ...he was just with us a couple days ago!" Tom stood and walked away. "I can't believe this...murdered on the same day he retired, and in his own apartment, yet! Who in the hell could have done that? And, *why*?!" He turned back to Danni. "Are you Ok? This must be one hell of a shock for you, and I'm glad we didn't drive back last night."

"I'll be all right. I'm just-...numb right now."

Putting aside his attraction to her, Tom went over to her and laid his hands onto her shoulders, as he was sure she needed a hug.

She let him take her into his arms and lay against him for a moment. "Harry was a good guy. A little rough around the edges, but he was a good guy, and a good cop."

"That's what I heard about him. He never married or had kids, did he?"

"No. Besides his sister, there's no family or known relatives." Danni pulled away from him. "Thanks- I needed that."

Tom nodded and smiled. "Um...are there any suspects?"

"Not at the moment. The forensics people were all over his apartment, and as far as I know, they still are. No clues as yet."

"No indication of forced entry?"

"I didn't ask right then. I guess we'll know when we get back and see the report."

"Yeah, I suppose so. Was there something else he-" Tom looked up as he heard movement upstairs, followed by some playful banter between John and Kim as they reached the top of the staircase and started down. "Well, it's about time!"

"Yeah, yeah!" John retorted as he and Kim joined them. "Are you two ready to eat?"

"Absolutely!"

"Well, fortunately we do have plenty of breakfast food," Kim said as she turned toward the kitchen. "I'll get it started."

84

"I'll give you a hand." Even though he knew they were safe now, with all the extra protection- not to mention the bulletproof glass they both were glad was in place-, John didn't want her to be alone in the room where she'd come under fire.

Kim figured his protectiveness was kicking in again. In this case, as with the last time, she didn't mind it in the least. "Just let me do the cooking, Ok?"

John laughed and put his arm around her. "That's a deal!"

"We might as well join you," Tom said, and stood up. "There's plenty of room in the kitchen, too." He and Danni followed them into the spacious room.

While they sat, quietly for a minute or two, Tom wondered if he was the only one who purposely avoided looking at the window with the distinctive mark from last night.

It was Danni who broke the momentary silence. She turned to Tom, but didn't try to hide what she was about to say from John and Kim since they already knew about the investigation, which what she was about to say was directly related to. "You were asking what else Lieutenant Miller told me. He said the anonymous caller phoned in again with a name and he's ninety-nine percent sure it's the identity of the John Doe we dug up. The caller also seems to be growing impatient with us." She told them everything else the man had said.

Tom perked right up. "No kidding. I wonder why he's trying to drive us- not that I mind the help, but...he really could have it in for whoever did this, couldn't he? Maybe some sort of double-cross happened- not enough bribe money or something. What's the name?"

Kim stopped what she was doing and moved next to John, who also looked intently at Danni, waiting for her reply.

"Ronald Novak."

As many times as Tom had looked over the cold files from the early '70s, including that one and others that stuck out for various reasons, his recognition of the name was almost instantaneous. "Ronald Novak?! You're sure about that?"

"That's what he said...why? Who's he?"

"You don't know that one? He was one of the four I told you about- the felony suspects in '70 who were charged, then they jumped bail and disappeared."

"Oh- right. Brain-freeze, I guess."

85

"Or overload, maybe." He turned to John and Kim. "To bring you both up to speed, Ronald Novak was suspected by some of our predecessors in a string of rapes in the spring and summer of 1970, most of which ended in murder. There was enough circumstantial evidence to hold 'em over for trial, but concrete evidence was lacking. Worse, they only left a couple victims alive, neither of which was willing to testify. It would have been tough to get convictions."

"You say 'them'; who else besides this Novak?"

"Ah, nice catch, John- got a little ahead of myself there. I tend to think about both of those scumbags in the same frame, since by all indications they worked together. Novak's accomplice was another charming individual named Ralph Wancowicz."

"Ralph *Wancowicz*?!" John cracked up laughing. "Christ, I bet he was picked on a lot; that's a stigma more than a name!"

The women looked at each other and shook their heads as they grinned, but Tom laughed with John before he went on. "I agree. Anyway, in spite of the lack of any hard evidence whatsoever against them, both of 'em disappeared late that summer. According to the files on 'em, they just took off. Wancowicz wasn't missed, apparently, but Novak's family filed a missing persons report on him. Nothing ever turned up; neither was heard from again. In Novak's case, we see why, and now I wonder about his cohort...

"Something else about these cases put the hook in me, though. Some of that research I did that you asked me about, Danni, was into that string of rapes. When those two left or disappeared, the rapes stopped. I know that's not definitive proof they were guilty, but it sure makes for a strong possibility. Whoever killed Novak- and maybe Wancowicz, too- might have done all the women in the Greater Baltimore area a big favor."

Tom noted his brother's demeanor. "John?" He'd been staring straight ahead, totally transfixed, until Tom gave him a bit of a jolt. "What's on your mind?"

All the humor he associated with the name was gone now; something totally different had replaced it. John almost could feel a nudge each time that very uncommon name was mentioned. "I was just thinking...that name, 'Ralph Wancowicz'- it sounds familiar all of a sudden..."

"Oh, yeah? How so?"

"I think it has something to do with-..." He slowly turned to Kim as it came to him. "You and I talked about this yesterday. Remember I told you that Hedges had an older brother who just left for no apparent reason?"

Kim picked up on that. "I do remember; you said he had a goofy-sounding name!"

"Uh-huh."

Tom's jaw fell open. "Are you saying Wancowicz was Hedges' brother?!"

"That's exactly what I'm saying."

"Holy shit..."

"Yeah. This whole situation is getting weirder by the second. Through the investigation surrounding that stiff we know was Ronald Novak, we've made a connection to Christopher Hedges, who in all likelihood is the same son of a bitch that kidnapped Kim and has had it in for me and my family for over thirty years...

"...what in the hell is going on here?"

Kim added, "And, what is it leading to?" She looked at John and Tom. "With everything I've learned over the past couple days from both of you and from my recollections, I'm starting to look at all of this together...I get the feeling your trails are converging, even though it appears you two are searching in different directions for what you see as different destinations."

Tom leaned in. "What makes you say that, Kim?"

"I might be way off base, but...that link John just pointed out- something tells me that won't be the last point in common you'll find..." With a shrug, she added, "I can't put my finger on why as yet. It's just a feeling."

"Stay on it, Honey. If there's any sense to be made of this, especially if no other corroborating evidence comes to light, I won't be the least bit surprised if you end up putting it all together." He turned to Tom and Danni. "Kim's intuition, memory and deductive skills are almost scary- more so since she's coming to a better understanding of them and learning how to use 'em."

"I believe you." Tom stood and stretched. "Well, for all we know right now- or what *little* we know right now, more like it-, you just might have something there, Sis. In the meantime, maybe Mister Jack will be able to help shed some light- hopefully provide another piece or two."

"That would be nice. All right, without further delay- and since we need to get moving-, I'll get breakfast started. We can take off as soon as we've eaten." Kim went to the refrigerator. "Is everyone Ok with omelets?"

"Oh, yeah. I hear on good authority yours can't be topped."

"Not that I'm partial, or anything," John said with a smile.

"No, not you!" The gist of John's remark reminded Tom of an important matter he had to take the first step toward resolving. Turning to Kim, he said, "I'll have the works on my omelet, if you don't mind. I need to give Donna a call- be right back."

"Oh- would you ask her if she'd like to meet us for lunch?"

"Sure, Kim." He walked out.

As he did, Kim observed Danni, who hadn't said anything since she revealed the probable name of the skeleton her team had found. The detective seemed to be pretty deep in thought...or was it something else? "What's your preference, Danni?"

"Hmm?"

"What would you like on your omelet?"

"Um, just cheese would be fine, thanks."

"Are you all right?"

"Yeah, I'm fine. Why do you ask?"

"I just...well, I wondered if you were feeling all right, or maybe troubled about something."

"I was just thinking about the case and...something else, too. I'm all right, though." She smiled at Kim, who smiled back and returned to her cooking.

You don't miss much, do you? Wonder what you're thinking, Danni mused as she observed her hostess for a moment. *I bet you're underestimated all the time...*

...not by everyone, though. Maybe you do *know more than you're letting on, especially if your intuitive powers are as strong as your husband believes they are...*

"Actually, I need to make a call, too. I'll be right outside."

She didn't see that Kim watched her with some curiosity as she walked out.

"Hello?"

"Hi, Honey. It's me."

"Tom! Is everyone all right down there?"

Usually when Donna was angry with him, like she surely was, her answers would be very curt. However, this wasn't a normal situation. "We're all fine- no one was hurt."

"Poor Kim must be scared out of her wits. No doubt John's worried, too, although the help Governor Collins is recommending sounds like a Godsend."

"Amen to that- no pun intended. At any rate, we're hoping the Assembly approves it, and quickly, so they might be a little safer, although I still worry. John's pissing off some powerful people. Worse than that, he's scaring them- enough so that he and Kim came under fire in their own home. It's not just some crackpot...I hope their security's up to the job of protecting them. I'm glad they're home."

"Me, too. It sounds like you hardly slept, if at all."

Tom smiled. "You know, you and Kim must be of the same breed. Nothing gets by you, does it?"

"Not when it comes to you."

"I love you, Baby. I'm sorry for last night and for the past few months. It wasn't so long ago when we had our twentieth anniversary, for God's sake."

"I know. I love you, too. This isn't all your fault; I should have gone with you."

"It's all right. I bet Jess was glad to see you. How is she?"

"She's fine- still asleep, of course, but she should be up soon. Look, I-...I was out of line when we went to dinner. I know how much you want to know what happened to your father; I just hope you'll find out someday."

"This has been rough on both of us, but that's gonna stop right now. I won't shut you out and allow this hunt to consume my life anymore- that's a promise. Finding some kind of closure sure would help, but alienating my wife and my children is not a price I'm willing to pay to bring that about."

"Honey, I do want you to find the answer, though, if it can be found. You definitely should keep looking. As for you and I, we just need to find some happy medium, that's all."

"That sounds good to me. We'll talk about it more when I see you. Actually, could you take the day off today?"

"I'm a step ahead of you; it's already taken care of. Shannon's covering for me at the hospital."

"Perfect. John and Kim are coming, too; Kim asked if you'd be available for lunch."

"Definitely. As shaken up as they must be, I'm sure they could use-...what was that? What's going on down there?"

"Damned if I know; let me take a look." He chuckled when he discovered why Kim had cried out, and why she was laughing hysterically and chastising John at the same time. "Well, apparently they're not *too* badly shaken- at least not right now. John has Kim pinned against the refrigerator and he's tickling her like nobody's business!"

"That's good to hear. I guess I should let you get going. How long 'til you get here?"

"We're stopping by to see Mister Jack at ten, so I figure around noon?"

"Great; I'll see you all then."

When Danni stepped out, John fired up his laptop computer.

"Checking the website?"

"Yeah. I haven't done that for a couple days."

"No surprise there. It has been just a bit hectic."

"Just a bit..."

They had a small staff of volunteers charged with monitoring and maintaining the 'Stratton For President' internet site, which they'd had to upgrade a couple times already due to the massive amount of daily hits, which was very encouraging. Better yet, that amount seemed to be climbing every week, and everyone who visited the site saw John's complete platform, in principle and with some of the specifics as well. There was no better way than that for John to keep his message fresh, keep it spreading and keep his finger on the pulse of the electorate. Even if he was in California conducting one of his forums, he still could respond directly to a question from a citizen in Rhode Island.

It also was a great way to bring in the donations.

"What's your question of the week, Baby?"

That was one aspect of the site John used to keep up the interest and encourage people to speak their minds, which the 'question of the week' feature certainly did. Ever since he started it back in July of 2002, there would be a full range of responses to every one from thousands upon thousands of people, and the one he'd posed for this week was no exception.

"One of priorities. I asked, 'Who do you see as a greater enemy to our nation: Iraq, or governmental actions that erode our middle class?' It's just another way to try to get as many people as possible to see that they need to tell Mister Black by way of votes next year that they want a President who will take care of his own country. They need one who won't divert their attention elsewhere to cover the fact that when it comes to domestic economic policy, he doesn't have a clue, or just doesn't give a damn. We are- and have been for some time- losing blue-collar and high tech jobs faster than the Exxon Valdez lost oil and our workers' wages are stagnant or dropping. Since the executives who support Black are profiting from that you can bet he won't do a thing to stop it.

"Their salaries go up, since they're exploiting all the cheap labor and thus their companies are benefiting. While it may be true that with our trade policies they have use cheap labor to stay competitive, they still don't seem to think twice about selling their citizens out and they sure aren't taking pay cuts themselves. They toast each other with Dom Perignon and watch the average Americans fight each other for jobs that don't even pay a living wage. I just hope, when I take office and we start to turn things around, that those vultures posing as executives are thrown out with the garbage and that their fucking golden parachutes fail when they get tossed out. Pardon my French, Honey. In this case, cleaning house would be a good move..."

"Your French is pardoned. What do the respondents say?"

"A lot of 'em seem to agree with me, but a good number also are buying Black's bill of goods, which I expect since the war was over so quickly, although now the occupation has begun. His smokescreen's working for now.

"That's all right, though- they're visiting my site, aren't they? That means they at least have an interest in what I have to say. When those Black fans wake up and realize they're getting screwed- that is, those of 'em in the middle and lower classes, who *are* getting screwed-, I bet a sizeable chunk of them will come over to our side. Frankly, I don't see why anyone in those classes would vote republican, or democrat, for that matter.

"Regardless of what happens in this war in Iraq, it doesn't hide the fact that the days of the plantation owners and slaves are coming back, and fast. That's what this administration wants. Same with their alleged rivals, the democrats, although they try to convince everyone they're for the working class while at the same time they also pander to the wealthy. In that respect they're even worse than the republicans.

"It's up to us, Kim. Every 4 years, or 8, we have a new set of sharks entering the ring, making false promises to our faces and then either doing nothing or the opposite of what they swore they'd do. Among other things, they encourage people who can't afford the 'American Dream' to live above their means and go for it, anyway, then they're nowhere to be found when that dream turns into a nightmare. That goes double for the politicians, who are in on this racket."

"How so?"

"Campaign contributions that lead to favors in the way of the politician's vote on a bill that affects the contributor's business. The politician looks out more for the lobbyist and executive instead of doing what's good for all of us, or just looks the other way when his or her contributor is involved in something illegal, or just plain wrong. Plus, like I mentioned before, they encourage people to live above their means, just like those mortgage brokers do. The politicians are more subtle about it but they're still guilty."

"They sure don't seem to care about all the jobs we're losing, either."

"You've got that right. One of 'em might say something about it, then have others join in and say they need to do something about it, but it ends in the usual finger-pointing for a while, then they just forget about it. I guess they just think it's enough that they talked about the problem briefly. There's no job security at all. They get downsized or shipped overseas, or a major illness hits someone with inadequate health coverage or none at all, and the person is screwed.

"The rich get richer by taking back the property and things for which they granted these creative loans they never should have made in the first place. They win both ways, because they have the properties, cars, boats, whatever, in addition to all the money the owner forked out along the way. Then, they turn around and screw someone else the same way by doing whatever they have to in order to make another loan. The beat goes on. The common folk keep losing ground in this system run by unconscionable, two-faced parasites, which will be the case as long as those two parties keep winning elections. We have to stop that, and we will."

"Hmmm...I like your position and your conviction, Mister Stratton, and in spite of your foul mouth you're awfully cute. I suppose I *might* vote for you," Kim teased as she placed his omelet in front of him.

"You *might*, huh? Come here, you!" He chased her around the kitchen, and she cried out when he caught her by the 'fridge, which he did rather quickly. He pinned her against it and started tickling her, and it wasn't long before she was begging him for mercy and cursing him at the same time, laughing all the while.

"What's all this? A new way of cooking?" Tom cracked as he came back in.

"You could say that." John ceased his playful assault on his wife.

"Actually, John was showing me how he plans to win over the voters," Kim retorted as she caught her breath.

John grinned. "Hey, if it works..." After kissing her, he said, "Go ahead and sit down. I'd say you need a breather."

Just then, the phone rang.

"So you're sure he's the one?"

"It can't be anybody else. All the rest who knew anything about it are gone now, except for two, and they won't talk. They can't, because they're just as wrapped up in it as I am, although the one might recognize that you and I are on the same team, which is why you need to make sure, if another opportunity presents itself, that you get him...

"...so, that leaves the bastard. The irony here is, he can't call the police on me and testify against me in court about anything, so he has to take this route. I'm sure he's smiling, though, damn him. It wasn't enough, what he had on me already, which is the same thing I had on him and what I thought was a mutual assurance that we'd never go against each other. He had to have more on me, so he stowed away in my fucking car on the worst possible night he could have. He saw plenty and therefore he knew everything. He even sent me the letter telling me that, and how I was going down and everyone involved was going with me."

"You still have no idea where he could be?"

"Nope- not a clue. When he doesn't want to be found, chances are you don't find him. He hasn't lasted this long being sloppy, but a few years ago he did show that he's human, which came as a surprise."

"You're sure he's not on your property in Virginia?"

"No way, Danni. Like I said, he's far from that stupid. He knows that's the first place I'd look since he hid out there, more or less, from late '72 until early '82. He was there again for much of '89 and '90. No one's been there since '94, which is the last time I saw the place. His tastes have gotten pretty expensive, anyway; a rustic house wouldn't do for him. He's probably hiding in plain sight somewhere. I never should have trusted that son of a bitch- biggest mistake I ever made. I should have shot him when I had the chance."

"Well, you're human. Unfortunately, it seems that was a bad time to show it."

"Yeah. Any sign of your other mark?"

"None. He has to turn up sometime, though; I'll be ready."

"I'm sure you will. Speaking of that, good job yesterday. I doubt he would have been a problem, but now we don't have to worry, which makes me feel a *little* better, anyway. Did you learn anything about who we discussed the other day?"

"I can see why you're worried about her- very sharp, yet just as subtle. I might have to make a move there, too."

"Ok. Call me after you're done there and let me know what happens. If anything of interest comes up this morning, I'll call you."

"All right. Talk to you then." Danni hung up and walked back into the house.

"John? It's Laura. How are you holding up?"

"Hey, Laura. We're fine; how about you?"

"Same as you, only better. Once I've told you why I've called, you'll be happier, too."

"Oh, yeah? I like the sound of this already."

"You should. In one of the most lopsided votes of this session, not only did the House approve of my measure- they went one better. They authorized the quadrupling of your personal detail. The vote goes to the Senate any minute now; I expect the same result there. I just wanted to give you a heads-up and let you know. Once this goes through, I'll have the Superintendent call Herb, unless he already knows of some potential candidates outside the force. This measure gives you complete control over who's chosen- no stipulations. It's your call and we provide the funding. This is one instance where I'm glad we had all the snow this year and were forced to delay the session."

"No doubt. That is great news, Laura; I think Kim and I will sleep a lot better now. Thank you again." He turned to Kim and

Tom. "According to my successor, it looks like we'll be adding twelve more to our security team."

"*Twelve* more?"

"That's right, Brother. Apparently the House of Delegates didn't think eight was enough, which is fine by me. The Senate agreed, obviously. I have to let Herb know; this'll be his show."

"Thank God," Kim sighed in relief as she hugged John. "I'll start cleaning up while you talk with him."

Danni walked in then. "Sorry about that. The call went longer than I thought."

"It's all right. I'll just nuke your omelet for a bit."

"Thanks."

Tom told Danni about the gist of John's phone call.

"So the Assembly approved, eh?"

"Bingo."

"Ah...well, I can see how that would strike the right chord, and it would explain the smiles all around." As Kim handed her the plate, she added, "I just might talk with Herb about a position- at least let him know I might be interested."

"You'll have at least this morning to think about it, anyway, before we meet out at Loch Raven," Tom added. "Although if you were to decide you wanted to do it, I know Ike Miller would fight tooth and nail to keep you on his team- and with good reason."

"Are these Stratton men always so flattering?" Danni asked her hostess.

"Oh, it gets thicker- trust me!"

"I believe you. I've seen lots of supporting evidence already, but I'm sure there will be plenty more," Danni commented, looking intently at Tom as she did. He shifted a little and faced away. That reaction made her smile inwardly. There were a number of possibilities as to what she could do with the notion that was making him uncomfortable. The next step would be for him to confront her about it, which she knew had to happen very soon.

At least one of those possible ways for her to handle that confrontation, if she handled it well enough, would help get her where she needed to be. She just had to be careful about it and play her hand as well as she could.

Danni glanced at Kim, who wasn't watching them. She was rinsing some dishes, which was a good thing. *If anyone will catch on, it'll be her- and probably at the worst time.*

You're a whole lot more dangerous than you look, but I'll be watching you...

...possibly from a much better perspective...

"What's that smile for, Danni? I hope it means you enjoyed your omelet," Kim grinned back as she took her empty plate.

Danni chuckled. "Well, yes, I did; it was very good! That's only part of the reason, though."

"Oh? What's the other part?"

"Well, the more I think about it, the more I see being your bodyguard as an exciting job, and also good experience. I'll check back with you and Captain Stratton when the picture becomes more clear as to how the selection process will go; I'm sure your team leader will have his hands full putting that together, in addition to still being directly responsible for your safety."

"I imagine Herb will be quite busy- I hope not overly so. You can tell just by looking at them how much of a strain they're under of late. I didn't mean to put you on the spot last night, but if you feel like being a bodyguard might be up your alley, it would be good to have you with us. Judging from what you did here, your instincts sure seem to be suited for that line of work!" She turned off the water and dried her hands. "Well, that does it for the cleanup. I have to go finish getting ready now; I won't be long."

"Uh-huh, I've heard that before," Tom said, winking at Kim.

Kim put on a show of shock and indignation as Tom grinned. With her hands on her hips, she shot back, "and after all those nice things I said about you! I just might have to put chili peppers in your next omelet!" She looked at Danni and added, "as you can see, they're not *all* about flattery; it's one part schmoozer, one part smart-ass!"

Amid their laughter, she walked toward the doorway. "I'll be back in a few, and before you make another comment, no, Tom, I don't mean a few *hours!*" She smiled at him as she left the room.

"There goes one impressive woman," Danni commented.

"No doubt about that!" The gist of that statement prompted Tom to shift gears. "I'm glad you and I have a moment, though. There's something I need to talk to you about."

Danni turned away. "I think I know what it is."

"I figured you might. First of all, I just want to say that you're a top-notch detective and a very attractive woman. With that in the open, I, um…wasn't in a very good state last night, and I think I might have-…well, I might have given you-…"

"I know where you're going, and I appreciate what you just said. I respect you, too, and yes- I think you're a very good-looking man. I can see you're pretty uncomfortable now, which is not how I want you to feel around me."

"I don't want to feel this way, either. I just-…I want to avoid any misunderstandings, but even more than that I don't want any bad feelings between us. I love my wife and my family, and in spite of the flare-up I had yesterday, I'm very happy where I am. I-…I'm sorry." He faced away from her.

"Hey, it's all right. I'm at fault here, too. I know you're married and I had no right to send those signals to you like I did. More importantly, we have a case we'd both love to solve, so what do you say we put this matter to rest with a handshake?" He was visibly relieved as he turned back and took her hand.

"Thanks, Danni. It would have been tougher all around if we'd let that go on."

"I couldn't agree more. Well, I guess I'd better take off; I have a few things to take care of this morning before I meet you all by the reservoir. I'll go thank our hosts first. See you at one?"

"You've got it. Catch you then."

"Although I still wonder why Donna didn't come down with Tom, I'm glad Danni was here," Kim said to John as they waved to Danni after seeing her to her car. "On the other hand, I also wondered if there was some sort of undercurrent between them. I know he and Donna have been going through a tough time lately."

"That they have. Plus, Tom did stray once; I just hope he doesn't again." John expanded on his comment when Kim turned away. "It was Vanessa Chamberlain, and it happened the night he went up and saw you dance, right?"

"How long have you known?"

"I suspected something the day she came down to his office to see me after Hedges had taken you- when she got the information from me that she needed. The way Tom reacted when he saw her spoke volumes. The clincher, though, was when we went to see him in the hospital after you pulled your Houdini act by getting out of that single glove, then you went one better and got *us* out of the mess we were in. He couldn't hide how upset he was that Vanessa was taken. I could tell she meant a lot to him and I had a good idea why."

"I'm not surprised you picked up on that. You never confronted him about it, though..."

"No, there was no point. Why cause him any more pain over it than he already feels?"

"I agree, and I don't think he'd do it again. I just hope he's not putting himself in a position to make that a possibility, especially with the tension between him and Donna."

"I'm with you."

At that moment, the door opened and out walked Tom. "Ah, there you are. You almost ready?"

"Just about, Brother. All we need to do is grab our things..."

Chapter 6

"You're awfully quiet, Honey- what's on your mind?"

John and Tom were engaged in casual conversation, and Kim had settled back to simply look out the window and enjoy the scenery as they rode along. She always enjoyed taking in the tranquillity and beauty of their community; it really did seem like they were on vacation whenever they were here. The stretch of road leading from their development to US Route 50 also was a nice drive; there were plenty of trees and open fields, and the occasional fox, deer or groundhog would add to the picturesque surroundings.

However, at this point of the ride to Baltimore, they were on US 50 and approaching the Chesapeake Bay Bridge. As soon as she saw the towering support spans, they served to jog her memory, especially given the recent revelations about past events that had stirred up a bunch of related memories- some good, some not. What the sight of the spans of the Bridge served up was something John had shared with her, and a possible meaning of it that she'd posed to him, which both he and she had ended up discounting...

...but now, as they reached the Bridge and started across it, her feeling grew stronger.

"Do you remember just after Election Day in 2000, when I asked you about the last thing your father said to you?"

"I do remember. I guess I'd better fill you in, Tom. I'm sure you recall a good bit of what happened the night Dad disappeared-meaning where we all were and what we did."

"That I do."

"Well, after you, Mom and Doug had left for the party, needless to say, Dad wasn't happy with me- and that's putting it lightly. I told you a little while back about the phone call that came for him, and also what he said to me about going back to our favorite fishing spot."

"Yeah, you told me everything that happened that night, come to think of it."

"I thought so. Anyway, Kim and I talked about it, too. She wondered if there was more to what Dad said than his desire for us to go back to that spot." He turned back to Kim. "Since you mentioned that to me I've wondered about it from time to time, but if that was the case, why wouldn't he just have told me? One of Dad's famous sayings was, 'never complicate the simple'. Why would he do the cloak-and-dagger routine, especially since I was only ten and the message could have been lost on me so easily?"

She shrugged. "That's a good question. Maybe he figured you were smart enough that you'd remember and eventually, when the time was right, you would find-…well, whatever it was he left for you? Oh, I don't know. I have no idea where this is coming from. I just-…I'm getting that feeling, maybe because of all we've brought to light recently. I almost feel compelled to bring that up- more so since seeing the Bridge made me wonder about it again. I know I might be making more of something than there is, but-…"

"It's Ok, Kim, you did the right thing letting me know. If you're feeling strongly enough about it, maybe there *is* something to it. Besides, I'd rather you tell me about something like this, even if it turns out to be nothing. Three years ago, on the same day Hedges kidnapped you, your friend Kelly came up with a little detail- something she'd seen in your dressing room. She told me how odd she thought it was to see corsets at a swimwear boutique. If I'd have followed up on that and investigated it right away, that little detail would have led us right to where Hedges was keeping you and the other women. You'd have been rescued a lot sooner."

"Well, maybe we would have, but…what if you'd found us and the police stormed the house at the wrong time? He could have gone over the edge and killed us."

"True, that certainly could have happened, too. At any rate, like I told you, I'll never overlook any detail again, no matter how unimportant it might seem. Maybe your feeling about what Dad said to me *is* nothing, but on the other hand, since you think enough of it to bring it up…"

John looked out over the Bay. "I talked to Bruce yesterday and one thing he told me was that my boat is seaworthy as of this past weekend." He turned back to Tom and Kim. "I think we need to take 'er for a spin, and while we're out, make a stop at a certain spot Dad and I went to."

"I think that's a good idea, John. Maybe see if ol' Bruce wants to join us."

"I'm sure he would have, if he and Anna hadn't left for their vacation last night. I tell you, those two take more vacations than anyone I've ever known!"

"Hey, if they can, why not?"

"My thoughts exactly. When we see Donna after we talk with Mister Jack, see if she wants to come with us, Tom. I'm sure she wouldn't mind a day out."

Tom grinned. "She won't mind that at all, provided she has plenty of Dramamine!"

"True. I remember when she turned every known shade of green there was, and even added a few more to the spectrum!" John added as he laughed. "How about you, Kim? I bet you're up for a day on the water, aren't you?"

"Absolutely! When can we go?"

"Let's make it tomorrow, if everyone's free- Saturday otherwise, although according to the weather report there's a possibility of rain this weekend. Too bad we probably won't get the chance today- conditions are perfect. It's supposed to be 82 degrees."

"82…I really like that number." Kim smiled at John and kissed him when he turned to her.

He smiled back when he caught her meaning. "September 1st of that year wouldn't happen to have anything to do with your partiality, would it?"

"Maybe a little."

John took her hand into his and resumed the prior conversation. "How are you and Donna set for tomorrow? Think you'll be able to break away?"

"I don't know. Actually, I doubt it. Donna took today off like I did, so it's not likely. I agree when you say this would be the day for it, but I guess we might have to wait 'til Saturday. You know, I haven't been out since the last time you and I went fishing."

"That was a nice trip, wasn't it? The last time Kim and I were out was last fall before Bruce put the boat in mothballs for the winter. I look forward to the next one, and the sooner the better."

Danni's cell phone rang.

Thought you might be calling soon, she mused as she looked at the screen and saw Lieutenant Miller's number at the station. "What's up, Sir?"

"Hey, Danni. I just hung up with Homicide's detective who's investigating Harry Lawson's death. Unfortunately he didn't have anything in the way of good news. Whoever the killer was apparently was pretty thorough. No clues of any kind have come to light, but he did tell me he thinks Harry knew his killer. No struggle took place and Harry wasn't the kind of guy who would just roll over. There were no signs of forced entry, either, and whoever it was might have been in the apartment for some time before pulling the trigger. A trusted acquaintance, at least."

"No kidding...well, I appreciate you telling me, Sir. You'll keep me in the loop?"

"I sure will. Enjoy your day off."

"Thanks..."

...for telling me what I already know, she thought as she hung up. She was glad to hear her boss tell her she'd done a bang-up job, though.

Danni pulled over to relay what she'd heard in another conversation to one who'd be very interested and, as a result of what she'd tell him, more on edge than he already was.

"Good morning, Cap- oh, Governor and Mrs. Stratton! I didn't know you would be here; I'm sure the Attorney General will be happy to see you, too."

"Good morning, Margie. Is he ready for us?" Tom asked as he closed the door behind them.

"He's on the phone right now, but I doubt he'll be much longer since he's expecting you. I'll go tell him you're-"

Just then, the door opened and Jack Weldon walked into his outer office. "Well, what a wonderful surprise! It's good to see you, John," he said, shaking his hand. Then he turned to Kim and embraced her. "And it's always a pleasure to see you, Kimberly. Needless to say, you're looking just as beautiful as ever."

She kissed his cheek. "Thank you, Mister Jack. I'm glad to see you, too."

"Come inside, all of you. Margie, would you hold my calls?"

"Sure will, Sir."

"Thanks."

* * *

102

"I know why you're here, Tom. What brings you two by?" Jack asked as he looked at John and Kim.

Tom answered for them. "They're here for the same reason, Mister Jack. I filled 'em in on the case. They're-" His phone rang. "Excuse me a sec...yeah, Danni?...It's all right- I understand. We'll reschedule soon, then. Gotta go now, but I'll be in touch...You, too. Bye."

"That was Detective Searles? I know you two are working together on the case."

"It was her. In fact, we were supposed to go check out the area where the body was found, but she had to cancel."

Jack nodded. "I knew her father. Damned good cop, he was. I don't know if you and John remember him, but he served under your father in the County."

"I didn't know him personally but I found out later he had. Did you know him well?"

"Very well. He and Ben Jacobson were partners on and off from '69 until '72, before Ben left the force that last year. The night he shot himself marked the end of a long slide down. What a shame that was. Maybe if *I'd* gone to see him that last night...I don't know."

"Danni never talks about that and apparently no one ever brings it up with her. Understandable, but we all know what keeping things buried can do to you."

I wish you'd have put that almost any other way, Tommy. "That we do. If '72 had been the last time Ray saw Jacobson, I still think he might have been around today, but that's another story."

"That was a pretty eventful period, Sir- particularly '70. I take it by now you know it's almost a lock that the skeleton found at Loch Raven was identified as Ronald Novak?"

"I was told late last night, yes. Seems Mister Novak didn't disappear after all."

"Apparently not. One reason why I want to go to the site where they dug up the skeleton is to conduct a search to see if any more bodies were buried there. Given what John, Kim, Danni and I discussed this morning, I have another reason to want to do that."

"I suspect you do..." Jack said in a distant tone of voice.

Tom just stared at him for a moment. "Huh?"

"What?"

"The way you just said that...it sounds like you already know my other reason."

"Well, you-…that is, it's obvious, isn't it? You and I discussed it, too."

Tom temporarily was at a loss, but then he caught on. "Oh-no, it doesn't have anything to do with my father. You really threw me there; I thought you might be having a psychic moment or something. I'm talking about Ralph Wancowicz."

"Wancowicz? What in the hell kind of-…ah, that's right. He was one of the four cases of suspected felons in '70 that jumped bail and never were brought to trial. What about him?"

"Together with Novak he was suspected of that string of rapes in '70."

"And…?"

"Well, since the county guys dug up Novak, who went missing about the same time as Wancowicz, I was thinking there's a possibility that whoever killed Novak might have killed his partner. I know it's just an assumption, but that string of rapes stopped right around the time those two went missing. It could be coincidence, but it also could be because the rapists were killed. Whatever the case, with Novak found, I think we have enough cause to at least check the area. He and Wancowicz were close buddies, from all indications, and they might have died together. I wanted to search that area further, anyway, because given the description, it seems to me it would be a good place to hide more bodies that someone didn't want found. In light of this new information, I have more reason to think that."

"Sounds like you've made up your mind. So, what are your questions for me?"

Tom frowned. "I get the impression you don't buy my take on this, Mister Jack."

Jack shrugged. "I don't know what to think about it. I try *not* to think about that period," he replied as he stood. "Look, I hope I don't come off as rude, but I do have a full day today. What are your questions for me?"

Tom glanced over at John, whose brows were raised. *Apparently, you're just as surprised as I am.* "Um…to start, what can you tell me about those four cases? What did your gut tell you? Did you think they were guilty?"

"At the time, we thought- that is, *I* thought they were, and Judge Tippett agreed there was enough reason for a trial."

"So, they were granted bail, posted it and were gone. It seems like you had enough to try them in absentia, based on that."

"It's true I could have, but considering the fact that we still had neither solid evidence nor any victims willing to testify, there was a good chance we'd have lost, which was a chance I wasn't about to take. What really did it was the unwillingness of the victims to come forward, which raised two possibilities: one, Novak and Wancowicz weren't our guys, and two, the surviving victims were so traumatized that they just couldn't have gone through a trial. We had nothing. Even if we'd gone forward and gotten the conviction, what would that have done?"

"It would have given every law enforcement agency, not to mention U.S. Marshals and the bail bondsmen whose money was at stake plenty of motivation and full justification to go find 'em. I don't get that, Mister Jack."

"That's one way to look at it, but…the way I saw it, that just would have been another slap in the face of the families of the victims- another reminder to them that the scum responsible for defiling and killing their loved ones got away with it. At best, it would have been an empty conviction, and at worst, a loss in light of not enough evidence, or some slick defense attorney like Parker exploiting the lack of witnesses and of the culprit.

"That was my real worry. You know how those cases go a lot of the time, Tom- and John, you especially know that. If we'd lost, the culprits could have resurfaced and lived scot-free, never again to be tried and held accountable for what they'd done. There was no way I was about to let that happen, so I put everything on hold indefinitely in those cases, hoping those two would be recaptured. Needless to say, they never were resolved."

John piped up. "Suspects, or culprits, Mister Jack?"

"Come again?"

"You said 'culprits', which tells me you were convinced they were guilty."

He looked at John, then away. "Like I said, we were pretty sure they were. I don't know, the glass we looked through might have been a little tainted, but…" He trailed off, then wiped his brow and glanced at the clock.

"Did you see the interrogation of him when he was brought in, or have any other opportunities to question him other than at the preliminaries?"

"Only the prelims. He was a cocky son of a bitch- excuse me, Kimberly. He *and* Wancowicz were like that; we all saw it.

Then, those two had that slimy defense attorney- same breed as Mark Peters, just an earlier version."

"Right. Curtis Parker, the one who was murdered in November of '74, just a month or so before Dad disappeared. That's another unsolved case; the killer never was caught."

"There were plenty of people who hated that guy, though, so the list of possible suspects read like a phone directory."

"I remember that one," John added. "Back in '99, when the 25 year mark of his murder hit, there was a story done on him and what evidence the police had at the time, and also how no more ever had come to light. That story stuck out because, like you just said, Tom, he was killed so close to when Dad vanished. They got some footprints, and the best they could determine was that it was a guy with size 9 feet who weighed 150 or so, I think."

"Good memory there, Brother." Tom picked up the questioning again. "You've said 'we' a few times- by that you mean you and my Dad?"

"Yeah, and Jacobson, too- he and Ray Searles were in on the arrest, along with your father."

His discomfort was clear to Tom. *I'd better tread carefully.* "I wanted to ask you about Jacobson; I looked at his file and there really wasn't much of anything derogatory in it. From what you insinuated about him, I expected to find some sort of bad evaluation, or incident report, or something like that, yet all I saw was that he left voluntarily. Was there something that should have been in his file, but was lost or taken out? Or buried?"

"That sounds like an accusation."

"It's not that at all, Sir. I'm only asking you."

"As far as that file goes, you're asking the wrong man."

"I understand, but I'm wondering if-"

"Tom, you know I had nothing to do with Jacobson's records and no access to 'em. You also know who did."

"And *you* know as well as I do that he's not available for me to ask. He hasn't been since December 31st, 1974, which is why I'm asking his closest friend in the off chance that my father might have shared something with him that could shed some light."

They both turned away at the same time. Tom took a breath to calm himself before he went on. "I'm sorry about that. Mister Jack, we have a thirty-plus year old mystery on our hands, and at this point we're stuck. Whoever this anonymous caller is seems to have plenty of info, but we still can't track him down. I know this is hard on you; it's hard on all of us, but I have a feeling this might lead to the resolution of a number of these unsolved cases…and maybe even some closure for my family and me."

"I know, and I apologize. Now you see why I don't like to talk about all this. Those bad memories just come flooding back in and hardly any of my friends from those days are around to help take the edge off…

"As far as Jacobson goes, I already know you don't like him, John, for what he and Peters pulled on you during your first run for Governor- all that crap about your supposed womanizing and the other personal attacks. You know what that was? Revenge. He accused you of one thing I knew he was guilty of- the womanizing part."

"What makes you think he did that for revenge?"

He took a deep breath and looked down. He opened his mouth to speak, but looked away again. "First, I want you to understand it wasn't her fault. He took advantage of-…"

Tom was on the edge of his seat. "Mister Jack, tell me what happened."

"The piece of-" he cut himself off as he looked at Kim, who along with John was staring intently at him. "He had an affair with your mother, which your father found out about." He paused to let that settle in. "Your parents were having some difficulties at the time. You have to understand, he-…your father was in a bad way for a long time, although he'd never have let you see it.

"Your Mom saw it, though, and she was upset that he wouldn't tell her about it, which he couldn't. He would have put her in danger, too. She suspected it all along, but no matter how much he wanted to, he couldn't confide in her- he couldn't do that to her, because it was bad enough what he went through because of it. They probably had your house bugged…"

"Mister Jack, you're-"

"Jacobson saw the friction all this caused in your parents' marriage, and that pig took advantage of a situation that was ripping your father apart. He went behind his back, pushed the right buttons, and-…Christ, I'm sorry to have to tell you this, but you deserve to know. It wasn't her fault- she was so upset with your father, who was in an impossible situation. Jacobson's to blame for that. It was all I could do to-…"

"Mister Jack, calm down. Take it easy for a minute. Do you need some fresh air?"

He settled back into his chair and shook his head. "I'll be all right. I'm just going to start from the point that changed everything, how it affected Tom, Sr. and what eventually it drove him to do. It's time you know how much more there was to your father than what was in his dossier; you deserve to know all of it."

The delivery guy knocked again and waited.

There was no answer. The girl wasn't home.

He double-checked the instructions to make sure the lucky bastard who made the order didn't specify that his purchase had to be signed for. He didn't.

The deliverer left the bouquet of flowers with the card attached on her stoop and took off for his next stop, thinking how nice it would have been if she'd been home to sign for it...

...especially if she is that cheerleader and bikini babe I have the calendars, pictures and posters of.

I wonder if she'd autograph 'em for me...

...nah. I bet she's one of those conceited bitches...

"You know your father spent almost twenty years in the FBI, but his file doesn't reveal all he did. It's correct in that it shows how outstanding and courageous he was; his character and integrity were impeccable. I don't think they'd have dared to say otherwise."

"Why would they have? And what did he do that the file didn't reveal?" Kim asked.

Jack looked at her for a moment, then smiled. "I always wondered why you didn't become a detective, Kimberly. You have all the right instincts for that line of work- you always did, especially your curiosity and your memory.

"Tom, Sr. was a very idealistic man in his younger years. He had a strong sense of obligation and the highest moral standards that he always lived by. He also believed in his government like mostly everyone back then did- always believed that they acted in the best interests of the people. He was naïve in that assumption, of course. He felt the same way about J. Edgar Hoover; he idolized the man...

"Tom played a role in the investigations behind the McCarthy hearings- by all indications, a pretty big one. He was driven; he believed the Communist threat was a big one and he was proud to play a part in helping expose them. In the early part of that, they did get a few spies that had done a lot of damage to the country with the secrets they sold to Russia and China, but McCarthy went way beyond them. Tom might have been a bit naïve but he also was a very intelligent man, so it was inevitable that the reality of those hearings would dawn on him. When it did, not long after McCarthy's censure in late '54, his bubble burst.

"He asked for the transfer back to field duty and was in a funk for a while. His performance still was top-notch, but that experience with the witch hunters really got to him. He thought about those lives he played a part in destroying and was disgusted with himself. He had some pretty bad bouts with the bottle for a couple years, but only his closest friends knew about it. I was one of 'em. No one inside the Bureau ever found out.

"The incident in '58 when he was shot served as a wake-up call in more ways than one. And, as you well know, that's when he and your mother came face-to-face for the first time. He was back on track; he recovered, married, became a supervisor and had his first son in a matter of two years. Better still, that was the start of the Kennedy administration.

"You really would have to have been there to appreciate how much of a breath of fresh air he was to the country. After eight years of McCarthyism, a do-nothing President and the Dulles brothers causing turmoil in Iran and Latin America for the sake of the big oil companies and United Fruit, we needed new blood. Naturally, the activities of those Dulles jackals were disguised pretty well, and I'm sure both got their palms greased with some of the boatloads of money those companies made since they virtually had free reign to pillage those nations. It was the CIA's dirty little secret.

"As for Tom and Judy, the early '60s were very good times. They were happy as larks and had their second son on the way when Camelot came to an end."

"I had a feeling the JFK assassination would come into play," Tom said.

"It wasn't just that. In fact, what happened afterwards had more to do with his state. The Warren Commission report was what everyone was waiting for, but your father had a bad feeling about it early on. As an insider, he saw the direction of the investigation and he was not happy with it. He already had a strong suspicion as to what had happened and he knew just as well that the government didn't want it to come to light. Tom, Sr. actually went down to Dallas a few weeks later- in mid-December- and did some fact-finding of his own.

"The Warren Report was released on September 27th, 1964. Your father retired from the FBI the following day. It was so obvious to many of us that that report was a cover-up, a lie. Tom saw it more clearly than anyone and he hit the roof. He didn't agree with *everything* Kennedy said and did, but he liked the direction we were taking as a nation and the renewed enthusiasm, both of which came to a halt. He suspected even then that this country would take a big turn for the worse after JFK was shot, and was he ever right. That did it for him.

"Hoover himself was walking by when Tom ripped his department head a new one after the guy told him he needed to put a lid on his opinions. He told me in detail what happened next; you'll understand why as soon as you hear it..."

September 28, 1964

"Those fuckers will get away with murder and that spineless piece of shit Warren and his hacks are accessories after the fact!"

"Stratton, you stand down *right now*!! If you ever say anything like that outside this office, I'll-"

Tom got right up in his face, towering over the shorter man, not caring that he stared down the Director of the FBI. "You'll what?"

Silence was his reply, so Tom went on. "No, Mister Director, I'm *not* going to tote the party line on this one. I'll never do that again. I spent three years fighting the Nazis and eighteen more fighting domestic enemies- real or imagined. Why? Because I loved my country, our way of life and those who stood alongside me defending it. I even bought that shit McCarthy and his committee sold us- those lies he concocted about the supposed Communist conspiracy. Communists supposedly were the enemies of my country, so I went against them and helped hunt them down.

"I didn't find out McCarthy was a liar and a grandstander until it was too late. If anything, *he* was more of an enemy to our country than every man and woman he blacklisted, times ten. Worse yet, I knew where he got his information- from none other than you, Mister Hoover. Worst of all, to my eternal shame, I took part in it. I learned an important lesson and swore I'd never be duped like that again. Now, along comes the Warren Report. It's a slightly different animal, yet similar in that a lie is being pushed on us. Unfortunately, many will buy it because their government wants 'em to.

"Six years ago I took a bullet for one of my comrades and almost died as a result. I'd do it again because he's my friend and friends look out for each other. We law enforcement officers live by a code of honor, which is a word the scum responsible for this so-called 'complete and honest' report know nothing about. I wouldn't wipe my fucking ass with that report! You know why? Because I went down there on my vacation week and did my own investigation. I didn't even need the whole week to put together a clear enough picture of what went down that day.

"Every Secret Service agent who was there should be brought up on charges, as should any son of a bitch that told them to sit on their hands and let the President be murdered, because that's exactly what happened. That whole area should have been sealed off and crawling with agents, neither of which happened. I know how presidential security's supposed to work. So do you, and we both know it wasn't there.

"As a commander in World War II, I picked out and set up my share of ambush sites, which I was pretty damned sure Dealey Plaza was from the moment I got there. There are a lot of people who were there that day who know what happened. The account they gave me couldn't be more different than what the Warren Commission said. I gathered enough evidence from those eyewitnesses to confirm my suspicion that Dealey Plaza *was* an ambush site.

"So, in the span of a few days, a single FBI agent who wasn't even in Dallas that day discovered what a whole commission couldn't find in almost a year. Of course, we have a congressman on it who probably couldn't spell his own name correctly three times in a row, even though it only has four letters.

"Then we have a piece of shit lawyer on it looking to make a name for himself by showing that he has one hell of an imagination. I'm sure he'll have a nice career ahead of him. That slimy son of a bitch pitched his lie, one of the most senseless theories I ever heard, and that worthless commission bought it- lock, stock and barrel. With the unscrupulous, the stupid and the spineless on the commission and working for it, it's easy to see why they'd reach such a conclusion, though, isn't it?

"To cap it off, that motherfucker Allen Dulles, of all people, is appointed to the commission to investigate the murder of the man who fired him. Johnson doesn't want the truth to come out, does he? And how about you, Mister Hoover? You have the President's ear; you helped pick out the members of that commission, didn't you? Am I right in concluding that none of you wanted to find the answer, or that you wanted to suppress it? That was the final bit of proof to my theory- how frightened a number of witnesses were to talk to me when I told them who I worked for. They were scared to death. Right then I started to worry about what this commission was going to put in its report.

"Well, their summary yesterday sure confirmed my fears and this bullshit about the evidence files being sealed for seventy-five years is the icing on the cake. That's not a matter of *national* security at all; it's a matter of protecting the assassins. It's a matter of those that are guilty covering their tracks and a panel appointed by John Kennedy's successor helping them do exactly that. The whole thing makes me sick. If it was up to me, everyone on that commission, every Secret Service agent and every decision-maker involved in the appalling lapse of presidential security on November 22nd, 1963 would be tried for treason and shot along with their fellow conspirators, because treason is just what they've committed!! The Warren Commission lied to us- you know it, I know it and everyone in this fucking government knows it!!!"

He had to take a breath and calm down. "I already see that no one will do anything about it. You're gonna let this lie stand. Worst of all, you're gonna stand behind it and propagate it as truth. Because of that, you're all going to damage our country for years to come, but mark my words: the day will come when you pay for what you did.

"You're looking the other way, which makes me wonder how much you really know and why you're not willing to tell the truth- not only that, but why you're pushing this crock on all of us. At minimum, you're turning your back and you're asking me to do the same. If you know anything about me, you know that's something I cannot and will not do."

With that, he pulled out his FBI ID and handed it to the speechless Director, along with his gun. A tear fell from his eye as his hurt came out despite his effort to stop it. "I used to love this job. It meant almost as much to me as my wife and my children. Now, I can't even stand to be in this building. We both know it's time for me to leave, Mister Hoover. I can't in good conscience work for this government anymore. We've turned a corner here. We're headed in a bad direction and I won't have any part of it."

He turned and walked to the door, but stopped before exiting it. "One last thing. I'll be watching over my shoulder, so if you or anyone else even thinks about trying to eliminate me, I feel sorry for the poor bastards picked for that job…"

He turned and looked the Director in the eye, then finished the statement. "…and I feel even sorrier for whoever sends 'em."

~ ~ ~

"In spite of the warning, they made some attempts on your father's life. People like him were problematic. There weren't many within the government who were brave enough to disagree with the Warren Report. Most just didn't want to face the truth- they didn't want to believe something like that could happen in their country, so out of cowardice, self-preservation or innocence, they bought it, too. Those who didn't were swept under the rug, discredited, dishonored, written off as lunatics- no one really listened, or wanted to.

"It was different with your father, given his credentials and record of service. They couldn't defame him in any way and he wouldn't kowtow, so he worried 'em. Tom, Sr. knew what he was up against, though; he knew there wasn't much he could do with no support from anyone else. Besides, he had to concentrate on his family. You'd just been born a few months earlier, John, so now he had two sons to provide for. Between his time in the Army and with the Bureau he had over twenty years of federal service, which entitled him to a good pension. That was back when they actually took care of their people. Since he didn't want to jeopardize that he chose to keep quiet about what he knew, which as you can imagine didn't sit well with him at all. He had to choose between conscience and survival, so he did what any responsible, loving father and husband would do. He chose his family.

"He couldn't stay out of public service for too long, though. When the Baltimore County Sheriff announced his retirement effective January 1967, he saw that as a perfect opportunity at the right time. He was much better qualified for that position than the guy he ran against in the '66 election, so that was no contest. He had his own turf at that point and a force under him, both of which made him feel a little safer."

"But they still came after him, you say?"

"That they did, John- three times in '65 alone. After that they averaged once or twice per year until '72, but the bad thing for mostly all of them was, we knew they were coming by way of your father's friends. He had an awful lot of 'em, and they were involved in every aspect of government and the military that mattered, so they gave him early warning. One guy slipped through the warning net- the last one to make an attempt before they stopped coming- but Tom sniffed him out and turned the tables. He was that good, your father was.

"Still, he was getting awfully tired of all that and he wasn't getting any younger, so on May 2nd, 1972, he took action. I'll never forget that day as long as I live. We had a meeting that morning and Tom was late getting to my office. It looked like he hadn't slept a wink; he was distracted, to put it lightly. You know how focused he always was- always concentrated on the matter at hand. It was an important case we had to discuss, too, but that was the furthest thing from his mind.

"All of a sudden, he smiled this…eerie smile, a cat-that-ate-the-canary kind of smile. He was quiet, too- didn't say a word. Finally, when I asked him what was wrong, he said we needed to postpone the meeting until the next day. No explanation, nothing.

"As he was walking out the door, he said, 'listen to the news. They won't give you the whole story, but I have a feeling you'll like what you hear.' He winked and walked out. It came over the wire as a flash report; they'd just reported finding J. Edgar Hoover dead about an hour after your father left my office. Nobody knew before then- *nobody*-, but your father knew. He never confirmed that he took Hoover out, but he never denied it, either. I believe he made good on the threat he made to that fat old bastard the day he retired from the Bureau in '64. When he had a problem, he dealt with it himself; that was his way. Hoover was one such problem, but not after that day.

"All those attempts on Tom's life ended, most likely as a result of his chief antagonist's death. There was a rumor that the old pervert was wearing a dress; can you believe that? This guy-the top law enforcement official for decades, who built his reputation during the Prohibition era, supposedly hard-nosed, tough as nails- and he's wearing a dress when he was taken out! Tom just smiled when I tried a few times to pry it all out of him; I wish he would've filled me in. Anyway, the war was over. Your Old Man had beaten 'em...

"...or, so we thought."

For a long moment, they didn't even blink their eyes.

John and Tom clearly were engrossed and had hung on every word. They glanced at each other, then straight ahead as they tried to digest all they'd learned.

Kim, however, had a different expression. When Jack regarded her, she looked away. She clearly was interested in all he'd revealed; her curiosity was apparent, but he had the distinct impression her attention wasn't totally focused on that. Right now she was somewhere else, which made him worry for a moment.

He wondered what was on her mind while taking in the green of her eyes as they darted around...

...and the swell of her soft, full breasts as she breathed in...

...and the shape of her smooth, silky, bare legs as she shifted in her chair and crossed them. The short, snug-fitting black floral print dress she wore did nothing to hide her many assets.

In so many ways, you haven't changed at all, Kimberly...
...as for one of those ways, that's most unfortunate...

It was John who broke the silence. "Are you kidding me?! You're telling me my father killed the Director of the FBI?!"

"I'm quite sure of it. Can you tell me who would have had better motive to kill Hoover?"

"I'm with John, Mister Jack- there is no way in *hell* I believe that! It's crazy; there's no way! My father wouldn't do that. He *couldn't* have!" Tom interjected.

"Couldn't he? Maybe you didn't know your father as well as you thought." Seeing their reactions, he backed off from that. "Look, you know as well as I do how reports can be manipulated and altered; it's the same as what you say about statistics, John. The media was vague with details of his death. For all we know, anyone could have killed him any number of ways. The death report never was released. All we heard was, he died in his sleep. Anything could have happened. I bet they knew, but didn't want

115

the report to be released for all the uproar it could have caused, just like why the truth of JFK's murder never came to light.

"I know I've given you an awful lot to chew on, but I hope you'll give it due consideration and that you'll believe what I've told you. I have every reason to believe that it's because of what he knew and what he was forced to do because of it that he disappeared." He looked from Tom to John. He saw their skepticism, but also their intrigue. He knew they'd be hooked. Why wouldn't they be? This was some very heady stuff and all of what he'd just told them about their father- to the best of his knowledge- was true...

...except for one part.

As for Kim, who gazed intently at him, he wasn't sure. She could be a problem in his last shot at damage control- in more ways than one. What he'd been told only minutes before they arrived made him worry more. If she realized she had all the answers...

...it's been so long, though, and those were very subtle hints she had- unrecognizable to virtually anyone...

...all the same, I just about had a heart attack when she said those things to me at her wedding. I don't know if I can bank on her not putting the pieces together...

He snapped out of that unsettling thought. There only were two ways to head her off- one of which he was attempting now-, although at this point he wondered if that would even work. There still was the chance that the 'anonymous caller' would reveal even more of what he knew, which might make what Kim could or couldn't put together a moot point...

...even though the direct approach never really was the bastard's style- and wasn't an option for him in this case-, Jack knew he didn't have a lot of time either way...

"...Mister Jack?"

He jumped a little. "I'm sorry, Tom. What did you say?"

"Are you all right? You don't look so good all of a sudden."

"Yeah. What was your question?"

"Do you know who killed my father?"

He stared ahead for a moment. "I can't say definitively, but I have my suspicions. It certainly could have been Hoover loyalists within the Bureau, it could have been people who still were afraid of what he knew and didn't want to chance him talking...those are the most likely choices. Considering the fact that no evidence of any kind ever was found, I'd have to conclude that. It's vague, I know, but I'm at a loss as to who else it could have been..."

He glanced over and caught Kim staring purposefully at him- again- so he finished his line of thought, hoping to derail her. "...except for one other possibility. Someone else who might have had enough reason to hate your father."

Tom's eyes narrowed. "Jacobson?"

"It's possible. He had the means and ability, I'm sure. He was a Vietnam vet- said he served as a sniper. Your Dad told me about that conversation he had with him. He certainly had motive, since it was your father who, for all intents and purposes, gave him the boot off the police force after giving him a boot up his ass when he caught him in bed with-..."

"Right. He was a sniper, huh?"

"A good one, too, if what he told your father was true. With the training those guys get, that certainly would have been a job he was capable of."

"Well, if it was him, he might have had help."

"What makes you say that, John?"

"Dad got a call the night he vanished- from somebody who sounded really young. It was upsetting news for him, from the looks of it, and something he had to deal with. He left just after that. I guess there's a chance that whoever that caller was might have set him up."

"Could be."

Tom took over again. "Speaking of Jacobson, he sure seems to have lowered his profile ever since his run for Governor in '94 never went anywhere, then his business was virtually taken right out from under him a few years later." He turned to Kim. "Have you talked with Jenny recently?"

"Yes, just the other day while John and I still were in Iowa."

"Did she mention anything about him?"

"Not a word. She hardly ever does. She really didn't have much reason to, I guess; he never was much of a father to her."

"But she should know where he is, anyway. Do you know where Jenny lives?"

"Mm-hmm. Maybe I should pay her a visit."

"I think that's a good idea." He stood and extended his hand toward the Attorney General. "Mister Jack, I appreciate your time and all you've shared with us."

Jack shook his hand and smiled grimly. "I can't imagine it's all been welcome information. I'm sorry to have kept it from you, but..."

"I understand why you did. I might be getting back with you as we learn more about these cases and, hopefully, about my father."

"I hope you find an answer. I hope we see each other under better circumstances next time, John," he said as he shook his hand, and turned to Kim. "Same with you, young lady."

"So do I, Mister Jack. We'll see you soon," she replied as he walked around his desk to give her a hug. "By the way, how has your nephew been?"

"My nephew? I don't have a nephew, Kimberly," he replied, looking at her sideways.

Her brow furrowed for a couple seconds. "Oh- that's right. I'm sorry; I don't know why I thought you did. I guess it was someone else I was thinking about." She smiled sheepishly and embraced him. "Anyway, we'll see you soon!"

As soon as they were gone, Jack reached for the phone, wondering what that last exchange was about.

She knows perfectly well that I don't have a nephew. I never even insinuated that I did. I even told her at her wedding how much of a shame it was that my brother never had any kids, so what in the hell could she-

When it hit him, he dropped the phone into his lap.

He went back to a day twenty-two years ago when he told her he *did* have a nephew.

He also remembered perfectly why he'd said it.

"Oh, my God..."

"I understand why he held it all back when we were kids, but...I'd have thought there'd come a time sooner than now when he'd have told us. And, *why* now, when we're asking him about those four cold cases in the same time frame? On top of that, did you see his reaction when I told him about the conversation you, Kim and I had on the way up?"

"Yeah. For a minute it looked like he had ESP, didn't it? That was weird, but that's what happens sometimes when you make assumptions. He sure did act strange today, though. I can't help but wonder if it was a natural progression from those cases into what he said about Dad. Like you just said, the time frame is right, and our father was the Sheriff in the jurisdiction where those crimes happened...either way, I'm still having a hard time with it. I can't imagine Mister Jack would lie to us- especially not about Dad."

"Neither can I. One thing's for sure: we definitely need to find out more about Jacobson."

"Agreed. I also think we should talk with Warden Steele. He was Dad's right hand for some time while he was Sheriff..."

John and Tom discussed all they'd learned while they rode toward Tom and Donna's, but Kim was silent.

Something didn't seem right...

...unless she was making too much out of something she thought she'd noticed, which she had to acknowledge was a possibility.

Then again, he all but forgot about his nephew...

"Kim?"

"Hmm?"

"I just asked, what do you think about all this? Did anything in particular stand out?"

"I was watching him when he told us all he did. For the most part, I think he was telling the truth. With all my counseling experience I usually can tell when someone's lying or holding back. I didn't see either while he told us about your father, but I did see a little inconsistency in his mannerisms was when he talked about how he thought your father was killed.

"Something seemed a little funny when he talked about Mister Jacobson, too. It might be nothing at all or it might mean that just like everyone else, he has no idea what happened and only is putting forward a theory based on what he knew. I mean, it *is* Mister Jack we're talking about...maybe it's more his way of trying to protect you somehow, or to lessen the blow. He's had to bear those secrets for an awfully long time."

"True."

"There was one thing I'm still wondering about, though..."

"Do you mean when you asked about his nephew?"

"Yeah, his face went-...wait a minute- he *did* tell me his brother had no kids!"

"Come again?"

"At our wedding while we talked- he said his brother had no kids!"

"Ok..."

"He didn't have any other brothers or sisters, right?"

"No, only the one brother. Why?"

"Remember when I told you about that day soon after I turned thirteen? When those neighborhood boys tied me up and kept me in the treehouse next to Mister Jack's place for most of it?"

"Oh, yeah. I won't forget that any time soon."

"I also might have mentioned that earlier on the same day I was walking past his yard and I saw the guy I thought was good looking working in his yard, digging."

"That's right, you did tell me about that. You asked about him and he told you the guy was-...his nephew..."

"Exactly."

"A bunch of kids tied you up and kept you in a treehouse?!" Tom asked with an expression that was somewhere between curious and astounded.

Kim blushed and lowered her head. "Well, it- it was a game, and-...it's a long and kind of personal story I'd rather not get into, if you don't mind."

"I understand completely. That's just not something you hear every day."

She giggled. "I don't suppose it is. It's also not something I expected to blurt out, even though it was meant to jog John's memory."

"I'd say you succeeded at that, Honey." He kissed her cheek, which still was quite red. "About Mister Jack calling the guy his nephew, I was thinking...you know how people call the sons and daughters of good friends their nieces and nephews? I wonder if that was the case with him?"

"Mmm- I never thought of that. It could be, but...I'd still have figured he'd remember, even if it wasn't his real nephew. If he was that fond of the guy..."

"Well, he is getting up there in age. Maybe he's slipping a little with some things, although you'd never know it with the details he laid on us about Dad."

"Exactly." Tom said, jumping into that one. "He also seemed a little too sharp with that moment he had when we first started talking. For an instant it looked like he knew exactly what I was going to say about our conversation before I even said it."

"It did, didn't it? As for this nephew- or whoever he was- maybe he didn't want to remember. Maybe it was the opposite of what we said; a case of that guy being someone he wasn't very fond of, although that wouldn't make much sense. It would be more like he was trying to hide the fact that he was associated in any way with the person, for some reason. However you look at it, it's pretty strange.

"On the other hand, there's that memory lapse he had with you, Kim, when at our reception you told him about the day in the dead of winter when you were little and you thought it was so funny, seeing him digging in his garden. He sure had the 'deer in the headlights' look when you told him that. Then he remembered, though, so we might get a call from him later and he'll be embarrassed because he forgot about that nephew."

"Funny you should put it that way...I've thought about the way he reacted when I told him about the digging incident, too. We do have to look at the fact that Mister Jack's almost eighty, so while these might be nothing more than mere memory lapses, they just as easily could be the onset of something worse...

"Although I can't imagine this to be the case, he also could be playing selective memory games with us, or making things up. I only bring that up because, as both of you pointed out, he seemed to remember the details about your father with total clarity. Of course, given what he shared with us, I suppose those details would stay with him."

"I know *I'll* never forget 'em. He's held all that in for all those years; that in itself had to have gotten to him. Did you see the hurt in his eyes, in his gestures? It was written all over him. As far as him playing games with us...I don't see why he'd make all that up. What would his reason be? Why would he do that to us? He's like extended family; look at all he's done for us. It just doesn't make sense. It's not impossible, but it doesn't make sense. I see no motive. I'll say this much; in light of what we saw today, I hope this is the last term he'll serve as Attorney General. He needs to get out of that and relax.

"Regarding the guy who was digging in Mister Jack's yard that day, do you remember what he looked like, Kim? Did he tell you his name when you talked with him afterwards?"

"Um...you know, he probably did. Unfortunately, my memory fails me sometimes when it comes to names. I do remember what he looked like, though. He was tall- definitely over six feet-, he had long, dark hair and he was a big guy- very defined muscles. I couldn't make out all the details of his face but I could tell his features were really chiseled. He looked like something you'd see on the cover of one of those romance novels."

"Sounds like a certain asshole we're trying to track down."

Kim looked at him. "I was about to say that; I've thought the same thing sometimes. Weird, isn't it?"

"Yeah..."

"At any rate, I never saw him again after that...come to think of it, Mister Jack never really talked about him again. Maybe they weren't close- maybe the guy was getting paid for the work, who knows?

"Oh- on a different subject, I still want to see those pictures of the real Joshua Strauss. Let's look at those when we get back, Ok?"

"Sure, we can do that."

"So, where's the next stop after lunch, John? Should we go talk with Warden Steele?"

John shook his head, then answered his brother. "There's somewhere else we need to go first," he replied as he looked at Kim.

Chapter 7

Donna had prepared a lunch for them- one of her homemade pizzas, which made those of any commercial place taste ordinary. With the grace and manners of wild animals, they made it disappear quickly, much to Donna's amusement. "Damn- I'd think none of you had eaten for weeks!"

"It's not every day you have pizza this good- especially when you're on the road as much as we've been," John replied. "In fact, the last time we had anything even comparable was the last time you made it, which was quite some time ago."

"Well, I'm glad you like it, and hopefully this makes up for me not coming down last night."

"Don't worry about that, Donna; you were needed here, too. Besides, as a result of Detective Searles having brought Tom to our place, we might have found a good prospect for our quadrupling security detail."

"Well, that's good. He has experience in that realm, then?"

John hesitated in his reply, so Tom answered for him. "Actually, we're talking about a 'she'. Detective Searles is a woman."

Kim chimed in, hoping to steer Donna away from the direction she was headed for, although she also began to wonder. "She is that, although she's a bit- well, different from virtually every other woman I've come across, with the exception of Dawn on our security team. She's athletic and pretty muscular, and she's a martial artist. She sure takes her job seriously, which is a good thing. She's *really* quick; she took me down and covered me before I could take a breath! I'll definitely feel safer if Detective Searles joins our detail."

"I imagine you will."

Kim and John saw the look Donna gave her husband, and they saw his reply. When they glanced at each other just after seeing that non-verbal exchange, they shared an expression that said 'uh-oh'.

Apparently, Tom had not told her all the details of last night, including the fact that the detective who drove him to Kim and John's place not only was a woman- she also was a fit, attractive, young and single one.

Tom made a belated effort. "I went to Danni's place to-"

"Her place? Hmm- I could swear you told me you were meeting your study partner at the library."

"Well...that was the original plan, but she called late in the afternoon and said she had to meet someone that evening. She had a date, so-"

"Oh, a *date*. I see. I bet he was right on time, too. Did you finish the assignment for your class?"

"Almost."

"Almost? You were 'almost' finished it before you went to meet her. So, you had a little diversion, then." She stopped herself there, and looked at John and Kim. "I'm sorry to subject you to that. All of a sudden I'm not feeling so well; I think I'd better not go out on the boat this time. I need some rest." Donna got up, and so did everyone else. She said her good-byes to John and Kim, then went upstairs.

Tom looked apologetically at John. "I'd better-..."

"Definitely," he replied. "Your wife is a hell of a lot more important. Kim and I'll be fine; we'll let you know if we find anything."

"Do you think something might have happened between them? Maybe before they came down last night?"

John knew she was asking about Danni. "I don't know. Christ, I hope not..."

"So do I. He looked a little guilty to me, but that could be because he didn't tell Donna about her- at least, I pray that's all. And then, Danni..."

He waited for her to go on but she was hesitant. "What about her?"

"Did you see the way she reacted when I made the comment about her date?"

"No, I guess I wasn't paying attention. What did she do?"

"It seemed as though I caught her off guard- like she had no idea what I was talking about when I said her date would understand why she had to cancel. Then, she recovered- it was the same kind of reaction we talked about that Mister Jack had when I reminded him of when he was digging in his garden that January. Maybe that was just a slip, but I don't know...I get the feeling there's an attraction between her and Tom. I'm worried, John; he's such a good man, but he's vulnerable that way. I can't imagine that she has any other agenda- at least, I don't *think* she does-, but what you and I suspect would be bad enough if it's true. When there's a certain chemistry between two people…"

"Yeah. Let's just hope it didn't get to that point, and that Tom and Donna will be all right. They've been married over twenty years; I can't see either of them with anyone else. I just hope they see it that way, too." He turned to Kim. "That look on Donna's face, and then Tom's reaction…it hurt me just seeing them like that. Love sure can become problematic, as you and I know, too. Really puts things in perspective, doesn't it? It also makes me appreciate even more what we have, Kitten."

"As far as what you said last, I feel the same way. Also, as for your comment about love being problematic, I'll paraphrase a certain man I happen to be very fond of; one thing the bad times do is help you appreciate the good all the more."

"Sounds like a pretty smart guy." She giggled as he kissed her tenderly, then pulled her close. "I just hope Tom and Donna see it that way."

"So do I…" Along with her thoughts about Tom and Donna came someone else she worried about who possibly was facing a different set of problems. "John, would you mind if we made a detour? Speaking of love and its effects, there's someone I'd like to visit to see how she's doing with it."

"Jenny?" She nodded. "Sure, we can do that. It would be nice to see her. Besides, we have plenty of daylight for our trip to the Bridge."

Jack knew he should do it and be done with it.

Physically it would be so easy- the only energy he'd have to expend would be to toss the small, faded journal into the roaring potbelly stove. Just like that it would be done…

…but he'd tried that numerous times already and every time he held back, like he did on this occasion. He simply couldn't do it- not before, not now, maybe not ever.

He closed the door of the stove, sat in his old rocking chair and stared out the back window into his garden.

* * *

125

"I was hoping she was just in the shower or something," Kim said with disappointment in her voice. "It's been so long since I've seen her."

"I know, Honey. We'll call ahead and try to arrange something with her next time we come up."

Just as they were about to leave, Kim spied the present left on Jenny's doorstep. "Oooo- look at these beautiful flowers! This guy does have good taste, although that's the only good thing I know about him so far. Let's see... these are pink camellia, and here's a gardenia..." She trailed off when the recollection hit. The flowers- and their layout- were exactly the same. "I've gotten this arrangement before."

"Oh, yeah? I don't think I've ever sent you these..."

"You haven't. The ones you get for me are my favorites, mainly because they come from you. As for who sent me these, let's not talk about him." She moved closer to him, partly in reaction to the memory. "I'll call Jenny later on; like you said, I'll set something up so we can meet. Well, I suppose we should be-"

As they were about to walk away, she spied the card.

"Hmmm..." She leaned down to have a look at it.

"Infringing a bit there, aren't you?"

"Absolutely not! We just happened to be here for a visit when I noticed these lovely flowers and I simply became curious as to who sent them to my former student- that's all. Then, I just happened to observe that the card is folded in half, thus rendering it readable by anyone, including me!" she retorted, grinning mischievously as she opened it and read it aloud:

'Dear Jenny-

Hope you like these. I can't wait to see you next week. Better yet, I can't wait until we make things permanent so I'll be able to give you your next bouquet myself. See you after the contest.

Love you. Chris'

"Augh!!" Kim exclaimed when she got to the name. "Another Chris, and therefore another coincidence. I'd hope this guy can only be better than the monster we're looking for. Let's go, Baby."

John took that lead-in to reopen their discussion of his nemesis and Kim's former tormentor as they walked back to the car. "Speaking of which, what was he like in the early stages-

when you first started dating him?" he asked as he helped her inside and climbed in behind her.

She went back to that period while they started rolling toward home. "You mean, other than the fact that he was a control freak extraordinaire, very obsessive, extremely possessive, insanely jealous, and totally domineering?"

John couldn't help but laugh. "You really should learn to express yourself, Kim- don't hold back so much! And yes, besides those wonderful qualities, did anything else stand out? Was he...I don't know- spontaneous? Ostentatious?"

Then he thought of something else. "Also, where did you live when you moved in with him?"

"He was as far from spontaneous as he could have been- a creature of habit if ever I saw one. Whenever we went out to eat he'd order the same thing every time, and we always went to the same restaurant. It was a very nice place but you'd think at some point he'd have wanted to try something else!

"That wasn't him, though; once he found something he liked or felt comfortable with, he rarely deviated. That was a pattern in more ways than one, needless to say. You saw what he did as a result of his relationship with me and wanting to recreate it. He wound up kidnapping eleven other girls with light-colored hair and green eyes, similar height and build as me, with each one representing a different phase of my life or one of my hobbies. Then he took me for the second time."

"That he did," he said, nodding slowly. "Creature of habit... sums him up pretty well, doesn't it?"

"Definitely. It always was the same routine in every aspect, too. He wanted me to be a total submissive, and I was. The whole thing really fascinated me for a while. I liked being what amounted to a kept woman in every way- until he showed his true colors and got so vicious, that is- but that's all there was. That's all *he* was. When I look back, I don't see anything else. He didn't like sports, wasn't interested in cars; he was far from the typical guy in so many ways. He never talked about law school when we were alone and he never wanted to be around any of my friends. We only had that one dinner with Vanessa and her boyfriend.

"Otherwise, outside of school and dancing, I saw very little of anyone else but him for several months. He never even had a job- for obvious reasons, I suppose. Now we know in all probability where he got his money from and why he had the luxury of doing nothing but ordering me around. That was what he lived for: to dominate me. What was he like when he was around you, John?"

"We seemed to have a lot in common at the time. It's no mystery now why he knew what interested me- subjects I liked to discuss, since he and I talked about them years earlier. As for what we did, come to think of it, he was inclined to follow my lead- strange as that may seem. I'd say 'let's do this' and he'd go along. He did see me as competition, of course. Looking back, from my perspective he was just observing, learning, and waiting for his chance to beat me in a big way to make up for me getting the last laugh on him. Bettering me academically wasn't enough for him.

"That rings true, given all he said to me on Suicide Ridge and more so now that we're very sure he's Christopher Hedges. Then, when I cut him to ribbons during debates it just made his need to get me burn even hotter. I got him good, and in front of an audience, like before. I pointed out his weakness and used it against him, first when I observed out loud that he'd pissed his pants when my father took hold of him and again when I shot his arguments down- piece by piece and time after time...

"...and he just could not recover. He couldn't muster a counterattack. He was safe and very effective in the environment that was controlled and closed- that being the classroom. However, in the open field- the debate-, where you have to apply your knowledge, be quick on your feet and sharp as a tack, he had nothing. He'd just stare at me, hating the fact that I'd beaten him again, yet he would not budge from his position. I found it funny that he wouldn't admit defeat, either- never saw himself as being wrong. He kept giving me that 'I'll get you next time' look and he kept coming back for more...

"...then, you and I upped the stakes when we were all over each other right in front of him during the Memorial Day '89 pool party. He couldn't take it; we both got him and he snapped. He had to have you in the controlled environment again because, given the choice, you wanted to be with me. He couldn't accept that and wouldn't acknowledge it. You got him even more when you escaped him, which became his biggest defeat; another one he couldn't get over. 'That wasn't supposed to be the way', he told me, yet even then he wouldn't admit he'd been beaten.

"So, for those years between 1989 and 2000 he did all he could to recreate what he had with you until he got you back so he could conquer you once and for all- and me as well. To his credit he got very good at his game, but yet again, you beat him. As a result, he lost most of what he had.

"His actions since then- the mass selling of the video footage of you, sending a copy of it to us on our first wedding anniversary, that strange 'like father, like son' message he sent to me- indicate that he hasn't moved on, either. He's sniping at us with all that. Wherever he is, I'd say it's probable that he's plotting something against us. I seriously doubt he's moved on at all. What else does he have? What other interests? Nothing, and none. He'll stick with where his talents lie and what he knows, part of which is intruding in and fucking up the lives of those he thinks screwed him over somehow or belittled him. That's his way."

He turned to Kim. "Somewhere in all that lies our answer; we just need to figure out where…"

Danni sipped her water as she casually observed the people around her.

She'd decided to stop off at the park and wait. It was right next to the Bridge, and put her close to where she wanted to be. As a bonus, she got to take in a little sun and relax.

There were worse things to do to pass the time and wait for the next move.

Kim stared at the DVD as she held it over the trash can.

After donning and adjusting her bikini in preparation for the boat ride, she'd looked up at the small box on the shelf in their walk-in closet that contained the half-dozen DVDs. The conversation about Hedges she and John had during the drive, and their recent focus on him in general, made her think of the videodiscs again.

For some time she'd considered throwing all of them away, and that feeling was especially strong with the one she was holding. After viewing a couple of the others shortly after acquiring them, she and John hadn't watched any of the discs depicting her performances at The Silver Palace since. She'd pulled them out of the suitcase full of her lingerie and shoes, not to mention the laptop computer with all the bank records, that day in July of 2000.

As for the disc in her hand, which was the record of her twelve-day ordeal in the hands of Christopher Hedges in the spring of 1989, she never wanted to see it again and she really didn't want John to see it, either. He didn't object at all- not that she expected him to.

I really can't see any reason why I should keep it...

John took hold of her wrist as she went to open the garbage can. She turned to him, obviously confused. "Is this the one?"

She nodded. "I want to throw it away, which I might do with the rest of them as well. A lot of bad memories, this one in particular." She went to throw it away again, and again he stopped her. "John, why are-"

"Do you think you could remember where it was that he kept you during that time?"

"I don't know...I really don't think so." She looked up at him. "I never told you about that period, did I?"

"No. Vanessa told me a little, but I'm sure she condensed it way down. Don't feel like you have to- believe me, I'll understand if you'd rather not-, but if you want to tell me, I'm here." He saw her answer and took her hand into his. "We probably should sit down," he said, then led her over to their bed.

Once they were sitting, she began. "I was terrified. Even today, just thinking about it makes me shiver sometimes," she lay against him as he drew her close. "It was a nonstop hell for almost twelve days- even worse than the 2000 incident. There was no one else to divert him from me. If I wasn't tied to his bed or some strange piece of furniture he'd rigged up, he'd keep me in this small closet. He knew the effect that it would have on me and he took full advantage.

"He always had me restrained in some way, like the last time, but back in '89 he-... he hurt me. He really got off on that, along with scaring me and humiliating me. His psychological warfare was unrelenting. He was so sadistic; he liked all that better than the actual sex- at least, that was the case with me. He said that more than anything, he hated how he would lose control of himself because of me, which was why he did all those things to me.

"I really saw him for what he was. He even convinced himself that it turned me on when he hurt me. With that twisted logic he justified all the ways he tortured me, and each time would be worse than the last. The only way I could stop him was to plead with him, which I did a lot of. Sometimes it worked, although not very often. He made me do the most degrading things, which I don't want to talk about. Toward the last I did them without hesitation to try to stop him from hurting me or locking me inside that tiny, dark closet. It was just horrible..."

John's fury would have boiled over if not for the fact that he was so tuned in to Kim, and thus heard and felt the lingering distress stemming from her ordeal as he listened to her and held her. She didn't need to see him blow a fuse.

Instead, after brushing away her tear, he gave her what she did need in the form of an embrace and a long, deep kiss. It was the way he chose to remind her that those days were long gone, and they never would come back. She pressed herself against him and her nails dug into his shoulders as she showed her understanding of and appreciation for that reassurance from him.

"Are you Ok, Kitten?" he asked as they finally ended the kiss. She smiled warmly and nodded, and he waited for her to continue.

"By the last night I had all but given up. He was right when he said I begged him not to leave. I was so lost- bound, gagged and blindfolded, facing the prospect of permanently being held captive in that house and crying because I was alone in every way.

"It was by accident that I noticed the slight bit of give in one of the leather straps he used to tie my wrists and ankles to his bedposts; it was the one holding my right hand. Believe it or not, instead of feeling a sense of hope, my first instinct was one of fear. I was afraid he was testing me and hadn't really gone- that he was just waiting for me to free myself so he could pounce on me and punish me like he threatened he'd do if I ever tried to escape.

"I just lay there for what must have been an hour, but gradually it dawned on me that I could be looking at the only opportunity I'd ever have to get away from him. I still felt that fear of what he'd do to me, but I knew being trapped there forever and wishing I'd taken the chance was something I just couldn't bear. I had to try, so I twisted and pulled for what seemed to be years.

"The worst feeling of all set in when my arm came free, and it wasn't just because my wrist was chafed. I was sure he'd come back before I was able to get away but that feeling of dread did make me work pretty quickly to free myself the rest of the way.

"The next problem: I couldn't run. Just like when you found me in the cage, he had those really high heels padlocked onto my feet, and my lingerie- including the corset- was all the clothing I had. I felt so desperate and pressed for time I didn't even think to try to saw through those straps holding my shoes on; I was on the verge of panic because I didn't know what to do next.

"I had no idea where I was, either. I was stupid enough to trust him to drive me back to my place at Princeton the morning after the Memorial Day party, and stupider still not to be suspicious when he told me he needed to stop by his apartment on the way. That was the same one we'd shared when I moved in with him- sort of- in the fall of '88; I did only to the extent of having my essentials and some clothes there, since I still was split between three places, really.

"Anyway, his apartment was where he turned on me. During the drive he told me his lease there was up at the end of the month, but he had another place. Then, when we got there, I did the stupidest thing ever by agreeing to go inside with him for some water. Before I knew it he pulled a gun on me and forced me into his bedroom. He stripped me, threw me onto the bed and tied me up. He informed me that what he didn't tell me about his other place was that it was perfect for the two of us. I went completely numb. Next, he gagged me and blindfolded me as he so often did and kept me inside until it was dark.

"Gradually he took a break from tormenting me to load me into the trunk of his car and, after a pretty long drive, there we were. I had no idea where 'there' was from that first moment until he left me the last night- not that it really mattered at the time.

"Boy, did that ever change. All of a sudden, as I stood in the kitchen wondering what to do next, it *did* matter- a lot. I had no idea where I'd run to, even if I could run in the first place. In the middle of that indecisiveness I caught a glint by the back door.

"I walked over to see what it was and found that it was a ring with a couple keys- car keys. Almost automatically I took the ring off its hook and walked to the garage where- thank God- I found a car. At first I was suspicious again and even more on edge, thinking it was just another part of the trap he'd surely set for me. In spite of that I had to get behind the wheel and start it, hoping it *would* start, which it did.

"Even though those high heels made it a bit difficult, I've never driven so fast in my life until I was sure I was far enough away, which was when I think I started breathing again. I just drove and drove- I still didn't have clue one as to where I was. For all I knew I might have been driving in circles, but finally I saw a sign for I-81. Once I reached there I thought I'd be all right, but the engine started acting up a while after I'd turned onto I-70 toward Baltimore.

"Well, someone must have been looking out for me, because just when I started to panic again, thinking the car would break down and he'd recapture me, I saw one of those emergency phones at the truck scales and pulled over to it. Better yet, the first person I thought to call- Vanessa- was home.

"She told me to stay where I was. I hid the car behind the little building and spent the longest two hours of my life waiting for her to get there. I couldn't stop crying or let go of her when she did. I was a mess for the next few months- most of all, for the first week-, but she took such good care of me. For a long time afterwards I did my best to forget about that whole ordeal."

As impossible as it seemed given how he felt about Hedges as things were, John's hatred of him grew deeper still. "No wonder you did; no one could blame you for that."

"I probably should have told the police, but...he had those videos of me. Plus, I was an exotic dancer; hardly anyone close to me knew, which was how I wanted it. I couldn't bear the thought of going through a trial and being chewed to bits by some callous defense lawyer. I was sure whoever it was would expose that part of my life and do his or her best to convince the judge and jury that I got what I deserved, so I dealt with it on my own."

"The sad thing is, that's exactly what would have happened in court. Sounds like you made the best decision you could have under the circumstances." John was glad she was able to remain relatively calm as she revealed all that to him; apparently she'd done a pretty good job of dealing with that experience since she could talk about it without breaking down. However, she did feel pretty tense, which certainly was understandable...

...as he cuddled her, a thought came to him. "I wonder what happened to that car..."

"I don't know. If he didn't claim it, which I can't imagine he would have, to this day it might be sitting in some impound lot."

"Maybe. Do you remember what kind of car it was?"

She shook her head. "I was wearing gloves, too, so I wouldn't have left any prints in it. No one ever contacted me about it, probably for that reason. Who even knows if that car was in his name, or if it was insured? Truthfully, I don't even know if it had any license plates. I'm sorry; I wish I could remember more."

133

"Don't apologize for that, Honey; the important thing is, you got away." He held her for a long moment, then backed away a bit, took hold of her shoulders and looked straight into her eyes. "Mark my words: we will find him and we will deal with him. He'll pay for everything he's done to you and he'll never hurt you or anyone else again. As for the DVD, the only reason I want to take a look at it is because he unwittingly might have left a clue as to where that place was."

"But, why would-...wait a minute: do you think he's back in that same house?"

"You said it yourself; he's a creature of habit. He needed a place to stay, so what would he do? Since he knew we were on the lookout for him, he had to be a little wary of the prospect of buying or leasing, and creatures of habit generally aren't too crazy about going into environments they're not familiar with. They tend to stay with what they know- where they feel comfortable.

"So, our boy comes back to his area; his old haunt. He doesn't want to chance renting, leasing or buying and he doesn't have to. I get the feeling he owned more than one house and he was smart enough not to put 'em in his name, like with everything else, it seems. I don't think the bastard ever owned anything legally. He probably used that apartment you told me about as a front, more or less. It's not definite that he's at the same house where he kept you, but it's certainly possible- more so if that place never was compromised...

"I also think we need to look into the ownership of the house outside Philadelphia again, where he kept you and the others. Maybe there's something we missed, or didn't look for in the first place."

He stroked her cheek. "You're sure you're all right?" She nodded and smiled again. "You really have healed a lot, haven't you? In so many ways, you'll make a great First Lady. The day will come when people will see you for how resilient, courageous, kind and good you are, and stop harping on one thing you did in the past." He emphasized his feeling with a kiss that conveyed every bit of it.

However, as he went to stand, he finally noticed he'd been sitting on something. A few silver keys of varying sizes, which had indented themselves into his leg, lost their hold and fell onto the floor. "What are these for?" he asked as he bent down and picked them up.

"Oh, I almost forgot about them." She sat back down, crossed her right leg over her left and reached down to the heel of the wedge sandal on her right foot. She removed a thin section from the middle of the three-inch heel, took the keys from John, placed them into the small, improvised compartment and slid it back into its place.

He regarded her with a curious smile. "Ok, *now* will you tell me what they're for?"

She giggled. "Well, this might sound silly, but considering all that's happened to me and how often I wear these shoes, I thought it might be a good idea to take a couple precautionary measures just in case I end up in handcuffs again. I also have a couple small blades stashed in a similar compartment in my other shoe in case I'm tied up with rope or tape. A girl can't be too careful- especially *this* girl- and what I just told you gives me even more reason to do this."

"While that is a good point, you also make me a little nervous by bringing it up. We have our security team in part to make sure you don't end up in such situations anymore. I'll tell you this, too: if you do anything to make their job of protecting you harder, you *will* find yourself over my knee, getting your ass spanked so hard that you'll need a cushion to sit down! In fact, I'll keep you inside this bedroom for a month!"

Her eyes lit up, and that smile he loved to see blossomed again. "Oooo!!" John shook his head and they both laughed heartily. "I'd think you'd know better than to make that sort of threat to me!"

"Yeah, you'd think. Maybe I should have said, you'll only get that treatment if you keep yourself *out* of trouble! Anyway, for now, let's prepare ourselves for a full day of sunshine," he said, reaching into her bag. "Considering what you're wearing, I have plenty to work to do, don't I?" he said as he eagerly opened the bottle of tanning oil.

"I still say you should let me do you first, considering the fact that your skin's maybe three or four shades this side of paste! It's too bad they don't make lotion that has triple-digit SPF; I suppose the factor thirty will have to do," she playfully retorted as she stood with him and turned so he could start the task that had him grinning from ear to ear.

"Yeah, yeah- pick on the white boy!"

* * *

"Good. I'll see you tomorrow, then."

Herb hung up with the latest prospect for the expanding security team. In more ways than one, the augmentation of his people was way overdue. His tiny team had logged in so many long days, particularly over the past several weeks during the last stretch of their long road trip when the death threats turned into more than just threats.

He closed his appointment book and leaned back in the easy chair to get as much shuteye as he could, which he knew wouldn't be enough. The rest of the team went down as soon as John and Kim took off on their run in the boat. Kim was very handy with the pistol and John was getting better with the rifle. They took one of each with them, along with the .45 John started to carry on occasion; Herb was curious as to where he'd gotten it. The little respite their ability with firearms gave the team was nice but it didn't change the fact that they needed to get the best of the new people and integrate them into the team as soon as possible.

He turned the ringer of the phone all the way up and placed it on the table right next to him, then drifted off quickly.

"This could have been some goofy impulse I had- just a knee-jerk reaction to what you told me. I didn't mean to bring you out here for nothing."

"You don't believe it was a knee-jerk reaction, though, do you?" John replied after regarding her for a moment. She seemed to be thinking out loud; she hadn't said that with much conviction.

"I don't know...it's hard to tell sometimes whether these inklings I get are warranted or not."

"Well, your intuition has proven to be pretty reliable..."

Kim looked at him and noticed he was frowning. "What's on your mind?"

"You said you were six that winter you saw Mister Jack digging in his garden, right?"

"Um...I think I was; I'm not sure. You know how those years when you're a child have a tendency to blend together sometimes."

"That they do..."

"Why do you ask?"

136

"I don't know. I keep coming back to that. If you *were* six at the time and he was digging in his garden just after New Year's Day, which is very peculiar no matter what the reason, that would make it January of 1975- days after my father disappeared. And you said his mannerisms were a little odd when he told us what he thought happened to Dad..."

Kim gaped at him. "Wait a minute; you're not suggesting-"

"I don't know, Kim. I'm only saying-...I don't know what I'm saying. Just that it would be a damned strange coincidence if it turned out that that was the winter in question when you saw him digging...no, this is wrong. I shouldn't even think such a thing. He and my father were best friends, for Christ's sake! He looked out for us in every way imaginable, too, after Dad disappeared. What in the hell is wrong with me?!"

"Settle down, Baby. That was the most traumatic event in your life, and worse, as yet we still don't know what happened to him that night. Of course, with all we've just learned...you're sure to be on edge- even more so than before-, just like Tom has been. I really do hope we're able to find out something this time."

She kissed him on the cheek and walked over to the cooler to grab some water. "I have to say, though, that *would* be a weird coincidence with Mister Jack's digging that day, considering all that's coming to light otherwise and how it's coming to light. Speaking of which, I just hope this little venture doesn't turn out to be a waste of time."

"Hey, like I said before, there's no harm in looking into it, right? I wouldn't call it a waste of time by any means. Plus, it gave us a good enough excuse to take the boat out."

"Yes, it did! And could we have picked a more beautiful day? Gosh, it's so warm!"

"It sure is- feels closer to ninety than to eighty. I'm sure that has a lot to do with the other reason why I'm so glad we came out," he added, grinning flirtatiously at her. Nearly every inch of her shimmered in the sunlight, compliments of the tanning oil. Better yet, she was wearing her sexy tiger-striped bikini, which quickly had become his favorite as well as hers.

She looked back at him and was very pleased with what she saw. "Yet again, there's that goofy grin of yours, which tells me you're probably not paying attention to what you're doing. You'd better stick to driving this boat, Mister!" However, after her scolding, she sidled up to him seductively and brushed against him. "Unless you'd like my assistance."

"Talk about an offer I can't refuse...although, that could become problematic, particularly if you think I'm not paying attention to driving now." He pulled her closer as she giggled. "If we don't find anything, we'll just make a run further south- make sure the engine's performing well. We have to give it a good workout every now and again, you know. Letting it sit too long isn't good for it."

"Very convincing argument- you've certainly won me over."

"All right, then. Case closed." He slowed the motor once more to just above idle as he piloted the boat as close as he could to the pilings where he, Tom and their father used to fish so long ago so Kim could search each one. The low tide certainly had helped, and the one he approached was the last they needed to check.

Tom and he had come here for the first time in many years just after John's birthday in 2000 and they'd returned for a few other outings since then, but each time they did a lot more talking than fishing. Little had changed in that regard, with the exception of Tom being much less peeved when they came up empty than he used to get. John jokingly pointed that out to him on that late spring day in 2000, only weeks before Kim was abducted for the second time in two months.

As it always did, his recollection of that period moved him to tighten his embrace on her a little.

"Ok, I think this is good. Let me have a look." Kim made her way to the front of the boat; the waves were quite gentle and made the short walk easy for her. She conducted her search of that last piling, scrutinizing every rock and every crevice for something that looked out of place as he slowly guided the boat around it.

As with the others she'd checked, she came up empty and returned to John's side. "I'm sorry; maybe I just read too much into what your father said. I wasn't even there, anyway. Maybe he did just want you to come back here as a way to bond with your brothers...and maybe so you could feel close to him as well."

"If that's the case, I'd say we carried out his intent- today as well as last summer when Tom and I were here. We'll come back again, too- and soon. Sure is peaceful, isn't it? The funny thing is, you're so close to the bustle of everyday life with the cars passing by overhead, which in a way makes it even better because you can see what you're missing. In this case, you don't mind missing it. After all the time that's passed, I think I'm coming to appreciate why Dad enjoyed it here so much...

"By the way, you don't owe me any apologies. At least we checked it out, which we need to do even when a potential clue seems silly or meaningless on the surface. As we both have said, it's better to do that than not act on it and have it nag at us. In this case, I haven't noticed anything out of the ordinary, either. All we've seen are these rocks and the same crab pot markers Tom and I remarked about when we were here.

"You'd think the guy who works the pots would touch up the paint on his markers, or that he'd break down and get some new ones. God only knows how long the damned things have been here. You can see how dark they are underneath that paint; there's a chance a boater might not even see 'em until it was too late. Come to think of it, maybe I should find out who works 'em..."

"That might be a good idea," Kim said as she moved in between John and the wheel. "As for now, I want to steer- with your expert guidance, of course." She leaned back against him and looked up at him invitingly.

What she really wanted was very easy to see, and just as obvious was that it didn't end with the kiss he gave her as he embraced her once more. It only was a moment before he began to caress her; his hands slid down along her slick, shining, firm and already-tanned body to her hips...

She reached up and held on to his neck, moaning as their kisses became deeper...

"Take that into your cabin, you two!"

"Get down, My Brother! *Damn*!!"

They hadn't even noticed as another boat carrying a group of fellow sun-lovers had approached, then slowed and veered off slightly to pass by John's boat at a safe distance. Several guys on it whistled at and lauded Kim as they and their friends cracked up at up at and clapped for the embarrassed couple, then waved as they pulled away.

Kim and John laughed and waved back as the other boat kept going. "On that note, are you ready to open this bad boy up?"

"I'm ready- let's do it!" She took hold of the wheel. John laid his left hand on top of hers and manipulated the throttle with his right. Together they guided the boat away from the piling and toward the channel.

Suddenly, he put the throttle on idle.

Kim looked up at him and saw that he was fixated on something. "John? What are you looking at?"

"That marker over there- on the other side of the piling. I didn't notice it before."

"What about it?"

"It's different from the others…"

Kim studied it for a moment. "Well, yes, it is, but that could just mean it belongs to another person, or that whoever laid them out ran out of the kind of markers he was using."

"Maybe, maybe not," John said as he moved the boat alongside it, put the engine back on idle and quickly grabbed his hook. He scooped up the line, got hold of the marker and pulled it closer so he could examine it.

"Couldn't we get into trouble for that?"

"We could, but I bet this hasn't been touched for a long time." He started to clean it off. "Look at all the algae and other buildup on-…"

Kim observed while he checked out the marker, then she saw him blanch. She touched his shoulder. "Honey?"

"Oh, my God…"

"John, you're scaring me. What's wrong?"

He turned to her, shock emblazoned into his face. "We used this jug when we went crabbing. This red ring around the top, and the big dot on the body of it…"

He grabbed the rope and began pulling it up rapidly.

In almost no time at all his frenetic effort produced a small box that looked every bit as untouched as the marker.

"It's been a long time since I've felt this good…"

Tom couldn't help but smile at Donna's statement. "Do I ever second that," he replied as he kissed her, then embraced her again. She'd unleashed every bit of her pent-up anguish on him along with her indignation over him not telling her about Danni, which Tom knew he deserved. It had taken a while for her to get that out of her system; her Italian temperament certainly had come into play, but so did her Italian passion afterwards.

Although that was the best sex they'd had in some time, he would do all he could from this point on to avoid the circumstances under which it had been generated.

The ringing of the phone brought them back to the present.

"This person's very lucky not to have called before now," he said, rolling over to get the phone as Donna giggled and agreed.

"Hello?"

"Tom, it's me. Is everything all right there?"

"Hey, Brother. Yeah, Donna and I are fine. What's up with you two? It sounds like water in the background...are you on the Bay?"

"We sure are and I hope you're sitting down."

Tom sat bolt upright. There only could be one reason why John wouldn't have waited until he and Kim were back home to call. "What did you find?"

"It's Dad's diary. He buried it underwater, close by one of the rock pilings around the Bridge supports; he marked it with a jug we used to tag the end of our trout line when we went crabbing."

"I'll be damned...Dad's diary. So, Kim was right."

"She sure was. Can you meet us at Sandy Point by the docks? I'll have Herb and our team meet us there, too; it'll save you some driving time."

"Yeah. I'm on my way. See you in about forty-five minutes."

When he hung up, Donna said, "you mean, *we're* on *our* way."

"That's exactly what I mean," he replied as he kissed her. "Let's get ready, Honey."

"Yes, Sir- we'll be right there."

As Herb had expected, the call came a lot sooner than he'd hoped it would.

Nonetheless, in two minutes, the team was up, fitted, ready and headed to the car. All four were sucking down some energy and caffeine as they rolled toward Sandy Point.

"This is in very good condition, considering your Dad had it since the '50s. Obviously the plastic wrapping he put it in did its job well."

John had killed the motor and dropped anchor, sat on the bench seat in back of the boat and pulled Kim into his lap.

Together they looked through the diary from cover to cover, after which he'd made his call to Tom. There wasn't an entry made every day, and the ones he made weren't overly long, or else he might not have fit all of it into one journal, let alone have had some pages left over. The first entry was January 19th, 1955.

The last was September 1st, 1970.

He hadn't responded to what she said. When she looked up she saw that his mind was elsewhere, as she figured it would be. Not wanting to get any oil on the diary, she put it off to the side.

"He was right, wasn't he?"

She looked back up. "You mean Mister Jack?"

"Uh-huh. Dad's diary backs up everything he said, just about verbatim. I can't believe I even suggested what I did about him while we were looking…"

"Well, remember what you said earlier; we have to consider every possibility, no matter how unlikely, in the absence of evidence."

"In this case, *extremely* unlikely. Let's forget I ever said it."

Again, his hand glided back and forth along her thighs. The more he did that, the more Kim began to smile. She was glad to feel him loosening up. "You never could keep your hands away from my legs, could you?" she teased, wanting to help cheer him up even more.

"That's a rhetorical question if I ever heard one," he answered in the same playful tone as she'd used, although there was nothing playful about the kiss he laid on her.

When they finally pulled back from it, another mood was kindling. He knew what he said next would have the effect of fanning it. "Being here with you in this spot where my father and I spent many a day just reminded me again of that dream I had the day we met. You seemed pretty sure that dream meant more than the obvious- that you and I are meant for each other. Well, I think you're right; there is more to it." All his love for her was crystal clear in his gaze. "If it wasn't for you suggesting to me the very same thing about what Dad said to me before he left that last night- that there was more to his words-, I probably never would have found his diary."

Kim was right there with him, sharing emotionally in the significance of the moment. Although he still had a way to go, John was closer now than he'd ever been to achieving closure when it came to the fate of his father. Her bittersweet joy from being able to help him to that end coupled with her love for him rendered her speechless, but her feelings came out another way.

"Yet again, you've shown me how extraordinary you are," he said, pausing only to kiss her tear away, "and yet again, I want to show you how much I appreciate you for everything you are and always were. Before I do, I think we should take some friendly advice we were given not too long ago."

"Oh? And what advice would that be?"

His right arm already was around her body, so he slid his left arm underneath her legs and stood, lifting her up with him. "Let's take this into the cabin."

"This one looks like John's."

Tom and Donna stood on the dock at Sandy Point State Park, located on the western shore of the Chesapeake and literally right next to the north span of the Bay Bridge where it met the shore. They'd been waiting for about ten minutes. Herb and the rest of the detail had arrived even earlier and cleared the area. Now they were staked out and watching.

Tom took a look at the approaching boat as it pulled in toward a slip. "Yep, that would be his." As it got a little closer, he added, "I think I see some evidence that'll indicate it's more a case of those two being late than of us being early."

"You mean how you can see the glint of the sun from the tanning oil that's all over Kim, but only on parts of John?"

He laughed. "Case closed, huh?"

Kim pointed them out and her unmistakable smile lit up the already bright day even more. She and John waved to them as John took over the controls.

Tom and Donna waved back and moved to where they were docking. "Toss me the mooring line, John; I'll hook you up."

In a matter of minutes the boat was secured. John shut the engine down and helped Tom and Donna aboard. Just as his little zinger about a certain condition of Donna's was formulating, she cut him off. "Don't you start with the seasick remarks or I'll throw your ass right overboard. Understood?"

They all cracked up, John especially. "Understood. Good to see you again, Donna."

She winked at him, then turned to Kim. "And you, Miss Hot Stuff, had better put some clothes on before you start causing accidents around here!"

"Yes, Ma'am!" Kim replied, smiling sheepishly as she drew on her cover-up. "On the serious side, I'm so glad you guys worked everything out."

"Thanks, Kim. So are we," Tom said as he put his arm around Donna.

"I wish I had my camera now; what a great picture of you this would make. I'd hug you both, but I don't want to get this oil all over you."

"Like you did to John?" Tom's remark drew more laughter and made Kim blush again. "Sorry, Sis. I just couldn't resist."

"Obviously! I'll have to think of what else I can add to your next omelet, wise guy! Anyway, if you two have finished embarrassing me, there's something John and I found that you both will be interested in."

John brought the diary over.

"How does it look, people? Coast still clear?"

Herb's detail reported in turn. Nothing out of the ordinary.

"All right, good. Keep your eyes open," he said as he watched a maintenance person who'd been emptying the trash on the grounds and now was heading toward the restrooms.

"I'm sure glad we're getting some help," Mel remarked.

"I'll drink to that, my friend." Fortunately, none of them commented on how tired they were, although the implication to that effect in Mel's statement was clear enough.

"Everything he told us- it's all here..."

Like John, Tom had slowly gone through the journal, trying to extract every last word, every last meaning, every last thought his father could have had while he wrote it. When he finally put it down, he added, "and it looks like we need to find one Benjamin Jacobson as soon as we can. I have a lot of questions for him, as I'm sure you do, John."

"You'd better believe I do. We also need to talk with Mister Jack again, and to Warden Steele. In fact, I'll call him now, if you

144

want to call Mister-" Just then he noticed the fading light of day. "Damn, the sun's set already! How long have we been here?"

Tom looked at his watch. "For some time, apparently. Wow, it's seven-thirty…well, let's call 'em, anyway. I know they'll want to see this."

"While you guys are doing that, I need to hit the head," Kim said, standing up.

She didn't pay attention to the boat passing by, nor did she notice it was going faster than the posted speed limit in the no-wake zone…

The standing around and waiting as the sun disappeared worsened Herb's fatigue, and he had no doubt the effect on everyone else was the same.

Finally, Kim stood and stretched, which was a good sign. *Hopefully this means we'll be leaving soon…*

A big explosion jolted everyone at the park…

…Herb in particular. The trashcan next to his car blew up. He dropped to a knee and scanned the area, pistol at the ready.

Then he looked toward the boat.

What he saw made him run full speed toward his charges, not at all mindful of any danger he might be in. "Derek! What happened there?!"

With Derek's response came the news he expected and feared: "Mrs. Stratton's down…"

Chapter 8

"I think she's all right, John. It looks like she bumped her head when she-...Kim?" Donna patted her cheek as she began to come around.

Kim opened her eyes, moaning a little as she did. "What happened?" she asked, looking up at John as he took her hand into his.

"We're trying to figure that out, Honey. Just relax, Ok?"

At that moment the realization hit her.

John saw it and headed her off before she could move. "Easy, Kitten, just take it easy now."

"Take it easy?! Someone shot at me! Someone just tried to kill me for the second time in two days!!" Immediately after that outburst, she winced and raised her hand to her head as it started to ache again.

"You have to calm down; you might have a concussion. Now, lie still while we wait for the ambulance," Donna said in a firm tone, but she lightened up right after that when she saw the fear seeping in. "You'll probably have to stay overnight at the hospital so we can make sure it's nothing major, which it probably isn't. I'm sure I speak for all of us when I say I'm glad this worked out like it did. For now, listen to your husband and your sister-in-law and relax, Ok?" She smiled as she reapplied the cold pack to Kim's head and checked the bandage on her shoulder from where the bullet had grazed her.

Even though it was a rather subdued one, Kim managed a smile as well.

There was no question that everyone there was on edge, especially the bodyguards, who maintained a tight perimeter of security as they waited for the police to arrive, which fortunately did not take long.

"Go ahead and get with the police, Herb. Let's find out what they know. We'll stay with John. He needs a few minutes; he'll be all right." John's head bodyguard was stricken with guilt. Even though it wasn't obvious, Tom still could see that was the case.

Also visible to him was Herb's deep fatigue. As he turned to leave, Tom added, "you'll be all right, too."

Herb nodded and walked away.

Tom joined Donna, who sat with John on a bench. John had said little since the incident happened.

His face was a tightly controlled mask of rage. The look he'd given Herb had said a lot, none of it good.

"Talk to me, Brother."

John glanced up at him, then stared back out over the water toward the spot under the Bay Bridge where he and Kim had made love not much more than an hour earlier. He drew in a deep breath, taking in the scent of the tanning oil he'd rubbed all over her, which he'd enjoyed immensely; some of it still was on him from where their bodies had touched.

The replay of those moments in his mind gradually steered him in a different direction.

Can't be angry- have to get over that. Have to calm down and think...

"John?"

He slowly released that breath. "This was planned with very little notice. Whoever pulled it off not only knew of our meeting here, but also must have been close by. Only six people other than Kim and I knew we'd be here and the timeframe during which we'd arrive. You and Donna obviously are ruled out, and even though it's remotely possible I'm wrong about this, I'd bet my life that no member of my security team played any part whatsoever in what just happened. That leaves two possibilities that come to mind: one, our phone conversation was monitored somehow, and two, one or more of us is or was bugged."

Tom was glad John had wrestled control of himself away from the seething anger and overwhelming dread. "If the only calls you made were to Herb and to me, I agree with all you've said. Whoever did this also must have a good knowledge of the area, and this park in particular, but talk about a small window of opportunity...the thing that worries me most right now is, we must be talking about a damned good crew."

They turned when Herb and a man wearing a suit approached them. Tom recognized the man and extended his hand in greeting. "Hey, Glenn. You know Donna, and I'm sure you recognize my brother John."

147

"I certainly do, Sir. Glenn Pierce, Mister Governor; I'm a detective in the counter-terrorism unit of the State Police. Captain Stratton and I are well acquainted. We've worked together on several occasions. I wish you and I were meeting under better circumstances."

"So do I, Glenn, but I'm glad you're here, anyway. What do you know so far?"

"Not much, I'm afraid. At first blush there's very little in the way of evidence."

"That's what I expected. The good thing is, Donna seems to be right about Kim's condition. The paramedics agreed that it's no more than a mild concussion. Thank God she's all right, but..."

Herb knew what was on John's mind as he trailed off. The bodyguard also was sick about what had happened, but for a different reason. "This was my fault, Sir. I-"

John cut him off. His earlier anger at Herb, which was pure emotion from his initial reaction, was gone. "No, Herb, I won't let you take all the blame. I never should have had you all meet us here. We should have gone back to the house where we know we'd have been safe...then again, we don't even know that we're safe there anymore. Plus, you and the team are worn out from the hours you've been logging and it's just before our augmentation.

"All those ingredients combined to form a perfect opportunity. I see that now and someone else saw it not even two hours ago, then planned and executed an operation that almost resulted in my wife's death, including a bomb blast that served as one hell of a good diversion. Someone knew we'd be especially sensitive to that after the explosion at the studio, where I was supposed to be the other day...

"What I can't figure out is, *why*? Why would someone want Kim dead?" John wiped the sweat from his brow. "Is there anything else you saw? Anything at all?"

"A car was pulling out when the trash can blew and it didn't stop. At first I thought that might have been the shooter, Sir, but one of the cruisers stopped it and searched it. A family was in that car and it was clean, so they were ruled out. I'm 100% sure the maintenance person was a major player, if not more."

"How long was it between the time I called you and the time you and the team arrived here?"

"No more than twenty minutes."

"So, whoever did this had twenty minutes or less to put it together before you and the team got here. That's not enough time for an amateur; I think we all can agree there. This was a very small and very good team- possibly one person, although I'd think this would have been a tall order for someone on his own...or, *her* own, in this case." He turned to Tom. "I met someone last night who struck me as very capable of pulling this off."

Tom caught his drift almost immediately. "Danni?!"

He nodded. "She cancelled on us at the last minute today- why, we don't know yet. Was she the first one up this morning?"

"Yeah, she was, but-"

"That would have given her opportunity to plant a bug."

"Hold on, John. Granted, the opportunity for her to do that was there, but...you should see her record. She's outstanding as a detective; I'm having a hard time believing she'd do that."

"How many other potential suspects do we have, given what we know? We have to track her down right now, while the trail's hot. If we *can* find her and she can account for her whereabouts we'll make a judgment call from there. Until then, I want her found as soon as possible."

He saw Tom's continued skepticism. "I can imagine how you feel and I have no doubt she is an excellent detective, which right now, in my eyes, increases the chances that it could be her. Kim sensed something about her that wasn't necessarily good and I trust her instincts more than anyone else's. I know it's possible she was wrong- and thus, maybe *I'm* wrong-, but it wouldn't do any harm to find out."

Recalling his similar effort after the mass murder in Baltimore three years earlier to convince a department head of the probable involvement of one of his officers in that bloodbath, Tom relented. "You make a good point."

"Why don't you give her a call while I check on Kim?"

"Are you going to the hospital with her?"

"It depends on whether we can have additional security assigned to protect Kim if she has to stay there."

"Consider that done. Remember, I'm a Captain in the State Police. You're not the only one with some clout around here."

John patted his shoulder. "I know." He looked toward where the medics were treating Kim. "Tom, I want somebody to burn for this- anyone and everyone who had anything to do with wanting to harm my wife. This has to stop, and if there's a chance I can help stop it, you'd damned well better believe I will."

Tom nodded. "I wouldn't try to talk you out of that, Brother. Go on and see to Kim; I'll get extra security for her first thing. As for Danni…I do need to look into this, and fast."

"John…" Kim reached out for him.

From the way she trembled in his arms, it was obvious to John that fear also had her in its grip. All the same, she tried to downplay it. "How do you feel, Honey?"

"I'm fine. They do want to keep me overnight, which I'm not too crazy about, but I'll get over it. Do the police know who did this?"

"Not yet. We're working on it, though; we'll find 'em."

Her headache didn't stop that from sinking in. "You said, 'we'? You're going with them?" she asked as she lay back onto the gurney.

"Now that I know you'll be all right, I think I will. Tom's arranging for extra security for you; I want you to be safe first and foremost, which he'll take care of." He looked her in the eyes very purposefully.

Kim picked right up on his vibes. "You think Hedges is behind this, don't you?" He nodded. "Well, that wouldn't surprise me a bit," she said as Donna joined them.

"You and Tom are going after that detective, right?"

"Yeah."

Kim's eyes narrowed. "Detective? I thought you were-"

"I also have a feeling Danni Searles had a role in what just happened. She might have been the one that took the- dammit, I'm sorry, Kim." A look of pain crossed her face when that blow settled in.

"I can't believe this! She was in our house last night as our guest, and today she tries to kill me?! Are you sure about that?"

"I'm pretty certain, yes. I don't have proof yet, but that's what my gut tells me."

Kim looked away. "At this point, nothing would surprise me. You probably should get going, then. You don't want to let her put too much time and distance behind her."

"And don't worry about my sister-in-law here; I'll ride with her and keep her company at the hospital," Donna added. "You guys get that bitch, all right? She caused a lot of trouble for Tom and me, but what she just did…I bet it was her, too, John."

"Well, if we're both right, you also can bet we'll get her. Thanks for staying with Kim, Sis. I know she's in good hands now." Even so, it pained him to leave her. *I should be with you…*

Kim saw that too as he gazed at her for a moment. She saw guilt materializing in his eyes and she did her best to head it off. This needed to be done. "Go ahead, Baby. I want you to help get them, too. If you can, it'll help make us safer," she said, touching his cheek. "Just…please be careful- both of you."

"We will." He kissed both women, got up and walked over toward Tom, who suddenly had a perplexed expression as he looked at his cell phone…

"What's up?"

Frowning, Tom replied, "I just dialed Danni's cell phone and it went right to voicemail. She's on duty today- at least, I thought she was…Danni, it's Captain Stratton. I need you to call me as soon as you get this message. I'm on my cell."

He hung up, then dialed her boss. "Ike? Captain Stratton here. Danni Searles is on duty today, right?…She is…Well, yeah, originally she was supposed to meet me at Loch Raven and take me to the site where the skeleton was found. She had to cancel, though- said there was something else that had come up. So she hasn't checked in with you?…No, her voicemail kicked right in…I didn't think that seemed like her…Ok, do that, Ike. I'd appreciate you letting me know as well…yes, my sister-in-law was slightly wounded. I'm at the scene now. You got the APB already, then?…That's good- we need everybody on the lookout. Hey, I need to go- thanks for your help."

"So, he hasn't heard from her, either."

"No." Tom wasted no time. "I know where her place is; we need to head up there right now."

The ex-detective drove up to the house at the end of the sparsely populated block, turned into the driveway on the far side of it and pulled all the way up into the open garage. She turned off the car, climbed out, walked over to the garage door, closed it…

...and finally breathed, muttering a curse as she did. She'd almost done it, but had missed her opportunity.

The side door to the garage opened and in walked her host.

"What happened out there?"

Danni stared ahead. "If it's all the same to you, Mister Jack, I don't want to talk about it just yet."

He nodded. "Well, come on inside. You can tell me after dinner, if you like."

"...yeah, and the darkness won't make this any easier. My brother put it well; this *was* a perfect opportunity, in just about every way. I just hope he's wrong about Danni. I'll see you there, Ike." Tom hung up with Lieutenant Miller as they rode back toward Baltimore, headed for Danni's apartment in Owings Mills.

He watched as John examined the contents of Kim's purse. Donna had called from the ambulance just before he, Tom and the security team left; she let him know that Kim's bag- with the purse inside- still was on the boat. John took the bag along with the intention of returning it to Kim when he picked her up from the hospital upon her discharge, which presumably would happen tomorrow.

They hadn't gone far before an inkling came to John as to how the assailant or assailants might have known they would be at Sandy Point.

Because of that inkling he'd dumped the contents of the bag, and then the purse, out onto the car seat shortly after they left Sandy Point. He checked every piece quite thoroughly. At one point John remarked about how surprised he was that she didn't need a duffel bag instead. It looked as though he'd gone through nearly every piece.

It was when he opened up a tube of lipstick that he found what he expected he would. "Bingo," he said as he showed it to Tom.

Sure enough, instead of lipstick, there was what looked to be a listening device inside the tube.

"This purse was downstairs this morning. I'd bet all my money that she dropped this bug in here first thing, when no one else was walking around yet. She listened to everything we said all Goddamned day long- knew everything we were talking about,

152

every move we would make. She knew we'd be at Sandy Point and she tried to kill Kim. Son of a *bitch*!!"

Tom stopped himself from telling John that they didn't know conclusively that Danni had planted the bug, primarily because he also had the feeling she did.

"You know, this was an effective move, but it also was pretty damned risky and hastily put together. I'd go so far as to say it bordered on reckless. Maybe she was pressed- felt like time was against her somehow...perhaps because she knew about the security augmentation that's in the works. If we hadn't gone to the park- if we'd have played it more safely- and if Kim had found that in her bag, the jig would have been up right then. She took a big chance and it nearly paid off, but already she's been found out.

"Apparently that was a chance she was willing to take. I'm sure she knows we've found her out, which we have to figure she planned for as well. We won't find her at her place; that much I'd also bet on," John said as he put the bug under his foot and crushed it. "What we need to figure out next is where she'd go."

He looked up as they merged from I-695, the Baltimore Beltway, onto I-795, the spur that would take them toward Owings Mills, bypassing the always-busy Reisterstown Road.

That was a good thing since now, time was working against them instead of Danni...

"Well, well..."

Chris sat forward in his chair as the report unfolded.

Someone had taken another shot at Kim- maybe the same person who'd tried to shoot her the night before. He had to laugh.

Looks like she has another devoted fan, he thought, as he decided he'd give the younger version a call.

"This certainly could rule her out as a suspect."

They stared at the very large bloodstain on her bed.

Upon arriving at Danni's apartment, they'd all but determined to break into the place when Tom decided to try the doorknob for the heck of it.

When it turned and the door opened, after exchanging expressions of concern with John and Ike, then drawing his weapon, they'd gone inside.

The living room looked no different to Tom than it had yesterday when he and Danni worked on his assignment. Same with the kitchen.

Although, fortunately, he hadn't seen her bedroom yesterday, he was certain that it looked considerably different then than it did now, in particular with that ugly stain. It was a sight he was all too familiar with.

"Maybe, maybe not. I guess the blood type will tell the story- part of it, anyway," Tom said in response to Ike's comment.

Ike himself already was on the horn getting a crime scene unit to where they were, along with a homicide unit.

John, however, was oblivious to all that. As he stared at the stain, he went back to the description of an event that had happened over thirty years ago.

The more he gazed at that stain, the clearer the way was becoming...

"John? Are you all right?"

There's one person too many here for what's on my mind... "Yeah. Ike, I guess you have things in hand here. We should get out your way."

Tom nodded. "That's just what I said." He turned to Ike again. "Let me know what the verdict here is, Ok?"

"Yes, Sir, will do. I wonder if your theory about this having something to do with Harry's murder, and therefore the investigation into Ronald Novak, has even more merit than we think."

"I guess we'll find out. Talk with you later." He and John shook hands with Lieutenant Miller and walked out.

As they made their way back to their vehicles, John stopped Tom when he found a spot out of earshot of anyone else. He didn't even wait for Tom to ask him what was up. "I have another theory that might or might not be related to yours. I couldn't say it in front of Ike; you'll understand why.

"I'll get right to the point. Think back to last night when Kim and I told you about Christopher Hedges, in particular when he supposedly died in 1972. Think about what the police found- blood everywhere and both his and his mother's bodies gone. We assumed he was dead and with good reason. As it turns out, he's far from it. Now, we see a big blood stain on Danni Searles' bed. On the surface it looks like she's been murdered, but I don't buy it. Do you?"

"Honestly, John, I don't know what to make of it right now."

"Well, consider this, too: we last saw Danni when she left my place around 8:30 this morning. That puts her back here no earlier than 10. She called you right around then to tell you she couldn't meet us at Loch Raven. Why? Because she heard our conversation about going back to the fishing spot. So, she keeps listening, waiting. She decides the time is now for her to disappear, which explains what you just saw in her apartment."

"What about the blood, John? Where did that come from?"

"I don't know. I haven't thought about the particulars and I'm not concerned with 'em at the moment. Listen to me. Based on what's coming together I'm wondering now if Danni and Hedges are in cahoots, and he figured since he couldn't have Kim, no one could. So he hires Danni to kill her and then disappear for good, only she screwed it up."

Tom was taken aback. "I can't-...you're really reaching there, Brother. I'm not sold on that part. You've presented a good argument that Danni might well have tried to kill Kim, but as for the why...I don't know. I think you're wrong about her motive- *if* this is the case at all. Plus, how do you figure Danni would be in league with the guy who kidnapped Kim? What could their connection be? Hell, we're not even a hundred percent sure Hedges is the guy we're-"

"No, *you're* not sure if Hedges is the one, but *I* am. As for her motive, theoretically it's possible I'm wrong, but I don't think so. You know his obsession with Kim and how he couldn't let go, even after all these years. The way I figure it, he's accepted that he won't get her back, so what better way to take his revenge on both of us?"

"Ok, I understand that part, but tell me this: how would Hedges, or whoever that guy is, come into contact with Danni, and then persuade her to do his dirty work? I just don't see it; Danni's nobody's fool and is not the kind of person who would be motivated only by money. There would have to be something more to convince her besides a good payoff. Plus, look at what happened to Harry Lawson. How do we know the same person who killed him didn't kill her, too? The crime scenes were similar- no sign of a struggle, indicating familiarity with the killer."

"Wasn't Lawson's body still in his place?"

Tom turned away. "Yeah."

155

During the moment of silence, for John another potential piece of the puzzle started to materialize as a result of a stop he and Kim had made earlier.

Now, this might be a reach, but under the circumstances I have no choice...

...then again, it fits right in with his flaw of being a creature of habit. Kim even said he got her those same flowers...

If he was right, he might have to wait for her, or do exactly what they were about to do at Danni's place before they discovered the door was open...

"John?"

Tom's voice served to shake him out of his thoughts and into action. He moved toward the car.

"What are you going to do?"

"Find that bastard. This feeling is way too strong to ignore, no matter how half-baked it might seem. Are you coming?"

A still-incredulous Tom nodded, knowing there was no way to dissuade John. "Yeah. Whatever you're about to do, I'm not letting you do it without me. Where to?"

"First we pay a visit to a mutual friend. Let's go, we need to get moving..."

"...yeah, I'm there now...Hmmm- I'm not sure about tonight. It's kind of late and it's about two hour's drive to your place...oh, did you? What did you get me?...*Now*, who's the tease? You won't tell me?...I'll find out soon enough, huh? Well, I can't wait- and thank you in advance. You're so good to me...Ok, I'll see you soon- maybe *really* soon. 'Bye."

Jenny had a big smile on her face when she hung up with him.

Sometimes I still can't believe how this all turned out. Who'd have thought? He really is good to me...

...but then again, I had a feeling he would be.

Her smile remained as she locked her car and headed up to her pad with an extra spring in her step.

"Christ, John- look at her. She looks just like-...sorry."

They'd decided to wait, although when they saw the flowers still sitting on her stoop, John had wanted to try to break in to

Jenny's place. Fortunately, although it took some work, reason prevailed. Tom and Herb had convinced him that that simply was not a good idea.

Their collective effort paid off.

John couldn't have missed her even if he'd wanted to. As she ran up the stairs to her second-floor apartment, her tight, curvaceous body was on full display, compliments of the high-cut, abbreviated spandex bottom and sports bra she wore. The shiny tights she wore called even more attention to her legs. It looked like she was returning from cheerleading practice or a late workout.

Her attire was practically the same as what she wore the day she was kidnapped almost three years ago.

The coincidences just kept on coming...

"No apology necessary. I was thinking the same thing. Actually, Kim told me on a couple occasions how scary it was that in so many ways Jenny reminded her of a slightly taller version of herself when she was the same age, which is exactly why we're here." He got out of the car and walked up to meet her, followed closely by Tom and Herb. "Jenny!"

She'd just read the card attached to the flowers and her smile had grown even broader when the call startled her. She sprang back up and whirled to see three big men walking up the steps...

...two of which she recognized, which made her sigh in relief. "You scared me for a moment! Hello, by the way," she said, hugging John and Tom.

"May we come in with you?"

"Um, sure." She went to reach for the flowers.

"It's all right; I'll get these for you." He picked them up and gave them a cursory look. "Very nice- looks like the boyfriend misses you. When do I get to meet him?"

She looked at the flowers, and then back at John. He was the last person she wanted to see the card...

...but John knows him as Joshua, so maybe he won't notice...

...on the other hand, if he starts asking-

"What's wrong?" John saw the change in her disposition, and thus saw his answer.

Yes, indeed- further proof that he's a creature of habit to the extreme. He can't stay away from Jenny, either- maybe because he can't have Kim...

...I'm glad you decided to be nosy and have a look at the card, Kitten. You may well end up leading us right to him.

"Um, nothing...I mean, I guess I'm still pepped up from my workout and surprised to see you here now." She pulled her keys out of her bag and dropped them as she tried to sort through them for the right one. Her hands were shaking a little and her breathing was becoming a bit more rapid. *I'd better change the subject, and fast.* "What *are* you guys doing here, anyway? What's going on?"

"We need to talk with you."

Finally she managed to open her door. They all went inside and the biggest of the three men- the one she didn't know- closed the door behind them. "Why-...why do you need to talk to me? What happened?"

"Someone tried to kill Kim a little while ago."

"Oh, my God..." She slowly sank onto her couch.

She was very disconcerted and John didn't give her a chance to recover. "Where is he, Jenny?"

"Who do you mean?" She didn't look back at him.

"You know exactly who I mean. Christopher Hedges."

Wide-eyed, she turned back to him. "How did you-..."

Even if there was any doubt remaining as to the identity of Jenny's boyfriend, which there wasn't, that reaction would have dispelled it. John had to purposefully refrain from ripping into her about being with someone who not only had kidnapped her, but also twelve other women. Although he was certain there would come a point when he'd do just that, now wasn't the time. There was something far more important and time-sensitive.

When she tried to turn away again, he took hold of her shoulders and made her face him. "Listen to me. You have to tell me where he is and you have to do it now. Kim's life might depend on you; he could send someone else after her. He won't leave her alone- he can't. Tell me where he is."

"He's changed, John. He-"

"He has, huh? Tell that to Vanessa Chamberlain; tell her how he's changed, if he hasn't killed her by now."

"But...but he wouldn't-"

"We don't have time for this! Tell me where he is!"

"*No*!! I won't!! You're wrong about him! He wouldn't do that- not anymore! I won't let you take him away from me!" She began to cry and tried to pull away, but he wouldn't let her go.

He pulled her close in spite of her resistance. Soon she gave up and lay against him. "Don't do that, Jenny. I'm sorry."

This is worse than I thought...

Obviously, that way would not work and now he was in danger of losing his cool. He couldn't allow that to happen. Apparently, she'd forgiven Hedges somehow, which reinforced the fact that berating her about her atrocious taste in boyfriends- especially this one- wasn't the way.

He saw only one alternative that might persuade her- that being her affection and reverence for Kim. At this point he wasn't even certain that would work, but he had to try. As she calmed down, he pulled back and brushed away her tears. "Honey, I can see he's come to mean a lot to you, and you know how much Kim means to me. I'm not positive your boyfriend tried to kill her, but I'm pretty sure he did. I can see you don't even want to consider that as a possibility; for Kim's sake, I hope you will.

"You might be my only hope of stopping the one who's trying to kill my wife. I need your help, and so does she. Her life can't mean so little to you- not with all the history the two of you have. Was she not there for you during high school and afterwards when hardly anyone else was? Did she not risk her own life three years ago to free you so you could escape and help rescue the other women? Did you not tell me you felt even closer to her than to your own parents?"

"Yes, and I still do. Everything you've said is true and I appreciate so much all she's done for me, but...John, I know him. He wouldn't do that- not now."

"I want to believe you but I need to see for myself. I need you to take me to him so he can prove to me- and to you- that he's not behind the attempts on Kim's life. Please, Jenny."

She looked away for a moment while she thought. "Let me call him and-"

"No- no phone call. He can't know we're coming."

"I just want to-"

"You can't call him." He saw her rising ire and cut it off. "I know you trust him, but I hope you can see how I don't. He kidnapped Kim twice successfully and almost a third time as well. He was- and might still be- completely obsessed with her. Maybe he's turned over a new leaf- I don't know- but I can't take that chance and neither should you. If he loves you and is devoted to you, I don't think it's too much to ask for you to confront him about this and get the truth out of him- good or bad. Do you?"

She took her hand away from the phone. "No."

"Ok. So you'll come with us and show us the way to his house?"

She nodded. "I have to shower first and-"

"There's no time. Please understand that we're really pressed; the shooting happened three hours ago and every second is critical."

With a sigh, she relented. "All right. We'll need to take my car so he'll know it's me." She picked up her purse and followed them to the door, but then... "Wait."

John turned back to her. "What is it?"

"I want you to promise me you won't hurt him if it turns out he wasn't behind this."

"Huh?"

"You promise me or you'll get nothing from me."

There was no wavering in her expression. She held his stare and he could see that he had no choice.

"All right. If he's innocent, I won't hurt him- provided he doesn't try to pull anything on any of us."

"He won't, I'm sure-"

"Ok, ok! We need to go."

Herb stepped in. "Hold on, Sir. Miss Jacobson only can fit one other person in her car besides herself, so we need to hash out how we're going to handle this." He turned to her. "What's the layout of his place? Is the driveway long? Open yard?"

"Yes, it's a pretty long gravel driveway lined on both sides with trees until you get to the yard, where it turns into sort of a circle. Actually, the trees are pretty thick where he is but there's a good bit of open space around his house- especially in the front yard."

"So, chances are he'd see us coming...I get the impression that he wouldn't react too well to seeing us pull in behind you."

"Probably not, but I don't think he-"

"You don't think, but you can't be certain. Even if you were, that wouldn't be enough for me- not by a long shot." He addressed John again. "Sir, this means the only way is for you to ride with Miss Jacobson, whose allegiance lies with the man who abducted and might well have ended up killing your wife, almost killed you, held twelve other women- including Miss Jacobson herself-

160

hostage for thirteen years and counting. I don't like this at all, especially since I'm responsible for what happened to-"

"Herb, I know you still feel like you're to blame for what happened to Kim but as I told you before, it's not all your fault. Now, we might have the chance to stop all this. I also know you don't like how we'll have to go about it but I don't see any other way. We have to act, and quickly. We just don't have time to make a plan, so we'll have to improvise. Plus, you know as well as anyone that this is as personal as it gets."

Herb knew his mind was made up. "I'll give you a radio and headset, Sir, which you *will* wear and use. That way you can let us know when we're there and I can figure out how we'll cover you…all right, this might do it. I want you to give us a few minutes to park our car so we can move on foot into covering positions for you. That is something *I* won't budge on. When we get to the place, you'll pull off to the side of the road, Miss Jacobson, and wait for word from us before you go in."

Jenny protested. "John, you promised me you wouldn't-"

"Miss Jacobson, my job is to protect Governor Stratton, and I don't take that responsibility lightly. I'll be blunt with you; if your boyfriend makes any aggressive move toward the Governor, I will shoot him down without hesitation. There is not one single aspect of what we're about to do that I'm comfortable with, but if it results in stopping these attempts on Mrs. Stratton's life, I will do what I have to. If she means as much to you as you say she does, you will do the same. Now, do we understand each other?"

Jenny lowered her head. "Yes, Sir."

"Come on, Jenny," John said as he put his arm around her. "Let's get going now." He glanced at Herb and gave him an approving nod as he opened her car door for her…

…finally, half an hour into the ride, John had to find out. "Tell me how you ended up with him, Jenny."

He sat in the passenger seat of her small, sporty car as she drove west along I-66 toward Chris's place. They'd made some small talk in the meantime that amounted to little more than a delay resulting from Jenny's reluctance to open up to him for obvious reasons and John's initial reluctance to press her in worry that she might stop the car.

Knowing it was inevitable and that she'd have to tell him sometime, she relented. "He's exciting, he treats me really well and there doesn't seem to be anything more he enjoys than spending time with me. He doesn't have to parade me around other people to gain their approval, he never ignores me and he's very attentive. In short, he's everything I ever dreamed of in a boyfriend- everything all the losers I ever went out with before him were not."

John just stared at her. "Does it not bother you that-"

"I know what you're going to say. All the abductions."

"Including you."

"This might shock you, but for me it wasn't so bad."

"It wasn't so bad?! When he forcibly abducted you, meant to keep you imprisoned for the rest of your life?!"

"*What* life?! What did I have other than cheerleading?! I still was meeting these boring, loser guys I couldn't have cared less about. Most of them were more into themselves than anything. I didn't even get lukewarm feelings when I was with any of them. And then, the ones I wanted to be with didn't want me- like you, for example."

"Now, hold on. You were-"

"Too young, I know. I'm not attacking you, especially since I know you and Kim are meant for each other, and I'm happy for both of you in that you have each other. You and she lead such exciting lives- you with your career, which might land you in the White House, and Kim, who's lived a life jam-packed with excitement! She's done more than I ever even dreamed of doing. As for me, my 'life', as you call it, was an endless circle of mediocrity. It's hard when that's all you know and all you expect. I wanted to be more like Kim and do things she'd done, which was why I did the bikini contests in 2000."

"I remember you told Kim and me that you wouldn't do those anymore after that year. Why are you doing them again?"

"I changed my mind."

"*You* changed your mind? Or, did he?"

"Well...he's right- I mean, I did so well in them before, so why not try again? I'm still in the same shape I was in then, so my chances of winning this time are really good. Look, John, I want some excitement in my life, too."

"There are other ways. Jenny, you don't know this guy. There's a whole-"

"Not now- I don't want to hear this. I gave him a chance and he's redeemed himself, even though as far as I'm concerned he didn't need to. He's always showing me and telling me how grateful he is that we're together. He even treated me well while he held me captive, and now...he's wonderful. He always liked me, and...well, I started to like him, too, but that didn't really dawn on me until after I'd escaped. Now, I love him. I have a feeling he's going to ask me to marry him soon. He wants me to move in with him, which I'm going to do as soon as my lease is up- if I wait that long. He wants to take me away somewhere for my birthday next month. I told him he doesn't have to do that; I'm happy just staying home with him."

She turned off the highway, apparently onto the exit that would take them to Hedges' place. "It wasn't him, John; I know he's innocent. You'll see. He's changed- he really has."

John didn't answer. This was a lot like the stories about other foolish and terribly misguided women who, probably for similar reasons as Jenny's, fell in love with and even married convicted murderers and rapists, all but ignoring the heinous crimes those wastes of humanity committed. It just didn't make sense any way he looked at it; how could those women overlook or simply dismiss all the carnage- the irreparable damage- such parasites were responsible for?

Shrugging that off, he looked ahead, waiting for the moment he'd anticipated for over thirty years. However, in spite of how ludicrous he thought Jenny's situation with Hedges was, he wasn't happy about the prospect of bursting her bubble.

She was sure to fall, and hard.

Danni jumped when Jack laid his hand onto her shoulder. Then she turned away.

Her disappointment was obvious to him. "You tried, but she got lucky."

"I don't know how they do it- Kim and her husband. It's like there's a magical protective field or something like that around them. It went fine; I wrapped the bomb in some newspaper, dropped it into the trashcan, and made it go off at the perfect time- so I thought. Another boat was pulling in, and it was moving pretty fast. I didn't notice it until just after I took the shot. Its wake might have made me miss," she grumbled as she watched the telecast. Her attempt was all over the news. "I blew the last chance we might have of taking her out. If she remembers everything…"

"I know. Of course, it could be too late, anyway- who's to say they haven't already? Things are getting out of control; we'll have to think of something else. I *hope* they haven't figured everything out on their own, but…ah, what's the use in worrying about it? I really wish the boat engine didn't drown out what John and Kimberly talked about most of the time while they were out on the Bay. If they know and they let it out, it's not only me they'll hurt. Even if a certain acquaintance of mine is taken out…"

"I don't know. We can't worry about it anymore. What's done is done. Tomorrow we'll ditch your car. You have your money and I suppose you'll want to be on your way before long, so you may have some thinking to do tonight as to what your next move will be. I suppose you'll want to be on your way before long, so you have some thinking to do tonight as to what your next move will be. I already know mine…"

"His driveway's not far ahead."

It had taken nearly two hours, like Jenny said it would. They were on a desolate looking road in a remote part of the area where Maryland, Virginia and West Virginia meet. She slowed the car as the road had become a bit rough; potholes dotted it intermittently.

John nodded. "Herb, kill your lights," he said into the transmitter. "We're getting close now." He turned back to Jenny. "Tell me when we get to his driveway, then we'll stop for a few. Does he have motion detector lights?"

"No. He likes it dark when he sleeps; he says with all the animals running around out here those things would be on constantly." They rolled on a little further until Jenny brought the car to a halt. "There it is."

"Ok, stop here." He touched the transmitter button. "Find a spot, Herb. We're about fifty yards from the driveway entrance. It's up on the right."

"Copy, Sir. I'll let you know when we're in place."

At the hospital, Donna got up to leave.

Kim was sound asleep for the time being. The nurse was monitoring her every two hours after the initial neuro-check; the doctor would come in at the two-hour interval and check her again just to make sure she was all right.

Donna confirmed with the guards that Kim would be protected. She learned that the squad of state troopers would be there until she was discharged. Donna was to pick her up if John and Tom still were tracking down the assailant.

For now, it was time to go home and get some sleep herself. She kissed Kim on the cheek and left quietly.

Chapter 9

"We're set, Sir. No sign of movement in the house, although there is a light on."

It only had taken five minutes for Herb, Tom and the team to set up, but for John and Jenny it was a long five minutes. They sat in a very uncomfortable silence, with Jenny staring straight ahead as the weight of what very well could happen settled in.

"Ok. Thanks, Herb." John was relieved as the wait was over. "Take us in, Jenny."

Chris saw the reflection of the headlights on his window and went right over to it.

There she was.

With a smile, he headed downstairs to meet her.

"Another light just went on, Sir."

"Copy- I see it." As soon as John acknowledged Herb's transmission, the outer lights also came on at the same time Jenny stopped the car. She turned off the engine.

Here we go...

Chris opened the door and stepped out onto the porch, smiling as Jenny got out of her car. He very much approved of the way she was dressed...

...but he did not approve at all of her passenger, who stepped out of the other side.

"You put a hit on her, didn't you, you motherfucker?!"

He dropped down behind the still-open car door, took aim and fired when he saw Hedges reaching into his pocket. The glass on the door behind him shattered, and Hedges immediately dove to the porch with bullets fired by the others zipping past him.

"*NO!!!*" Jenny screamed and took off running for the house.

"Jenny, don't-" He saw it was too late to stop her even before he opened his mouth.

When John saw the front door open, then close again, he knew Hedges had gone back inside- to get a gun, no doubt.

John didn't waste a second.

Chris ran up to his bedroom for his shotgun. He'd stay there, as it was the best defensible position he had. No one could come in or out without him getting the drop on whoever it was.

It's times like this when the ability to call the police would be a plus, he thought as he chambered a round in the twelve-gauge, grabbed more clips for his ten-millimeter automatic pistol, which he'd tried to pull while outside, and prepared himself.

If he was going down, he fully intended to make that as costly for his old enemy as he could...

...and for the one who brought him here.

John managed to tackle Jenny just after she opened the door and started inside. He heard Hedges running up the stairs.

"You *lied*!! You promised me you wouldn't hurt him!!"

"Jenny, he was reaching for a gun! Did you think I'd just stand there and let him shoot me?!"

"John! Are you all right?" Tom quickly reached him and crouched next to him, pistol drawn and covering him as he tried to subdue the struggling girl.

"Yeah, I'm fine. I need you to take hold of her and keep her here. Cuff her if you have to and do what you can to keep her quiet, but keep her here, and safe. I'm going after him."

He went to stand but Herb stopped him. "Like hell you are, Sir! You need to stay put."

His blood's up right now. This is the only time he's really susceptible to making mistakes...

...maybe- just maybe- this could work...

"Herb, I need to get him! I *know* he's the one!"

"Chris! Help me!"

They looked at Jenny and Tom spoke up. "I think you're right, John; we need to restrain her or she'll try to go to him."

Dawn, who'd just come in, took hold of her. "I'll take care of her, Sir." She quickly cuffed Jenny's wrists and ankles, then grabbed a roll of duct tape from a nearby table, tore off a strip and used it to seal Jenny's mouth. That took all the fight out of her.

"Take her over there behind the sofa, Dawn, and stay with her." While she did that, Herb turned to John, made him take cover as well and continued. "Mel and Derek are keeping watch outside to make sure he doesn't try to slip out a window or something."

"Good. Now we need to-"

John's blood froze as he heard her...

...it was the same muffled cry he'd heard her make when Hedges had her in the cage three years earlier...

"Hey, Johnny-boy! There's a very beautiful woman here with me; I think you two know each other."

"How in the-...that's impossible. Kim's at the-"

"Hospital? Sorry, wrong answer. I have her right here. She's a little banged up, but she's all right- for the time being."

"If you shoot her, by the time I've finished you off once and for all you'll think you died a thousand deaths, just like the coward you are!"

"Enough with the pleasantries, ol' buddy. I'm talking, you're listening."

John took a breath. "Go on."

"Seems we're in a similar situation as we were three years ago, only this time you didn't get to Kim first. I'm very impressed with the way you figured out where I am; maybe you'll get the chance to enlighten me as to how you accomplished that. In the meantime, if you don't want a river of your wife's blood flowing down my staircase, you'd better come upstairs right now. Only you, John; everyone else will stay where they are."

"You're not going up there, John! It's a bluff; he doesn't have her! Your first instinct was right- it's impossible!"

"By now, you should know better than to say something like that to me, with everything we've had happen."

"Think about it- she and Donna are at the hospital. We saw-"

"What's the matter, John? Aren't you man enough to deal with your own problems? Do you need your brother and your goon squad to take care of things for you? I'll tell you this; I see any sign of them coming up with you, Kim dies. If you're not on your way up here in ten seconds, Kim dies. That ten seconds starts now."

"*John*!! Call the hospital- call Donna! Get a fucking grip here!!" Tom hissed, still with a firm hold on his brother's arm.

He was still for a moment, then he turned to face Tom. "You're right. I just had the same thought but I'm glad you said it. He's trying to pull my strings again," he whispered back.

John stood and walked over to the base of the steps with his .45 automatic at the ready. "What do you say we knock off the bullshit? If you really have her, let her walk to the top of the stairs. We both know that won't happen because you don't have her, right?"

Damn...

"Of all the times for you to exercise restraint. Not quite so impulsive and hotheaded now, are you? Oh well, you can't blame a guy for trying, eh?"

"Not when he's as slimy as you are. There's not enough salt in the world to dry you out." John actually got a laugh out of him with that remark.

"That sounds funny coming from you, Mister Politician."

"One thing puzzles me. You know we have Jenny down here, yet you haven't said a word about her. You didn't offer to make an exchange or make any demands at all for us to let her come up there with you. You're supposed to be in love with her, aren't you?"

"What, after the stupid bitch led you right to me?! How many minutes did it take for her to sell me out to you?!" After that burst of anger he took a breath. "Look, what do you say we talk a little bit and figure out what we're going to do here? I think we both know where all this is heading, anyway; between you and

169

me, one of us won't survive the night. You have the numbers but I know the layout, and now I'll even the odds a little more."

No one was surprised when the lights went out and, like the others, John also wasn't surprised to see the stricken look on Jenny's face from Hedges' remarks just before they did.

Poor girl...

...at least he didn't draw things out with her, though. I think she'll come to see him for what he is. I just hope she can get over him- and soon...

"Look, Hedges, I don't have time for games. This isn't a siege and I won't let you make it one. In fact, I'll just call the police now."

"No!" He thought for a moment. "Then again, call 'em if you like. If you do, you'll never know who's trying to kill your wife."

"Nice try, but I bet you don't know who's behind that any more than we do."

"I know who *might* be. In fact, this person has just as much motivation to take her out as I would- if not, more."

"And this person is...?"

"First, tell me how you found me. By the way, this is where Kim and I spent our time together in early June of '89...thought you might like to know that. Anyway, I'm very impressed with you tracking me down- curious, too, as to how you accomplished that. Hopefully you didn't leave any marks on Jenny."

"Not my style. That's more up your alley- imprisoning women, beating them, raping them and controlling them completely to try to make up for your, shall we say, inadequacies?"

"Inadequacies, huh? Is that your take on it? I don't know what your wife told you, but I imagine it wasn't everything- and her own slanted version, at that. Deep down, she knows the deal, too; she understands that I'm far from the only man who dominates women. That may scare her, like it does a lot of 'em who keep trying to deny reality, but it doesn't change the fact. Unfortunately, a lot of feminized men don't get it, or they've surrendered their masculinity in order to be politically correct.

"I wonder which of those is the case with you. Have you turned into a 'modern man', or do you pretend to in order to pacify your wife? If either of those conditions is true, you're a liar, a coward or both. That's our nature, my friend- that's what we do. All this psychobabble, feminist bullshit to the contrary is exactly that- bullshit! Every man- no matter who he is and what background he comes from- is naturally dominant over women, and the most dominant of the men is the one the women are attracted to. The most popular, good-looking actor, the best athlete, the wealthiest businessman. Darwin's theory at its best and it's proven every day."

"So where do you fall in that spectrum? The best kidnapper?"

"Say what you want, but the ways of old weren't so bad when you look at how things are now. All these rules, a legal system designed to protect the ones who'd fall by the wayside otherwise. The way it is now, the brightest and best are not the ones who are in charge. It's the sleaziest manipulators and liars that make the rules now, and everybody else just-"

"Look, spare me the raft of bullshit; we've had this talk before. Coming from you that speech couldn't ring phonier, since you're one of the manipulators. All your life that's what you've been: an arrogant, lying identity thief and murderer- the worst kind of scum there could be. As for your position about men and women, what a crock of shit- and for more than one reason! On that topic I think it's funny how you changed your mind so quickly about Jenny; first you call her a stupid bitch who sold you out and now you pretend you're concerned."

"Oh, I'm not concerned- not since she's shown her true colors. That was just a figure of speech and a bit of humor."

"Nice. I'll give you this much- you are consistent. No one's damaged her more than you have and it won't be long before she realizes that. To answer your question, you fucked up. All you had to do was not leave your name on the card you sent with Jenny's flowers. Kim and I stopped by her place to see her; we were concerned because we've hardly heard from her lately. Obviously our concerns were well founded.

"She wasn't there but your flowers were. Kim was curious, especially when she recognized the flowers as the same kind you used to send her, so she bent down and read the card. She saw the name 'Chris'. We didn't know then that it was you; we thought that was another coincidence, like the flowers. See, we put our heads together and figured out that it was you who killed Joshua

171

Strauss and his family, then assumed his identity. It made the most sense. We didn't have physical evidence to back it up, but we really didn't need it.

"Then, when Kim was shot at and Detective Searles' apartment was made to look like a murder scene, which I don't believe it is, I thought back to your first staged disappearance. By then I suspected that and the other ingredients had to add up to more than coincidence; I thought about the flowers and the card and made an assumption that it was you she was seeing. It made perfect sense, given your history with Kim. I knew it was more than possible that you were behind the murder attempts, so I gambled."

"You were wrong there, but you did find me. Yes, indeed- very impressive. You went completely on gut instinct and here you are. You have to admit, though, I covered my tracks pretty well. It took over thirty years for someone to blow my cover."

"What did you do in the meantime? Where did you hide?"

"Oh, here and there. Different places. I worked on developing the skills I'd need to make it in today's world, including my ability to create disguises. That started with one Joshua Strauss, who I happened across by accident in October of 1980, not long after his eighteenth birthday. We talked and had a few beers. He got a little too tipsy and blabbed things to a total stranger- me- that he shouldn't have, those being his last name, the fact that he was the son of millionaire parents, the fact that he was their only child and the fact that he had no other relatives. He also didn't have very many friends. Once I gleaned all this about him, I put my plan into motion. I just had to wait for the right time."

"Which was July 22nd of the following year…"

"Yep."

"Where did you bury Josh and his parents after you killed them?"

"You'd love to know, wouldn't you?"

"I'm surprised you're not telling me, as much as you like to toot your own horn. Why would you keep that to yourself?"

"Right now, it serves the purpose of making you wonder- of being one of many questions you want an answer for that you might not get. Just a measure of power I have over you, whether you choose to acknowledge it or not. Apparently, you don't know as much as I assumed you did…so, you and Kim put your heads together, eh? Speaking of 'heads'- or just 'head', in the singular-, did you tell her how good you are at giving it?"

John bristled and turned to Tom, who glared toward the upstairs, then looked sympathetically at John. He was adjusting to the darkness and he could barely discern his brother's features. He rolled his eyes and shook his head, indicating to Tom that he was brushing the comment off. The good thing for John was, that jab didn't make him nearly as angry as he thought it would- primarily because he knew the opportunity to even the score was at hand.

"At long last, we get to the heart of the matter. I have a feeling you were about to shove that in my face- if you'll pardon the pun- the last time we spoke, which was three years ago on Suicide Ridge. Just like when you would laugh at me when I was seven, after what you did, you had that same look of triumph in your eye just as you were about to shoot me. That is, right before Kim shot the gun out of your hand.

"Well, since you ask, I did tell her what happened- how you were fifteen at the time and I was seven. Talk about sorry and hard up... you couldn't get any girls to do that for you so you went after a young boy who didn't know any better. What does that say about you? I'm surprised you didn't kidnap a bunch of men instead of women. In fact, I'd think jail for you would be paradise- all those guys to choose from. Hell, I bet the boys in prison would love to hear that male dominance rant you just gave me while they're ramrodding you, or you're ramrodding them. Why wouldn't you want to go?"

"No way. I'm not going there- ever. You hear me?!"

"Yeah, I hear you. I don't know, though; I might only wound you, so I'd say there's a chance you'll go. Hey, if that happens and you've really had a change of heart in your sexual preference, maybe you could just tell the fellas there that you have a secret weapon: you can squeeze your ass cheeks together so hard that you'd rip their dongs off, so they'd better watch out!"

He waited a moment and heard Tom and the others snickering or laughing out loud. "You're quiet all of a sudden, Chris. What gives? No witless comebacks, like you usually have for me? No? It might surprise you to hear this, but I've gotten past that little episode. Better yet, I'm the one who'll get the last laugh. You're not walking away from this. What you did to me is minimal in comparison to what you'll get in the very near future. I have to say, though, if you weren't such a pussy, I'd challenge you to a bare-knuckle fight, man-to-…well, whatever it is you are, which sure isn't a man."

"Sure, John, you and your gang against me."

"I wouldn't need them. A one-on-one fight against you would be good for the soul; I'd welcome it. Of course, you wouldn't go for it since we'd be on equal terms- not like the last time we were face-to-face. We talked about this before, on the Ridge as I recall. A fair fight is the last thing you'd want. You know, since you went to the well of the past, I'll go there myself- back to '72, before you pulled your disappearing act. Remember when my father chased you down? Remember what you did? That's what you're afraid of: having two generations of Strattons beat the shit out of you…or, should I say, beat the *piss* out of you."

Tom gave him a curious glance, but John shook his head.

Time to back off, at least for now. Maybe he does know something that could help us find Kim. It couldn't hurt to see what I can get from him- if he'll part with anything. "All that aside, I'll return your earlier compliment. I do have to hand it to you- that was quite a ruse you pulled with your first staged death, which was seventeen years before what turned out to be your encore."

"Thank you. It was tough to pull off."

"Obviously you did even better the second time, but I'm interested to hear about how you and your cohort did it in '72."

"It wasn't hard, really."

"Pray, tell."

"I'm a little confused here, John; I thought you were all gung-ho to find out who's been trying to kill Kim. Now you're trying to glean some information from me. You're even flattering me, which is something you just don't do under any circumstances. Why so interested in how I convinced the world I was dead?"

"The police are on their way. We're turning you over to them so you don't have much time. I'd like to know how you two did it."

"No…you want to know who it was that helped me, don't you? That seals it; you *don't* know everything…it seems I gave you too much credit for what you knew. You want me to make it easy for you- give you all the answers. That, ol' buddy, ain't gonna happen. You get nothing from me. I've lost, but so have

174

you, only you'll get the worse end of it by far when the one who wants Kim dead is successful, which only is a matter of time."

Chris opened his safe and took out the notebook. Everything he'd done and everything he knew that would help John in any way in his quest to learn his father's fate and maybe even lead him to who was trying to kill Kim was in that book. He lit a match and held it up under the corner. Once the flame caught, he leaned the book against the wall and watched it burn, smiling in the knowledge that John's chance of finding out what he wanted to know was turning into a pile of ashes.

There'll only be one man left who knows once I'm gone and he sure as hell won't talk, either. I bet he's the one, in which case...

"My suffering is over, but yours has just begun. Your wife is as good as dead- that you can take to the bank. I could have helped you, most likely, but the prospect of you living the rest of your life never knowing who was behind Miss Kimberly's death, or that of your Daddy dearest, is one I just can't resist.

"Speaking of your father, he's already paid for what he did to my brother. Now, so will you."

John had had enough. It was worth a try to see if he could trick Hedges into revealing something, but since he'd caught on, John knew it wouldn't work.

Plus, Hedges' words about Kim were the final push.

By that time his eyes were fully adjusted to the darkness. The final chapter in this long saga had begun.

He turned to Tom and said in a low voice, "follow me and keep me covered. I'm going up. Don't argue- just bear with me; I have a plan. It's time to get this asshole."

They started up the steps slowly.

"As sweet as it would be to see the look on your face if I told you what you don't know, I wouldn't help you to help myself. We have a common enemy, but you'll have to find out for-..."

He heard a creak.

"Tell me you're not coming up the steps, John." He aimed the shotgun at the doorway. "Tell me you're not that stupid...then again, tell me you are. I've been waiting for this moment..."

* * *

John reached the top of the stairs and leaned against the
barrier, pistol at the ready. By listening to Hedges' voice, he knew
his longtime nemesis was in a room on the left side.

He touched the transmitter button. "Mel?"

"Sir?"

"Take a look in that shed out back and see if you can scare
up some gasoline. I'm sure he has a lawn mower in there. See if
you can find some oil, too. Once you do, find a bottle and a rag. I
think you know what to do with all that."

"Yes, I do, Sir. I'm on it."

"John? What-...what are you doing? You didn't call the
police at all, did you?"

"Nope. As for what I'm doing, I'm just having Mel whip up
a little cocktail for you, compliments of a Russian gentleman you
might have heard reference to- his name's Molotov. Sound
familiar?"

"Can we talk about this?"

"Guess you *have* heard of him, then. Gee, Chris, I thought
you were done talking. Didn't you just say you wouldn't help me
to help yourself? I could swear you did. That being the case, I
figure we might as well stop wasting time here. You even said that
my father paid for what he did to your worthless brother- who was
every bit the shit sucker you are- and that I'd pay as well. You
learned a lot from him, didn't you? Followed his lead to the letter,
you did, except you actually kept your victims alive, for the most
part- other than Vanessa, right? You killed her, didn't you?"

"She killed herself; that was an accident."

"Oh, an *accident*, like when you abducted her, I guess."

"It *was* an accident! I didn't-...I didn't think she'd go that
far. She ended up strangling on the tethering rope around her neck.
Her hands were tied behind her but she was on the bed. All she
had to do was climb back up but she didn't."

"You sound all broken up over it, too, even if that *is* how she
died. You'll forgive me if I don't believe you. As far as I'm
concerned, a pile of dog shit is worth more than anything you have
to say. At least the dog shit has some substance. As for Ralph

176

Wancowicz, if my father did kill him, which I also don't buy- to me it's just another of your delusional rants-, then he gave your brother what he deserved. If it wasn't my father who killed him, I'd like to meet whoever did and shake his hand.

"Soon, you'll follow his lead one final time, now that I know by your own words it was you who killed my father or played a supporting role in it. You know the best thing about me ridding the world of you once and for all? To everyone else, you're already a corpse; you have been for over thirty years. So, in the final analysis, it doesn't even matter, does it? I can't kill a dead man, can I? As you would say, you have to love the irony! How does it feel to know the last smell you'll experience is that of your own flesh burning?"

"Sir, I have a couple gallons of gas here and a quart of oil. He also has a couple old whiskey bottles in here along with a box of rags; some of them are already oily."

"No kidding! Sounds like a one-stop shopping place to me; I'll pass on a big 'thank you' to our generous host. Excellent, Mel- go on and prepare as many cocktails as you can."

"One more thing of interest, Sir. There are a couple fifty-five gallon drums here, and a bunch of sulfuric acid and lye. One of the drums is full of lye, and...I see what looks like the top of a skull."

"Jesus...we'll have to take a close look at-"

Suddenly the hairs on John's neck stood on end.

Hedges wasn't talking; no sound was coming from the room.

He turned to Tom and signaled for him to move down a few steps as he brought his .45 up to the ready.

Something was about to happen.

Chris was shaking uncontrollably. He envisioned everything around him engulfed in flames, and terror was taking over.

By all indications, John was not bluffing.

Why would he? This is his revenge. This is the end...

...but I won't tell him what he needs to know. No way.

Plus, there still was time for Chris to end it on his terms.

He slowly stood, leveled the shotgun and charged.

With a scream, he pulled the trigger...

BOOM!!!

177

John felt a slight sting in his right shoulder, then heard the cocking of the shotgun.

He didn't hesitate; he took a deep breath and rolled forward into the open onto the floor, aiming his .45 as he saw the muzzle flash from the second shot and heard the barrier next to him virtually explode. He fired right at the flash as Hedges was coming toward him.

That first bullet stopped him in his tracks and caused him to drop the shotgun. Despite the maddening pain Chris tried to reach for his ten millimeter. Even as he did, he knew he'd never get to it.

Sure enough, from just a few feet away, he saw three more flashes and felt the jolts as he heard the thunder from John's pistol.

The second, third and fourth rounds knocked him down.

John watched as he raised his arm, then bent his knee to plant his foot on the ground, apparently attempting to get up.

His arm flailed weakly back and forth, then dropped.

Hedges settled back to the floor.

He didn't move any more.

"John?! Are you all right?!"

Tom's words and hand on his shoulder shook him out of the daze. He hadn't moved from his position and still had the gun pointed at Hedges. "I'm good."

"O.K. Let's see if we can get the lights on again."

"I'm a step ahead of you, Sir," Herb said as he moved to the fallen criminal, gun trained on him just in case. The four holes in the man's bare midsection and chest were quite obvious, even in the faint moonlight. After a quick check, Herb relieved him of the gun in his waistband. "He's secured, Sir. No more weapons on him." As Herb went on into the room from which Hedges had emerged, he instructed Derek to get their car.

Seeing that John's legs were wobbly, no doubt resulting from the adrenaline rush wearing off, Tom helped him up. The brothers moved to where Hedges lay and stood over him.

John's need for vengeance that stemmed from all the humiliations Hedges had caused him and the suffering he'd caused

Kim- the need that would not be buried or denied- now flowed from him in proportion to the blood that flowed from his former nemesis.

It quickly was dying, just like Hedges was...

Chris began to wheeze, but he needed to get his last barb in. "You know, John...I get the distinct impression that...I just might have turned you into a monster...or better yet, made you realize you're every bit like your old man was," he said, grinning. "Oh, yeah, Papa Tom would be...proud of you; you're a chip off the ol' block. You solved your problem...just like he would have. And, he *did* kill my brother...my father had no reason to lie...or, did he? Wait a minute...did he send you?! Did he-" he grimaced as a horrible jolt of pain tore through him.

It was possible.

Now, there are only two living witnesses left...

"You'll make out best of all...won't you, you son of a bitch?"

John's eyes widened. "What did you say?! Your father's making out- what does that mean?! *Who is he*?!!"

Chris looked up at John, who'd grabbed a fistful of his hair and was holding him up so they were face-to-face. He was fading fast. He just realized he'd voiced that last thought, which was all that was supposed to be.

However, it still didn't matter- not really. Soon, *he'd* probably be dead as well...

In spite of how difficult it was becoming, he had to get his last curse out. "You'll *never* save Kim. Even though...I had nothing to do with what just happened, I was your last chance to find the culprit...and you blew it," he said, laughing as he gurgled blood and coughed some up. "Best of all...I'm going out on my terms- not yours. *I've* gotten the last laugh-..."

Christopher Hedges seized up. Although it was a struggle, he managed to get what would be his last words out through clenched teeth: "...and it's on you." He tried to spit at John but couldn't draw another breath to do it.

* * *

"*Dammit!!*" John shoved the lifeless body back onto the floor. Just then, the lights came back on.

"You did what you had to do, Sir," Herb said as he walked back to them. "There are people who by nature bring out the worst in some others. Then, there are those like him that bring out the worst in everybody. He definitely was a cancer; there was no way around killing him. He never would have surrendered to the police and sure as hell not to us."

"He never would have told me anything, either, even if he did have the answer. He might have been screwing with me again with what he hinted at. He never changed- hated me right up until his last breath. The problem is, we're still no closer to finding out who Kim's would-be killer is."

"That's not the only problem we have, Sir."

He turned to Herb and nodded. "Let's go downstairs so we can discuss it. There are a couple things we need to take care of."

"You're bleeding," Tom observed as he followed John down the steps along with Herb. "We need to get you checked out."

"It's all right, Sir; Dawn's a trained medic. She'll take care of him while we decide how we'll handle the situation." Herb turned to her. "Derek's bringing the car in, so grab your kit. The Governor might have some buckshot in his shoulder and arm."

"Gotcha. Be right back," she replied as she freed Jenny.

John sat on the couch next to Jenny, who was morose. He touched her hand, but she didn't acknowledge him. "I'm sorry, Jenny. I'm sorry it had to turn out like this for you."

She didn't say a word. She simply stared straight ahead, considerably more distraught than she'd been at any point this evening, or maybe ever.

John exchanged a worried glance with Tom. Her whole world had collapsed; from the looks of her, she'd retreated inside herself. It was too early to tell how far gone she was, but whatever the case, it didn't look good.

He looked up as Dawn appeared next to him.

"I'll need you to take off your shirt, Sir."

He did so with only minor discomfort. "How does it look?"

"Not too bad, really. Is it painful?"

"Stings a little, that's all." As she went to work, he moved to the matter at hand. "We don't have much time here, gang, so I won't waste any. For starters, we're not calling the police. Hedges got what he had coming for the hell he put Kim, Jenny, Vanessa and those other women through. Justice was served tonight, so there's no need to complicate things."

He looked at Tom, who unease was apparent as he shifted around. "I know you must be torn on this, Brother. It goes against what you're supposed to do, but I think you agree deep down that the world is a better place without him. There's the personal dimension for you as well. If we had any doubt as to what happened to Vanessa, he put 'em to rest."

Tom held his gaze for a moment, then turned and walked over to the doorway.

John stopped Dawn's first aid work for the time being, stood and went to where Tom was, which was out of earshot of the others. "I've known for a while now. Look, there's nothing for you to be ashamed of, Tom. You're human; it happened. You and she shared a moment and that was it. That was all it could be. Even so, that moment means something to you; *she* means something to you, as she should. When you were in the hospital three years ago after having been shot chasing Rollins down, I saw how upset you were when it settled in that he took Vanessa with him and that he'd probably kill her, which as we know now, he did. He didn't show a bit of remorse, either. It was like-"

"I was with you, John. I heard him."

"Are you with me now?"

He was silent.

"Until about a hundred years ago, what I did tonight is how such matters were settled. I wonder sometimes when people say we solve our problems in a much better way now. These days, when someone commits all the crimes Hedges did- even when the guilt is obvious- so many try their utmost to emphasize the criminal's rights. We have to go to trial, which takes months to even get to, and then- even if he's convicted- chances are the punishment doesn't fit the crime, like it would have in the olden days. When the circumstances are questionable, of course we have to have a trial, but when the guilt is clear I don't see why we should waste our time and money.

"Back then, in this case, he'd have been hanged, and quickly- no questions asked. It wouldn't have been the usual

181

instance nowadays of ten or fifteen years passing before the sentence would be carried out- *if* he even was sentenced to death.

"Or, if it came down to apprehending him once guilt was established, they'd have organized a posse and gone out after him with the purpose of bringing him back- dead or alive. We were the posse, we got our man and we were right in doing it. Hedges *was* guilty. You know it, I know it, everyone here knows it. Of that there can be no question, unless you sanction what he did, which I know you don't. He chose death and he got it.

"Look, Tom, there's what society and the law tells you is right, and there's what you know is right. Sometimes the two agree, sometimes they don't. When they don't, you have to go with what you believe is the right thing, which is what I did. Everyone who knew that guy knew he was the worst possible scum, and based on all his actions he got what was coming to him. I had full justification in killing him.

"To be blunt, I'd have been very uncomfortable handing him over to some judge or jury that had no knowledge of the case and would apply their own generalized and objective standards- their own measure of justice. As we know, that easily could have been far *from* justice as far as thirteen women- my wife included- and I are concerned. I had the evidence, I knew what needed to be done, I did it and I'll live with it. End of story.

"You know this doesn't mean I don't believe in the trial system. That's how I made a living for a while, as you remember. In a lot of cases it's necessary and it works, but in this case, it *wasn't* necessary and it would have been a waste of time and money. How would you have felt if this had gone to trial and some defense attorney got him off? That would have been a travesty. No way would I have allowed it.

"I feel like I was in the same situation Mister Jack faced when he weighed the pros and cons of trying Novak and Wancowicz, only I had another option and I used it- just like Dad did with Hoover, if Mister Jack was right about what he did. What happened tonight was inevitable. I needed this and so did you. I'll sleep a lot better tonight knowing that fucking disease never will get the chance to ruin another person's life.

"The sentence was carried out and justice was served. You think about that before you give me my answer." He paused a moment. "But also know that whatever you decide, you're still my brother and I love you."

John went back over and took his seat next to Jenny so Dawn could finish her work. "One last thing. When Mel was searching through the shed for the stuff I told him to get, he found a couple big oil drums. One of 'em was full of lye...and a skeleton- or, part of one, at least. I don't know if it's Vanessa, but...I thought you might want to know."

Tom turned to him and John clearly saw the anger had descended over him before he started out the door. "Don't go out there, Tom; you don't need to see-"

"Yes, I do. You know I do."

John looked at the empty doorway for a moment, and then at Herb before he turned away.

"You don't feel good about what you just did, do you, Sir?"

He winced as Dawn extracted a second object from his shoulder. "No, and don't ask me why. I think Tom's on board with us but I want to be sure. He's a good man and a top-notch cop, which is part of the reason. I had to give him my side to hopefully alleviate any doubts he might have that we're doing the right thing here and that Hedges had to go. If I didn't feel that way, I wouldn't have bothered with any of this.

"All the same, no, I don't feel good about what I did with Tom just now, but with Hedges I did what I had to do."

"I know. You needed closure. For what it's worth, I'd have done the same thing and so would the rest of the team. We're all with you, but I want to be sure you understand something. You just as easily could have come out on the short end of this and you put yourself in that situation. That is something I'll never let you do again, even if I have to punch you out to stop you. Do I make myself clear?"

"Yes, you do, and I apologize for making your task more difficult. I appreciate all you've done, Herb. I knew I made the best choice when I took you on; you've been a good friend to me for many years- as good a friend as you possibly could be. You picked a hell of a good team, too. Once we add on our twelve newbies and get whoever's responsible for trying to murder Kim, I have every confidence we'll be fine. Speaking of my wife, I have an exception to what you just said; when it comes to nailing those responsible for tonight and last night, don't even think about keeping me out when we get our chance."

Herb nodded. "I thought you might say that. Fair enough."

Dawn finished patching him up. "You're all set, Mister Governor. Only two pellets, both of which were close to the surface. You'll be fine."

"Thanks, Dawn."

"So, what's next, Sir?"

"Why don't you two take a look around? Mainly, check his bedroom. See if you can find the videotapes or discs of Kim- those he sold copies of and made his money on. I want 'em destroyed." He looked around the room. "I also want this house burned- right down to the ground. He kept Kim here, Herb. I want every trace of this place gone, just like its owner."

"You've got it." He stood, then he and Dawn moved toward the stairs.

"One more thing: see if you can find any documentation on it. Title, deed- anything along those lines and any other important-looking papers he might have."

Both nodded and headed up.

For the first time since the attempt on Kim, John sat back and relaxed, although he knew he wouldn't be doing that for long. The next step was disposal of Hedges' body, and he already had a good idea as to the best way to accomplish that.

"Are you going to kill me, too?"

He turned to Jenny, incredulous at first, but the more he thought about it, he understood a little how she might feel that way. *She was within earshot of a killing and the victim was somebody she loved. This will take some time...*

As for the present, he moved quickly to reassure her and gently squeezed her hand. "No, Honey- of course I won't kill you. All you did was fall for the wrong guy; it happens all the time. Ultimately, I hold him responsible; he took advantage of you in the worst way. While it was very poor judgment on your part to go to him in the first place...I'm sorry for saying that and I won't dwell on it. That's part of being young and inexperienced. We all make bad decisions when we're young- I know I did when I was.

"The important thing is, we got to you in time so you didn't have to regret this one any more than you already do, which you would have- believe me. I suppose we didn't make it by much, if you were about to move in with him, but thankfully we did make it. He drew Kim in with his charm and he ended up hurting her in so many ways, like he'd have done to you. He was a true sadist."

She touched his shoulder. "You're hurt..."

There was a lot more he wanted to tell her that was meant to the end of easing the pain she surely was feeling and help her learn from the mistake she'd made, but presently they weren't in the best environment for such a talk. In this house, with Hedges' body upstairs and another skeleton in the shed, it just wasn't the time or the place.

He smiled at her. "Oh, I'm fine. That's nothing."

The whole time they'd been sitting, she hadn't looked at him. When she did, John saw nothing but guilt and pain in her eyes, and no small amount of shame.

Almost immediately she burst into tears.

She didn't resist as he pulled her close. "I hate that you had to be here for this, but...I guess there was no other way." He held her as she sobbed uncontrollably.

"I'm sorry, John. I was so stupid."

"Don't beat yourself up, now. You'll be all right..."

"Well, look at this..."

"What's up?" Herb inquired as he walked over to Dawn.

She didn't answer verbally; instead, she swung the door of the safe the rest of the way open to let him see.

It was a rather big safe: two-and-a-half feet wide, two feet deep, four feet high...and nearly overloaded with money. There also was a small top shelf with documents and a couple DVDs.

"Jackpot," Herb said with a grin. "Looks like in all the excitement he forgot to close it. Well, well...I bet this is what he made off that footage of Kim, which I'd also be willing to bet is either or both of these discs," he said as he held one up. "Why don't you have a look at 'em to make sure, Dawn? Check the VCR, too- he might have the tape in there. Actually, he might have played that to make us think Kim was up here at first. I'll load the money into a box or something.

"I'm glad that world-class asshole made one thing easy for us. I don't like the looks of that pile of ashes by the window, though, especially with the metal spiral in it..."

Tom walked in with Mel. "What do you want to do, John?"

John looked up at him for a moment. "Mel, would you mind taking Jenny out to our car and waiting in there with her? I won't be but a few minutes." When Mel acknowledged him, he turned back to Jenny. "We'll be leaving soon. I want you to stay with us at least for tonight, ok? You shouldn't be by yourself; it's been a rough couple hours for you."

She nodded and sniffled, then walked outside with the bodyguard.

When he and Tom were alone, John answered. "First of all, I'm sorry."

"I know. I am, too. It was her, by the way. I found a ring she always wore; it still was on her finger. She deserved a lot better than what she got."

"No question about that." He was quiet for a moment. "As for our next step, I think it's best we douse Hedges' body in that gasoline Mel found and light him up. We'll use the oil, too; that combination should do the trick. Then we light this place on fire. It's all wood, so it should go up like a torch- just like he will. By the time it burns itself out there should be no trace of him left. That's the way I want it."

"There won't be any trace of him left?"

In his expression John saw what he was getting at. "None."

"I hope you're right about that."

They looked around as Dawn and Herb came back downstairs. "Did you find the tape he made of Kim?"

"That we did, Sir, along with his computer and an awful lot of money. We found some papers, too."

"Good. It all comes with us except for the footage of Kim, which will burn with its maker."

"Sounds like a winner to me. By the way, I also saw a pile of ashes right under his bedroom window, which was open. It's a fresh pile, too- looks like he burned a spiral notebook before we could get up there."

"Shit. I thought I smelled something burning."

"Yeah. It's quite possible that was something important. Speaking of burning, I heard you talking about how we should finish it. That is the best way. This house will go up quickly, especially since it hasn't rained in a couple weeks."

"That's what I figure. Let's get it ready; we need to hurry."

"No, Sir."

John turned to him, puzzled.

"You and your brother need to go to the car now, send Mel back in and wait with Miss Jacobson while we handle this."

Fifteen minutes later, they were rolling down the driveway. John looked back and saw light inside the house, which wasn't a result of electricity. As he knew it would, the fire spread quickly. Chances were it only would be a matter of minutes before that house was engulfed and the world would be a better place...

...at least, in his own eyes it would be. He'd had enough of the look on Tom's face and had to find out where he stood. "Tell me what's on your mind."

"John, I want you to know that I'm with you. You're my brother and I stand with you. I also want you to know there might come a day when what you did will weigh on you, if it's not already. I'm not sure I believe you when you say you'll sleep well tonight. A man with no conscience would, but you most definitely have a conscience. This wasn't merely a matter of you taking the law into your hands; you took the life of another man and the fact that that man was reprehensible in every way is beside the point."

"What?! That's *exactly* the point! He deserved to die and I killed him!"

"Clyde Davis deserved to die, too, and you had no choice but to kill him. Even so, that troubled you for some time afterwards; I wouldn't be surprised if it still does. This time you did have a choice. Things didn't have to go the way they did and you know it. I understand why you did what you did and I'm not standing in judgment of you. I'm just saying that you *do* have to live with it and it won't be as easy as you think it'll be."

Now, it was John who was silent for a moment.

Tom thought back to an event of the momentous year of 2000- an event that had been all but forgotten. "I always wanted to ask you about this and now seems to be an appropriate time. Do you know what happened to Wally Daniels?"

"He got what was coming to him, just like his mentor did."

"Is that all you know?"

He turned and looked Tom in the eyes. "I don't know exactly *what* happened, but I knew something *would* happen. I could have stopped it but I didn't. I saw no reason to, especially since Kim would have been put through hell on the witness stand, compliments of some lawyer and Daniels himself. I even know who probably killed that backshooter, who was every bit the coward that James Dougherty was- the one I got the murder conviction against and for whom I denied the clemency appeal just before I was shot. Dougherty did to his victim exactly what Daniels did to me, only I was lucky enough to survive. It took ten years for Dougherty's sentence to be carried out.

"In Daniels' case I saw an opportunity to shorten that time significantly, and better yet spare Kim the damage that trial might have caused her- another trial that would have been unnecessary since guilt was established. I saw the opportunity and I took it by failing to stop a transaction that already was set up- ironically, by one Christopher Hedges. It was a transaction in his bank account that I came across when we found his computer with Kim's lingerie in that suitcase- a transfer of money that brought about the end of Daniels' life. Other than Hedges, I was the only one who knew about that matter. He and I were in accord on that one point.

"Now he's gone, so besides me, you're the only one who knows. After we gave those portions of Hedges' money to his former captives, I made sure to keep the computer long enough for that million-dollar transfer to go through. I deleted the record before I turned it over to the police. Again, justice was served. I hope you're not trying to make me feel guilty about my actions then and tonight. Can you not understand why I did what I did? You say you're not standing in judgment of me...are you sure about that?"

Tom looked away. "Yeah, I'm sure. I don't stand in judgment of you because I'm not in your shoes. None of those terrible things Kim had to suffer through happened to Donna, but if they had...I'd have done the same thing you did. Don't get me wrong here, John; I said I'm on your side and I am. I'm just asking you questions that I have a feeling you'll be asking yourself one day. You've personally killed two men and by omission played a part in killing a third. That's an awful burden to carry around, no matter what the circumstances are."

"I see your point. I appreciate where you're coming from, Brother, and what you're trying to do. You might be right; that could happen. Then again, it might not. I have no doubt that I was completely justified in killing Hedges and Davis, and in allowing Daniels to die. It's no different than when I denied Dougherty's appeal; for all intents and purposes, I threw the switch and killed him myself. I don't regret that, either.

188

"Does that make me a bad person? Maybe to some, but as I've said, I think society's better off without the likes of them. I don't believe in waiting for God or whoever to judge murderers and rapists. We need to take care of that here; we need to keep those bastards off the streets and there's no better way to accomplish that mission than to kill 'em. I've always believed that and I always will. They show no mercy to their victims, so why should we show them any?

"When it comes down to it, someone has to make the decision. I won't tell you it's an easy one, but it's one that has to be made for the good and the safety of every decent person. When those who die deserve to die, I don't see it as a crime or as being morally wrong. The alternative is doing nothing- giving those cowards a slap on the wrist or excusing their behavior somehow.

"Hedges had to be dealt with. You can question my method all you want but don't question my motive. At this point I don't even care so much about what he did to me, but…after all those years, Kim told me what he put her through in '89. We just talked about it before we took the boat out this afternoon- well, yesterday afternoon. She told me how scared she was even when she got away from him. Plus, for all those years afterwards, she was so ashamed that she couldn't even tell anyone about it.

"Seeing her anguish because of that piece of shit was like a knife twisting in my gut. I never hated anyone so much in my life. I couldn't have let it go, Tom- what he did. There was no way."

Tom nodded. "You looked out for your wife, and for Jenny."

They both looked at Jenny, who was fast asleep. Her head rested on John's shoulder. She was swallowed up in Herb's jacket, which he'd draped over her shoulders when he saw her shivering.

"You always look out for family above all; Mom was right on. Jenny hasn't had that luxury for some time but she has us now." He looked back at Tom. "You said it before, Brother; you and I are the only blood relatives we have. There's no one else."

"That's right. We need to look out for each other and we will. Everything that was said and done tonight stays between us. I want you to know that you never need to ask again whether I'm with you, John."

John smiled. "I know."

"Now, what will you do with this money?

"Since we'd never be able to track down everyone who bought that video, we might as well see what Kim wants to do with it. It's more her call than ours. Besides, even if we did find the majority of those who had a copy, I doubt very much that they'd destroy 'em or send 'em back."

"I'm sure you're right about that. As for the broader scale, there's no need for guesswork when it comes to the next step."

"None at all. Needless to say, I thought for sure he was responsible for what happened to Kim. I bet he knew who was, though. Now we figure out what he meant when he said that he was my last chance to find out, which I don't believe for a second. Remember Kim's feeling that our paths were converging in regard to what we both were looking for? I've reached my destination and it could turn out that yours is close by, like she said. Somewhere along the way, we'll find out who's behind this.

"The clincher that landed Hedges in his funeral pyre came from Kim reading the card he sent with the flowers for Jenny. I made the assumption Hedges was the one she was seeing and I went with it. Another reason we found him is the similarity between what the presumed crime scene in '72 at his house looked like when he supposedly was murdered compared to the scene tonight at Danni's apartment. I had a feeling the correlation of those phony murder scenes meant something and as it turned out, it did. As for Danni herself, I bet you she's still around and that she knows something...

"...or, whoever the mastermind is knows. You and I both figured Hedges had to have help with his disappearing act over thirty years ago and it wouldn't surprise me in the least if the same son of a bitch is behind Danni's. Hedges didn't gloat about it being his idea; you know he'd have been too quick to do that if he'd come up with it himself. A sixteen-year-old might think of something like that- maybe- but I doubt he had the wherewithal to pull it off alone. I don't think he'd have thought it out as thoroughly and chances are he'd have screwed up the execution somehow. Once we figure out who orchestrated those scenes, which could turn out to be his father, we'll be closer to finding our answer. Then, with that talk about his father just before he died..."

"Yeah, I was about to mention that. I also would love to know what was in that notebook Hedges burned before you got him. Your answer probably went up in the smoke, unless he stored it on this computer, which I doubt," Tom noted.

"He said he'd never help me with any information and he meant it, so I bet you're right. Anyway, we'll be talking with

Warden Steele tomorrow; maybe he'll be able to shed some light- who knows? Same with Mister Jack- I need to call him in a few hours. Time is against us, but we're close, Brother, and we need to stay on the trail."

"Definitely." Tom remembered something he was curious about earlier, but when he noticed it, it wasn't a good time to ask. "That gun you have- it looks familiar. Let me see it."

"Sure," John said as he produced it. "It should look familiar. It's Dad's. He forgot it the night he disappeared- left it on the table."

"You've had it all this time?"

He nodded. "It was the last thing he touched before he left. I wrapped it up and hid it away. Every now and again I'd take it out and look at it; I kept it clean and serviceable just in case the opportunity materialized for me to get the one who got him. Hedges played a part, at least- I'm sure of it. I don't know of anyone else who had a more negative impact in my life in so many ways than he has, so even if the prime directive wasn't carried out…well, this is a very close second."

"That it is, John." Tom handed the pistol back to him. "Well, there's still a chance it might yet serve that main purpose and get whoever else was responsible. A lot of clues are surfacing of late; perhaps one of 'em will break the secret wide open…

"For now, we need sleep; it's been a hell of a night. A long one, too."

John yawned. "I second that, Brother. After we look in on Kim and make sure she's all right, we'll grab a few hours."

Back at the house they'd left, a man stood in the woods around it and watched it burn. Even from the distance of at least a hundred yards, 'Ray' could feel the intense heat of the blaze. Amazingly enough, he still heard no sirens, although forty minutes had passed. From all indications, in another hour or so there would be nothing left of this house.

That was a good thing, apparently to many people- now including him.

Given what he'd just learned, his eyes had been opened.

If he had pulled the trigger, she would not have been saved.

A very unexpected twist of fate had taken place.

Somehow, I will return the favor…

Chapter 10

Kim awakened slowly and looked around. Her head felt heavy with the lingering effects of the sedative.

However, to her surprise, when she looked toward the chairs set up next to her bed, she didn't see Donna with the nurse who'd been assigned to her.

Instead, she saw one of the last people she'd have expected.

"Hi, Kim. It's been a long time."

It took a moment before her mouth would work. "Jill?"

She nodded and smiled ruefully, but after she did an uncomfortable silence settled in. Both women looked at each other and away a few times until Jill Weldon spoke up again. "I, um...I hope you don't mind me coming. I-...well, needless to say you and I don't have the best history, which was my fault- more so than you even know..."

Her remorse was apparent to Kim, who said what she felt needed to be said. "I think it's about time we put that behind us. It was so long ago, and-"

"Could I-...if you don't mind, I came here to- to tell you-..." At that point it became too much for her.

In an action that was very uncharacteristic of her former rival, Jill moved over to Kim and hugged her, bursting into tears as she did. Momentarily stunned once again, Kim was slow to react, but she embraced Jill in return.

It took a little time before Jill was able to speak again. "I got here about fifteen minutes ago; the nurses said it was all right for me to wait with you until you woke up. While I sat here watching you I thought about all I did- all those hateful things I said about you just because I was so jealous, which were bad enough, but..."

Sensing there was more, Kim waited for her to go on.

Jill sat up, determined to look Kim in the eyes when she made the revelation that undoubtedly would be shocking, not to mention as terribly painful to Kim as it was to her.

Worst of all, given all she'd found during her time with him, she knew her theory was right.

"Are you Ok?"

Jill nodded and took Kim's hands into hers. "I just hope *you'll* be Ok after I tell you this..."

* * *

"I thought you might be looking through that again."

Tom was the first besides Donna to wake up. Everyone had stayed at their place that night. He was examining the diary John and Kim had found, but not the content. He was looking at the book itself. "Yeah, John, I just finished up. I agree with you how strange it seems that the last entry is on September 1st, 1970. I wonder about the entry itself: 'I can't sit still and watch this anymore. I just can't.' What does that mean?"

"I wish I knew. I also wonder about what Mister Jack told us yesterday about Dad's activities in the FBI up until the time he left and why so little of it was in his diary. You'd think he'd have been more descriptive, especially if he did know about what happened to JFK. Then, I'd definitely have thought he'd have an entry about what he did to Hoover."

"You're right; that *is* pretty strange. And how about this: Dad and I ended up with the exact same sort of journal. This one looks just like the one I got when I was about thirteen or fourteen. I made entries in it until shortly after I got out of the Marines. In fact, just out of curiosity I'm gonna call the manufacturer while we're riding out to see Mister Henry."

"Hmmm...it does look just like yours, doesn't it?" John remarked when he looked at it.

Tom turned to him. "How in the hell would you know-...you *dirtbag*! You did read my journal, didn't you?! *That's* how you knew I had a crush on Louise Compton when I was in ninth grade! I oughtta knock your lights out!"

"Louise Compton, huh? Maybe I should knock *your* lights out!" Donna made her presence known with that remark after having rejoined them. John cracked up, along with everyone else there while Tom sat, shaking his head and quite red-faced as Donna kissed him.

"One of these days, Little Brother...anyway, I just thought that was a strange coincidence about us having the same kind of journal. I guess we'd better hurry and eat so we can meet with Warden Steele. I know he's anxious to see this."

"That he is. Oh, I need to call Mister Jack now, too."

John dialed and the phone kept ringing until he got tired of waiting. "He's not at home and his answering machine must be

193

full. Well, he deserves a day off every now and again, although this is one of the times I wish he'd modernize and get a cell phone. One thing that surprises me is that he hasn't called about Kim. That bothers me...when she was taken a few years ago he called me as soon as he heard, and this is all over the news."

"You'd think he would have, as close as they are. By now he must have heard what's happened to her. He really hasn't been himself over the past couple months since Novak's body was found, but that especially rings true over the last couple days. I'd say he *needs* a day off, or several. You and I definitely should have a talk with him and see if we can persuade him to cut back and maybe groom his replacement. Hey- did you call the records keepers about those documents Herb and Dawn found in Hedges' safe?"

"Yeah, they're looking into that. It shouldn't be long before they have the list of everyone who's ever owned that place and the grounds; hopefully that one will be more helpful than the one from the house of his that we found all the women in three years ago. Did you hear anything on the news about the fire?"

"Nope- nothing. I checked the internet and nothing at all was mentioned there, either. It was a pretty isolated place; he didn't seem to have any neighbors closer than a mile away, maybe more. Chances are the fire burned itself out before the sun came up. It had a good six hours and conditions there have been dry for a couple weeks, just like we thought, so the wood probably *was* pretty dry. My guess is it went quickly. I checked the weather, too; a big rainstorm's due to hit that area late tonight. There might even be flooding, so if no one gets there before tomorrow I'd say we're all right. I think we are even if it doesn't rain, but that'll just give us more peace of mind."

"Good morning, everyone."

"Hey, Jenny. How did you sleep?" John inquired as she joined them.

"Pretty well, thanks."

"I'm glad you did- guess you needed it."

She nodded. "I'll be out of your hair soon; I need to get back to my place."

"You say that like you're intruding, which you're not. You're welcome here anytime. I hope we'll be seeing more of you now."

"Same goes for me, Jenny," John added.

"Thank you- both of you."

Donna jumped in next. "For now, have a seat. I'm sure you know me better than to think I'd allow you to leave here with an empty stomach."

She smiled and thanked Donna as well, then sat at the table.

Although John was a little reluctant to open the next topic with Jenny, his curiosity got the better of him. "I, um, need to ask you something; it's about your father."

Her expression changed to one of indifference, at best. "What about him?"

"How long has it been since you've seen or talked to him?"

"I haven't seen him since-…gosh, it's been so long that I can't remember when the last time was. I think I last saw him in '98 or '99 and I haven't spoken with him since last year around the holidays. Why do you ask?"

"Well, Tom and I are looking into some cases back in the early and mid '70s. I don't know if he ever told you, but he was on the police force back then." Her reaction gave John his answer before she even said anything.

"He was?"

John glanced at Tom, who shook his head and looked away. "Yes. He served with the Baltimore County Police from '68 until '72; he was one of my father's deputies by the time he left the force. Before that he served with the Marines in Vietnam, apparently as a sniper. I see he didn't tell you about that either," he noted as her mouth fell open.

"Are you sure we're talking about my father?"

"We're sure. I had a background check done on him and that's what I was told," Tom answered. "We don't know for certain about the sniper part; his military personnel file was a little vague there. We heard that from someone else. He definitely was in Vietnam, though- and apparently he was highly decorated."

Jenny just stared straight ahead. "Why would he not have told me about that?"

"Good question. I'm sorry to drop that in your lap like I did. The reason I'm bringing it up is because we need to find out if your father can help us in any way with some cases in the early '70s we're checking into."

"What happened in those cases?" When John and Tom filled her in, her surprise over what they'd revealed about her father's past gave way to worry. "Does this mean you think he might have played a part in their deaths?"

John only had revealed to her what they knew; he held back much of what Jack had told them since they only had his word- not proof. "We don't know anything of the sort, Jenny. The fact of the matter is, we don't know much of anything about what he did then- whether he was involved in those cases or not. All we have is hearsay. That's why we need to talk with him; we need to hear from him what he knows. If you'd rather not have any part in this, I understand- and I mean that. The bottom line is, he's your father."

"So you want me to let you know if I hear from him? Or should I try to call him?"

"I'll leave the decision to you. We're just looking for information; we're not accusing anyone of anything since we have a hell of a lot more questions at this point than answers."

"John…is one of the cases you're looking into your father's disappearance?"

He nodded. "He was involved directly in the arrests and interrogations of those suspects, so we're trying to figure out if their disappearances and his are linked in any way. It's the first time we've had any sort of a potential lead. We don't know if there's anything to it but we'll do what we can to find out."

"I'll do what I can, too. You all have been so good to me for all these years and I want to help you now. I'll call him today."

John smiled. "Thanks, Jenny. Now, you know that your father and I have been at odds for a long time, so it could be a pretty hard sell. I don't expect him to jump at the opportunity to talk to us, but having you put the bug in his ear might help." He stood, and so did Tom. "We have to take off now to see an old friend. Enjoy your breakfast and we'll catch you later. You, too, Donna- great pancakes, by the way! Is there anything you *can't* cook well?"

"Now, surely you don't expect me to say something other than 'no'! As for you, Thomas, remember the old adage that silence is golden- particularly now."

"Trust me, I'll remember, Honey," Tom replied, laughing as he kissed her.

She turned very serious after that. "You guys do what you have to so Kim will be safe," she said to John as she hugged him.

"We will."

* * *

The shock she'd felt upon seeing Jill was nothing compared to that which she felt after hearing all she had to say. At the same time Kim was telling herself that it just couldn't be, deep down she was pretty certain it was true.

She had to consider the possibility that none other than Jack Weldon, the long-time father figure in her life, wanted her dead- or worse, if what his daughter had revealed was true.

"I know, Kim. I feel the same way," Jill said, observing her. "You sure shaped a lot of sexual fantasies that day- one in particular, unfortunately. It makes me sick every time I think about it. I've been so torn. I mean, he's my father, but-...I couldn't let this lie."

"You did the right thing. As much as it disgusts me to hear it, I'm glad you told me. It must have been so hard for you."

"It was, but it had to be done. What happened to you yesterday helped make the decision for me. I'm so glad you weren't hurt too badly."

"Thank you."

Jill went to say something else, but stumbled as she tried to get it out. "Do you-...do you think we might- that we could-...I shouldn't ask you this now, but maybe-..."

"Are you trying to ask if we could be friends again?" She turned away and fell silent, so Kim went on instead. "I would love that, Jill." Kim smiled as the woman who'd once been the best friend she had turned back to her.

The women embraced once more as emotion got the better of both of them.

"I'll be damned..."

Henry Steele, the longtime warden of Maryland's maximum-security federal penitentiary, stood and walked over to his window after closing the diary. He was quiet for a moment before he continued. "This sure brings back some memories, boys."

"I imagine it does, Mister Henry. It raises a lot of questions, too, though. For example, there's what Mister Jack told us about what Dad did during the McCarthy hearings and his private investigation of the Kennedy assassination. The more I looked at

197

the journal, the more I realized that Dad hardly mentions anything in there. Was Mister Jack exaggerating, or what? What can you tell us about that?"

"First of all, tell me what he told you." He listened intently as John and Tom relayed the story to him.

When they finished, the bald, muscular and intimidating man who would turn 61 this year nodded. "That's the way I remember it; your father told me the same thing. Jack told you what your Dad told us and I don't think he was lying or overblowing it. I always took Tom at face value- trusted his word completely. He was a man of impeccable character; if anyone ever said something to the contrary I'd knock him flat. I see your point, though; it's very strange that he would have kept a diary, which you usually use to record your innermost thoughts and feelings, without making any mention of those events that ended up playing a big role in some life-changing decisions he made. It doesn't make sense to me. I have to tell you, I expected to see all that in here...

"Based on what we learned about him, I'd say Jack was right in his assessment; your Dad's innocence and sense of duty and honor blinded him to the fact that we had a bunch of shady, crooked people running things, which still seems to be the case today. They led a lot of well-intentioned people down the wrong path. McCarthyism, big oil, United Fruit, the Warren Report, and later, Watergate- the predecessors of the massive S & L fraud in the '80s, the Enron collapse, the Wall Street criminals manipulating earnings forecasts and all these CEOs looting their companies- gave those of us who saw it all for what it was a real wake-up call. Some didn't see that, some did but chose to ignore it for various reasons, and some saw it but *couldn't* ignore it.

"Your father fell into that last category. It took a good bit of time before he realized the two-faced nature of those 'leaders'. When he did, his innocence was gone and he felt like a fool. He'd hoped to atone for his part in the McCarthy witch-hunt when Kennedy took over and things looked so much better. Then came the assassination, which was bad enough.

"Next came the lie, which was the final straw for your father. When Tom, Sr. told Jack and I about his take on what happened there and how he was sure a cover-up was in the works, at first we didn't believe him. Hell, if all that evidence was there, how could they cover it up? Why would they *want* to cover it up? Well, as we know, he was right. The ball started rolling at that moment.

"He stewed, which was about all he could do. I admire how he was able to shield all of you from that- from the looks of you two during that time you never knew the hell he was in. You boys and your mother were all that kept him sane- of that I'm sure. If he didn't have all of you, it would have happened a lot sooner. Even so, it was inevitable. He couldn't hold all that in; even his love for his family, as strong and deep as it was, couldn't stop it."

Tom leaned forward in his chair. "Couldn't stop what?"

Henry glanced at him, then turned away. "Before I tell you this-...no, I won't put any conditions on it. You deserve to know and I think he'd have wanted that. I'll be honest; I thought you'd already read about it in the diary and were coming here to confront me about it. I really am surprised it's not in there, but be that as it may, it's time you knew."

Henry sat back down. "His wrath was what couldn't be contained. He had so much of it pent up for all those years with all he'd seen- from the betrayals, the lies, the crimes he bore witness to. It infuriated him how the perpetrators never were punished-how they got away with it. I think that had the biggest impact on him. He became Sheriff because he wanted to have just one corner of the world in which things would be as they should.

"It was good for the first three years, but the peace didn't last. I guess for him it just couldn't, no matter how much he wanted it to. Injustice followed him like his own shadow; he couldn't escape it and finally he had to try to stamp it out wherever he could. The turning point came with the start of a string of rape/murders."

"Novak and Wancowicz in 1970."

Henry nodded. "After the second one, they turned to murder. They were some of the worst filth I ever came across; they just toyed with us. They committed their crimes for the thrill of doing it and cared nothing about human life, and we didn't have shit on 'em. Even though they were guilty as sin, our case against them would have gone nowhere. They knew it and we knew it. That was the last straw, which I have no doubt is what prompted Tom to make that last entry in his diary. He'd seen enough; he wasn't about to let that happen in the place he was in charge of. And make no mistake: he *was* in charge.

"I found him at the morgue a few days after the arraignment. He had one of those drawers open and had rolled the body out; it was that of the latest victim, whose body was found early in

August. I'll never forget those cases as long as I live and I knew he never would. I don't know how long he was there before I arrived, but he just stood there and stared right into that girl's eyes. He was seething; I was sure he was about to go off. The look on his face scared the hell out of me- turned my legs to stone. I was afraid to move any closer to him, so I just waited for him to come back from where he was, hoping he would- or could- come back, but in one way he never did. I knew right then something had snapped inside him.

"When your father was angry, he made people shake in their boots- including those who were on his side, in part because they were grateful that they weren't the targets of his wrath. He's the only person who ever had that effect on me. From then on, his wrath was nothing less than deadly. Once that wrecking ball was swinging full force, no one could stop it- not even Tom himself.

"He couldn't bear the thought of those animals getting away with what they did. He was sick of not being able to do legally what had to be done. It seemed to be turning into a trend as well; we were moving toward the Miranda era, and more and more criminals were becoming more and more brazen, like the two we were dealing with. They were the type that got a kick out of the terror they saw in the women they assaulted; neither surviving victim would finger them, so up to that point they would have gotten away with it.

"A couple nights after we were in the morgue, he and I were out patrolling in his car. He didn't say much and I got the impression that he didn't want me to say much, either, so I took the hint. Gradually I noticed that we were cruising in areas where Novak and Wancowicz were known to hang out. Given that and Tom's disposition then and in the morgue, I started to worry about what he might be thinking. They were out on bail and the trial still was weeks away.

"In retrospect, I probably knew what was coming but I didn't say or do anything to stop it because…well, I agreed with your father." He unintentionally raised his voice a little. "You boys need to understand the state your Dad was in. It wasn't on some whim that he did what he did, and he still was a good man- the best I ever knew."

"You're right; he was a good man," John affirmed. Seeing that Warden Steele was becoming increasingly agitated, he added,

"Do you need something to drink, Mister Henry? We can take a little break if you like."

"No, thanks, Johnny. After all the years that have passed since then, I want to finish this and get it off my chest. It's been hard as hell, keeping all of it in. Plus, I know you and Tommy need to get back to finding the shitbag that tried to kill your wife as soon as you can. Anything I can do to help, say the word and it's done."

John smiled and nodded. "Thanks."

Henry leaned back, clasped his hands behind his head and went on. "Wancowicz was the one we happened across. We saw him drive up to a bar, so we pulled into the lot behind him and watched him go inside. We sat there and waited for the skinny bastard to come back out. After an hour and a half, there he was. To my surprise, he did us a favor by taking a little spin out Loch Raven way, along the reservoir. He made it really easy for us. It almost seemed like invisible forces were helping guide Tom toward the inevitable- nudging him that way, just in case he was on the fence about what he had to do.

"Tom made sure no one was around, then he made his move. He put his light on the dash, turned it on and pulled Wancowicz over. He took the driver's side, I took the passenger's. Tom didn't say a word to him; he reached in through the open window, grabbed hold of him and yanked him out- never even had to open the damned door. He stood him up straight and knocked him out in one shot, which Tom was very good at doing. He grabbed a handful of hair and dragged that dead weight back to his car, threw him into the trunk, cuffed him and shut him in there.

"Then we took a drive deeper into the Loch Raven area- out toward the Warren Road Bridge. It was quiet there- wooded, isolated. He found the spot he was looking for, parked the car well off the road and pulled that scum out of the trunk. He had me bring the pickaxe and shovel, and he grabbed a baseball bat, slung that guy over his shoulder like a sack of potatoes and off into the woods we went.

"It turns out Tom knew about an old cabin out that way that hadn't been lived in or used in any capacity for years. It served a good purpose for us. After about fifteen minutes of walking we got to it. Wancowicz was coming around and starting to sputter a little when Tom set him down onto a chair, fired up a lantern and sat across from him at this old wooden table that looked like it was made in the 1800s. Mister rapist and murderer was drunk, so he showed some bravado, demanding to know what in the hell we thought we were doing and where we were.

"Tom still had yet to say a single word to him. He just sat there and stared at the guy. Wancowicz was too drunk, too arrogant, too stupid, or a combination of the three at that point to figure out what lay ahead for him. He said stuff like, 'what, are you tryin' to scare me or somethin'? Tryin' to scare a confession outta me? Well, you need to do better than this!'

"Even that had no effect on Tom. In fact, the longer he sat there in silence, staring that piece of shit down, the calmer he seemed to get. You see, it was becoming more and more clear to him that what he was doing was necessary, and right. Gradually, I think Wancowicz started to get the picture, too, and the bravado faded. He was sobering up, and pretty fast; his forehead and upper lip were getting sweaty and he shifted around.

"Finally, Tom spoke. I still remember every bit of what followed..."

September 1, 1970

"You know why you're here, don't you?"

The complete lack of expression on the Sheriff's face was grinding down Ralph's nerve, but that first sentence the man uttered served as a glass of ice water thrown into his face. It was at that moment when he realized how much trouble he was in. "Wait a second, man- this ain't right. You can't-"

"I saw at the arraignment that neither you nor your partner has any concern for those poor girls and you definitely have no regret or remorse about all you did. Even now I don't see any, but I'll give you a chance to show some. Just bear in mind that if you do, it had better be genuine or you'll just make me hurt you more."

"We didn't do nothin'!"

"You didn't do nothin', eh? Well, that's what's called a double negative. I'm sure you have no idea what I'm talking about, so I'll fill you in. Since you 'didn't do nothin', that's the same as saying you *did* do *something*, which I already know to be true. You're helping me and you don't even know it. I don't suppose you did very well in English class, did you?"

Right then, Tom produced his bat. He stood and walked slowly toward Wancowicz, who looked less defiant by the second.

"Let's talk about Jeanine Roberts, your last victim. How many times did you and your buddy stab her? It was about fifty, right?"

"I told you, I didn't-"

"Didn't do nothin'. Yeah. I thought we'd gotten past that, but maybe not." With no warning, Tom swung the bat and hit him right in the stomach. He bellowed in pain and doubled over. "The next time you say that to me, I'll pick a more sensitive area to hit. Now, I'll ask you once more: how many times did you stab Jeanine? For the record, it doesn't matter whether you did it or Novak did it, because you both will pay equally. Now, at least be man enough to admit what you did. You stabbed her about fifty times, from the looks of her."

"You gonna take these cuffs off me?"

"Nope. The cuffs stay on. You know what they say; turnabout is fair play. The girls you raped and killed were restrained, right? So, why shouldn't you be?"

Tom saw the recognition on the guy's face; he understood fully where this was going and he was afraid. "Ever hear of a guy named Hammurabi? Or, a *dude*, as you doper freaks would say? No? Well, let me give you a little history lesson to supplement the one in English that I gave you a minute ago.

"Hammurabi was one of the earliest legal minds- not like these lawyers today that only seek to twist laws and make themselves famous and rich. Plus, with the help of psychiatrists they want to make everything excusable- like what you did, for example. They'd probably love to use some argument like, 'oh, he was on drugs- he didn't know what he was doing, therefore it wasn't his fault'. Well, I don't buy that crock of shit and I doubt Hammurabi would have.

"His code was simple: the punishment you receive should equal the crime you commit. In other words, you're held accountable for what you do, and that which you cost your victim in turn will be taken from you, or taken out on you. Very fair, equitable system, don't you think? It's the one I believe in. If we had it in place, I bet that would deter criminals like you, since you'd know what you'd get would be every bit as bad as what you dished out. It's true justice and it's simple. I like simplicity; things are just getting far too complicated in the world today.

"I think you know where I'm going with all this, but then again, you still might be wondering, 'what does all this have to do with me?' Since you don't strike me as the smartest guy in the world, I'll explain it to you. You committed the crimes of rape and murder in my county. Worse, you did both numerous times; unfortunately I only can punish you once."

"You got no proof, Jack. This ain't no court and I'm gonna tell my lawyer-"

"My name isn't Jack and you're wrong- on all three counts. I already had enough proof before you gave me even more just now with what you said. I see in your eyes and in how you act that you're guilty. Plus, with that last spiel, you didn't even try to deny what you'd done. Instead, you told me I have no proof, but I do.

"You also claim this is no court. I beg to differ. This is my court and you just convicted yourself. All that remains is for me to execute your sentence. Execute…that has a nice ring, doesn't it? At least, *I* think it does. As for you telling your lawyer anything, I just don't see that happening." Tom stood still, looking down at him. "What's wrong? Just a few minutes ago you were full of vim and vigor, but now you look pretty damned scared to me."

"You-…you can't do this…please, man, don't-"

"Now, this is fitting, isn't it? I bet Jeanine Roberts begged you to spare her life, didn't she? She begged you to stop, right?"

The kid sniveled and stammered, which triggered Tom's anger. "ANSWER ME, YOU FUCKING COWARD!! *DID JEANINE ROBERTS BEG YOU TO SPARE HER LIFE?!!!*"

"*Yes!!*" Next, immediately after he answered, he screamed as the next blow from the bat struck his collarbone and crushed it. Another came right after it- the lumber connected with and splintered his right shoulder, knocking him to the floor. He was howling in pain.

"Just think: we still have forty-seven blows to go yet before I put this bat- or what'll be left of it- in an appropriate place, given what you did to Jeanine besides killing her. You got off on hurting her, didn't you? Making her beg for her life…pretty psychedelic, eh, *dude*?" Another blow, this time to the ribcage.

"Well, I hope you feel good knowing that I'm enjoying hurting you- probably every bit as much, if not more. This is one hell of a pleasure, taking shit like you off the streets and making sure you never come back and hurt anyone else. You know, I could get used to it." He hit him again, and again. "A lot of your lily-livered contemporaries think the death penalty is cruel and that it's not a deterrent. On the contrary, I'm willing to bet you'll never hurt anyone again. The punishment most definitely fits the

204

crime. You even have time in between beatings to reflect on what you did and to realize that you do deserve what you're getting.

"But, those who want to spare the likes of you see it as vicious, and archaic- that means outdated, by the way. You can bet most- if not all- of those peckerwoods never lost a family member to some rapist and murderer like you. I bet they'd feel differently if they did. Instead, they want to look out for the rights of filth. They don't seem to give a damn about the rights of the victims and their families. Well, I do give a damn and right about now I have a notion you're starting to, in some way. Speaking of rights, you're right-handed, aren't you?" Tom didn't even wait for the answer before smashing his elbow.

"Ok, enough talk. It's time to finish with your sentence. I just wanted you to fully understand everything that's coming down on you and my reasoning behind it all. In this case it's a lot worse knowing than being surprised, isn't it? And don't worry; I brought a nice, big buck knife along, too. Wouldn't think of depriving you of that part…

"I hope you enjoy your, uh, 'trip', *dude*…"

~ ~ ~

John and Tom were speechless for the moment.

For John, the weight was heavier; he wasn't only thinking about what they'd just learned for its own sake.

"I never saw anything like that- and it happened right in front of me." Even now, nearly thirty-three years later, it still made Henry shiver. He saw every detail just as clearly as he did then. "At first I was sure he'd gone completely insane, but the more I thought about it the more I realized how methodical and purposeful he was in how he killed that punk. When he finished and turned to me, he was as calm as he could be.

"I couldn't move; I was scared out of my wits. He sat me down, gave me a drink and we talked about it. Tom insisted on that. The first thing he did was reassure me that he wasn't going to kill me, which, to be honest, I briefly wondered about.

"So, we talked about what he'd done and he explained it all to me, but I think that also was for his own benefit. He needed to reassure himself that he'd done the right thing by taking care of Wancowicz. He believed he had and I came to feel the same way. Tom's brutality put the fear in me, but the more we talked about

205

those poor girls and all those two had done to 'em, the more convinced I was that Tom did what had to be done.

"He vowed that he'd only hand out such treatment to those who deserved it- the worst of the worst, and especially those that might slip through the cracks in the system that kept getting bigger. Frankly, once I understood where he was coming from, I had no problem with helping him in that. I had total faith in his judgment and his sense of justice, both of which were beyond reproach. We buried the body about a hundred yards from the cabin and that was it."

Tom finally spoke up. "So, Dad's next target was Novak..." When Henry nodded, Tom wondered about something. "Why did Dad not give him the same treatment? I'm sure you've seen the story on what happened to him."

"I didn't just see the story, Tommy. I was there- and that time, so was Jack. The difference was, Novak didn't break like Wancowicz did. He was a little smarter and cockier. The report was right when it said Novak probably died as a result of being continuously pummeled by a very strong and enraged man. That's exactly what happened. He made Tom see red; your father just started punching the guy and kept on punching him. By the time he finished we couldn't recognize Novak. Tom didn't even make sure he was dead before we threw him into that box and buried him. In all honesty, I don't know if he was."

"My God...and they weren't the only two, were they?"

"No. As we came across more that deserved such treatment, we dealt with 'em and buried 'em there. We had it down; we'd gather enough evidence against 'em- legally or otherwise- to the point when there was no doubt we had the right person, or people. Instead of charging 'em with the crimes they were guilty of, we just took 'em out. We cut out the middleman and in the process made our county the safest in the nation at the time. Your Dad made sure they got as bad as they gave. Worst of all was what he did to the arsonist..."

"How many overall did he- ... how many were there?"

"As many as thirty that I know of."

"This is unbelievable...I had no idea. I never even would have suspected it."

"That's how your father wanted it. Like I said, one of the great things he did was to shield his loved ones from what he'd done, but in turn he must have paid a terrible price emotionally. I don't know how he did it; in a way it seemed like he had split personalities. Day after day, when he really sat back and thought about it, what must he have thought of himself and of people in general? How they could become so depraved and why the powers that be almost seemed content to rationalize the crimes and not punish the criminals like they should have been?

"In one way you could look at it as politicians wanting that fear to be there so they could take advantage of it and use it to help get themselves elected. Tom voiced that belief on a number of occasions. I guess he figured that if no one else was going to punish them, he would. He believed his cause was right and that by removing parasites like them, he made the body of America healthier and safer. He didn't want to risk having the legal system let the really dangerous ones off on technicalities so they could rape and kill again, which in those days happened more than I care to remember. It still happens today, especially when the criminals are wealthy, like you've pointed out in your forums, Johnny. The beat goes on.

"As for how Tom dealt with it, maybe he was able to do what some people do and just bury it, although I can't see how he could have. How do you bury something like that? There's no way to make the executioner's job easy, even when he's justified in doing what he does, but it's a job that has to be done." He said the last part with slightly more emphasis, looking John in the eyes when he did. "I have no doubt that you know how that feels. You were in your father's position, in a way. You did the right thing, too, when you turned down the clemency appeal for Dougherty. He was an embarrassment to the human race."

"I know," John said, finally breaking his lengthy silence. "As for Dad, he wasn't always able to hide his pain. When I saw him sitting by himself days before he disappeared...I have a feeling all you just told us figures in to why he was so despondent that day."

"Yeah," Tom added. "You could be right."

"He was in the War and he did his share of killing, so maybe that helped him deal with it for a while, but toward the end I was seeing some cracks in the armor, too, John. He insisted on doing the executions himself; he accounted for nearly all of 'em. It sure is likely that after four years it could have been getting to him. Having that fucking asshole lawyer hounding him didn't help, either. He suspected what was going on; we could tell by the way he looked at Tom."

"That was Curtis Parker, wasn't it? The one that was murdered in late '74?"

"One and the same. I won't lie to you; it was a happy day when we were rid of him. He was representing Novak and Wancowicz in '70. That's where the bad relationship between Tom and him started. Tom hated his guts. That guy was as unscrupulous as they come- a young hotshot punk looking to make his mark. He saw a big paycheck coming from Novak's family and you could see the confidence he had that he'd get them off. Like his clients, he didn't give a damn about those young girls who were murdered and mutilated. You still see a lot of these damned defense lawyers who are that same breed of parasite; they just don't care about anything but winning their cases at any cost.

"Parker cared just as little about the victim of a client he'd represent in the summer of '72, who was another real sweetheart named Larry Patterson. This one kidnapped a girl and was keeping her in a box buried underground. He was a copycat- saw a popular cop movie at the time and thought it would be really neat if he could do the same thing. We had his ransom notes and we worked our asses off trying to figure out who it could be, narrowing the field down. Your Dad, Ben Jacobson, Ray Searles and I were on the case. We did a damned good job on that one, too, if I do say so myself; it was one of our best efforts. Better yet, we were pretty sure we'd caught him in time to save the girl, but there was a problem.

"We got him into the station and Parker was right there with him, advising him not to say anything- not the least bit concerned that the girl could be in danger of suffocating. I tell you, Parker tried to show up the police at every opportunity, and he had a real hard-on for your father; that was his game. However, on this day he went too far.

"I remember that one clearly, too; it was little Doug's second birthday. Your mother set up a party for him which, because of this guy, Tom was late for. He was not happy about that. It was stifling hot, too- had to be a hundred outside with the humidity about the same. Then, Tom had the air conditioning vent off and the windows closed in the interrogation room where we had him. There was no fan, either, so we were sweltering. It felt like hell in there, which was just how Tom wanted it..."

"Is somebody gonna turn the A.C. on in here? And how about takin' these damned cuffs off so I can fan myself, maybe?"

"A little hot, are you, Patterson? Personally, I love this weather- can't get enough of it. I'm from lower Georgia originally, about 80 miles southwest of Savannah, not far from the Florida border. We had it plenty hotter down there. In response to your questions, the answers are 'no' and 'no'. Why should I make you comfortable while you're keeping a girl buried underground in a box? In fact, I'm thinking about bringing a heater in here to make it hotter still- give you a taste of what your victim is going through."

"Sheriff, you're way out of line. First, you have no proof he's guilty, second, this is cruel and unusual-"

"That's funny, Parker. You couldn't care less about Allison Mitchell's conditions, could you? She's in a box, probably with a limited air supply, and here you are handing me lines about the way I'm trying to get the information I need to save that girl from this unconscionable piece of shit- information I *will* get." He turned back to the suspect. "I know you have her, in spite of what this...lawyer of yours says."

"You have no right to-"

"You shut your mouth, lawyer!! I'm not talking to you; I'm talking to him. I know that he knows where she is," Tom turned back to Patterson and leaned closer to him, "and one way or another, you will tell me where she is."

"I got rights here, pal- like Mister Parker says, you're way outta line."

"Allison has rights, too. Above all, she has the right to live, which supercedes the right you think you have to not tell me what I need to know to save her life- if you haven't killed her already."

"Sheriff, I'm drawing the line. This inquisition stops here and now. You're accusing him without any proof at all. Mister Patterson, as your attorney I advise you not to answer any-"

Not even allowing the lawyer to finish his sentence, Tom reached over and took hold of his collar, then pulled him across the small table and slammed him up against the wall. "I told you to shut the fuck up, didn't I? The next word out of you will be your last. Do I make myself clear?"

Parker, shaking, looked at Deputy Steele, who shrugged his shoulders. The attorney fell silent.

Tom let him go and turned back Patterson, who started to shiver as well. "Now, let me explain to you how I'll convince you to come clean. First, I'll use these pliers to rip your fingernails off one by one. See this piece of sandpaper? Guess what I'll do with it?"

The man's eyes widened and Henry saw him clench his hands into fists, no doubt to protect his nails.

Tom smiled. "Starting to get the picture, are you? Now, if you still want to be tough, there's another step I'll take. I haven't had to go this far yet, but we'll see. Take a look at that can of hairspray. When you hold a match up and shoot the spray into it, the result is a flame-thrower effect. Have you ever smelled burning flesh?"

"N- no."

"Neither have I, but I'm really curious about what it would smell like. I hope you'll be a hard ass so I can experiment on-"

"All right!! Jesus Christ, I'll tell you where she is!! Don't bring that on me, *please*!!!"

~ ~ ~

"So, Patterson talked, we found the girl and she still was alive. Your father's way worked, but...Christ, you should have seen his eyes. In every other way he was as calm as he could be but his eyes burned holes through that guy. The degree of hatred in them was one I didn't think was humanly possible. Honest to God, it looked like madness, which he might even have done for effect, although no one knew other than Tom himself.

"Whatever the case, it worked, and in the end he was right. He had the right guy and the outcome was the best it could have been. To my knowledge, everyone he ever gave such treatment to deserved it. He had that way of knowing guilt- of seeing it, or sniffing it out. I trusted his judgment completely. He was the right man for the job; our community was safer with him at the helm. Your Dad was viewed by everyone as the hero he was."

"Parker came after him hard later on, though..."

"That he did. Nobody paid him any mind for some time, mainly because of the outcome to that case. Anybody who spoke out against Tom was reminded that Allison Mitchell was alive only because of our investigative efforts coupled with Tom's… persuasiveness, for lack of a better word.

"However, the public's memory is short. Once that case started to fade into the background and the pendulum swung further toward the rights of the accused, Parker picked up on that and renewed his campaign to discredit Tom. In '74 he did some investigating into some of our cases. We started to worry; this guy was an asshole from the word 'go', but he was smart and he was ruthless. He was asking a lot of questions and although your Dad had an awful lot of friends, not everyone was in his camp. Then, Parker was killed and that was all she wrote for his investigation. They never found any files or anything else Parker had on your father, so they figured he was just blowing smoke.

"Still, there were loose ends, including Ben. I doubt he was on your Dad's side; Tom made him leave the force late in '72, mostly because of his drinking problem. By then he'd gotten bad with it. He reported for duty while he was in the bag one night and that was the last straw. There was some friction that developed between your father and him earlier in the same year, too, which certainly didn't help matters."

"Why?"

Henry was reluctant to delve into the subject, but then again, he'd come this far… "Look, I don't know if this was fact, but word in a very small circle had it that Ben…had an affair with your mother. I hate like hell to bring that up, and frankly, I always wondered if it was even true, but you know how your Dad felt about your Mom. Even the insinuation drove him nuts."

"Mister Jack told us about that, too; he's convinced that's what happened."

"I'm sure he is."

"Why do you say it that way?"

"Because he's the one who started the rumor."

It was time.

Kim and Jill, after more than twenty-five years, finally had made amends, but amid that good feeling there was another pressing matter at hand that had to be resolved.

"I need to get out of here. Would you take me to your father's place and let me inside? He's probably at work now."

"Um, yes, of course, but shouldn't we call the police?"

"No. I just thought about that, but your father is the Attorney General and he has lots of connections. Who's to say someone wouldn't tip him off so he could go back and destroy the evidence? For the same reason, I think I'll have to come up with a story to get away from the troopers outside. I can't take any chances." She got out of bed, shed her hospital gown and donned her bikini again.

Jill nodded and took a breath. "Ok, Kim, I'll give you my key. I'm ready when you are." She raised a brow. "Are you going like that?" She remarked as Kim put her cover-up on.

"No choice. I can't wait for Donna and my change of clothes; she's not due for another hour. Let's go…"

Chapter 11

"Make sure you call me, all right? I don't like this at all."

"Don't worry; I'll be fine. Besides, he called you and told you he'd be out much of the day. I'm just here to get the evidence I need. I won't be long. You'd better take off; I don't want you around in case he comes back. Chances are he'll know it was you who told me everything."

Jill nodded in reply. "Just call me when you're ready."

"I will. Thank you again, Jill."

Kim watched her leave, mainly to make sure she didn't stick around. When her car disappeared, Kim shook off the jitters she'd done a good job of hiding and went right to work.

"Mister Jack started that rumor? Why? *Was* it just a rumor, in your opinion?"

"I don't know. I can see how it might have happened, but Ben was a good cop and he had a solid career ahead of him. He wasn't a dumb guy by any means; it just didn't make sense to me why he'd do something so stupid- especially with none other than Tom Stratton's wife! Furthermore, he knew what was going with our supplemental justice system, to put it one way.

"He was one of the eight who knew about it. Other than Tom, Ray Searles, Ben, Jack and me there only was Harry Lawson, who came into the fold after Ben left the force; we were the primary players. Judge Tippett and Ed Wilson, who owned the bail bonds place we dealt with, helped us out in other ways but didn't play an active role. Now, as far as I know, they're all dead except Jack, Ben and me, although in a way, Ben seems to have been dead for some time. I haven't spoken with him in years."

"Neither has his daughter."

Henry nodded in acknowledgment. "I bet Jenny's suffered from Ben's misfortunes every bit as much as he has."

"She certainly has, in more ways than one." John changed gears for a moment. "So, Harry Lawson was in on that, too?"

"Yes. I have a feeling that's why he was killed, which also is why I'm taking precautions myself. From the report, there was no struggle. Harry just would not have rolled over and let somebody kill him- that much I know. I have no doubt he was acquainted with his killer. I can't imagine any other motive for someone to take him out besides what he knew about our squad and our activities."

"So, who, then? Who could have killed him?" Tom asked. "I know it wasn't Mister Jack; he was in his office during the time in question...guys, I'm having a hard time with this. He's the Attorney General, he's been a family friend for years and here I am wondering if he killed a retired cop. Plus, he dropped that bomb on my father like he did...I just don't get it."

"I've been trying to understand it for years, Tommy. I always wondered if Jack had some kind of motive for starting that. Yeah, Ben and your Mom were in bed together one night after both had gotten pretty drunk, but we all were pretty well tanked-"

Tom's face turned white. "He and my mother were in bed together?!"

"I'm serious when I say this, boys; I don't think it was anything more than them taking a break in spite of what it looks and sounds like. Ben swore to me they were a little tired of drinking and needed to rest for a bit. He said they just talked and I believed him, but he couldn't even approach your father about it. Tom would have beaten his head in. The seed already had been planted and it had taken root. Jack usually did the right thing but he also had a lot of pull with your father. They were best friends, as you know. There's a chance he might have used that relationship to influence your father in a couple ways and possibly divert Tom away from his own agenda."

"How so?"

"You know how protective Jack always was of you boys after your father disappeared, but he was even more...protective of your mother. The way he looked at her, though, it just seemed to me that he was feeling more than protectiveness toward her. It was more along the lines of covetous, I thought, and that was the case even before what happened to your Dad. The bottom line is, I can't help but wonder if Jack was the one who-...well, made advances toward your mother and she turned him down- I don't know. He always went on about how great a couple they were, but the way he looked at her sometimes..."

"Funny you should put it that way."

Henry turned to John. "What do you mean?"

"He says that about Kim and me, too, and frankly, I've wondered about how he looks at Kim...so you think he had the hots for Mom?"

"I had a feeling there was something there- on his part- but I never could prove it. I wasn't going to confront Jack or Judy about it when I had no proof and I sure as hell wasn't going to tell Tom that about his best friend when I had no way of being sure I was right. I don't even like telling you two about it now for the same reason. I never would say anything bad about your mother, either. She was a terrific lady in every way.

"All we had was Jack's word, and that was the only time I ever doubted it. I hated like hell seeing all the damage done, but I just couldn't be sure he was lying. He was one of us, so why would he? There's only one possible answer: the one I gave you."

John's mind was back in the timeframe of the mid-'70s. *Jack was at our place quite a bit during that time, wasn't he? Then, after the Bicentennial, he scaled his visits way back...and Mom never looked at him the same way...*

"You might not have been off base with that, Mister Henry." He turned to Tom, and saw that he probably was thinking the same thing.

Once Kim had gotten into the house with the key Jill had given her, she wasted little time reflecting on past memories here. Those days were long gone in more ways than one.

She knew exactly where she had to go. Without delay she went upstairs to Jack's bedroom. It had some sturdy old furniture, including a big four-poster bed with a nightstand right next to it.

She couldn't help noticing the rather large photograph in the gold frame that sat prominently on the nightstand next to a very weathered-looking book of some sort.

She walked over and looked at the photograph...

...when she did, her blood froze in her veins.

"What makes you say that, John?"

"For about a year and a half after Dad vanished, Jack came over pretty regularly. He and Mom spent a good bit of time talking, and alone. We never suspected anything, obviously, because Jack was our friend. Mom never said anything bad about him, but after the little Bicentennial get-together we had, we saw a good bit less of him. He and Mom didn't spend any time alone again, either...

"And, like I said, there's been an occasion or two on which I've wondered about the way he looks at Kim. Granted, I know it's hard *not* to look at her, but...Jack was more of a father to her than anyone else, so I wouldn't think anything of it. There didn't seem to be any reason to before, but now you're telling me he might have wanted Mom...or could it have been that he was jealous of what they had? His marriage wasn't a good one and didn't last long at all, so that would stand to reason. He seemed to fancy himself as a father to Tom, Doug and me after Dad disappeared, and there was the time he spent with Mom initially..."

John jumped to his feet and walked away. "I'm with you, Brother; I don't want to believe any of this, but..." He turned to Henry. "You don't know if Jack had designs on Mom and neither do I, yet here I am putting this scenario together based on an assumption. Worse, I'm starting to think it might not be so far-fetched...

"...on top of that I find out my father killed as many as thirty men, possibly including J. Edgar Hoover...Jesus *Christ*!! I feel like the fucking roof's collapsing over my head!!"

Henry walked over to him and laid his hand onto his shoulder. "I'm sorry I kept this from you..." He trailed off, at a loss for words.

"If I were in your shoes, Mister Henry, I'd probably have kept it from us, too. Do you have any theories about what happened to Dad?"

"No. It's possible what Jack said could have happened; those FBI people did have motive and he's right about all the errand boys they sent to kill Tom, but I don't know. As incredible as it seems, Jack himself might have had motive...God *damn* him for stirring that up about your mother and Ben!! I probably should have told your father my feelings about it, but what in the hell *could* I have told him?! It was Jack's word against Ben's- of course he was going to side with Jack! Ben was a drinker and he did some questionable things but I honestly don't think he was guilty of what Jack accused him of and Tom convicted him of.

"I know how he tried to sabotage you when he ran against you in the Governor's race in '94; I was pissed at him for doing that just like you were, but look at it from his standpoint. His

216

career was ruined on hearsay; it took him years to earn some sort of respectability again. What he did to you was an attempt at some payback for what your Dad did to him- not the right thing to do, of course, but a human thing to do considering what he must have gone through. That's the only time I felt that Tom had made an error in judgment; it was costly to a lot of people. Besides what he did to Ben, Jack compromised your parents' relationship."

"Which would give him motive, wouldn't it? Maybe it's not so incredible, if you look at it that way." He turned and looked Henry in the eye. "We still don't-"

John was interrupted by Tom's phone ringing.

"Hello?...Yes, Miss Leeds, thanks for getting back to me so quickly." He covered the mouthpiece for a moment and said to John, "the lady about the diary." He took his hand away from the mouthpiece and resumed the conversation with her. "You have an answer, then?...You're sure about that?...Ok, thank you very much, Miss Leeds- you've been a big help." He hung up, then took hold of the diary.

"What did she say?"

"My hunch was right: this version of the diary was made from '72 until '80, which means this is a fake made by someone who knew a lot about Dad, including where he hid the original. It sure looks like this person got the real diary and replaced it with this one. Whoever it was must be a damned good forger because this handwriting looks just like-…"

"…oh, Jesus…"

Tom's mouth hung open and John walked over to him. "Tell me."

"The conversation he and I had a couple days ago…Jack told me about when he and Dad used to play hooky from school and how he'd forge the notes so well that no one knew the difference. He might have forged this one and kept the real one, which could have damning information about him in it that he doesn't want to come to light. Or, he could have burned it." Something else came to mind. "Yeah…he also went crabbing with us several times; he probably remembered that marker jug, just like you did. Who else would have had motive to switch the diary?"

John practically collapsed into the seat next to him.

For some time, neither said a word.

* * *

217

Kim was equally paralyzed as she sat on Jack Weldon's bed, surrounded by pictures of herself and feeling sick to her stomach while she watched the videotape.

The framed one of her on the nightstand was taken from a bird's eye view of her as she sunbathed. She was certain it was taken on the very day the neighborhood kids overpowered, tied and gagged her as part of their so-called game of cops and robbers, then held her captive in the treehouse, which was visible from where she sat.

At least, in the daytime it was visible. Kim wasn't even aware that night was falling- that she'd been sitting in that spot for quite some time.

He had scores of pictures of her: bikini shots numbering in the dozens and various ones of her in other tight and revealing clothing. Disturbing enough was the fact that out of all those he seemed to have gotten using his own camera, the vast majority were taken when she was thirteen. The exceptions were a number of them he'd taken of her cheerleading during her junior year of high school, but even then she only was sixteen.

Worse than that were the ones she found in a separate envelope, which caused her to tremble uncontrollably. Those photos of her had been snapped while she lay helplessly bound inside that treehouse. To her horror, she realized the feeling she'd had that night that someone was in there with her was right on the mark- and it was the man she'd looked up to for so many years.

However, the final straw was the tape. It lay among all his personal snapshots of her and those he'd apparently collected of her during her cheerleading days at Princeton and in D.C. for the pro football team. There also were photos of her during her time on the bikini circuit, including some so-called 'cheesecake' shots of her and the calendar she'd done. The drawer was laden with those pictures and the single videotape.

Initially, she paid no attention to the short message written on the label.

Although deep down she knew the tape's content, she felt a morbid desire to make sure.

She inserted it into the VCR on top of the television that sat on his dresser.

The tape had started to play automatically. She turned on the TV…

218

…and watched herself being secured to Hedges' bed.

The man who'd looked out for her for all those years, who was most vocal in the attacks against, had betrayed her in the worst way. At her wedding he'd referred to whoever had made and sold this videotape as the 'perpetrators of such filth- the vermin that would further exploit such a wonderful young woman'.

That man, none other than Jack Weldon, owned a copy of the footage of her in captivity to go along with all the pictures…

…yeah. You really looked out for me, didn't you?

A tear rolled down Kim's cheek as she just sat there, staring at the screen and not yet realizing that it had gone blank.

"Guilt." With that word, John finally ended the silence.

Tom turned to him. "Huh?"

"When you remove the cloak of perceived irrationality by considering situations in which the impossible becomes possible, you just might find your answer underneath. No matter how superficially nonsensical the scenario seems- or how unlikely the suspect- in a vacuum of tangible evidence everything should be considered…"

"What are you talking about, John?"

"That's part of a position paper I wrote for a college course. I brought it up as part of my conversation with Kim after she and I figured out that the phony Joshua Strauss was Christopher Hedges- when we started trying to fit some things together, like the three of us are doing now. I said 'guilt' a moment ago in answer to the question we asked ourselves yesterday- that being, why would Jack want to deceive us by making up some or all of what he said to us? What would his motive be? The answer is, guilt. *That's* what I saw in his eyes yesterday, along with the anguish.

"He either killed Dad or he played a part in it, and he's carried that around for thirty years. What Kim saw when she was six was Jack burying Dad's body a day or two after he killed him, so the possibility of him being behind the attempts on her life is pretty damned high. He was afraid she'd figure it out. He pulled the cloak on by doing all he's done for us- helping us along in our careers, lending us moral support when we needed it, always being there for us. All that considered, why would we ever suspect him?

That's what he banked on- that we *wouldn't* suspect him, or if we did it would be too late…

"…which I hope isn't the case. Come on- we need to take off. I don't know for sure if everything we've come up with is true and that Jack did try to have Kim killed, but I'm damned sure gonna find out." He and Tom stood, but when he turned to thank Henry, he saw that the man was on the phone.

"Les? It's the Warden. You're in charge here for the rest of the day; there's something very important that I need to do. I'll see you tomorrow." He hung up and said to John, "you *do* think he put out a hit on your wife, don't you?"

He nodded.

"I agree and I'm coming with you. I'll follow along in my car. Don't bother trying to talk me out of it; you'll just be wasting time." He grabbed two extra speed loader clips for the .44 Magnum revolver he carried in his shoulder holster, just in case things got out of hand.

John nodded. "Ok. Let's go."

Kim jumped a little as the tape ran out and the VCR went into automatic rewind.

At that moment she finally noticed how dark the room had become.

"Oh, my God- I have to get out of here!" She jumped to her feet and went over to the VCR to retrieve the tape. With it in hand, she moved back to the bed and gathered together all the photos of her. *No way I'm leaving them with you so you can-*

She stopped mid-thought when her attention was drawn to the old book on the nightstand- the one that was next to the first picture she saw.

Curiosity got the better of her and she decided to have a look.

When she opened the book, another shock befell her.

It was a journal.

The date on the inside page was January 19th, 1955.

The name on that same page was Thomas J. Stratton. She read the first entry, which was the same- word for word- as that in the one John and she had found yesterday.

The same terrible feeling in her stomach came back, only now it was stronger.

An overwhelmed Kim had to sit down again. Even though she knew she had to leave this place, and soon, it all was just too much and her legs refused to work. She had to know.

She paged through the very thick diary and on impulse went to the end.

The last entry was December 29th, 1974. She wanted to read what it said, but there wasn't enough light in the room.

Without thinking she turned on the lamp, which sat on that same nightstand.

"What do you mean, she's gone, Maggie? Where is she?"

Donna was incredulous as she stood at the nurses' station with the bag of clothes for Kim. "I was supposed to ride home with her. Do you know where she went and who she went with?"

"Um, she left with another woman and a couple state troopers."

"Ok. Thank you." Donna walked away from the station and pulled out her cell phone.

She tried Kim's number. "This is not good," she said when it went to voicemail after four rings.

After leaving a message, she dialed Tom.

What in the…?

He almost dropped his rifle when the light in the window gave him a jolt.

He was even more surprised to see her sitting there.

What is she doing?! And why isn't she leaving?

Whatever the case, he had an opportunity to get her out…

…he was about to leave his position in the old treehouse and go inside when the situation changed.

Jack and Danni, who were pulling up in front of the house, saw the light go on as well. It filtered through the upstairs windows.

For a moment they looked at each other in stunned silence.

"I'll check it out, Mister Jack. Give me two minutes, then come in."

* * *

After reading the last words John's father ever wrote, Kim finally got herself together. It was time to leave, to tell John what she'd found and to sick the police on Jack Weldon and Danni Searles.

In fact, I'll call him right now. She picked up the phone on the nightstand and dialed...

...and got the 'not available' message. "Dammit," she muttered as she waited for the spiel to end. "John, it's me. I'm at Jack's house, and I've found-..."

As she picked up the pile of photos and put it on top of the diary, she looked at the videotape again.

This time, what was on the label jumped at her.

It said, 'Enjoy the show, Dad. I know you will!'

The phone dropped and her hands flew to her mouth.

As if Jack's other betrayals weren't enough...

"Hang the phone up, Kim."

She looked up to see Danni holding a gun on her.

Her heart sank even further and she also felt very stupid. She'd been caught, and she had no idea where John was as she put the receiver back in the cradle.

Worse, she felt no will whatsoever to resist.

All she did feel was desolation and she hurt all over.

Danni approached her carefully, even though she sat almost perfectly still with a very forlorn look on her face. "Well, it seems to me that you'll be smart about this, anyway. Once again I was all set to shoot you, but it looks like I might not have to- that is, if you show me you'll keep on being smart by facing away from me and clasping your hands together behind you."

She has a gun on me and she's a black belt in martial arts. I don't have any choice.

When that cold, hard fact settled in, she dismally followed her instructions.

"Very good. Stay nice and still."

That was the last thing Kim heard before the lights went out.

"We have a lot of pieces, don't we, John?"

"Yeah, a bunch of 'em. It starts with Kim telling us at our wedding reception how she saw Jack digging in his yard one

January day a long time ago. He freezes, then comes up with a smokescreen. He tells us it was a mild winter. He was backpedaling and the only reason he'd do that is because it was just after New Year's, 1975. Otherwise, there would be no need for him to create some bullshit cover story. Contrary to what he said, it was bitter cold that winter, as we well remember. I didn't pick up on that before because I didn't have reason to think he'd lie, which is exactly what he did- on the biggest scale possible. He was digging in his garden when the ground was rock hard. He was desperate; he did that to hide what he'd done, where no one would think to look.

"Next, he lied to Kim about the guy she saw digging in his yard in August of '81- the guy he told her was his nephew, again when we were at the reception. He denied even having a nephew when we were in his office yesterday- had no idea what Kim was talking about. Plus, he was giving her the eye while we were in there. I didn't think anything of it then, but now...as sick as it seems, I can't deny the possibility that he's in the same league as Hedges as far as Kim goes. I see two possible reasons for him to have had Danni take her out: one, to prevent her from telling anyone if she figured out what he was doing in his garden in January '75, and two, because he couldn't have her. If Danni knew that her father was part of our father's killing squad, maybe *that* figures in somehow; maybe Jack used that knowledge to manipulate her. It stands to reason that he could have a history of manipulating people, like he seems to have done to us...

"Along those lines, I had to find out through the TV interview he did three years ago that he knew Kim was involved in the sting that netted Rollins and his crew. He never told me. I know what your reasons were for holding that back from me, Tom, but until now I had no idea why he did. He worked with me all along on that case, which Kim was a crucial part of and actively involved in. He even asked me about her and whether I'd seen her anymore. I told him how much I missed her and how much I'd have loved to see her again after those fireworks we generated at the Memorial Day pool party...he knew where she was and how to contact her, and I bet the son of a bitch knew she wanted to get back with me, too. She always did confide in him, so who's to say he didn't try to dissuade her from that?"

He ran his hands down over his face and took a breath. "Add those factors in with everything we've learned over the past twenty-four hours...we don't have the whole picture yet but I have the feeling we know what it'll look like when we do, even though what we have is almost purely circumstantial. Hypothesis."

"Yep. You know, that's the same thing a lot of people said about the case you just mentioned that made you famous."

"They did, didn't they?"

"You were right about the theory you put together then, you were right about who kidnapped Kim and all the others three years ago, and...well, along with my feeling that he forged Dad's diary, your arguments have convinced me that you're right about Jack. As you said, the impossible has become possible, and then some."

"It's the only thing that makes sense, isn't it? I never would have believed it and I still don't want to, but it's all we have."

Tom picked up his phone as it rang again. He looked at the screen before answering. "Hi, Honey, what's up?" He didn't like the news he got from Donna.

John liked it even less. He pulled out his phone to dial Kim and saw there was a message from her that he wasn't aware of, which was as short as it was alarming...

...what made it worse was seeing the number from which she'd called, which made his blood run cold.

"...and we need to hurry."

When Kim came around upon hearing those words from Danni she found herself in a familiar state, which the detective was just putting the finishing touches on. She wasn't the least bit surprised about that or the fact that Danni had relieved her of her cover-up, leaving her only in her bikini.

"Ah, welcome back, Kim. I hope you find your accommodations comfortable. Thought I'd relieve you of that excess clothing, too- for your comfort and our pleasure," Danni said with a smile as Kim glowered at her. The stifling leather gag sealed her mouth, preventing her from replying. She quickly realized there was no chance of escaping the restraints Danni had fastened onto her wrists and ankles, holding her in a spread-eagle. The shackles were bolted into the padded floor on which she lay.

Danni turned back to Jack. "This is quite a nice place you made for her- looks like you finally got your chance to test it out. Fitting that it'll be her last residence after all, isn't it?" She backed out of the very small cell Jack had built into the wall of his bedroom. It only was about four feet high and wide, and about seven feet long, and was padded all around.

"Whew- it's already warm in there, and it'll get warmer still soon enough, won't it? Speaking of which, I'll leave you two alone for a few minutes; I have those preparations to take care of. I won't be long," Danni said as she exited the room.

Kim didn't like the sound of what Danni had just said, but that thought was whisked away when she looked at Jack, who now crouched in the doorway. She wanted to lay into him for all he'd done, but the gag wouldn't allow that. *I doubt anything I said would have any effect, anyway...*

All she could do was scowl at him as she noted his almost indifferent expression. Her anger swelled exponentially- and quickly. While she looked at her longtime father figure, Kim felt the same urge to kill as she'd had with his son. However, all she was able to do in reaction to that urge was yank at and writhe within her bonds, twisting and pulling in a frenzied struggle to break free and strangle him as her eyes shot laser beams of hatred at him. The gag stifled the curses she tried to lay into him with.

His further silence and apparent lack of any sympathy or remorse made her fight on with all her strength for as long as she could, but the manacles continued to serve their purpose of binding her and holding her in the vulnerable position she was in.

Gradually they sapped her strength along with the anger that supplemented it, reducing the degree of her struggling. Finally, as much of her energy was spent, she gave up and began to cry.

"That's why you're also gagged, Kimberly; I didn't expect a good response. I guess your question for me is, 'how could you?' You probably know the answer already. It's why men 'befriend' and 'mentor' beautiful young girls and women. To put it one way, those of us who aren't as desirable have to resort to siege warfare as opposed to the quick strike- like John and his father obviously were capable of- to conquer them. We try to create an opening to exploit- to find a weakness in the fortifications. If the siege fails, we have to resort to sneak raids or surprise attacks to secure our objective, which is what I resorted to in order to have you.

"You already know it was me in the treehouse with you the night of August 18th, 1981, but there's a lot you still *don't* know. Since we have a few minutes while Danni sees to her preparations, I'll explain to you the events of that day, including how and why you ended up in there.

"Simply put, you were the prize, Kimberly. You were *my* prize. A woman such as you doesn't come along very often- maybe once in a generation. You're that one whose beauty is so unique, unparalleled and utterly irresistible. Just looking at you makes men melt, and want to possess you. Your presence- your aura- commands the attention of everyone. I saw that magic in you early on, when you were little; even then I knew you'd turn every head when you matured. Then came that summer when you hit thirteen and became a woman in every way. You started wearing your hot pants and the tight tops, teasing all of us...that was what got the ball rolling, so to speak.

"Women always were my weakness; I hated how vulnerable you all made me feel and hated even more the fact that whenever I tried to reach out to one, she'd slap my hand away. It was my own fault because of the bad choices I made, but eventually, who's to blame becomes irrelevant. The fact that you're where you are, meaning miserable- that's what sticks, and festers. You only can be rejected so many times before something changes inside you. Either you become angry and want to lash out somehow, or you turn to stone and withdraw, which is what I did for a long time.

"I kept to myself, kept within my circle and just went about my work. I succeeded for a while, until you came along. I doubt anyone else would have changed my course, but what I saw in you did. It didn't even matter that I was in my upper fifties and you'd just become a teenager. It should have mattered, but it didn't. You brought my weakness back to the surface; for that I hated you. I hated how you made me feel that way again. It would have been so much better for everyone if I'd been able to keep shutting myself out when it came to women, but I couldn't do it.

"There was another factor in the actions I took when it came to you- that being what you knew, what you'd seen. I guess you know the nature of the digging you saw me doing on January 2nd, 1975. I have a feeling you and Johnny already have figured out that Chris and I killed Tom, Sr.- even without the benefit of the diary. Also, back to that August day in '81, I suppose you remember seeing Chris out back, digging. I saw how you looked at him, too; I wasn't sure if you were more curious about him or what he was doing, so I had to find out. I pulled you aside for that reason. Although by your body language and the way you blushed it seemed that your curiosity came from your attraction to him, I still worried that there was more to it. It's appropriate that you're wearing a tiger-striped bikini now; you know what curiosity did to the cat, which I'm sorry to say is what it will do to you.

"That's why you didn't run away when you had the chance, wasn't it? It was that curiosity of yours. Your need to know everything outweighed your desire to escape. You're still such a bright girl; you were back then as well, so I didn't want to take any chances that you'd raise questions about the purpose of my bastard son's digging.

"You do know now that on the day of your treehouse caper, Chris was completing his transition into his new identity: Joshua Strauss. Danni told me you and John figured that out. He was burying the former holder of that identity and I was helping him in return for what he'd done for me at the end of 1974. I couldn't take the chance of you asking questions and doing some digging of your own, so that's when I hatched the plan that would have served the dual purpose of silencing you and satisfying me.

"It won't surprise you to know that Jill, who most definitely hated you back then, was the one who convinced all her friends to play the cops and robbers game. Of course, they jumped at the chance to tie you up and humiliate you- bring you down a few notches, just like I knew they would. That's why I posed the idea to my daughter and suggested they lock you inside the treehouse as well and leave you there for a while to teach you a lesson. I had no idea of the other effect it would have on you...at any rate, they did quite a job, didn't they? Jill had told me about the party they were going to that night, so it was great timing. I suggested to her that they leave you in there until they came back. It was absolutely perfect in execution; it couldn't have gone any better than it did.

"The way I saw it unfolding was, when all the kids came back from their party and went back up to the treehouse to get you, they'd discover that you were gone and would figure you'd escaped. Then, in a couple days when you were reported missing, no one would know what had happened.

"The kids who'd tied you up and stashed you away certainly wouldn't talk for fear of incriminating themselves. Even if they did, they wouldn't have been able to shed any light on what had become of you. The neighbors would have portrayed you as the little tease you were, dressing provocatively and enjoying all the attention you got. Eventually, the police would have deduced that you ended up teasing the wrong one, who abducted you as a result and probably ended up killing you. In a way, they'd have been right, although they'd never have known. No one would have.

"Then, as all that played out in my head, I started thinking about you- looking at the pictures I had and grinning ear to ear when I thought of how much better it would be to have the real Kimberly Francis instead of just her images. I was ready for you.

"So, I waited until after all the kids had left you alone, then I went out to the treehouse with my key for the lock and crept up the ladder nice and quietly. I'd made the food that Jill took out to you, and I mixed in a special ingredient to make you- shall we say- more docile and amorous at the same time.

"From what I heard as I climbed that ladder, the ingredient was working even better than I thought it would. I undid the lock and went inside, and there was the most erotic and beautiful sight I'd ever seen. Your scent was noticeable and your, um, activities and your cries helped me get inside without letting you know I was there. I went against my instincts, which told me to scoop you up and take you inside right away. I just couldn't resist watching you; what a passionate girl you were- and still are, as evidenced by that videotape Chris sent me. He really captured you- no pun intended- at your best. Aside from differences in position and wardrobe, you reminded me of that night...

"I had you, Kimberly. I literally had you in my hands. After you passed out I had to feel you- get a little taste, but I let you distract me so much with the show you put on and that exquisite young body of yours that I lost track of time.

"Then, those damned little boys interfered and ruined my plans. I barely got out of there before they climbed up and rescued you. I knew I'd blown it. The ultimate irony was when I helped you down from the treehouse. Then, you decided against spending the night at my place, and that was that. I'm surprised I was able to hide how furious I was with myself for letting you slip through my fingers. I felt sick for weeks afterwards- months.

"The more time passed, the more desperate I was to have you- so much so that I went to your stepfather with an offer to buy you. I knew he didn't want you around, anyway; he never cared for children and really, you weren't even his child, so I offered him the money and he agreed right away." He paused to let that sink in.

It was yet another emotional dagger buried into her. Even though it made sense, given how little Steven Francis had cared for her- if he ever had at all-, it was a terribly painful blow nonetheless that he'd agreed in effect to sell her into slavery. She turned away from him and closed her eyes.

"All we needed was the opportunity, and we were close. He was to hand you over to me not long after you finished eighth grade. By then I had a place all set up in which to keep you- restraints, gags, the works. As you've figured out, it's the one you're in right now. It's been set up like this since the spring of 1982; it's where I'd have kept you during the day when I went off to work. I thought it would be fitting to give you a taste of what almost was. I can assure you, you'd never have escaped had Steven handed you over to me. I even offered to let him come and, shall we say, 'visit' you from time to time, which he was looking forward to. I'm sure you detected the undercurrent there, didn't you? As for Jill, even if she'd found out I was keeping you I doubt she'd have objected, given how she felt about you. No one ever would have known you were here. Victory was in my grasp again.

"Then, just before you graduated middle school, a problem arose. You met Diane Watkins. Because you and she were in such close contact, you would have been missed. Your mother probably would have believed a stranger had taken you, especially with the Ted Bundy story fresh in everyone's minds. It wouldn't have been such a stretch for *her* to believe that, but Diane- she might have had doubts, so Steven got cold feet. I assured him we'd still be able to pull it off, and we could have, but his paranoia took over. He backed out.

"That was it. You were gone, and as things turned out it would be more than two decades before I had another chance. As I said, I hated you for having that strong of a hold on me- for driving me to take those measures to have you- and I hated myself for being so weak as to allow you to have that power over me. Worst of all, my efforts failed. I just couldn't handle another Judy Stratton scenario- she had the same hold on me-, but that's exactly what ended up happening. Eventually I got past it, although that took some doing.

"I lost what I figured was my last chance, but you also left a lasting impression on someone else that fateful day we had you in the treehouse- my son, of course, who saw you talking with me. He also saw you as the ultimate prize, just like I imagine every man sees you. You're the trophy we all want and he most definitely wanted you, especially when I told him you were attracted to him. He knew about my plan and he wanted in, but he couldn't help me that day. He had other matters to attend to.

"Eventually, Chris took over where I left off. You remember the Rollins sting, of course. Well, when you came to me with your information and we set that up, I had to tell Chris. Together we came up with the plan to take all Chris's accomplices down. He ended up making it worth my while to the tune of two million dollars. We also collaborated on a follow-up plan. We achieved the primary goal without a hitch- with your assistance, of course.

"Unfortunately, our follow-up didn't go so well. We waited down the road as it all went down. Subsequently, we planned to ambush the car carrying you and your friend away from the scene so we could take both of you, but to our mutual chagrin, another car followed right behind that one. It was a worthwhile long shot, but we couldn't have taken both cars down, so we aborted that.

"Chris had later successes with you. In fact, the place where Danni and I are meeting after we leave you here holds some special memories that you and he shared, but eventually he screwed up, too- got careless. Like father, like son, I suppose, as much as I hate to use that expression now. We were civil back in those days, but things changed...

"So, for the added reason of self-preservation, I took my last shot to get you and I finally *did* get you, but yet again I can't keep you, just like my son can't seem to keep you. You're like the Hope Diamond: the most precious treasure one could possess, but you bring trouble, misfortune and inner strife to whoever tries to possess you. You'd have brought all that on John as well.

"You already have, really. You distract him; you always did. How could he possibly concentrate on running the nation when he knows you're in his bed, waiting and willing? How could any man who had you think about anything else *but* you? In a way, I'll be doing him a favor. Your death will be nothing less than a tragedy, but then his full potential will be realized. His focus on his work will be absolute, which will benefit all of us.

"As for me, I suppose I'll have to settle for all my memorabilia of you since I can't have you, either." He left her for a moment to gather all the photos together along with the videotape and Tom, Sr.'s diary. He deposited all of it into the open drawer from which she gotten them and pulled the drawer out, then returned to the doorway.

He noticed a look of anxiousness in Kim's eyes now as she squirmed in her bonds. There could be little doubt that she realized where all of this was leading.

"I'm sorry, young lady, but you know too much. Plus, all the memories you conjure up- all the failures...there was a small chance for me to keep you alive, which was why I asked Danni to kidnap you instead, if it was possible. Unfortunately, it wasn't then, and now it's too late. You'd be a complication now. I suppose it had to end this way."

He turned when he heard Danni walking up the steps to rejoin him, then looked back at Kim. "To satisfy your curiosity, we're going to burn the house down- with you in it. You'll be dead before the fire starts, though; Danni will see to that. We're not sadists, but we do have to be practical and taking you with us just isn't an option."

As he went to leave, he said, "I truly am sorry it has to end like this. No one ever had to know about all we did, but my son couldn't let it lie. It was my hope that John would assume he tried to kill you, then somehow find him and kill him. That would have closed the loop for good but I suppose Chris is buried too deep. I just hope *I* can find him. If it's any comfort to you, if I do, I will kill him."

With an expression of sadness, he took one last look at her and simply said, "Farewell, Kimberly."

With that he left her. As Jack's revelations sank in, all the emotions they brought on combined once more to paralyze her temporarily. Even had she not been restrained, Kim couldn't have budged.

"...he hasn't checked in since this morning? So you have no idea where he is...Yes, have him call me on my cell phone, if you would. Thanks."

Just as John hung up with Jack's secretary his phone rang again. "Hello?...Oh- hi, Doctor Hughes. How have you-...you've found it? Well, that's good news. Look, I want you to take that sample and do a paternity test for me with what DNA you can find on Jack Weldon...Yeah, that Jack Weldon. Let us know what you find. Thanks for letting me know right away, Doctor Hughes."

John hung up with her and another phone began to ring. "Man, this is unbe-...oh, shit- it's Kim's. I forgot I still have hers, too; no wonder she used Jack's phone," he said as he took it from his pocket. He turned to Tom and said, "this was in her bag." He looked at the screen out of curiosity, and what he saw made his skin prickly:

Weldon, J.

"Kim?!"

"Um…no, it's- who's this?"

John was confused, and didn't reply right away. *J. Weldon… it must be-* "Jill? Is that you?"

"Yes. Who are-…John! I was trying to reach Kim; I told her to call me when she-…do you know where she is?"

"I just got a message from her. She called from your father's place, which is where we're headed."

"Oh, no- you mean she's still there?"

John's stomach tightened. "Jill, you have to tell me what's going on- right now…"

"I won't be too far behind you, Mister Jack. See you at the ranch." After he acknowledged and walked out, Danni gave all her attention to Kim. "As for you, I'm not sure I agree with him as to the reason why you took matters into your own hands and came here."

She smiled and said, "no response, eh? Well, that's all right. I wouldn't be interested in hearing it, anyway. The predicament itself is what brought you here. You get off on all this; it's just too intoxicating for you, isn't it? The little housewife became bored, but now she has excitement in her life again. Your past experiences with this really have a hold on you, Kim- don't even try to deny it. You wanted to be caught, didn't you?"

It always seems to come down to someone thinking that, Kim ruminated as she waited for the inevitable.

"I can see your answer in spite of your efforts to hide it. The position you're in suits you perfectly, along with the way you're dressed. You get a big charge from this. You're a typical, submissive female- just another girly-girl with all the right tools: your face, tits, ass, legs and the sex kitten persona to go with it.

"You sure capitalized on it, too, didn't you? Why, you were Aphrodite herself. Of course, you sure don't seem very formidable now, being a goddess and all. I'd never have thought mere shackles could hold you, but apparently they do. You are just a girl after all, in every way. I really find it depressing that such an exceptional and brilliant person is happy being the woman behind the man. That being the case, I don't feel so bad about killing you. No big loss, really.

"Contrary to Mister Jack's wishes, I want you to die slowly. I know how to make your death as agonizing as possible, which I'll take great pleasure in bringing about. I think you know what I'm getting at. It's about to get *really* warm!

"Look on the bright side, though. You're getting what you really want, which is one final opportunity to play your best and most appropriate role of damsel in distress- all tied up and locked away, this time inside your tomb. Enjoy yourself, Kim."

After a moment of savoring the fear in her captive's wide eyes, Danni closed and latched the small door.

Dammit...

It had happened too quickly and he wasn't ready. Even though in a matter of seconds he'd set up again, she moved back out of sight.

Come on...one more time...

Danni was about to strike the match when she froze.
From of the corner of her eye she caught the glint...
...she turned and looked out the window...
...and knew what was coming.
She saw the flash, and then nothing.

Before Kim could begin to think about how to get herself out of yet another potentially deadly situation in which time for her was running out quickly, she heard the crash. She lay still and listened, but couldn't hear any movement. She had no way of knowing what had happened since she was locked inside the pitch-dark room. Apparently her improvised cell wasn't soundproof.

In a way she wished it was as speculation- none of it good- took over.

What's going on? Is someone else out there? If so, I hope it's someone who knows I'm here...

...or, do I?

233

Her next thought aroused her fear. She tugged at her restraints as another possibility came to mind…

…and when she heard another rather loud noise followed by another lesser one coming from downstairs that fear grew worse. It sounded like a door had been kicked open.

She bucked madly in the unyielding bonds, fighting desperately, but again to no avail.

The footsteps she heard on the lower level triggered a terrifying déjà vu for her…

…that horrible night of November 22nd, 1989, when she lay in bed at her Princeton apartment, bound and gagged and waiting for her chief tormentor to return for her…

When the footsteps grew louder, coming up the steps and nearing the bedroom and the enclave in which she lay completely helpless, she realized the futility of fighting anymore.

Unsure of what to do, Kim fell silent and still.

Maybe he won't know I'm here if I keep quiet, but…what if the house is on fire already? What if-

She held her breath as the footsteps came closer…

…and closer…

…and closer. Her heart was pounding as she heard the intruder stop at the doorway…

Chapter 12

"What in the hell was that flash?"

John and the rest of the group had parked the cars a few doors up from Jack's place and were about to take their positions when they saw it.

"I don't know, Sir, but we're gonna find out. Captain Stratton, if you and Warden Steele would circle around the left side of the house, Derek and Dawn will take the right side and you can link up in back. Be careful- I wouldn't be a bit surprised if that was a gunshot."

The four acknowledged, Tom formulated a quick plan of attack and they took off.

Herb turned to John and Mel. With the distinct possibility of Kim being held inside, he knew better than to ask John to stay put, which definitely would not happen. Besides, the man had proven that he could put his .45 to good use if he had to. "Sir, Mel and I will breach the door and go in. Stay behind us and don't come inside until we give the signal."

"Ok. Let's do it."

Herb got on one side of the doorway and nodded to Mel, who kicked the door open and charged in. Herb went in right behind him. A small lamp on the ground level where they were provided some light, and there appeared to be a light on upstairs.

On his bodyguard's signal, John went inside, then moved to the steps and stayed close behind Herb to cover him as he went up. He waited near the top of the staircase, crouched and with his .45 at the ready while Herb checked and cleared the rooms. During that time he heard Derek give word that they'd apprehended someone out back.

The big man emerged from the last of the four rooms and gave John the thumbs-up, at which time John clicked off his headset and moved into the doorway of the first room on the left. He pocketed his gun and walked over to the part of the bedroom wall where the conspicuous latch was- the one Jill told him about- hoping he wasn't too late…

* * *

235

"Freeze! Move and we'll shoot!"

Tom and Henry provided cover as Dawn and Derek made a quick check of the yard, looking for anyone else while they moved to a better position to apprehend the man in the tree, who, by his lack of action, showed that he believed what Tom had just told him.

"Now, listen carefully. Drop the rifle, *slowly* come down the rest of the way, and once you're on the ground, put your hands on your head and walk slowly into the open until I tell you to stop. Mess up once and you're a dead man. Move."

Tom watched as the man did exactly as he'd been ordered. He approached the open space between the tree and the house. A few steps later, Tom said, "halt. Get down on your knees, clasp your hands behind your head and stay still."

As soon as the man complied, Dawn and Derek moved over to him and secured him very quickly while their counterparts covered them. "Ok, Captain Stratton. We're good here, and we don't have any other company."

Tom and Henry went to them to get a look at their prisoner.

It was Henry who recognized him first. "What in the hell are *you* doing here?!"

Kim remained perfectly still when she heard the latch on the door go up. An instant later, the burst of light as the small door swung open made her squint and turn away initially.

"Kitten? Are you Ok?"

"*Mmmm!*" Elated, she tugged at her bonds as John entered the room, crawled up next to her and unbuckled the gag.

"It's all right; you're safe now. Hold still so I can get this off you." He quickly got rid of the leather device and tossed it aside.

"I'm so glad to see you, Baby," a very grateful Kim said as John went to work on freeing her. "I heard something after Danni locked me in here. What happened?"

"Someone did us all a favor and killed her. Tom, Warden Steele, Dawn and Derek are out back and we got word that they've captured whoever it was. We saw a flash and as soon as I walked into this room I saw the result of it," he said, glancing back at Danni. "She pulled a fast one on us; she took a page out of Hedges' book and made her apartment look like she'd been murdered in it to cover her tracks, but it looks like she got hers. It stands to reason that the same one who taught Hedges that little trick taught it to her, too...

"Just relax now, Honey. I'll have you free in a minute..."

"If you'll be so kind as to have 'em go easy on me and get these cuffs off, Henry, I'll be glad to tell you," Ben said as he gestured to the bodyguards.

"I think you'd better tell 'em first, Ben, especially since you came with a sniper rifle. John, Kim and their people have been pretty antsy lately with the security situation."

He nodded. "That's a good point."

For the benefit of the security team members, Henry said, "This man is Ben Jacobson; I know him well." He turned to Tom next. "What do you say we get him inside?"

"Sounds good to me. Is it all right to go in yet, Derek?"

"Yes, Sir. They just cleared the upstairs and your brother's untying his wife now; she seems to be fine."

"That's great news! Ok, let's get inside."

"They were going to kill me, John; Danni was looking to get an in with us so she could take me and I wonder if her eventual plan was to kill you. She and Jack originally planned to keep me, but they couldn't pull that off. So, Danni was about to burn the house down, and instead of shooting me, like Jack said, she wanted me to-...I can't even say it." She shuddered as that thought of what would have been her end took root. "Funny how her cruelty ended up helping save my life, isn't it?

"Jill came to see me in the hospital, told me what she knew about the treehouse incident and gave me the key to this place. I had to come here. I know it wasn't the smartest move I ever made and I'm sorry I made you worry, but I had to."

"I know. I probably would have done the same thing. Speaking of Jill, she was worried about you, too; she called your phone and told me all she knew, including this...room he made, and why he made it."

Even if she'd wanted to, there was no chance Kim could have held back her wrenching pain and anger as John worked to release her. "How could he have hidden how abominable he was and how obsessed he was with me?! He was the one who gave those kids the idea to tie me up and keep me in the treehouse, and he was in there with me at one point- remember when I told you I thought someone was?! It was him; he'd planned to take me down from there and keep me in here partly because he was afraid I might have known what was happening! Hedges was burying Joshua Strauss in the yard that day; that's who I saw digging! Weldon even drugged me, which was why I ended up passing out- *damn* him!!

"Then, after Davie and Darren rescued me, he talked my piece of shit stepfather into *selling* me to him!! I couldn't believe it when he told me; he's absolutely disgusting- they both are!! He told me Steven would have come here and-...no, I won't say it, it's so revolting, and it's probably true! All that religious bullshit he fed my mother and me; I'm not a *bit* surprised he would-...that hypocritical *pig*!"

John knew what she was getting at and she was right; there was no need to elaborate. Instead, he waited for her to go on.

"It just kept getting worse, the more Jack told me. I still can hardly believe it. His plan was to keep me locked up in this little cell, which is the same thing his son did to me! If Diane hadn't adopted me when she did, I would have been sold to the very man I looked up to ever since I was little! I trusted him, and if it wasn't bad enough that he almost ended up enslaving me, he almost had me killed without thinking twice!

"But worst of all, he killed your father, John; he told me he did! When I saw him digging in his yard that day in January 1975, he was burying his body! It made me sick to hear him say that and he was so matter-of-fact about it, even though he called your father his best friend...*God*, how I hate him!! He has the diary, too- the real one! I read part of it and there's so much more to it than the one we found, but he took it! We have to get the police after him. I know where he's going, but I don't know where the place is, though, dammit..."

Once he'd freed her, which was much easier to do this time as opposed to last, he pulled her against him. Tears of relief came pouring out of her as he rubbed her shoulders.

"Thank God you all came. Baby, please get me out of this place; I want to go home."

"I'm with you there. We'll be leaving shortly. Now, you say you know where he's going?"

"I'm pretty sure; he said it's a place where his son-Christopher Hedges, no less- and I had some fond memories...*augh*!! It burns me up just thinking about it! Remember when we wondered who his father could be and I said I wouldn't be surprised if it was Satan? Well, evidently I wasn't far off the mark!"

"I agree completely. That sure answers a lot of questions we had, doesn't it? Doctor Hughes found the sperm sample from Hedges; I have her matching that against Jack's DNA, but I guess we already know what the result will be. What did he mean, though, when he said what he did about the place you think he's headed for?"

"Oh- the only places Hedges had me, which I'm sure is what his father implied, were the house outside Philadelphia, the apartment we shared and the cabin I told you about where he kept me in '89. I can't imagine he meant the place in Philly and the same goes for the old apartment. That leaves the place not far from I-81; I wish I could tell you where it was."

"Jack Weldon is Hedges' father...I'll be damned. He will be, too- literally- once word about everything he's done gets out..."

...that is, if we let the word get out. Right now, no one knows, other than us...

...all the damage he's done- to my family and to my wife. There can be no question of his guilt. He will pay. The only questions are, to what degree and by whose hand?

I know I'd love to empty Dad's .45 right into that black heart of his- there could be no more appropriate ending than that...

"I know, and I'm glad," Kim replied as she cuddled closer to him. "Soon the whole country will know what a monster he is. The only thing he seemed to regret was that he'd been found out; he said 'no one ever had to know, but my son couldn't let it lie'. He also said he was going to kill Hedges if he found him, which he wasn't sure he'd be able to do. You've tried and so has the FBI, but no one can seem to unearth him. This is so *frustrating*!"

He touched her chin and turned her head upward so she faced him. "It was, until last night. We already found that place, if it's the same one. We visited there and came across an old friend-none other than our boy Hedges."

Kim backed away and grasped his arms. "You found him?! What did you do?" He didn't respond verbally, but she caught his meaning clearly. "I'm not surprised it ended that way. It was you who killed him, wasn't it?"

He nodded. "Although he deserved it, I didn't go there with the sole intention of killing him. It was his decision- the way he wanted it. I won't tell you I'm sorry it turned out like that, but there was no way he'd have let us take him alive so I did what I had to do."

"I believe you. Did you find Vanessa?" she asked, in a voice that reflected her hope for good news that was intermingled with her feeling that, in this case, she wouldn't get any.

He nodded slowly. "He killed her, Honey. I'm sorry."

Kim let him pull her against him again as the emotional roller coaster she was on took yet another downward turn, this time because of the fate of her very close friend. "I knew it; I knew that was how it would end up for her. He never did like her, probably because she recognized him for the twisted, evil bastard he was...she was a good person and no one had better *dare* say she wasn't!"

"I sure wouldn't say otherwise, especially after all she did for you." He had a thought right after that. "You know, it might be a good idea for you to call her parents or relatives pretty soon and let them know what happened. I'm sure they'd much rather hear such news from someone who was close to her as opposed to hearing it on TV or the radio."

That helped calm her down. "You're right; I'm glad you thought of that. I'll call her mother as soon as I can. So, how did you end up finding that place?"

He explained it to her, after which she said, "I can't say I'm happy about the reason. Why on *earth* would Jenny want to see him?! She was petrified of him when he had us; I don't understand her at all! I mean, wanting some excitement in your life is one thing, but...well, I'm just glad we dropped by her apartment when we did."

"So am I. You saved Jenny with that impulse you had to look at the card; she was right on the verge of moving in with him. Another month and we'd have lost her. We wouldn't have bagged Hedges, either, and now we just might know where ol' Jack's going. He's in for a big surprise if that's where he's off to..."

They turned when Herb came into the room. "Let's go downstairs, Sir. There's someone your brother wants us to meet."

"Ok, we're coming, Herb." John helped Kim to her feet but noticed she was a bit unsteady. "Still woozy?"

"Yes, but only because our friend lying on the floor knocked me out earlier before she put me in that sweatbox and shackled me down."

John lifted her into his arms, carried her out of the room and downstairs, preceded by Herb. She turned in toward John when he sat down. Having ridden in his arms, she ended up in his lap. She didn't waste a second before voicing her appreciation to the others. "Thank you all so much for-" She fell silent immediately, astonished when she saw the man with Tom, Henry Steele and their security contingent.

"Hello, Kimberly."

"Mister Jacobson?! What-…what are *you* doing here?"

Ben smiled at her bewilderment. "Lending assistance to a lovely maiden who was in peril." He still saw the confusion all over her face. "Actually, the primary reason why I came here tonight had little to do with you, but when I saw you, my main purpose changed completely. I never would harm the one who cared so much about my Jenny, nor would I allow anyone else to harm you. You were the most positive influence in her life; actually, it could be said that you were the only consistent positive in her life. The fact that her father wasn't much of one really hindered her- and still does, I'm afraid, based on some of the decisions she's made. You were right about me. Alcoholism all but destroyed me and it took a heavy toll on my daughter, but I was too selfish to even see that, let alone do anything about it. As a result, Jenny suffered and it's my fault. If it wasn't for you trying to help her I don't know what would have become of her.

"She called me just today and told me all that happened, including the talk your husband and brother-in-law had with Henry, which was my reason for coming. I came here to have it out with Jack; with everything coming to light, he has a lot to answer for.

"I got here a little after sunset and found a good vantage point in the treehouse overlooking this room. That was when I saw you sitting on the bed. I didn't know what the situation was- when they'd be coming back or what you were doing, so I waited. It's good I did because when I decided I might try to go inside and get you out of there, that's about when they showed up. I stayed put, hoping I'd get a chance. I had a hunch that time was at a premium and at that point I wanted to help you any way I could.

"I saw movement through the window and quickly found out that you had company; the next thing I knew, you were knocked out. Detective Searles, who supposedly was dead, must have come in from the front. I never even saw her, but she gave me my first break when she didn't close the curtain. Needless to say, if I had any lingering doubts as to who ultimately was behind the attempt on your life, right then those doubts disappeared. That made me want to kill Weldon all the more and I hoped to get a shot at him, which I never did. After a while I heard his car leaving but there was no way I was about to leave you there, at the mercy of a woman who'd tried to kill me and probably had no compunction about killing you.

"I couldn't get a clear look for some time after she knocked you out, but when the opportunity came I positioned myself for a shot. I had to be certain I'd kill her and I knew the best chance I had to do that was the way I did it. I couldn't have come inside; I know she'd have gotten the drop on me. She made her final mistake by lingering just long enough in front of the window. In her last moment she sensed what was coming and knew she'd screwed up. That was it."

Kim got up from John's lap and walked over to him. "Herb, would you take the cuffs off him, please?" She embraced Ben and kissed his cheek. "Thank you so much, Mister Jacobson."

John followed Kim. "I second that. We've had our differences but it seems to me there's a good chance we all were deceived in that process. All the same, I'm glad you were here, too, Mister Jacobson. I owe you one hell of a debt." he said, extending his hand.

As Ben shook it he said, "no, you don't, John. You've done right by Jenny; she told me everything. I thank you as well."

"I'm glad I could help. If you don't mind me asking, where have you been?"

"Mainly in the bottle. Otherwise, just here and there, trying to forget everything. It didn't work very well."

"It never does. You can't run away from your troubles; they always catch up with you, which you know as well as anyone, I imagine. So, Jenny told you everything?"

"Yes. From what I gathered, because of you there's one less vermin in the world."

"Well, I guess you also know we have a lot of new information, too- just about every question we had before is answered, thanks in large part to Kim. We know the identity of Dad's killer, Tom. We also know where our father's buried."

"That's what Jack was doing when you saw him digging in his yard that winter, wasn't it, Kim?" Tom asked as he turned to her.

"I'm afraid so. Plus, he told me he's Hedges' father and he made off with your Dad's real diary along with a bunch of pictures of me that he took while he was stalking me. He also has a copy of that video his son made of me while he had me a few years ago."

It was on everyone's mind and where all the talk eventually would end up. John was the one who put it out into the open. "So the question is, what do we do about Weldon now?"

Tom didn't hesitate; all he'd learned made the solution clear. "Easy answer: we should do to him what we did to his son, particularly if he puts up a fight."

Henry wasn't paying attention the first time it was mentioned. Seeing so much of Kim's remarkable body, compliments of that sexy bikini, almost was too much for him. He never saw any women at the Pen and didn't see many of them otherwise, especially none so drop-dead gorgeous. He felt guilty eyeing up the wife of his mentor's son, but in spite of his inability to stop himself from stealing a few glances at her he made certain not to let on that he was checking her out after learning that another old man's obsession with her had put her in danger once more. Although she probably was quite a distraction for nearly everyone there, if they were looking like he was, they also did well not to be obvious about it. Nevertheless, this time he got past the distraction and what was said registered. "Jack's *son*? He never had a son..." Henry's comment was ignored for a moment.

"Do we know where he's going?"

"I bet he's headed for the place we burned down last night."

"Wait a minute- you did *what*?! Look, one of you boys needs to tell me what's-"

Tom explained. "Christopher Hedges was his son, Mister Henry. We all knew him better as Joshua Strauss, whose identity Hedges stole. Kim and John figured him out. I'll explain everything when we're on the way. For now, what do you say about Jack?"

Henry looked around the room for a moment. "This is starting to feel like how it was with your father and our small group thirty years ago. Strange how we're deciding the fate of a man who used to be one of us- stranger still that we're deciding that in his own house. Believe it or not, it was in this place- in this room where we would meet and decide what we'd do about the criminals we dealt with. After Novak, we always came here…a lot of memories. The fates of scores of people were decided- not just of those we killed, but of those whose lives were saved as a result of what we did. We avenged plenty of victims of rape and murder, too.

"You know what my only regret was? That we couldn't go to every one of those victims and their loved ones and tell them that they'd been avenged. We couldn't give them closure," he looked John in the eyes, "but you were able to do that, John. You gave Ben's daughter closure and you also gave it to your wife. It was your decision to go after him, wasn't it?"

He wasn't surprised in the least when John nodded. "I'd have done the same thing, and so would your Dad. That bastard's the one who kidnapped all those women; no one else could have caught him, but you wouldn't give up, would you? You had to track him down and make him pay, which you did. Tom, Sr. would be proud, and now we can get to the root of all that evil; we can settle this once and for all.

"I always knew Tommy had a lot of your father in him. The more time passed I began to see a lot of him in you, too, and now…you're every bit like he was. I'm starting to wonder if his soul left his body and entered yours. I always thought how ironic it was that you were born the day before he turned forty. Your birthdays were so close together, yet for the longest time you couldn't have been further apart, or more different- so you thought. Some of us knew better all along; we knew you were one and the same, which certainly can cause friction. With you two, it was like trying to force the same polar ends of two magnets together, which doesn't work. Finally, I guess you see it, too, Johnny. You did exactly what he would have done."

Henry walked toward the kitchen. "I owe you an answer, Tommy, and here it is: like Ben, I say Jack needs to pay for what he did. You boys lost your father to him and John almost lost his wife to him. I'm on board with whatever you decide."

"I want in, too."

244

Tom stared warily at Ben for a moment…

…then again, he certainly has reason…

"I also lost a lot because of him. I want him to explain to me why he lied. That was my primary reason for coming here today; I was going to get the drop on him, put a bullet in him and make him tell me why he tried to ruin me. And yes- he did lie. Your mother and I did not have an affair and we didn't have sex that one night, either. I admit I was attracted to her- Judy was a beautiful woman- but your father was my friend. I respected both of them too much to do something like that. Weldon owes me answers and I want 'em, so I hope you'll count me in on whatever you decide to do."

Tom's internal deliberation didn't last long. He felt pressed for time anyway, so he gave his verdict. "Ok, you're in, too, Mister Jacobson. I also want to hear his side of that. He does have a lot to answer for, but we have to go before he slips away. John, Kim, you don't have to be in on this if you don't want to be; I know we'd all understand. Come to think of it, it would be better if you weren't. Too many of us being there wouldn't be a good idea."

"No, Tom," Kim answered. "I want closure, too, but I want you all to promise me that you'll only kill him if you have to. We know he'll get his in court. His son might have had a chance for some lawyer to dig him out of his hole but Weldon has no chance. Once we get the police here and have them dig up his yard, he's finished."

"I agree with you, but even as fitting an end as that would be, we can't call the police. There's no way. John's already killed Hedges, which is something that must not leave this group. I understand your point and normally I'd want to do it that way, too, but unless something changes, it's not an option. If he's going to the cabin, he'll probably know what happened as soon as he gets there, and there's always the chance that someone else was there and called the local police. I do not want my brother's future compromised by what he rightfully did to that piece of shit."

He turned to John. "This is the right way, Brother, even though I have no doubt you want to be in on what we do. You have more important matters ahead of you, and Herb and the team need all the rest they can get. Plus, they have to do the work to augment your team, which I know you all want to make happen as soon as you can.

"Most importantly, you and Kim need to be together and alone in your home. Kim, you've been through yet another ordeal and I think it's best that you sit this one out. It might get ugly. You know I'm not implying that you can't handle it; I just think this is best."

"He's right, Honey," John said. "I'm with you in wanting closure but I also know we'll get it. Our team does need rest and frankly, so do I. It looks like you could use some, too, especially since you've been banged up over the past couple days, so let's go home. Tom will let us know what happens."

Kim assented and the group said their good-byes.

Just before they separated to go to their cars, Tom thought of something and pulled John aside once more.

"Give me your gun, John."

"My gun? Why?"

"Because one way or another, it just might end up serving the main purpose for which you've kept it all these years."

"Tell me how," he said, handing their father's .45 to Tom.

"After I take off, you need to call the police and get 'em over here. This is what I want you and Kim to say to them..."

Once he'd made sure that Kim was in the car and surrounded by Mel, Dawn and Derek, Herb waited for John to finish talking with his brother. After just a couple minutes, they parted and John came over.

"All set?" Herb asked, opening the car door.

"Yeah." John hesitated a moment before climbing in. "I noticed the way you looked at Mr. Jacobson a few times. What were you thinking about?"

"I thought I'd seen him somewhere before, but the more you all talked and the more he revealed, I think I must have mistaken him for someone else. I don't know- one of those weird déjà vu kind of things that hit you, some of which turn out to be false alarms...

"Anyway, I'm sure you and Kim want to get home, so what do you say we hit it?"

"How are you feeling, Kitten?"

"Oh, I'm fine now. I meant to tell you, as he released me from the hospital the doctor said all my readings were perfectly normal and that it almost wasn't even a *mild* concussion.

Finally, after they were finished giving all the information to the police, who mercifully didn't keep them for very long, they were on the way home. As they rode south on I-97 toward the Bridge a great sense of relief was settling in for Kim, which she voiced in her response to John as she relaxed in his lap. "As for the big picture, which is probably what you meant, I feel the same way. It's really over now. Tom was right when he said we should concentrate on each other; I'm glad we didn't go with them. I never would have expected Jack to turn out like he did, but at this point I think we can say with certainty that the circle is complete- at least, that one is."

"Yeah, it sure is," John replied as he stared straight ahead.

He'd managed to keep himself in check as he and Kim talked with the police, but now, while they were alone, it started. "I guess it's safe to say we…won't be seeing him anymore."

Before he even realized he was crying, he became aware that Kim was soothing him. When the anger came, it hit him hard. "That mother*fucker*!!! He was Dad's best friend- they knew each other since they were *kids*!! How in the hell could he *do* that to him?!! All this time- the days, the months, the *years* we waited and hoped; he was right there with us and the son of a bitch *knew*!! He had my father buried in his fucking yard while he was consoling us and telling us to be strong while he tried to move in on my mother…Christ, I can't believe this…and if that wasn't bad enough, there was everything he did to you…"

Kim kissed him and waited until he started to cool down before she talked. "We've said it before- there are some horrible people out there. I know how much you're hurting but I also know that you and I are much stronger than to let the Jack Weldons in this world bring us down."

"All along I wanted to know; I kept wishing that we'd find out what happened. Now I know why they say be careful what you wish for. I don't think the truth could have been any more brutal."

"Well, you can take away one positive; you won't have to wonder anymore. We never thought you'd be able to make peace, but now you can. That's not to say it will stop hurting completely- at least, not any time soon- but it'll hurt less over time. You'll get past this; everything will be all right."

247

Eventually, he wiped at his eyes and sat up. When he turned to Kim, she smiled tenderly and kissed him.

He returned her smile, then told her what had just come to him. "That's not the only positive. It's clear to me now, what it meant- my dream, the one I had the day you and I met. What Dad said then and you said just now sums it up: everything *will* be all right. I agree completely with both of you. You know what else? It's only that way because we're together. I know I've already said this but I'll say it again: the truth never would have come out if not for you. I'm just sorry you had to be so…involved in all of it."

"I'm not. I wouldn't have missed this. The good you and I have outweighs the bad by so much that it breaks the scale. Out of all the men who've played vital roles in my life- or *any* role, for that matter- you're the only one who never betrayed me and I know you never would. Well, there was Billy Drake, too, even if only briefly."

"He did look out for you, though. Imagine if he'd have been one of the shady characters we usually associate with those clubs."

"I know. He certainly could have done a lot of damage, couldn't he? To take your point further, it would have been so easy at any point between thirteen and now for me to believe that Jack, his son, Danni and a lot of others were right in that everyone looks at me as nothing more than a sex object or a trophy.

"That really could have brought me down if I'd allowed it to, like I nearly did many times in the past. Even now, sometimes I have to remind myself that they're wrong, like Billy told me on a few occasions and you, our family and our friends let me know so often in so many ways. As we know very well, there are times when those outside our circle try to drag me down in that way. It doesn't get to me as much as before and it doesn't happen as often as before, but sometimes it still hurts.

"In spite of all the negativity I do have to admit, there still is a part of me that enjoys the spotlight and probably- to an extent- always will since I'm past the point where it can do any real harm to me. My flashy, vain side seems to be less prevalent now- at least, in public. I guess I've grown up a little in that way."

"Not just in that way," he added with a smile.

She cooed appreciatively. "I'm sure you realize Aphrodite isn't dead by any means; you have seen- and will continue to see- *plenty* of her." Kim followed her words up by giving him yet another taste of that side of her that she knew he loved, along with

248

the rest of her. With the inevitability of what lay ahead when they got home and their ever-increasing mutual hunger for it, it was becoming more difficult by the second for them to hold back.

"You came for me again, Baby. Things weren't looking good just before you did; it was a lot like the last time that happened to me. I was just thinking about that night...I wish I could put into words how safe and how loved I felt when you were there with me, holding me. And then, when you touched me, how electrified I felt- even though I was in that cage, all chained up when you came...if it was possible for me to combust, I would have. You helped me forget, even if just for a moment, about the danger we were in.

"That was a defining moment for me, emotionally and sexually, combined with what we did in the van after it all was over and we were safe. Another circle had been completed; his hold over me in that regard and every other was broken. I knew I never again would allow any sleazeball like him to dictate what I did, how I felt and what I liked! For the most part, those terrifying moments with him were whisked away, almost just like that.

"It was absolutely mystical- magical. It still is, John. Whenever you tie me up and dominate me, it happens again; I think of all the moments we've had and how amazing they've been for both of us. In spite of the negatives, that hasn't lost its appeal in the least. I know it has the same effect on you, too."

She shifted in his lap and tightened her embrace on him. "Mmmm...in fact, just thinking about our episodes is making me *really* horny, which right now is not good, so I'd better stop!" John cracked up and she laughed with him. "I'm just awful..."

"In a good way, though."

"You're supposed to disagree with me!" She gave him a soft, playful jab into his chest. "You know, the way I feel right now makes me believe that nothing Jack revealed to me will have any ill effect whatsoever. I mean, how could I look at anything negatively, considering how great things are for us? Add in my benefactors who helped make sure that his twisted plans for me were ruined: Davie and Darren when they rescued me from the treehouse, and my Mom when we met and became close friends before she adopted me, preventing my enslavement contract to go through. And then, you came for me- tonight and three years ago." She cuddled closer and kissed his neck.

He didn't doubt the sincerity of what she was telling him, but all the same John began to wonder if, for some reason, she was belaboring this point...or perhaps holding something back. "I'm glad you're able to rise above all that. For now I think we should concentrate on the positives, and the future. What do you say?"

She smiled yet again. "I like the sound of that," she said as she planted another hot kiss on him. Kim had to make a conscious effort not to get carried away and she knew he was doing the same as they pulled out of that one.

Then, with a sigh, she pondered a bit more. "I will say this, though; it's funny- and definitely ironic- that what should have been one of the most frightening events of my life ended up turning me on to some incredible sex with the man I love. Ignorance truly was bliss, in this case..."

Something else was on her mind, too. "As much as I hate to say this, in a way Danni might have been right when she said I enjoyed the excitement. Maybe the danger even turns me on a little, I don't know. I mean, I didn't want to be caught- she was wrong about that- but...if I hadn't been so affected by all I discovered in Jack's house, I probably would have gathered it together and gotten out of there almost right away. I'd love to have been able to call you and Tom and tell you everything I knew so we could have set a trap for him, which is how I did want that situation to turn out. All things considered, it wasn't a good move to not call you right away after all Jill told me, but I wanted to help. I was so angry and hurt, and I wanted to get him.

"Remember, in his office the other day, when he said that I should have become a detective? I'm not so sure I agree with that, considering how I let them get the drop on me, then found myself tied up and locked inside a closet after having been knocked out. That certainly wasn't the outcome I had in mind. I might have made a good investigator at some point, but as for the detective work, I think I'll leave it to the professionals. I've gotten myself into enough trouble."

"You sure have, and you're not out of it yet."

"Really?" She caught his meaning, and that only served to heighten her already-raging libido.

"Definitely. It looks like I was right before; I just might have to keep you under lock and key after all in order to tame this adventurous streak of yours...but then again, I don't know if that would bring about the desired end. I recall warning you that there would be repercussions if you ever put yourself in such a situation again, but even the threat of *not* punishing you hasn't worked!"

They shared a laugh, but it wasn't a long one, or a hearty one. The gravity of Kim's latest close call was omnipresent.

She tried to keep the tone reasonably light, if only for a while longer- until they made it home, which was why she held back and didn't give him the kiss that was burning on her lips: the one that most likely would lead to much more.

"I don't know, Baby, maybe I'm making more of this than there is. Maybe it was just a last attempt to do something exciting. I'm sure my perspective will change in a big way when we have children...*if* we have children."

"I'm not so sure about this being some sort of whim. We both know that adventurous is something you've always been; it's in your blood. Maybe this episode itself was an isolated one, but we still should find you another outlet of some sort. Our bedroom play seems to help a good bit, but even when we have children- and I do mean when- you might need something else to keep you out of trouble, like you pointed out. Your adventuresome streak isn't something that will just go away. We just have to find something a little less perilous that still will satisfy you in that way, and we will. I want you to be safe, but just as importantly I want you to be happy."

Her appreciation was deep, and immediate. "Do you know how much I love you?" Unable to hold the kiss back any longer, she laid it on him and the coals were stoked even more. "This sure has been an eventful couple days. Believe me when I say I'm glad they're over and that things ended up the way they have.

"Like you said, we should focus on the positives and the future, which is exactly what I intend to do. As for the present and all we've learned, since I really feel closure, that will help further diminish the negatives brought on by the gruesome twosome and the little toady: Jack, his son and Walter Daniels. However," she said, cuddling closer to him, "the best therapy of all will come when we get home- if we ever *get* home."

She looked out the window when they slowed for the toll plaza. "We're only at the Bridge?!" Kim whined. "I thought you said you told Mel to drive *fast*! This is torture! It must be the longest ride home we've ever had!"

"*Shhh*!! Damn, Honey, go easy on the guy!" John couldn't stop himself from laughing as he admonished his barely dressed and particularly amorous wife. He could tell by the way she kept shifting around in his lap that she was right on the brink. "A little patience goes-"

"Oh, shush *me*, will you?! As for patience, if there's anyone in this world who knows there are times when that is not a virtue I possess in certain situations, it's you!" she playfully retorted.

Try as she did, Kim was failing in her effort to keep the mood light. She couldn't stop reflecting on all she faced, all that had happened and her craving for the release she needed badly.

The current flowing through her kept gathering momentum-the one that started immediately when John opened the door of her tiny, stuffy cell...

...which so easily could have been her tomb. She couldn't shake the thought of how close she'd come to never again being able to do what was coming, let alone to relish the feeling of being in John's arms- her favorite place in the world.

Finally, realizing it was an exercise in futility, Kim gave up in her effort to restrain herself and the torrent of passion rushed out of her.

John saw it coming, from shortly into their drive until just before Kim lost control, and he'd quickly figured out where it was coming from. He was just as appreciative of how everything had turned out, and of how fortunate he and Kim had been once again.

He wished they were twenty feet away from home rather than twenty minutes as he made sure the radio was just loud enough...

Tom was pushing his car as hard as he could in the other direction. He had his dash light up and flashing, and the accelerator was buried along with the needle on the speedometer.

He didn't say a word the whole way; there really was no need for talk since all three men knew the score and were in agreement as to what the outcome would be, although Tom hadn't sprung his plan on them yet. He'd decided to wait until they were almost there.

The only real question was, would he be there?

By all indications, that was his destination.

If that was the case, how would he react when he saw it? Would he take off?

That possibility prompted Tom to try to go faster still.

* * *

"Son of a bitch…"

It couldn't have been more than a couple days since it happened. What was left of the place still was smoldering, and it wasn't much more than its frame and foundation.

Jack sat on an old bench that was in the front yard, wondering what it was that had caused his place to burn down.

He also did something that he was growing more and more weary of- contemplating what to do next. Going back to the home he'd had since the early '50s no longer was an option, since by now what had happened here undoubtedly was happening there. Back at his home, the firemen most certainly were responding to the call, whereas here it didn't look like they'd come at all. With no nearby hydrants, there was little they could have done, anyway. The fire went unchecked and rendered his place a total loss.

The last thing he wanted- the task of having to rebuild or find another place- stared him in the face.

In a way, it was fitting. Much of what he had and what he knew was gone. His son, whose whereabouts still were unknown to Jack or anyone, seemed intent on destroying him and the families of everyone else involved in the killings so many years ago- the killings he and the others had kept a lid on for so long. It stood to reason that John and Kim were his ultimate targets, and Chris probably didn't care who else he destroyed in the process.

The funny thing was, three years ago he had both his targets and still screwed it up.

As much as I hated to, I took care of part of your work…

…and that's something else I'll never forgive myself for. I let this thing destroy me and everyone around me.

I should have just killed that son I wish I'd never had, like my instincts told me to, and then turned the gun on myself. Everyone would have been better off…

As he waited for Danni, it really started to settle in.

Jack was tired. Tired of bearing the secrets, tired of the guilt over Tom, Sr. and the others, tired of the state of decay he was in- tired of everything. Worse yet, the whole reason for everything- the justification- seemed to be losing importance and relevance for him. The secret was intact- for now-, but all things considered, it just didn't seem to matter very much anymore.

253

Many a day had passed- especially recently- on which he wished he was the one in the ground. That feeling was particularly strong as he sat there, waiting.

There was no question about what it was he was waiting for.

At that moment, he was shaken out of his ruminations by the sound of tires crunching gravel and dirt. He turned, saw the headlights of an approaching car and stood to greet Danni.

However, there were three people in the car, which was not Danni's. This one belonged to the son of his best friend, who Jack killed almost thirty years ago.

When Tom, Jr., Henry Steele and Ben Jacobson stepped out of the car, Jack's first feeling was one of relief; he actually smiled for a moment. There could be no question that it was over.

Even if he'd brought a gun he wouldn't have drawn it.

The time of reckoning was at hand.

Tom didn't waste a second. "As you've probably figured out, Detective Searles won't be joining you. If anything, she's probably joined your son, whose remains- if there are any- are in those ruins behind you."

Jack nodded and lowered his head. "Is Kimberly all right?"

"She's fine, contrary to your intentions. Strange you should even ask me that. After all you did to her, you have your hired gun try to kill her and now you ask if she's all right."

"I agree with you; it is strange. I always was fond of her-you couldn't help feeling that way about her. From the earliest age she always was a delightful girl, but the more she matured, the more I saw the woman she'd become emerging. Everyone who looked at her saw it, especially those who knew her. I wanted her and I took some extreme measures to have her but she eluded me for various reasons. That's just part of the story, though.

"Things got...twisted along the way. I don't think I could give you a full explanation of why I did what I did to her if I tried. Nothing makes much sense anymore and to tell you the truth, when it comes to myself, I've stopped caring." He looked back up. "So Chris is dead? How did you figure out he was my son?"

"We didn't know until you told Kim, but given your ownership of this place, we'd have figured it out that way, too. Plus, the FBI has a sperm sample from him, which they're

254

checking against your DNA for paternity. We already know what the finding will be.

"And yes- fortunately, he's dead. He overdosed on .45 slugs. It was a long time coming but better late than never."

"It should have been a lot sooner; I never should have let him escape his teens."

Tom momentarily was unable to respond. *I just told him his son is dead and that's how he reacts?!* "We didn't know you at all, did we, Mister Jack? You don't care that your own son is dead. Furthermore, you imply that *you* should have killed him…I want to hear about that. I want answers from you about a lot of things, but first tell me about Christopher Hedges."

"He was born on October 29th, 1956- the anniversary of Black Tuesday, the stock market crash of 1929. That was a bad sign in itself and very appropriate. He was no good- that much I knew. I never had anything to do with him or with his mother after I knocked her up. It was a mistake- a stupid mistake that I should have corrected. I was drunk, she was there and that was it.

"In '72 she was about to make things hard on me- she demanded more money or else she'd tell the world who the father of her second son was, which was the last thing I wanted. My ex would have loved that and used it to drain more money out of me herself. That was the situation the day I decided I'd end my problems with her once and for all- Chris's sixteenth birthday, by chance. The older son, Ralph Wancowicz, already was in the ground as a result of your father's first foray into the administration of true justice, so I figured I'd ship the remaining members of that family off to the underworld myself.

"I should have stuck with my plan in its entirety. Things sure would have been different in that case…"

October 29, 1972

Jack had picked the perfect night and the perfect time. She was on the couch, passed out, probably from drinking. The TV was on, and pretty loud. He didn't even have to break in; apparently she'd forgotten to lock the door.

He walked right up to her and drew his pistol.

"There's a right way and a wrong way to do things, Sally. In this case, you picked the wrong way. Now, you get no alimony." He fired a single shot right through her forehead.

She jerked a little and was still again.

He heard a noise behind him, whirled around and drew a bead on his son.

The two locked eyes.

Much to his surprise, the expression of shock on the boy's face faded quickly.

His first thought was not that of pulling the trigger, like he'd intended.

Instead, given what he noticed, he wanted to know where the kid stood- to test him. "How do you feel about this, Chris?"

Jack saw a look of disdain take over and he began to smile.

Chris shrugged. "She was a pain in the ass. Always bitching about something, always trying to intrude in my life because she doesn't have one of her own. Fat, disgusting pig- just ate and ate and ate, and watched TV all the time. She always ranted about you, too- 'your father' this and 'your father' that...she never told me who you were, though."

He turned to Jack. "Are you gonna kill me, too?"

Jack stared at him for a long moment.

His own mother had been murdered right in front of his eyes and he'd barely flinched.

There aren't many people like you and me around; you're my son in more ways than one, aren't you?

For that reason, I'd better keep you at arm's length...

"You're not well thought of around here, and for good reason. I see certain...gifts in you. You're bored, aren't you?"

Chris's eyes narrowed. "How do you know?"

"It's written all over you. Highly intelligent but rebellious, cold and cruel. You don't like things as they are, so you're lashing out. Tom Stratton, Sr. told me what you did recently- how you peeped at his wife, then threw a rock at his cat." A mask of hatred descended upon his face as soon as Jack mentioned that name. "You know, I might have use for you, if you're interested."

This time it was Chris who took a moment to respond. He shrugged again. "Whatever you have in mind, it can't be any worse than my existence so far."

Jack nodded. "All right. Understand this- your life as you know it is over. To the rest of the world, you *will* be dead, along with your mother." With that he put away his gun.

"Come on, Son- we have work to do..."

"…so, we made it look like both of them had been shot and killed. When he told me they had the same blood type, that made the job a lot easier. There was no DNA back then, of course, so the blood typing was all we needed. We put her in his bed for a bit and let a good bit of her blood run out so it would look like the same thing happened to him. Then, we dragged her out twice for further evidence that both of them had been murdered. It worked like a charm. Best of all, Henry and Ray Searles investigated the scene and bought off on the appearance, which anyone would have done. Needless to say, the murders never were solved.

"Ironically, I had him stay at the house in the country I'd just acquired that same year. It used to be a nice place until you all burned it down. The really funny thing was, I never even thought to look for him here- never suspected he'd be so brazen as to hide out here. I haven't had cause to come out for years- practically forgot about the place. I expected to find it in a state of disrepair, but not this bad…

"Anyway, that's how it happened- the biggest mistake I ever made. I'd have gotten away with killing Chris, too- who would have suspected me? There was nothing tracing me to him or her. As for Danni, we used the same strategy. I had her drain a pint of her blood, store it and use it when it was time for her to disappear as well."

"John didn't buy that she was dead; he figured she'd pulled the same act Hedges did."

"Ah. Smart boy, Johnny is; he always was. Since he found himself and his confidence he'll make a great President." He looked at Tom and smiled grimly. "To answer the question you posed to me earlier, no, I suppose you didn't know me at all.

"Truthfully, I don't think *I* ever knew me, particularly after we started the killings. That affected us all, needless to say. We had the ultimate power. The more we used it, the less conventional rules applied to us and the less I started to care about everything else. How much further can you go than what we did? After the first two, it got easier- for your father and for us. You can kill dozens of men, hundreds, thousands, millions- at that point, what's the difference?

"And what that does to you…tell me, Tom, what else is there if the most basic, common link you have with others- the value of life- is gone? Regardless of whether they deserve it or not, eventually you grow cold; you become an iceman. It happened to me and it happened to your father although he'd never have admitted it. Same with you, Ben, and you too, Henry. It happened to Danni as well. She killed Harry Lawson without blinking an eye...

"It also could happen to your brother, Tommy. In fact, who's to say it's not happening now? I see it when he talks about the death penalty. His philosophy is your father's; it's the same damned thing. Also like your father, he's killed before. Chances are he'll kill again."

"He might, if he has to. I worry about the effect that will have on him in the future- only a little, though. It would have been different if he was like he was a few years ago, before he and Kim got back together. The killings he was involved in were justified- no one can deny that. Throughout history we've seen that there are those who can handle the task of killing. As long as they keep the right perspective and only dole that punishment out to those who deserve it, they do all of us a great service.

"That's how John sees it; he acted as an exterminator, ridding society of destructive pests. For him, murderers like your son have no humanity to take. John will be all right if he continues to exercise good judgment and doesn't let that power go to his head, which I doubt he will. Along with every other aspect of life, Kim will help him enormously in that one. I could be wrong, of course, but I don't think I am. You pointed it out yourself; John is much stronger and more confident than he ever was."

"So was your father when he was Sheriff."

"Yeah, so I've heard, and so I saw. I don't buy what you say about him turning into an iceman; that couldn't be further from the truth. I can't believe after all you did to him and to us that you'd try to malign him-..." Tom held up his hand. "Enough about my father and my brother. John will be fine and so will his wife- no thanks to you. You, on the other hand, have to pay for what you've done to my father and my family."

"You're wrong- this *is* about John. Don't you see he's becoming every bit like your father? If I were a betting man, I'd bet everything I had that he will be elected President. What will happen when he does? Will he stay on course, or will he go the way of his father? If the former happens, all will be well except a bunch of rich people will want his head. If the latter happens, who knows what disasters could come?"

"Just because you couldn't handle it doesn't mean John won't be able to, and as I said, you are way off base with your implication that Dad couldn't handle it. More to the point, you have one hell of a nerve even mentioning yourself in the same breath as him or Dad. You shot a defenseless woman while she slept just because she was going to expose you for the pile of shit you are and get money out of you that she deserved, so don't you fucking dare preach to me about character and morals when you don't have a trace of either one!!

"As for John, he'll take care of himself. Along with Kim he'll be much better off knowing that you're gone, which you will be. Furthermore, if you say another word about him, my father or any of my family without me asking you, I promise you this: I'll make your exit from this world as slow and painful as I possibly can." Tom waited for a moment and saw that Jack understood. "Now, I want you to tell me what you did to my father. I also want you to explain why you told him Ben had an affair with my mother."

Jack shifted around and wouldn't look at Tom.

"I'll answer that for you, Tommy," Ben said. "He passed off on me what he was guilty of. Isn't that right, Jack? You're the one who had designs on Judy and you felt guilty about it, but instead of admitting that, you made me your fall guy. You knew nothing was going on between Judy and me other than some mild flirting that neither of us was serious about, but you convinced Tom that there was more to it.

"Then, I was unlucky or careless enough to be in the same bed as she was the night when we both were pretty hammered at that party. You jumped right on it, didn't you? You knew I had a problem with the bottle, you put the bug in Tom's ear about us, and then you had your slam-dunk at our little soiree. You turned him against me, and not long after that I was finished in the police department."

"What did you do after that, Mister Ben?"

"I had to start all over. It took some doing, but by the late '70s I was on the right track- married and doing decently with the firearms business I started with a guy I knew. Then, on June 20th, 1980- when Jenny came into the picture- I became more focused than ever.

"The '80s were very good for me business-wise, but for quite a while, as it turned out, Annie was seeing my partner behind my back. How's that for some irony? She knew the story about what you accused me of, Jack- I told her- and she did it to me, knowing how much it would hurt me. After I finally found her out in '92, I *kicked* her out and she moved right in with him. I made him pay, though- beat the living shit out of him one night. He played me for a Goddamned fool all those years. I bought him out and bade him good riddance.

"The buyout wasn't cheap, though, so I went into debt. Then, business started to fall off a little and things got tight for a while. Jenny and I were on our own, which was hard on her. Things had gotten ugly between her mother and me; she saw and heard things she shouldn't have. A lot of arguments, shouting...no kid wants to see that. Jenny and her mother became estranged, too, mostly because of how bad things became between Annie and me.

"I was glad in a way that Jenny took my side, but I wasn't happy that she had to take a side. Unfortunately I started drinking again and that made it even worse for her. Not long after that my business was ripped out from under me when the bank called in the debt prematurely. It was their right, but it was a shitty thing to do nonetheless. I could have dug myself out, but...well, I guess it just wasn't in the cards."

He frowned when he saw the look on Weldon's face. "Do you know something about that? Wait a minute- did you play a part in it?"

"We took over the note on your business- my son and me. Shut the doors and sold everything. We used aliases so no one would know, especially you." Not a second after the last word left his mouth, Ben's fist struck his jaw and sent him spinning to the ground.

He was about to do more damage but Tom stopped him. "Hold on- not that way. He'll get his, trust me on that. Let him tell us what he knows first."

"If you're going to kill me anyway, why should I tell you what you want to know?" Jack inquired when he stood up shakily.

"One, this is your chance to finally come clean. Two, if you do, you'll have the opportunity to end your own life as opposed to one or all of us doing that for you. What you just got is a very small taste of what at least two of us have in mind for you. We have thirty-plus years worth of bad feelings to unload on you. I'm sure I speak for all of us when I say we have no problem with taking restitution out of your hide. Does that answer your question?"

He nodded and Tom went on. "Good. So I take it you're the one who turned Danni Searles against Ben?"

"Yeah," he said, rubbing his jaw.

"Jack poisoned her against me, just like he turned your father against me. It was a similar situation; who'd have believed the word of an irresponsible drunk who'd hit rock bottom over that of the highly respected Attorney General? You say you don't care anymore, Jack? That's how I was at that point. Danielle came to me and when she accused me I all but threw her out. I said, 'sure- why not blame me? What difference does it make?'...

"...well, she did. She tried to kill me a couple years ago, but she failed. By that time I'd finally crawled out of the bottle, but all the bitterness still was there." After a moment of silence, he said, "why, Jack? What in the hell did I ever do to you to make you want to destroy me at every opportunity you got?"

He didn't answer and kept his head lowered.

"You still owe me one more answer, too," Tom reminded him. Just as he was about to prompt Jack to spill, he spoke again.

"I knew you'd find out eventually, Tommy. In a way, I'm glad you did. It's been hard, hiding it for all these years. What I told you is true; your father always was my best friend. When I killed him, I killed the best part of myself. It's haunted me ever since. At the time I thought it had to be done, but...

"As for you, Ben, I was afraid your drinking problem would loosen your tongue around the wrong people and, whether you intended to or not, you'd bring us all down because of that. I was afraid you'd let the secret out; I saw it as my job to protect it and us. I didn't agree with Tom that we should bring you in. You were good, but you were too young and you had that weakness with liquor. I was looking out for all of us...at least, I thought I was. And yes, Tom, I was fond of your mother. The last thing your father said to me was to make sure you all were taken care of and I did that. I saw to it that none of you ever needed for anything and that you were comfortable."

"That we were comfortable- that's almost funny. Yeah, you sure looked out for us. You saw for yourself my mother's torment from never knowing what happened to her husband- how that kept tearing at her until it finally killed her. *You* killed her, Jack- just like you murdered my father, you're responsible for killing her, too. You could have admitted your sin so at least she'd have known, but you took the coward's way out. You always did, didn't you?"

"I *did* look out for her!! You think you know everything, but you don't! I admit I was guilty of desiring her, even while your father was alive, but I protected her after she-..."

"Don't do it, Jack," Henry said, joining into the conversation. "There's no need to bring that up."

Tom, however, wasn't about to let that go. "After she, what?" More uncomfortable silence. "After she *what*, Jack?!"

Jack turned back to him. "Do you think she didn't know what your father was doing? Do you honestly think a man and a woman who loved each other as much as they did could keep such a secret from the other? She knew, Tommy; she knew everything. Not only that, she tried to help when your father needed it."

"What are you talking about?! Helped him how?!"

"Remember how we talked briefly about Curtis Parker? Well, he was out to get your father in a big way, and-"

"I already told Tommy and Johnny about him. Leave it alone," Henry said.

Jack turned to him. "Well, obviously you didn't tell 'em who killed him, did you?"

Chapter 13

Henry laid into the Attorney General. "You son of a bitch, don't you-"

"What are you talking about, Jack?"

"You said you wanted to know everything, Tom. Well, you wanted it and now you'll get it, like it or not. Think back to the fall of '74- early November, specifically. Do you remember your mother wearing a brace on her knee?"

"You're asking me about a knee brace my mother wore while you're leaving me hanging on who killed Parker?! What kind of sick game are you-"

"This isn't a game!! Do you remember the brace?!"

Tom thought back to that time. "No...I can't say I-"

"You asked her about it, Tommy- does that refresh your memory? You asked her the day she put it on, when I was there- you wanted to know what happened and she told you she had a household accident. Well, it *was* by accident she sprained her knee, but it sure wasn't in the household...at least, not her own."

Tom took hold of his collar. "Enough with this fucking tiptoeing around!! You tell me- *right now*!!!"

"All right, all right! Back off a little, huh?" When the big, angry and very strong man let go of him, he went on. "Judy knew everything and she followed the news. She saw Parker's press conference just before Election Day; he said he was conducting an investigation into certain police activities in Baltimore County. He said he was close to an indictment and we knew who he was after. We were as nervous as we could be- Judy most of all...

"...what she did next showed me what true devotion is. On the night of November 6th, 1974, she went up to Curtis Parker's back door and knocked. He answered and there she was, wearing all black. Apparently, he made some sort of smart remark about the significance of her coming to his back door and asked her if she believed that would stop him from sending her husband to jail. Judy answered him by putting a bullet through his eye."

Tom clearly was staggered; it took a moment before he could recover. When he did he turned to Henry. "Is what he said true?"

Henry nodded and lowered his head.

Tom walked a few feet away. "The report said the suspect was a male who weighed about 150 and wore a size 9 shoe."

"Your mother put forty pounds of Tom, Sr.'s weights into a backpack and wore Johnny's shoes over her own. She put some paper inside them to fill them out. Judy's footprints started and ended at the little creek behind Parker's house. She sprained her knee while picking her way along that creek back to her car."

"Always look out for your family, above all..."

"What's that?"

"She always told us-...never mind. Go on."

"Well, if that's the case, she certainly lived by what she said. She did that for him because she loved him and she also understood why he did what he did- with the killings.

"Anyone close to her knew she abhorred killing and violence in general, but she told me later that she'd accepted his rationale in spite of her feelings. She put herself on the line and compromised everything she believed in to take that sanctimonious, arrogant bottom-feeder Parker out before he could indict your father. She even had the foresight to take all the paperwork he had on Tom, Sr. Parker never told anyone else about what he was doing because he didn't have enough proof, as we found out. He couldn't have accused your father with what little he had, so he was using more scare tactics than anything at that point; shaking the tree to see what would fall. He was close, though- too close.

"Well, just like that, he was gone and no other investigation would come. We burned Parker's files and that was it. The investigators they sent to Parker's place never found any evidence- no one ever was charged and one more shark in a lawyer's suit was out of the picture. Nobody ever thought to consider her- why would they have when there was no reason to? It was perfect...

"...until your father found out on Christmas Eve. He should have been riding high. The Governor-elect recently had told him he was the designee to take over as State Police Superintendent. Parker, the only fly in the ointment, was gone, so he had every reason to be happy. Truth is, he was starting to slide, anyway, which you'll see in his diary. I wasn't kidding about that, Tommy; the situation really was getting to him.

"Then, he found Johnny's shoes that Judy had used the night she killed the archenemy, and the paper she'd used to pack 'em still was in 'em. They were in her trunk; she'd forgotten to throw 'em away, and he saw 'em while getting the Christmas presents out of Judy's trunk. Later she told me she tried to keep it from him but he'd caught her off guard. It was starting to eat at her; it was inevitable that she'd have told him, anyway. A few days later she confessed to him and he blew his stack. They had a fight- a pretty bad one, and-"

"That must be the one John saw."

"It probably was; she said he peeked in afterwards. It was at that moment- with their fight- that everything started to unravel and it happened quickly. The shame of it was we'd already stopped with the killings. The last one Tom deep-sixed was in early September and we were pretty jumpy about doing that guy. He needed to go, no question, but…on the whole, it was time. We'd agreed upon that late in spring. A mistake somewhere along the line was inevitable; frankly, I'm amazed we didn't screw up somewhere. Besides, he knew the Governor was considering him for Super and I was running for Attorney General, so we had to stop, anyway. Then, there was Judy.

"It was hard enough on Tom that she knew about what we'd done, but when she iced Parker, Tom just couldn't handle it. He was in meltdown and…something had to be done."

For the whole time Tom had paid close attention not only to his words, but also to how he said what he did and his tone of voice. Remembering Kim's remarks about Jack's change of mannerisms that day they were in his office, which now seemed to be ages ago even though it was a couple days, Tom already had caught at least one significant discrepancy along with a few inconsistencies. Although it all was academic in terms of the outcome for Jack, Tom wanted to know the truth and he was waiting for the best opportunity to trip Jack up and see how he'd react. If he tried to cover his tracks, well, the end simply would come about quicker.

When he stopped talking, Tom didn't allow him time to regroup. "So you killed him."

"He was contemplating suicide. Would you rather have had him do that? He was sick with himself for what his bond with Judy had driven her to do in order to preserve that bond. She did you boys a great service as well by saving your father from dishonor, but Tom knew what she'd sacrificed- that being her principles, specifically the most vital of them. We talked the day after he'd put away a lot of bourbon and he spilled everything to me. He told me he wanted to kill himself."

265

There it was. His voice went slightly higher when he mentioned suicide. Remembering what Jack had told him about another former cop he'd been friends with, Tom made his feint, which also was for the benefit of the man standing next to him. "Just like Ray Searles did, I guess. Must have been hard on both of 'em, huh?"

"It was the same thing, Tom. I was with Ray that last night. It was hard as hell, but I did what had to be-"

Jack's eyes went wide. Tom and Ben looked at each other, then back at Jack. Ben spoke up. "Funny, Jack- I thought you blamed me for his suicide."

Jack knew he'd been caught. He didn't respond to Ben.

Then it was Tom's turn. "When we were in your office, you told us that you wished you'd been there with him and now I find out you *were* there. You said it only was a matter of time before he killed himself, but that wasn't the case, was it? You sped up the process, didn't you? You were afraid his guilty conscience would become too much and that he'd crack and reveal what you all had done. That's when you stepped in, right?"

Again, no response. He just stared at his feet.

"Then you told John, Kim and me that my parents were going through a rocky point in their relationship and that Ben exploited that. Tonight you've made no mention of it, even though that came across as a primary motive as to why you stabbed him in the back. Why would you not mention that now? Because it was a lie, wasn't it?"

He moved in close to him again. "How much of what you've told me is bullshit, Jack? Or, don't you even know anymore? Have you told yourself so many times that the lie was the truth until you believed it, or are you just slipping in your old age?"

He shifted gears and tried another way. "Look, you know there's no way you'll save yourself, and I bet right now you're at the same point as you say my father and Ray were. Therefore, what do you have to lose? Why not come clean, Jack?"

It took surprisingly little thought. "All right." He looked Tom in the eye. "Your father was very distraught, but no, he did not want to commit suicide. There were very few things Tom could not have done and that was one of them. However, as far as I was concerned, what he wanted to do instead was worse..."

He had to turn away again as the shame of trying to defame his best friend in the eyes of his son was hitting him. What he'd done to the man himself was bad enough. "I will not try to justify what I did- not now. At the time I thought I did the right thing for everyone, although when I saw, every day, the extent of the damage I'd caused...

"...but what he wanted to do would have caused much more damage for many more people than just him, and I don't know if he realized that! It would have-...I'm starting to do what I just told you I wouldn't. I want you to understand everything, though. It's my side, yes, but I'll give you as much of the whole picture as I'm able to.

"He had too much to live for, which was my motive and my means to convince him to come to my house and meet me that last night. I had Chris call your house and get him on the line. He could have been the one, Tommy; your father could have gone the distance himself. FBI Director, Governor, maybe even President. He had the right stuff, too, just like you and John.

"A few nights before New Year's Eve he tells me that he's considering spilling the truth- about everything. The way he said it and the mere fact that he'd told me about it indicated to me that he was leaning heavily toward doing that. The bottom line was, I couldn't let him do it because it would have done a hell of a lot more than to bring *him* down. I wasn't just thinking about myself, either.

"In the end he felt guilty about doing the right thing and he would have sacrificed the lives and careers of those who helped him and all their families, including his own, for the sake of that guilt. You don't do that to those you love! The worst part about it was, he was right to kill those bastards and make 'em disappear-*we* were right! The community was safer because of what we did; we all knew it! Judy understood that, too- look what she did for him to prove that, along with her love for him!

"And he would have thrown it all away- just like that. I tried all I could to convince him he was wrong but it didn't work, so...I killed him. He never saw it coming, but...in a way, maybe he did. He stared out my back window into the garden- never moved a muscle when I came up behind him and-...

"I made sure he didn't suffer. I had to wait an additional day to bury him because I had commitments elsewhere. When I did bury him on the 2nd, little Kimberly happened across me. That's the truth; that's how it went down.

267

"Henry can vouch for everything I've told you about what your mother did to Parker; it's also true. We were riding in his patrol car when by chance we saw Judy's car, then Judy herself as she limped out of the woods by that creek. Really, she had no choice but to tell us. Believe me, I wish that never happened but at the same time that's why I loved her, Tommy, and why I wanted her to love me. I can't deny that played a role in what I did to your father…" Jack started to choke on his words, and wiped at his eyes before he continued.

"He was my best friend. All those years we were like brothers. I enlisted with him to go fight the Germans, but the Army wouldn't accept me because I'm flat-footed and I also had chronic back problems even then. The pain already was bad and it steadily got worse. I did all I could back here to help the war effort, but I still felt guilty. All those boys over there dying, and here I am stateside because I wasn't good enough. That hurt, Tommy; the pain in my back was and is nothing in comparison. What made it worse was having so many people asking me 'why aren't you over there?' I got tired of saying 'they wouldn't accept me' since that got me so many dirty looks and comments, so I just stopped saying anything about it.

"As for Tom, we always wrote back and forth. I made sure to write him at least once a week. I worried about my friend, but he sure came out all right. He never had a contrary word or thought for me for not fighting in the war and he'd threaten to beat the tar out of anyone who did. He never had a problem with that, but I did. I tried in so many ways to make up for it through law school and what I did with my degree- all the prosecutorial roles I played. I was good at it, too, and I silenced the voices of every critic that got on me about not being in the War…every one except my own.

"He was a good man, your father. As for a friend, no one ever could have had better. Things didn't even change when a beautiful nurse came into the picture- not for him, anyway. Neither Tom nor I had ever expected we'd marry but then came Judy, who just glowed. Tom fell as hard and fast for her as a man could. Even though it seemed like she played hard to get sometimes, she was every bit as gone as he was. I was smitten with her, too; she always knew that but she never told your father because she didn't want to compromise his and my friendship. Not that I have to tell you, Tom, but she was that good a woman. There couldn't have been a better match than her and your Dad.

"Well, I wanted what they had, too, but I rushed into a big mistake. My wife and I never really loved each other; we weren't even close to what Tom and Judy had. I'd sabotaged us even before we'd met, anyway- with Chris and his mother, of course. I think the water from Jill's christening and the ink on her mother's and my divorce papers dried at about the same time. So, I'd fucked up again. I looked for escapes and didn't find any, all along becoming more fixated on Judy and starting to realize I was wishing my life away. I also envied my best friend more and more.

"In retrospect, I probably started to look for a way to kill him when we started our extracurricular activities with Novak and Wancowicz. I had no right to think such thoughts and it could well be that from there things went downhill. My friendship with Tom was undermined more and more by my love and desire for his wife. Four years later I betrayed my closest friend in part because of that, but as strange as it may seem, the main reason I killed him was to prevent the devastating impact on his wife and sons of the fallout from the confession I believe he would have made.

"It was bad enough that he would have thrown away all the good he could have done for our country because he felt guilty about doing the right thing. It would have been worse if his guilt destroyed the futures of his sons. That's also why Kimberly had to-... she held the pieces, and could have caused just as much damage to..." He trailed off, unable to continue.

"I don't get it. You say you loved my mother, yet you killed my father because of your belief there would be ramifications-"

"It wasn't just my belief! Think about it; what would life have been like for the sons of the killer of a couple dozen men as opposed to the sons of a revered Sheriff who disappeared?! If that story had gotten out, do you think the public would have cared that those animals deserved death for all they'd done?! Would they have cared that he made his county a lot safer to live in?! No- none of that would have meant a damned thing! Worse, you and your brothers would have been the real victims. You never would have come as far as you have, and John? No way in hell would he have become Governor. He wouldn't have been able to win a race for school janitor. Even so, your mother would have suffered most.

"I think Judy might have come to know- or at least suspect- what I did, which more than anything is why I rarely came to your

269

home anymore after the Bicentennial. It was then when it got to be too much- trying to seduce her and all the while knowing…everything. I wanted to tell her what I'd done and why, but I just couldn't. I've never forgiven myself and I don't expect you to forgive me.

"Even so, as much as you must hate me, you can't possibly feel as much contempt for me as I do for myself. You also were right when you implied that I'm slipping. I am forgetting a lot of things I said before- a lot of alibis. I wish I could forget it all, but I can't. In the final analysis, as much as I despised him, I seem to have become an old Walter Daniels."

There it was. Tom didn't see any guises or attempts at diversion. The truth was out and the evidence was right in front of him- most of it, anyway. "Where's the diary, Jack?"

He gestured to his car. "You'll find it inside the drawer sitting on the back seat. All the pictures of Kimberly are inside it as well."

"I already know you forged the one John and Kim found, which was in the same place you found the original. How did you know where it would be?"

"Bugs. I had a few planted in your house. I heard your father's last conversation with Johnny. I knew I had to find the diary. If it had surfaced, you and your family would have been damaged every bit as much as you would have been if Tom had confessed verbally. I had to get your Dad's journal because I couldn't allow that to happen- not after everything else I'd done.

"Tom's death was bad enough but having everything come to light in spite of the measure I took to prevent that would have been the worst travesty of all. I hope you'll do the same thing I did in that regard: never let anyone outside your family read it. What your father wrote is for your eyes only; no one else needs to see it. Go on, Tommy. It's yours now."

Tom went into his car and pulled the old wooden drawer out. He made a cursory examination and found everything to be there.

He placed the drawer inside his own car and walked back to Jack. "You always said you wanted to do right by us; you wanted to look out for us. Well, now's your chance." Tom produced John's .45, wiped it clean of fingerprints and handed it to him. "There's a round in the chamber. This is the gun John used to kill that pestilence of a son of yours. From all you've told us, it doesn't sound like there was much of a father-son bond between you, anyway- not even close to the bond John, Doug and I thought we had with you."

"We did have that bond. That was no lie…at least, it wasn't for me. You boys came to mean everything to me. You were my only chances to try to atone in some way, and not just for what I did to your father. I loved all three of you like you were my own; you, John and Doug were what I wanted Chris to be, but I knew for him that was asking far too much.

"When Doug was murdered a few years ago, I hurt like I should have upon hearing that Chris was dead." After a moment, Jack accepted the gun.

He smiled when he recognized it. "Your father's .45."

"That's the one."

Jack nodded, quickly understanding Tom's intention. "Very good plan. Anyone conducting an investigation will conclude that I shot Chris, then burned the house and killed myself. I see only one problem: how will my suicide be explained?"

"Easily. You heard that Kim had been rescued and you panicked because you'd told her everything before you left her for Danni to kill. Danni didn't show up like she was supposed to, so you had to assume something went wrong. Then, you listened to the news and learned there was an APB out on you, which sealed your fate."

"Very good indeed; you've covered everything and it sounds to me like it'll fly. A good, airtight plan that won't bring any heat down on anyone living."

"Right. It's what you had in mind when you-…" He didn't want to say it and he could see that Jack didn't want him to, so Tom moved past that and got to his main point. "You can end all of it. You can separate yourself from Daniels by doing what he never would have done- that is, like you just said, to atone to the extent that you can. The pistol is your way out unless you want to face the music, which I can't imagine you do.

"It would be awfully hard for you to explain those bodies buried in your yard, along with an eyewitness who saw you and your son burying two of them. On top of that, we have the diary. You're finished and you know it. The next move is yours; I think you'll do what's right. You'll have to click the safety off but don't do it until you get over there. That should be all."

"Tom, there's one last thing. I wouldn't ask you on my behalf, but I will on my daughter's. There's a bag on the floor in the back seat, right below where you found the drawer. You'll find a lot of money in it- over a million dollars. She has two children and a deadbeat for a husband. If there's any way you could-"

"I'll see that she gets the money."

He nodded and, for the benefit of all three men, said, "for what it's worth, I'm sorry for everything."

"So am I," Tom replied.

Jack saw the sincerity of what he just said. He instantly felt worse than he ever had at any point in his life- even after he left Judy's Bicentennial party. Never before had the sting of everything he'd done to the Strattons hurt so much.

Tom saw that and turned away for a moment. His knowledge that he was in the right didn't make what he was doing any easier. However, he faced Jack again, knowing he had to see this through. The souls of his father and mother demanded it. John and Kim demanded it.

Most of all, Jack himself demanded it. The longer he put it off, the harder it would be, but there was one last thing he needed to say to Tom. "Don't let what I've done, along with the justified vengeance you're taking out on me, consume you and bring you down. You are doing the right thing, but let your anger die with me. Don't let this twist you, because it-" he cut himself off from going too far down that road.

There was no sense in making Tom, Jr. feel any worse than he already was and would for some time- maybe for the rest of his life. "Take your mother's advice; above all else, look out for your family, especially your brother. He'll need you, and more than he realizes."

"I will."

Jack extended his hand to Henry, who shook it with his right and wiped at his eye with his left. He saw how upset and torn Henry was and didn't want to say anything to push him over the edge, which he was teetering on as things were. The firm handshake the warden gave him said more than his words would have. That was his way.

Next he turned to the man he'd maligned so badly. "I can't apologize enough to you, Ben. As horrible as this may sound, if I'd have killed my son I'd have spared your little girl all the trauma he caused her. If given the chance again I'd do it without hesitation. I also had no right to bring all the hardship on you that I did. I'm sorry. I can see that you don't forgive me and frankly I don't blame you. I wouldn't forgive me, either."

Then, one last time, he faced the son of the best man he ever knew.

"Goodbye, Tommy."

"Goodbye, Mister Jack."

The men watched him slowly walk over to the porch of his gutted house and sit on the porch. In the darkness they barely could see him taking a long look around his property.

Then they saw him raise the gun, put it inside his mouth and fire without hesitation.

His body fell backwards and he lay still. It was done.

On the brink of death, the man had shown acceptance of his guilt and, at the very end, the contrition he'd never shown in life. Even though everyone knew that undoubtedly was in part because he'd been caught, he still could have taken the 'spit in your eye' approach, which he did not do. There simply was no fight left in him. More than anything, each of the three witnesses saw how worn out he was.

Just to be sure, Ben went over to the porch where Jack Weldon's body lay. When he rejoined the others, the look on his face was all the confirmation anyone needed.

Seeing Tom's expression, Henry said, "give me your keys, Son. I'll drive."

Tom gave them to him without objection, and they got into his car and left. The drive home was a very long and quiet one, as the drive there had been.

"We interrupt this program to bring you breaking news regarding the case surrounding Maryland's Attorney General. With the latest, here's Nancy Jamison live at the State House."

"Good morning, everyone. This twelfth day of May 2003 is shaping up to be chock full of revelations and it's barely underway. Maryland's longtime Attorney General, John C. Weldon- better known as Jack-, was determined to have been responsible for at least three counts of murder and one count of attempted murder. Also, two days ago Mister Weldon's accomplice, Baltimore County Police Detective Danielle Searles, made an attempt on the life of Mrs. Kimberly Stratton. She told police at the scene that she phoned her husband to tell him of a

273

discovery she'd made, but before she could leave the house, Weldon and the female detective arrived and subdued her. Also according to Mrs. Stratton, the Attorney General was completely irrational and rabid with anger; a state she'd never seen him in. He ordered the detective to kill her and burn the house down.

"Upon receiving his wife's call, Governor Stratton and his team immediately went to the Attorney General's home. They broke in and found Mrs. Stratton upstairs, bound and gagged but fortunately unharmed. They also found Detective Searles lying dead on the floor; she'd been shot in the head by someone in the back yard, who the police are looking for as well. The Strattons have no idea who the shooter could have been- neither saw the person. The Attorney General himself was nowhere to be found, and for good reason.

"After showing the police the small, improvised cell she was locked inside of that from all indications Mister Weldon crafted himself, Mrs. Stratton then relayed information of an even more shocking nature that brought an end to an unsolved case.

"In January of 1975, Mrs. Stratton, who was six years old at the time, saw Jack Weldon digging in his yard. That struck her as highly unusual since it was the dead of an especially cold winter. As it turned out, he was burying the body of Thomas Jonathan Stratton, Sr., who'd gone missing as of New Year's Day that year. Weldon told Mrs. Stratton that he'd killed her husband's father and that his worry over her seeing him burying the body all those years ago, and possibly figuring out that was what had happened, played a big part in why tried to have her killed.

"When Mrs. Stratton showed the investigating officers the spot where her husband's father was buried, she gave them another shocker from the past. She showed them where she'd seen the Attorney General's illegitimate son, Christopher Hedges, digging in the summer of 1981.

"As it turns out, Hedges assumed the identity of Joshua Strauss at that point; the digging in his father's yard that thirteen-year-old Kimberly witnessed that August day in '81 was Hedges burying the real Joshua Strauss. You'll remember this was the same man who abducted eleven young women between 1990 and 2000, all of whom bore physical and characteristic resemblance to Mrs. Stratton. Ultimately, Mrs. Stratton herself became his twelfth captive, and he held all the women inside a Pennsylvania dwelling.

"The Governor's wife also revealed to the police how the Attorney General had figured out the location of his son, whom he believed to be the anonymous caller who phoned the Baltimore County Police and divulged the burial spot and name of Ronald Novak. She said Weldon was very agitated about that; he said he wouldn't let his son pin that on him. Apparently he played a role in Novak's death, but it never became clear to Mrs. Stratton what that role was. Mister Weldon also told his captive that Hedges assisted him with, among others, the murder of the elder Thomas Stratton, which Weldon planned because he was afraid the distinguished Sheriff was close to discovering his longtime friend's involvement in Novak's murder.

"From all indications, Hedges knew Weldon was trying to eliminate those who knew of his killings. As he was about to leave her to be killed, he told the Governor's wife about driving out to another house he owned in rural northern Virginia not far from Interstate 81, where he determined his son was holed up.

"He then informed her that his son had paid for his betrayal with his life and that after killing the son he'd burned the house down to destroy that reminder of his own stupidity and cover up what he'd done. That was when he told her she would die next because she knew too much even before all he'd told her, so he left her to Detective Searles. Then came the shot that killed the detective as she was about to kill Mrs. Stratton, who expressed her heartfelt thanks to whomever the shooter was. Not long after that was when Governor Stratton rescued his wife.

"As for the Virginia dwelling, according to Major Todd Stone of the Virginia State Police, all the physical evidence at that dwelling seems to corroborate what Mrs. Stratton said. The house was burned down and a charred body- believed to be that of Hedges but thus far unidentified- with four bullets in the torso was recovered inside. The skeleton of a female, also as yet unidentified, was found inside a 55-gallon drum in the shed in the backyard of the property.

"In the final twist, Weldon himself was found on the remains of the front porch, dead from a self-inflicted gunshot wound. Police are confident that the .45 caliber pistol lying next to him, which by all indications was Thomas Stratton, Sr.'s official sidearm as Sheriff, will turn out to be the same handgun that killed the man inside the house. The same handgun, presumably, that Weldon took from the Sheriff after killing him thirty years ago.

"The last thing police discovered was a bag on the floor of Weldon's car that contained well over a million dollars. None of the notes was newer than the 1977 series. Coincidentally, an open and empty safe was found inside the remains of the house.

"Keep in mind that Christopher Hedges, while posing as Joshua Strauss, was responsible along with five accomplices for the armored car heist in 1989 that netted over $9 million in old notes that were on their way to the Federal Reserve to be destroyed. You don't have to be a detective to see a motive for Weldon there. The next year was when Hedges embarked on the decade-long run of abductions. After Hedges was rooted out of his house in July of 2000, ironically he took up refuge in Weldon's place in Virginia until his father happened across him.

"The police believe that Weldon cleared out the safe and might have gotten away with all that money, but instead he committed suicide, probably fearing his apprehension by police upon discovering that Mrs. Stratton had been rescued and thus the jig was up for him. Perhaps he had nowhere else to go, knew his photo was being widely circulated and escaped capture the only way he felt he could. Police say that explanation makes the most sense, especially given Mrs. Stratton's recollection of his irrational behavior just before he left her. If his reason was otherwise, he took the answer with him.

"Whatever the case, it was a violent ending to a very bizarre and chilling sequence of events. Then, there's the matter of the Bahamian bank account containing over $85 million that's in the name of Joshua Strauss, which federal authorities will attempt to claim once they've established that the account holder is dead and was a multiple felon. Boy, do I see a mile of red tape in that process!

"Governor and Mrs. Stratton have asked, understandably so, that the press keep its distance and allow them privacy so they can recover from this latest spurt of excitement of the negative kind. We at Channel 11 will honor their request. If there are any changes or further developments, which I can't imagine there would be as this whole thing is crazy enough already, we'll let you viewers know when we know. Back to you in the studio, Melissa."

"Thank you for that report, Nancy. I'd say I hope life normalizes for the couple, but then again it won't be long before they're in the thick of a presidential race, which is far from normal. Public scrutiny on them, already heavy as things are,

276

surely will become heavier still in the months to come. Since this story broke, we're getting bombarded with e-mails, mostly from well wishers for the Strattons, which we certainly echo.

"As for the political environment, the gubernatorial races in Kentucky, Louisiana and Mississippi are heating up and the Progressive candidates are drumming up support. Governor Stratton is expected to campaign hard for all three of his candidates, starting next month.

"As previously reported, everyone is viewing those races as precursors for the presidential election next year and they're already licking their chops in anticipation of hard-fought contests. If you love political dogfights, well, we have three of 'em brewing for you, Southern style! It's really getting interesting, folks, so stay tuned and let's see how much pull our native son will exert 'a-way down South, in Dixie.' We now return you to your regularly scheduled programming. Have a great day, everyone."

"…hello?"

Tom wasn't surprised to hear the grogginess in Kim's voice when she answered the phone, even though it was after ten. "Hey, Kim- sorry I woke you."

"'It's Ok; we need to get up, anyway. How are you, Tom?"

"I'm good, thanks. I take it you two are a lot better?"

"Definitely. I think Herb's already sorting through candidates for our team," she said amid a yawn, "and given what he told John and me it shouldn't take long at-…"

Her dialogue dropped off, and it was pretty obvious why from what he heard, which was reminiscent of their little episode in the kitchen when John had her pinned against the refrigerator. With a smile, he waited a moment until Kim came back on.

"Sorry about that! I'll let you talk with your bully of a brother now. 'Bye, Tom."

John came on. "Hey. What's the word?"

"It's all over the news. They seem to have gone for it, hook, line and sinker. It all adds up, anyway, and most of it is true. How's Kim? Is she still alright?"

"All things considered, I doubt she could be better. Like I am, she's just happy things worked out like they did."

"I couldn't agree more. Oh- one thing I want to ask you. Of the $6 million Herb pulled out of the safe, would you consider

277

giving a million to Jill? Jack's last request was that the money the police recovered from his car go to her. She and her children probably will get a lot of grief from what her father did as things are and he said she's not doing so well otherwise. Plus, he did make things easy on us by taking himself out and tidying everything up in the process."

"I don't think that'll be a problem at all, especially since Jill and Kim seem to have buried the hatchet. Jill did spill on her father, too, which is why Kim went over to his house. I'm sure Kim won't have a problem with helping her and her kids out. With the reason you gave, she'll probably insist on it. Question is, how will we get the cash to Jill without raising suspicion?"

"Good point. We'll have to think about that."

"That we will. Speaking of plans, that sure was some kind of scheme you came up with- nothing less than genius at work."

"Thanks, but it wasn't much more than logic at work; all the elements were there and I just needed the string to tie 'em all together. Add in the maxim Mom always drove into us."

"You sure did look out for the family, Brother."

"I'm glad I could; it was the right thing to do, especially in this case. Ike Miller told me he sees no need to investigate further on the 'anonymous tipster's tidbits. Of the other bodies they dug up, most died of .45 wounds, anyway, and since Mister Jack had the gun as far as Ike knows, that's good enough for him. All we have to do now is make sure Jenny's on board, which shouldn't be a problem, either."

"I think she'll go along with it, especially since all she has to do is stay quiet. She won't even be involved. It sure seems to me that she wants to forget about all of that as soon as possible. Her father will help to that end, I think."

"It sure is strange how all of this went down, isn't it? And we never would have known if Hedges hadn't made those anonymous tips about Novak. That's what shook Weldon's cage and set the whole thing in motion."

"Yeah. Wherever Hedges is now, if he can see what happened I'm sure he's kicking himself in the ass."

Tom chuckled. "No doubt. Then, Ben Jacobson, who we were sure was our enemy, saved Kim's life. Quite a ride, this was. By the way, there's more good news for us: Todd Stone told me he'll have Dad's .45 returned to us once the lab people are finished with it."

"Ah, that is good news. I meant to ask you about it."

"It shouldn't be long before we get it back. Well, I'll let you go; I'm sure you and Kim want to kick back today, which is what Donna and I will do. One last thing- I want you two to come here tomorrow night. It's been a while since we've had a family dinner."

"That sounds terrific, especially with Jess back in town. Put it to Donna and let us know what she thinks."

"Will do. Catch you later, John."

"See ya, Bro."

John hung up as Kim emerged from the bathroom. "Hey, you! Come here so I can say 'good morning' properly."

Kim smiled and climbed back into bed. "Yes, you do need to redeem yourself," she retorted. The kiss he gave her did that and then some. "I overheard some of your conversation; you mentioned something about Jill. What did Tom ask you to give her?"

"A million dollars. It's about how much Jack had with him last night and it was his last request that we give it to her. Obviously she won't get the million he had, but Tom thinks we should give her some of what we recovered from Hedges."

"I think it-...hold on. What do you mean, what we recovered from Hedges?"

"I'll be damned; I completely forgot to tell you that! I guess there was just a bit too much happening over the past few days. After I got him, Herb and Dawn went upstairs and found his safe open. He had almost $6 million inside."

"Oh, my God..."

"It was quite a discovery. I don't think there's any doubt it was all the money he made from the videos of you he sold. As far as I'm concerned, it's your money to do with as you see fit."

"Wow...I suppose I'll have to think about that. One thing is for sure- a bonus is in order for the core of our team, considering how hard we've worked them. In spite of what happened to me, I think they deserve it. As for Jill, you agree with Tom that we should give her the million, right?"

"Yes."

"So do I. She and her kids have had a rough go of it for some time, and it's bound to get worse with what her father did. As for

Jill, our past animosity is just that- the past. I want to live in the here and now, and look toward the future, too."

"That sounds good to me, Kitten."

They lay together in the silence that ensued and were about to drift off again until the phone rang again.

"Jeez, people sure don't seem to want to let us sleep in, do they?" Kim said, picking up the receiver. "Hello?"

"Kim- I'm so glad to hear your voice! Are you all right?"

"Oh, hi, Jenny. Yes, I'm fine and I'm glad you called. Actually, I was going to call you today. How are you feeling?"

"I was pretty low because-…well, you know."

"But you're better now?"

"Much better."

"Good- you shouldn't let him drag you down even after he's gone. He *is* gone, too; he'll never have another chance to hurt you. Plus, you have John, me and our whole family pulling for you."

"My father, too- that's why I'm calling you. John wanted me to let him know if my Dad called, and he did. We talked for a long time. I just hung up with him a few minutes ago. It was great to talk with him. Best of all, we actually did talk with each other instead of to each other. That hasn't happened for years."

"It sounds like you two had a very productive conversation yesterday, too; you must feel good about that."

"I do. It was a long time coming, that's for-…wait a minute, you said *yesterday*?"

"Well…yes, he said he'd spoken at length with you yesterday."

"No, we spoke earlier this morning. Like I told John- before today I hadn't heard from him since Christmas. He told me everything that happened, including what you told the police about how that jerk I almost moved in with was killed. He says he loves me, then drops me like a hot potato. Dad said I wouldn't even be involved, which I'm totally fine with, especially since I'll be helping you guys out by not saying anything. He also told me about when he shot that woman who was going to kill you. He really did that?"

She turned to John with a perplexed expression, but held up her finger indicating she wanted him to wait a minute when he gave her an inquisitive look in reply. "Yes, he did. He saved my life, Jenny, and I'm very grateful to him…"

Kim wasn't made aware that she was virtually frozen and had drifted, wondering how Jenny's father knew what he did when he did, until John shook her a little and she heard Jenny calling her name. "Yes, I'm- I'm still here. Sorry about that; I must have zoned out. Anyway, are you still by yourself down there?"

"Mm-hmm. I'm just vegging- resting, more than anything."

"I'd like for you to come stay with us for a few days or maybe more; I don't want you to be by yourself. Besides, I've seen too little of you. It's so nice here and you haven't visited us yet. I think you'll love it. It'll be a nice respite for you."

"I wouldn't want to intrude; you two need some time alone."

"Oh, trust me, John and I will be fine. He's making noises about taking me away for a vacation next month, and yet again he refuses to tell me where, so I'll be hard at work to convince him that he needs to enlighten me and stop his teasing! Anyway, pack what you'll need for a week and plan on coming here Monday. You and I can hang out while John takes care of some campaign-related matters he needs to attend to. We can even help him here and there, if you like; it's really exciting stuff! Most of all, though, I want you to relax in a nice, peaceful and safe environment among friends."

"Well, I know better than to say 'no' to you."

Kim laughed. "You certainly should! Now, all I need to do is make my husband see the futility of that as clearly as you do! I'm so glad you'll be coming, Jenny; I'll make sure your room's all ready. Oh- hold on a sec." She covered the mouthpiece and turned to John when he nudged her.

"Tell her to keep tomorrow evening open; we might be having dinner at Tom and Donna's. If we do, I'd like her to come."

Kim smiled and kissed him. "That sounds great!" She went back to her conversation with Jenny and passed John's message to her. "If that comes together, it would make things easier since you could follow us home afterwards."

"They won't mind having me?"

"Of course they won't! I'll let you know as soon as I can if that materializes. I'll call you later when I do, Ok?"

"Ok, talk with you soon!"

"'Bye, Jenny." She hung up and turned to John, with the puzzled expression on her face once more. "She told me she didn't talk with her father until this morning."

Now, John was equally confused. "You're kidding..."

"Absolutely not. Jenny said- and reiterated- that he called her this morning, *not* yesterday morning. Until a few minutes ago, she hadn't heard from him since Christmas."

"Then, how in the hell..."

Kim finished the sentence for him. "...did he know what he knew last night?"

"I have no idea. It's not possible he could have bugged- ...no, I won't say that. If there's one thing I've learned- particularly over the past few days-, there's virtually nothing that's impossible. Who could have told him, though? Only Tom, Jenny and the team knew about what we did to Hedges, so unless Jenny isn't telling us the truth...but I don't think that's the case.

"Then, there's Herb telling us how Ben looks just like a guy he saw at our forum in Dubuque, Iowa- a guy he didn't like the looks of..." He rolled onto his back. "Just when I thought we'd solved all the mysteries, up pops another one."

"It sure seems that way, although at least this one isn't insidious; it's just strange...I think we need to talk with Mister Jacobson again, now that you're on much better terms. I'm sure there's some explanation for that. It also seems like Jenny will be seeing more of him, anyway."

She got out of bed. "For now, let's get moving. I could use a good workout and I bet you could, too, so snap to it!"

"Yeah, I suppose you're right. That would be a good start to the day."

"Hmmm...I don't sense much motivation in that response."

"I can't imagine you're surprised, since in more ways than one you *did* keep me up for much of last night."

She giggled. "I didn't hear you complaining then! Besides, you contributed to that just as much as I did. I'm sure you've heard the saying 'it takes-"

"-two to tango. Yeah, yeah," he replied with a chuckle. "Well, sleeping in for a bit wouldn't be a bad thing, either."

"Tell you what: we'll have a nap later to make up for that. For the next hour and a half, Mister, you belong to me! Remember: you charged me with keeping you in shape, which is a job I take very seriously."

"I never would have guessed!"

"Oh, wise guy, are you? In that case, you can add another half-hour to our session today, since we already have a day to make up for." She laughed when he groaned at that, then climbed back into bed and got on top of him. "Will I have to employ my most effective weapon in order to talk you into this?"

By way of his lascivious grin it was obvious to her that he knew she meant the white spandex thong and sports bra set she'd kept from a time she thankfully never would relive. She was glad to have put that outfit to good use with John, which apparently she was about to do again. Naturally, she would add the tan shimmer tights to further play upon that certain weakness of his she took so much pleasure in exploiting- not that he minded, to put it in the mildest way.

Besides being so motivational for him, her scanty exercise outfit and a few other reminders of that time that she'd kept served to help her cherish even more the life she and John were making together. Their life stood in stark contrast to the perpetual hell for her that easily could have been.

That thought prompted her to show her appreciation. "I'll take that as a 'yes'," she said, returning his grin after giving a signal that clearly conveyed to him that there was much more to come- *after* their workout. "On the serious side, Baby, I know staying in shape always has been a priority for you and time has been at a premium, which probably will continue to be the case for us- that is, if it doesn't get worse. We have to take advantage of it when we have it."

"I know; I was only messing with you."

"Well, you still owe me the extra half-hour."

"Damn- no slack at all!"

"Absolutely not, but don't worry- I'll count our time in the hot tub afterwards, not to mention any *other* physical activities you might feel inspired to perform. Now, let's go- up and at 'em!"

"How are they?" John asked her.

Kim had just hung up with Rachel, who'd called to make sure her friend in 'Mary-land', as she called it, was all right after having heard what had happened. "She sounded good and as sweet as ever, but she said her Mom's feeling sick and is sleeping, so she couldn't talk for long. I hope they're doing all right since the wonderful husband stuck Linda with all the credit card debt he racked up."

"Nice. Another example of why we should set standards that have to be met before someone can become a parent."

"Definitely."

"Kim? Would you mind giving me a hand with this?" Donna called from the kitchen.

"Sure, I'll be right there. Excuse me, guys." She left John and Tom alone to help Donna.

The conversation they'd been having prior to little Rachel's call was about Jack. The emotional damage from his actions and deceptions was pretty extensive. With that in mind, Kim had brought the topic up with the intention of getting it out in the open and dealing with it while they were face to face so nothing would be left to fester.

It didn't surprise her or John that Tom was the hardest hit out of the three of them, which Donna had forewarned them about. John resumed their conversation. "It's tough to put it all in perspective- that's for sure. The worst thing was how he just went about his business, knowing he'd done all that. I couldn't carry around what he did- not the way he did it- yet he covered it up for over 3 decades. He did try to compensate us for what he'd done in every way he could, though. There's no denying that he did everything in his power to help us in our careers. I doubt seriously that I'd be where I am today if it hadn't been for Jack's help."

"I know; I feel the same way. All the encouragement he gave us in addition to the influence he wielded from his office...Christ, you should have seen the look in his eyes at that last moment. As much as he wanted to, he couldn't block everything out. He tried and tried for all those years but inside he knew he couldn't rise above it or distance himself far enough from it. From all indications, he was glad it was over for him. He'd suffered enough. He didn't even think about pulling the trigger on himself, either. He just did it...

"...and I watched him."

John laid his hand on his brother's shoulder. "When I learned the extent of all he'd done I felt nothing but hate and disgust for him. I guess to some degree I always will, but...I know where you are now, Tom. I'm there with you. For all his sins, he still was an important part of our lives. I can understand how the further we get from the day of his death, the harder it'll become for you to keep hating him. Maybe that'll even happen for me, I don't know. I do know I'll never understand him. He killed his best friend, yet without hesitation he fell on his sword for the sake of the man's sons. As fond and proud as he was of Doug, you and me, it was no surprise how much it hurt him that he'd never have that kind of relationship with his own son.

"Plus, there's what you told me about what he endured physically, mentally and emotionally because he couldn't fight in the War. He wanted to contribute but he couldn't, which had to be a lousy feeling in itself. Then you factor in the blind criticism from stupid, ignorant people that couldn't or wouldn't see beyond the surface- that it wasn't his fault the army wouldn't take him. Those critics probably weren't even interested in getting his side. I've seen plenty of that kind of asshole. They like to point out the faults of others to try to take attention away from their own shortcomings. He got a bad deal- that much is for sure.

"But, you also have to look at what he did. He was all set to disappear and he meant to kill Kim or take her with him. He was afraid she'd bridge the gap and figure him out. He ordered her death when she did; we were seconds away from losing her. As badly as I feel for him, in the end I cannot and will not forgive him for betraying Kim like he did. He also would have left us in the dark about Dad and he'd have let Ben Jacobson go on wondering what it was he'd done to deserve all the crap that was thrown his way. Jack even forged a copy of his lifelong friend's diary and conveniently left out the fact that he was every bit as involved in all those killings as Dad was.

"Then, think about what he did to Hedges' mother- even aside from the fact that he killed her. Who's to say she wasn't a decent lady before Jack screwed her over like he did, saddling her with another kid she wasn't ready for? Who knows how much Jack contributed to Hedges turning out like he did, or how differently the guy would have turned out if only he'd been accepted by his father, and had gotten some attention and encouragement? Every time I start to think about that…it's safe to say his upbringing- if you can call it that- played a big part in turning him into what he was. Apparently the stepfather was a real piece of work, too…"

As incredible as it seemed, when his thoughts drifted in that direction- in spite of everything Hedges had done- John would feel a twinge of guilt over having killed him. But then…

"Consider this, too; look at all the directions I could have gone off in based on what Hedges did to me. I could have become a closet pedophile or sexual predator, resorting to abducting children, men or women to take revenge on them for the damage and the humiliation he caused me. I could have allowed the repulsiveness from his act to turn me off from sex and wound up blaming myself in some way for his crime against me, letting it get to me so much that I felt no recourse but to commit suicide. I could have allowed that single act to determine my course in life and totally twist me, but I didn't.

"Granted, it took an awfully long time for me to tell someone about what Hedges had done to me and I did let it get to me in some ways, but I didn't allow that to become the moment that shaped the rest of my life. I knew there was a lot more to me and there was a lot I could do and needed to do. The only regret I have about my episode with Hedges is that I let it fester inside me for so long- same as I did with my feelings about Dad and what I thought happened to him.

"It's all about the choices we make, Tom. We have to be responsible for 'em, no matter what's happened to us in life; it's part of being an adult. Jack reaped what he sowed, just like his son did. Mom probably saw him for what he was, which would explain why we didn't see much of him at the house after '76. Some people should stay unattached since relationships seem to bring out the worst in 'em.

"I'd say that was the case with Jack. He wanted what the other guy had- until he got it, that is. For him, the thrill wore off quickly. He was like a benign substance by himself, but when mixed with another he became toxic. Even though he knew that, he still couldn't or wouldn't improve himself, or simply acknowledge that he was no good with- or for- women, and just move on. The bottom line is, as hard as this is to take, he had to go down."

Tom gave an assenting nod. "You know, I almost wish we didn't find that diary. It was bad enough hearing everything from him and Mister Henry, but-...seeing all of it in his own words...I just don't know how Dad did it. Frankly, I don't know how you can handle it, either, John, which reminds me- you haven't said a hell of a lot after seeing Dad's real diary." He couldn't help thinking about Jack's admonition about the ramifications that his role in the killings John had taken part in or had carried out himself could have on him.

286

"As for the killings, I'm surprised by what you just said. You killed a few enemy soldiers in Grenada when you were there. When you think about it, there are similarities between what you did and what I did. Those I killed were combatants in different wars, one of which was personal."

"There's a big difference, though: I was in Grenada because I had to be. It was my duty."

"Well, I see what I did as *my* duty- to Kim, to the family of a murder victim, to my country and to myself. I didn't like it at any point and it's a hell of a burden to carry, but I did what had to be done in each case, just like Dad."

"The question now is, will court justice ever be enough for you again? I can't imagine it was for him. How could it be?" How would this affect John's judgment, especially if he ended up in the White House and an international incident arose?

Or, was he making too much of this? After all, what John had done was personal, and it was justice. Maybe this was the end of it for John- maybe nothing like it ever would happen again…

He decided not to ask for the time being and see how it played out. Maybe he'd never need to broach the subject…

When John didn't answer, Tom moved on. "Speaking of Dad, I called the caretaker at the cemetery; he's putting the inscription on the stone, so that'll be done before the burial." John nodded in reply.

They'd made arrangements for their father's remains to be buried alongside those of their mother. A private ceremony for family and close friends was scheduled to coincide with the burial, which only was days away. John was right about Jack, how it all had to end and why. He also was right in that it hurt and would for some time.

As for the diary, John had answered his query in a way. He stuck to his decision to let that go, hoping Jack's assessment of John's future was wrong. However, not helping was his recollection of Warden Steele's comment on that fateful day about John and Tom, Sr. being exactly alike.

He tried to shake that off. "We've dealt with a lot of death recently. I hope he stays away for a long spell."

"Amen."

Seeing John's disposition, which was the same as his own, Tom knew it was time to change gears. Fortunately it was easy to find a much better topic. "Looks like Kim's handling everything as well as you said she would," he noted as he watched her and Donna chatting very jovially with Jenny and Jessica, who'd just finished exam week.

I'm glad we're off that subject, John thought as he replied. "She sure is; I don't think she's ever been better or more together. She doesn't hide anything from me and I've vowed to myself never to do that to her again. She knows all there is to know about me, which is exactly how I want it. I think we'll both need a getaway after the ceremony, so I'm taking her to England the beginning of next month. Neither of us has been and I think it'll be a great trip."

"No doubt! That also sounds like the perfect way to get yourself ready for those Governors' races you'll be taking part in from June until November. I bet you'll be good and tired when all that's said and done. Donna and I are planning a trip to the Florida Keys; we could use a getaway, too."

"I believe you- you really look worn out, Tom. How long will you go for?"

"Two weeks. We want to see south Florida, too, and we have a Caribbean cruise laid on for the last part of it. The kids are coming with for much of it; Jess has a good friend in Orlando who invited her to come stay for a while, so that works out really well for all of us. From all indications, her sophomore year will have gone even better grade-wise than her freshman year, which we all were happy with. She definitely deserves a good vacation."

"That's great! She really has stepped up, hasn't she? Another curve-buster in the making, in the spirit of her Uncle John."

Tom cracked up. "You said it! She's becoming well acquainted with the Dean's list and she's setting a great example for her brothers. Tommy and Jake are seeing how well things are going for Jess and they're all gung-ho to get to college themselves."

"Don't forget the example their Dad's setting, juggling a busy career with law school, which he's close to getting his degree from- not to mention being a good man." *Once I get to where I'm going, I'll make sure that all pays off. I have the perfect job for you...*

"Thanks, John. Hey, back to those campaigns coming up, do you feel the same way as before about which is the best prospect?"

"Pretty much. Louisiana still strikes me as the best chance by a good margin, especially since we've already won three seats in

Congress there, including one in the Senate. What makes it better still is that it's the most important of the three because we can win it early. If we get the majority in the open primary on October 4th, then our guy is in and there's no need for any other election.

"That could have a huge impact on the two other races. They remember Huey Long very well down there; redistribution of wealth originated with him, after all. I'll do my best to help us win all three states, but as for right now I see The Bayou State coming into our fold. Kentucky's the real question mark and probably will be until the results come in. Then again, even that bodes well for us. It shows that we've come a long way in not too long a time.

"Ol' Miss is the least likely. That's a pretty solid republican bastion but I'll still give my best effort there just like I know our candidate will. Who knows- maybe enough of the enthusiasm of their Cajun neighbors to the west will spill over the border. If at the least we can make a strong showing, I'll be happy with that. I know this much; it's bound to be a very interesting fall…"

"Ray, I haven't heard from you for a few days. Thought I'd call and check in to see if you've made any progress."

Ben had to remember to keep in character, since he hadn't used his own name in some time. He answered Raines. "No, nothing yet. They're being smart and keeping a low profile, just like we figured they would. Frankly, I don't see us getting any opportunities until they start campaigning again. Plus, now that they have so many more security personnel…"

"I imagine it'll be tougher. Any chance of you infiltrating?"

"No. The head of their detail is hand-picking his people, so that's out. We'll have to wait and see."

"Are you getting cold feet, Ray?"

Here it is. I thought you might be growing impatient… "Why are you asking me that?"

"I just want to be sure you're still with me. I don't have to remind you what's-"

"That's right. You don't."

"Well, you can't blame me for worrying a little, so I'm sure you also won't blame me for giving you a little help."

"What are you talking about? I thought you left the hiring to me in that area."

"You're a proud man. As such, you might be hesitant to admit you need help. You're still on the payroll, though, and you will be until the job is done. This isn't meant to make you uneasy, either; you have nothing to worry about. I just think some competition is a good thing, and whoever completes the job will get a nice bonus in addition. The bottom line is, I want to be certain this job is done."

"I'm sure you know I don't like this, but I'll take you at your word. I guess I'd better get back to work, now that I have a rival. I'll talk with you later."

Tight with money was another trait Raines had; that was why the red flags were waving in Ben's mind. There was no way the man was happy about paying two people to do the job of one...

...if that was the case. There was another possibility as well.

That phone call could mean he'd been replaced. As a result he might have become expendable upon the other guy's hiring.

Who's to say his first job isn't to get rid of me? Raines already has demonstrated that he's impatient...

...question is, how impatient is he?

Ben wasn't about to take any chances. It was time to put all the components and the summary of his insurance policy together and get the package to a safe place. At this time more than any other, he was glad no one else knew what he'd done, on and off, for many years. He especially was glad Jenny didn't know.

Most of all, he was grateful that no one he had contact with in his line of work even knew he had a daughter, which he'd taken the utmost care to make sure of.

The next step would be the contingency plan for the worst case scenario...

Chapter 14

"Gosh, it really gets dark out here, doesn't it? No city lights to take away from the effect- that's for sure! I'm glad we have a full moon tonight."

After a moment Kim turned to him, curious about his non-response. Intertwined with his calm expression was something rather mysterious. In a matter of minutes it would be June 10th and thus his 39th birthday. The trip to England was in celebration of that and a chance for them to get away for a couple weeks. They'd seen quite a few of the multitude of beautiful sites the country had to offer, but again Kim wondered why he wanted to come to this spot in particular.

They were in the county of Dorset in the southwest portion of the island kingdom in a charming little town called Cerne Abbas. During the day, both were amazed by how lush and green the British countryside was, and by how many sheep and cows they saw. They'd also spent a very enjoyable afternoon at a pebbly beach overlooked by a rather high and impressive natural rock arch called Durdle Door, a popular attraction that also was part of Dorset county.

Finally, she had to know. "You still haven't told me why you wanted to come here. Any chance I'll know sometime tonight?"

He turned into a small parking lot and switched off the lights and engine. There were no cars around besides his and those of his bodyguards, who were nearby. The augmentation couldn't have gone better; now he and Kim were surrounded by sixteen well-trained, highly skilled veteran bodyguards that Herb had selected himself. They felt much safer than ever before, although Kim and he made sure to maintain their proficiency with handguns as well. Both insisted on being able to help defend themselves if another situation were to arise that would require it.

However, tonight wouldn't be one of those cases. Herb said he'd only come to John and put a halt to his plan if there were other people around, or another problem of some sort.

A minute or so passed and no Herb. The coast was clear.

When John turned to Kim, he finally enlightened her.

"*No way*...do you hear me?" He didn't respond verbally and his half-smile remained. That in itself gave her his reply, which was reinforced by his next action of getting out of the car, walking around to the passenger side on the left of it and opening her door. Kim still wasn't accustomed to the driver's and passenger's side being switched. She figured by the time they did get used to it, it would be time to return home and see the opposite again.

For the moment, Kim stayed put in her seat on the wrong side of the car, with her arms folded and a contrary set to her chin. "John Kenneth Stratton, we are NOT doing that!"

"It's too late for arguments, Milady. We're already here, so yes- we are."

"You are absolutely insane!! And no, we're *not!*"

"Oh, come on- look how dark it is here. No one will see us."

"That's not the-…no. No discussion *at all.*"

"Good. I'm not much in the mood for talking, anyway."

She gasped as he reached in, gathered her into his arms and swept her up, then carried her down the embankment.

All she could do was gape at him, momentarily at a loss for words. He just kept walking past a few bales of hay, totally nonchalant as they neared the upward slope of the smooth-faced hill. Even so, there was some distance to be covered before they'd reach their destination. "There are times when I could just-…"

"I know, Kitten."

"You know, huh?! I'm not so sure you do. I don't think you see how positively ridiculous this is or else you wouldn't be carrying me up a hill in a foreign country so we can make love- not only in public, but inside the genitalia of a giant traced out in chalk!"

"I love when you talk dirty."

"*Oh*!! You are impossible!! It looks like those old myths about what the full moon does to some people might have some merit after all!" Kim eased up a little, though, when she realized there was no talking him out of this.

Then, he started to laugh.

"You really are asking for it, aren't you?"

"Of course I'm asking for it; that's the whole point!"

Even as flustered as she was, she started laughing, too. It wasn't long before he had to stop and set her down. "I swear to God, if we get caught you will pay dearly for this!"

He only smiled at her in reply as he went about undressing her, which was a rather easy task in this case, then kissed her. "You know, the locals of olden times believed pretty strongly in the fertility power of this guy, so why not give it a try? We have nothing to lose."

She sighed, finally having gotten her breath back. She allowed him to unzip the short, tight white dress she was in, pull it down, then unhook her bra. "You make a very good case. I have to say, though, I never thought you of all people would lend credence to a piece of Dark Age folklore like that."

He chuckled again. "Touché."

"I also can't help but be disappointed in one respect," she said as she finished undressing- almost. She backed away and stood, now wearing only her racy panty. When he was about to ask her why she was disappointed, she said the rest as she hooked her thumbs around the sides of the thong, then wiggled her hips as she slowly, teasingly worked it down over them, then her thighs. "So far, Mister, other than the injection of your twisted humor, I find your foreplay very deficient. It's usually one of your strengths, too, so in light of that, there's one little thing you'll have to do before you can accomplish this mission of yours…"

Her panty was low enough to where she could let it fall, which she did. She stepped out of it with her right foot, then raised her left leg, with her piece of lingerie draped over her foot, and kicked the tiny white thong to him. She laughed as it landed right on top of his head; apparently his focus on her little display temporarily had robbed him of his reflexes.

With a smirk, he took her silk undergarment off his head. She stood only a few feet away from him, hands on her hips, wearing only that wicked grin he loved to see. Her hold on his attention was absolute. "What is it that I'll have to do?"

Her grin broadened into a full-fledged smile. "Catch me!" She turned and took off running up the hill directly toward where the chalk-traced, mythical Giant was.

That got him moving again- and quickly. Immediately upon shedding all his clothing, which he'd probably never done so rapidly in his life, he was in hot pursuit.

Also running faster than he ever had, it wasn't long before he caught her and pulled her down with him. He subdued his gleeful, struggling and extremely turned-on wife.

The state she was in was highly contagious…

* * *

...afterwards, they lay still together, their bodies slick with sweat, panting and basking in the glow of the moonlight.

As warm as it was, it seemed like the moon was just as much a source of heat as it was one of light. There wasn't even the slightest disturbance of the peace that surrounded them, and for a good spell of time, they simply lay there and enjoyed it.

After enough had passed, Kim broke the silence. "Talk about a role reversal...this is, without a doubt, the wildest thing you've ever done while I've known you. I have to say I'm very impressed, not to mention very happy with how it all turned out."

"Well, you sure were reluctant at first, to put it lightly!"

"And that surprises you?!" He laughed heartily. "I definitely was in the beginning, but the more I thought about it while you carried me up the hill, the more I came to realize what was behind this idea of yours." She looked up at him, and just beamed as her eyes began to glisten. "If I ever had any doubts, which I didn't, about how much you want children, too, this wonderful surprise would have dispelled them. That's why you did it, isn't it?"

John caressed her cheek and only smiled in reply. She kissed him tenderly, then nibbled on his earlobe as her hands coursed along his chest and shoulder, then moved down.

Shortly she found herself on her back again with him on top, which was her intention.

After all, it *was* the most favorable position for conception...

"Happy Birthday, Baby. I'm sure it's after midnight now," she said as she embraced him with her arms and her legs. "I love you, and I hope you enjoy my first gift for you..."

August 12

"...I remember coming through this beautiful state late last year and having Marc and Justine pull me aside at the end of our forum in Baton Rouge. They'd been pretty hard on me at times during the q & a period, so I wasn't sure what to expect afterwards. We got to talking and I discovered that they shared a lot of my beliefs. The more we discussed things, the more I began to think, 'you know, I would love to see this man and his wife as the First Couple of Louisiana'. The funny thing was, no sooner was I starting to hint at that when Justine said to her husband, 'so, Honey, when do we announce your candidacy?'"

John smiled at their reaction as he went on. "I felt the same way you do- then and now. I couldn't have been happier to hear that. The next day they began to amass their signatures to get Marc on the ballot and today, here we are in the thick of the race with support for him growing by leaps and bounds. I can't help but have total confidence that come January this man will be addressing the Bayou State legislature as your next Governor." The exuberance of the crowd was obvious by way of the deafening applause and cheering that followed John's address.

While he and Marc waved to them, John wondered how Kim was. Earlier in the morning she became so ill that she threw up, which was far from how she wanted to start off her 35th birthday. Her first thought was that it probably was a bit too much of the delectable but spicy food they'd had while they dined with the gubernatorial candidate and his wife the night before. Still, as a precautionary measure, Herb, Dawn and a couple volunteers took her to a doctor for an examination. So far John hadn't heard anything.

On the heels of his thought he got a tap on his shoulder. It was Herb, who gestured to him to follow him off stage.

He hurried off behind his head bodyguard, more than a little worried. He quickly spotted Kim, who was waiting for him in the left wing. The first thing he felt was relief; apparently, she was fine.

"What a sight. How much luckier could I be?" he said, remarking on her exceptionally brilliant smile as he went to her and kissed her in greeting. He took her into his arms and held her close for a moment. When they pulled back, he noticed her smile still was every bit as glowing and he couldn't help but return it. Her eyes stayed locked on his but she said nothing, which made him a little curious. "What is it, Kitten? What's behind that-"

What he thought next made his mouth fall open; there only was one reason why she could be so happy after coming from a hospital. "Was it...morning sickness, by any chance?" Her expression remained constant and in an instant his smile mirrored hers. What else would make her happy to the point of bursting, which it looked like she was on the verge of? "So, you're-..."

She nodded, still unable to speak, as her lips trembled and a couple tears spilled from her eyes, which conveyed the depth of her joy in a way her words couldn't.

He drew her close and held her tightly as her exultation, which couldn't possibly be kept within her, poured out. He summed up the moment very succinctly: "we did it."

"I'm really happy for both of you, John," Herb said, taking a couple seconds to pat him on the shoulder before he went back to his job. "Better yet, Kim's expecting twins."

John smiled broadly in reply. "Well, I'll be…I wonder if our friend, the Cerne Abbas Giant, had anything to do with this?"

"We know he sure didn't hurt the cause!"

Marcus and Justine Andrews walked over. "Is everything all right, Mister Governor? How are you feelin', Ma'am?" After only a brief observation, his concern was gone. "Or, should we just say, 'congratulations'?"

Marc, a highly respected professor and head of the Political Science department at LSU- also an activist and one-time legislator-, was a Southern gentleman through and through. Justine, an elementary school teacher for twenty years and Vice Principal for five more, was held in equally high esteem and epitomized the Southern Belle. With three children of their own, they recognized instantly what was taking place between John and Kim, having shared that wonderful feeling three times themselves.

"We have over 10,000 good friends out there who I believe would be very pleased to know that not only is this lovely young birthday girl perfectly well, but she's also expecting and we're the first to know. Shall I tell 'em, or would you like the honor?"

Since John was unable, he deferred to Marc, who said he had a little surprise in the works and promised he wouldn't keep them long. They walked out to center stage where Marc made the announcement. The crowd erupted into applause once more.

Next came the 'surprise'. "Now, I'd like y'all to join with me in wishing the soon-to-be Mom a happy birthday! One, two, three- 'Hap-py Birth-day to you…'"

Sure enough, the crowd joined into the song while Kim blushed.

September 21

"…so, here we are, only two weeks to go before what could be Election Day in Louisiana. Some of you political enthusiasts might know that here in the Bayou State they hold their elections in a unique manner. It's called an Open Primary, in which

296

virtually anyone can throw his or her hat into the ring. As such, they're not bound by the formalities of conventional primaries; there seems to be a more grass roots kind of appeal to it. This Open Primary will be held on Saturday, October 4th.

"Now, what's really interesting is, if one candidate garners 50% or more of the vote, that candidate is declared the winner and Governor-elect, and that's it. However, if no candidate secures the majority of the vote, a subsequent runoff election for the post in question is held between the top two vote-getters in the primary. In the event one is needed, a runoff election will be held on November 15th.

"As you might recall, a runoff election was necessary last year in the senatorial race when the democratic incumbent was pitted against the Progressive contender, who barely edged out a republican challenger for second place. Now-U.S. Senator Beauregard, a descendant of the famous Confederate General, shocked everyone with her victory over the heavily favored incumbent in that runoff election. Her brilliant campaign fittingly capped off the party's successes last year.

"With that in mind, Governor Stratton can't help but be highly enthused about how things are looking for his party and that spirit appears to have spread pretty far! The latest polls among registered voters here show Progressive gubernatorial candidate Marcus Andrews a whopping eighteen percentage points ahead of his competition, which is up six points from a couple weeks ago!

"Normally, a Governor's election wouldn't hold nearly as much national attention but these are far from normal circumstances. There is considerably more scrutiny on this one because it's the first contest since the interim elections last year and is being played up by many in the political world. This is seen not only as a contest between the candidates themselves and their party ideologies, but also as a contest of clout between the President and his one known challenger at this time: John K. Stratton, of course.

"We have Progressive candidate Matthew Bell in Kentucky in a statistical dead heat for the lead with the republican challenger, but in Mississippi, candidate Rita Malloy of the new party still trails by twenty points, although she has gained ground pretty steadily. It's really getting interesting, everyone, so stay tuned!"

Brimming with confidence, John clicked off the TV, but yawned right after he did that. As much as he loved campaigning, it did take a toll.

"Baby, would you help me with something, please?"

"Sure, Kitten, what is-" The rest of his sentence never made it out when he turned to see his gorgeous wife standing before him, totally nude, smiling and- better yet- holding a bottle of lotion that she handed to him.

"I thought you could use a little break- you've been going pretty hard lately. Now that I'm beginning to show, I was hoping I could talk you into rubbing me down with this lotion each night, at least, so I might be able to avoid stretch marks."

"Like you'd have to talk me into that!"

"Well, I'm glad I can provide you with a diversion."

"Indeed you have; I'll get right to work. Here, hold this for me." He handed the lotion back to Kim, then- much to her delight-scooped her up and carried her into the bedroom. "Looks like you have everything ready." He remarked as he laid her down onto the towel she'd placed over the comforter.

He squeezed some lotion into his palm and looked at Kim, who by every indication was very eager. "Are you ready, Mrs. Stratton?"

"Mm-hmm!"

Not wasting a second, he went to work, starting with her abdomen. Probably for the first time ever, it had a slight paunch. He took care not to rub too forcefully, given the cause- causes, rather- of that paunch. "You took your vitamins, right? And-"

"I sure did. I ate all my meals, drank plenty of water and exercised. And no, I'm not annoyed because you're asking me that again," she replied as she touched his cheek.

"You know, I don't think you've stopped smiling ever since we found out."

"I doubt I have. Isn't this wonderful? I'd still like to know exactly when it happened, but that's not so big a deal. As many times as we made love in that span, I guess it would be tough to nail it down. Just that it did happen is good enough."

She was quiet for a moment and when John glanced at her, he saw a tear forming in her eye, although she still was smiling. She went to say something, but held back, which made him curious. "What's on your mind?"

"Oh, nothing, I-..."

"What is it?"

"Well…I was just thinking about-…you know what I look forward to most? The first time my children call me 'Mommy'. Be warned- I know I'll probably be a mess when that happens, so I hope you and they will bear with me."

"Not that you're emotional or anything," he jested, and winked at her. With that, he moved up to her breasts, which were highly sensitive because of her pregnancy. She winced in discomfort when he started on them, even though he was far from rough in his handling of them. After apologizing, he became even gentler.

She closed her eyes and moaned softly as his touch, which never failed to arouse her, was doing it again. She shifted around and clutched at the towel as he went on, and her back arched when he focused his efforts on her nipple. Looking up, she saw in his eyes how close he also was, so she did all she could to keep him moving in that direction. "I was glad when the doctor said we can make love up until close to the 8th month."

His eyes narrowed. "What's this 8th month stuff- are you kidding? They'll have to pull me off you when you're in the delivery room!"

She cracked up. "And I thought *I* was awful!! We sure make a perfect match in more ways than one, apparently!"

"Do I ever second that." He finished with the lotion rubdown. With a grin he climbed into bed with her and started to give her a demonstration of what he'd alluded to…

…until Kim's cell phone rang. Groaning, she reached over to the nightstand and picked it up. "Hmm, it's Linda and Rachel's number. It's pretty late for them to be calling," she observed before pushing the 'talk' button. "Hello?"

She frowned and turned to John. "Yes, this is she. Who are-…" Her query, which had been cut off, was quickly answered. "Oh, no…"

John moved close to her. "Honey, what's wrong?"

"Absolutely. Thank you for letting me know. Can you give me directions from the airport?" She gestured for John to get her a pen and a sheet of paper, which he did quickly. She scribbled down what she needed. "Thank you again; we'll be there as soon as we can…"

October 3

John and Kim sat quietly with Rachel, and Mrs. Shaw from the Child Protection Agency in New York City. It was hard for any of them to believe it had come to this so soon.

Rachel's mother Linda, unbeknownst to anyone, was in an advanced stage of intestinal cancer, which had spread throughout her system. Having to work two jobs in order to support Rachel, Linda worked herself to the point of exhaustion and collapsed on the job on September 19th. The next day, when her tests came back, the doctors quickly had found what the HMO doctor had missed while conducting his routine- and obviously superficial-annual examinations. Even though a couple tumors showed up in Linda's last exam, they apparently were ignored or dismissed by the HMO physician.

What incensed the doctors at the hospital was that the disease absolutely should have been detected, and most likely could have been cured completely. Linda's doctor at the hospital subsequently filed the most derogatory report she could charging the HMO doctor with gross negligence and outright incompetence for turning what should have been a routine tumor removal into a terminal condition. On behalf of Rachel and her mother, John and Kim were contemplating pressing charges of malpractice against that doctor.

Fully appraised of her situation, Linda called her paralegal friend into her room on the 20th and that same day completed her will. The next day it was notarized and official, and Mrs. Shaw from the Agency was called in. In between taking care of her affairs to the fullest extent that she could, Linda spent as much of her last days with Rachel as possible.

It was on that last day that Kim and John were informed of the situation and left New Orleans posthaste for New York. In her hospital room during the last night of her life, Linda asked the couple if they would adopt her only child, which they agreed to without hesitation. That was the main provision of her will; she and Rachel already had discussed it, and Linda had made that provision only after Rachel had shown and expressed her approval. With Rachel's father a convicted felon and Linda's wish that he never see his daughter again in light of what he'd put her through, there was no chance of him getting any custody whatsoever, or visitation.

With that knowledge, Linda was at peace. She kissed her daughter good night and went to sleep forever sometime during the first few hours of September 22nd, 2003.

Now, two weeks later, their case was before the judge. It was the last case she'd see for the day. Suddenly the door opened and her assistant came into the antechamber.

"The judge will see you now."

"...I can tell you both want very much to adopt Rachel, but won't you be busy traveling during your campaign? That most intense part of it would coincide with the fall school session next year, when she's due to start Kindergarten."

Kim answered. "Yes, Your Honor, which is why, given what's happened, I'll be staying at our home in Maryland with Rachel while my husband travels during that final stretch. Since we'll have two more little ones by then, John, Rachel and I will have all the time in between to come to know each other and do things together."

"One more thing, Your Honor," John added. "I've already planned, as of mid-December, to spend the last two months of Kim's pregnancy at home with her and Rachel, plus the first two or three months after she delivers, depending upon how quickly she recovers and becomes self-sufficient again. What we've wanted most for some time now is to have a family of our own and I want to do everything possible to help make sure they're all right."

The judge nodded and turned to the representative for the state. "What are your thoughts, Mrs. Shaw?"

"Well, Your Honor, as you see in the will, Rachel's mother clearly expresses her desire for her daughter to live with the Strattons. Based on that, Rachel's affection for them and all we've learned from and about them, plus my observations of them when they're together, I recommend we grant them full, unconditional custody and approve the adoption."

"I agree completely. So ordered, case adjourned. Congratulations, Mr. and Mrs. Stratton, and to you too, Rachel. Please accept my best wishes for your life together."

"Thank you so much, Your Honor, and you, too, Mrs. Shaw." With that, Kim went right over to Rachel, knelt in front of her and hugged her.

"Does this mean I can come home with you?"

"It sure does, Honey. Are you ready?" She nodded 'yes' and Kim stood and took her hand. Then, John moved to her opposite side and took her other hand. They said goodbye to their benefactors and off they went...

...late that night, as Rachel slept in between them while they flew back to New Orleans, Kim watched John for a while as he stared out the window into the night. He hadn't moved for some time, even to shift; he was so still that it was hard to tell that he was breathing.

"You haven't said much of anything the whole flight, Baby," she said, finally disrupting his reverie. "What's on your mind?"

Finally he turned to her, and she saw the emotion in his eyes.

"I don't think it really hit me until just now."

"What?"

"She never stopped smiling..."

Kim caught on quickly. "You mean Linda." When he nodded, she went on. "At the same time my heart was breaking for her, I also saw how happy she was. She knew Rachel would be in good hands. She wasn't the least bit bitter about what had happened to her; all that mattered to her was her daughter's well being. It was so strange, but... as soon as she went to sleep that last night, I knew she wouldn't wake up again. This thought kept going through my head: 'she's at peace'."

As he thought more about Kim's words, he began to look at the situation in that way as well. Although he still hated what had happened to Linda he also knew a couple positives had come of it.

Besides the obvious and bittersweet one, another had just dawned on him. "The judge never even brought up your past as a dancer. Neither did Mrs. Shaw, and like you said- this was the time someone would have. You know what that tells me? People in general finally might be moving beyond it and not letting it influence their opinion of you nearly as much as before. It might even be turning into an afterthought."

"I hope so."

They both watched the sleeping child for a moment. "How about that, Kitten? You went into the store for an ice cream and walked out with a daughter."

"I guess I did, although I sure don't like the circumstances."

302

"Yeah. Needless to say, losing her mother will haunt her; that's an awful lot for anyone to bear, let alone a four-year-old."

"We both know that, which is why we'll be able to help her there. Rachel won't have to bear it alone. I think she'll be all right." She smiled and stroked her daughter's hair.

"So do I. Wonder how she'll react to her first Election Day?"

"We're about to find out, since the day is upon us officially," Kim noted as she glanced at her watch and saw that it was a couple minutes past midnight.

"...so, that's where we stand at this point here in Baton Rouge. It looks like the clock reads...right about at 9:30 PM local time. The polls have been closed for an hour and a half and with 75% of the parishes reporting in this gubernatorial election, we have the Progressive candidate with a big lead over his republican challenger. The question is, will he take the majority of the vote and thus win the Governorship tonight?

"I have to tell you, Angie, I haven't seen this much enthusiasm over non-presidential elections in some time. We finally have a real competition going on here involving not only a legitimate third party, but a strong one. The popularity and charisma of Governor Stratton most definitely have had an influence in this contest. His Populist message clearly has resonated- understandably so in the home state of the man who previously was identified as the foremost Populist: Hugh Pierce Long, better known as Huey, or The Kingfish.

"It was believed that then-Senator Long would have presented a big threat to Franklin Delano Roosevelt's presidency in the 1936 election, which he'd have been a part of, having declared his intention to run against FDR that year. However, in September of 1935, an assassin's bullet ended his aspiration along with his life. In April of 2000 we came close to losing Governor Stratton to an assassin's bullets, but fortunately he didn't follow Senator Long's lead in that regard.

"Nowadays, it's looking a lot like Governor Stratton presents an equally- if not, more- serious threat to President Black who, like FDR was in the '35-'36 timeframe, is in his first term and gearing up for a bid for reelection. From all indications, Governor Stratton has revived that Populist spirit and means to ride it all the way to the White House, helping as many like-minded candidates

303

as he can into office along the way. The 39-year-old former Governor of Maryland, elected to that post in 1994 and reelected overwhelmingly in '98, seems absolutely determined and unshakable in his quest.

"His well known, attention-grabbing wife is proving her worth to his campaign, too. She's become very popular herself; the negative opinions of her appear to be dying down, especially given the effect her pregnancy has had on her. Mrs. Stratton's delight over her state is obvious to anyone. Also factor in the couple's adoption of four-year-old Rachel Williamson, the very child Mrs. Stratton rescued from an imminent abduction by her non-custodial father back in March; it reads like a storybook ending. Finally, there can be no question of her absolute devotion to her husband. How people view Kimberly Stratton now is decidedly different from how they did when her past came to light in 2000 until as recently as earlier this year.

"In addition to the Strattons' efforts, if you add in the tireless campaigning on his behalf by Louisiana's Progressive U.S. Senator and both Representatives while in the midst of their congressional duties, that amounts to an awful lot of pull around here for Mr. Andrews!

"As for President Black, his popularity is going in the other direction with the growing dissent about the economy and the occupation of Iraq, the questions that have been raised about the pre-war intelligence, what the President knew about it and whether he or those in his administration exaggerated it. Add to that the fact that our forces have yet to capture Saddam Hussein and Osama bin Laden, which certainly doesn't help the President, either. Already we're seeing the effect of those consequences on the races at hand; you have to wonder if his coattails are shrinking.

"You also have to wonder what's happening with the democrats, who don't seem to be doing much more than wringing their hands and pointing fingers while trying to find some direction. Given how poorly the democratic candidate is faring-

"Ok, here we go. The latest numbers are coming in and- well, how about this, everyone? With 94% of the parishes in Louisiana reporting, we can project Progressive candidate Marcus Andrews, with 54% of the vote, as the majority winner and Governor-elect of Louisiana! They've done it! I think it's safe to say that any lingering doubts about the Progressives being a legitimate national party instead of just a flash in the pan, or a party with only regional or marginal appeal, have been dispelled.

"On the contrary, with this huge victory they are even stronger now- definitely a force to be reckoned with! President Black's personally endorsed candidate finishes a distant second-twenty-five percentage points behind! Not only is this a victory; it's a decisive one! The big losers here appear to be the democrats, whose candidate as it stands has collected only 12% of the vote!

"The independents, the swing voters, the previously unregistered voters and the registered voters who usually do not turn out to vote all seem to have come out in force for this one! As far as I'm concerned, Governor Stratton wins the award for best impression of the Pied Piper, because he really brought 'em out! The President and his party, the democrats and most of the pundits dismissed the Progressives before; they all must be in a state of shock now! Back to you, Angie."

"Thank you, Katie. Wow, what a night huh?" She turned to her camera. "Ok, folks, we need to take a station break here, but stay tuned. Hopefully we'll hear from Governor-elect Andrews, and also from Governor Stratton in a little while. I'm Angie Dobson, bringing you continuous live election coverage. We'll be right back."

"…yes, Barbara, that's exactly what we want, too. If what Doctor Hayes at the hospital said is the case- that those tumors were obvious and all of this would have been avoided if that HMO doctor simply had done his job-, I want to do all I can to help make sure that guy never practices medicine again. We'd be saving other peoples' lives by taking him out of the picture, so yes, my husband and I are in agreement with you and the board…that's why John's as passionate as he is about that subject.

"He hates HMOs and the whole state of health care, just like most of us do. That's another reason why he's come to look so badly upon the Reagan administration, and I'm with him. The healthcare system never should have been turned into a profit-based business. Insurance companies are running it, for all intents and purposes, and it's such a mess. In this case, Linda's company didn't help, either, going for that bargain basement HMO like they did in order to save a few bucks. I'll be so glad when John gets rid

305

of that system and provides good care for everyone. Well, keep us in the know, Ok?…Thanks- you, too. 'Bye."

When Kim hung up with the attorney looking into the matter of Linda Williamson's death, she turned and was surprised by Rachel, who stood in the doorway. "Oh- hi, Sweetie. Gosh, you sure are quiet; I never even heard you! Come sit with me."

As she did, Kim clicked the TV on. "I have to get used to having you here, don't I? It's only been John- your new Daddy, that is- and I for as long as we've been together, but now," she kissed Rachel on the top of her head, "we have you with us and we'll have two little ones in a few months. Did you have fun today, seeing your brothers or sisters inside me?"

"Yeah! That was really neat, but why did you say you didn't want to know if they would be little sisters or brothers?"

Kim giggled. "All your Daddy and I wanted to know was that they were healthy. We'll love them just as much, no matter if they're boys, girls or one of each. We're very happy we're having twins, but we're even happier that they'll have a big sister."

"Well, I hope you have one of each. I don't want two brothers; I don't think I could handle them. One brother would be nice, though, because my sister and I can keep him out of trouble."

Kim laughed out loud. "I will keep your request in mind!"

"May I feel the babies again?"

"Sure. Let's lie down first, though." When they did, the child lay her head onto Kim's stomach. They smiled at each other for a moment, but then Rachel's began to fade.

Having been there before herself, Kim knew exactly where she was. This seemed to be the right time to let her daughter in on something they had in common. "You know, Honey, I haven't told you this yet, but I had two Mommies- just like you."

"Really?"

"Mm-hmm. My second Mommy, who's your Grandmom now, adopted me when I was fourteen. I became her daughter the same way you've become mine."

"I miss my Mommy and I'm mad at the angel for taking her away, but I'm glad she told me to come and live with you. She told me you would take good care of me."

"Your mother was very good to you, wasn't she?" Rachel answered by nodding. "I don't blame you for being angry with the angel for taking her away. To tell you the truth, I'm angry about that, too. It's hard to understand sometimes when good people are taken from us- harder still when the reason why is so-..." she purposely cut herself off there.

I'd better not go any further with that; it'll only rile me up again, which is the last thing Rachel needs to see. She's hurting enough as it is, Kim thought, recalling how she'd found Rachel earlier in the day. She hated the mere thought of the child crying, even though she knew it was better she do that than hold the pain of her loss inside.

It was time to help her on the way to healing. Kim's natural instincts toward that end kicked in, helped by the personal dimension, since she was picking up where Linda left off.

Rachel is my daughter now.

That gave Kim a very good feeling. "I'm glad you're living with your new Daddy and me. We're both so happy that you wanted to be with us. Your Grandmom feels the same way. She's the nicest lady you'll ever meet and you will meet her very soon; tomorrow we'll be going home for a while. She's really excited to know she has a Granddaughter and she can't wait to meet you. You didn't have a Grandmom before, did you?"

"Mm-mm," she shook her head.

"Well, you'll like her very much."

"What happened to your first Mommy? Did the angel take her away, too?"

She sighed. "Yes. I wasn't as young as you are when it happened, but it still made me very sad."

"Did you have another Daddy?"

Kim wasn't ready for that. Just as she was trying to formulate an answer, one of the twins made his or her presence known. *Your timing is impeccable,* she thought, not wanting to discuss Steven Francis at all. This also didn't seem like the right time to tell Rachel the whole story about Jake, Kim's real father. "Whoa, did you feel that? We might have a soccer player in the making, huh?"

Rachel laughed, but turned and looked at the TV screen when she heard John's name mentioned. "There he is!" she called out as she saw his image.

"That's right, and he's about to speak to all those people. Let's listen..."

* * *

307

"...so I'll give the floor to Governor Stratton first, for without him, all he's done and all he'll continue to do, there would not be a Progressive party, my victory would not have been possible and the state of decline we're in surely would continue, but all that is about to change! Take it away, Mister Gov-...well, I suppose I can call you John for now, can't I?"

John laughed, then embraced him and clapped him on the back. "Well, you can call me that for a year, anyway!" He accepted the microphone and addressed the jubilant throng. "Thank you, Marc. All right, everyone- how about a rousing, Cajun-style welcome for your next Governor and First Lady?" Their applause became even louder- something John didn't think was possible- and lasted for a good thirty seconds.

"You also should give yourselves a round of applause, because primarily this is your victory. *You* made it happen!" They reached the same decibel level with their response. When they finished, he went on. "So much for those political analysts who for much of this year claimed the majority of you were against what we stand for, huh? Apparently they only polled a bunch of republicans and some democrats!" The gathered supporters laughed, then cheered again.

"This is our opportunity, everyone; the wheels officially are turning! You, the voters of the great state of Louisiana, have given everyone further evidence that the days of the two-party system in America are coming to an end! You also did it last year by sending a Senator and two Representatives to Congress. You've told the powers-that-be, who are on their way out, that you're sick of their endless bickering, smearing and failed policies.

"You have joined hand-in-hand with the citizens of my home state of Maryland and those of Arkansas, California, Delaware, Illinois, Iowa, Indiana, Michigan, Minnesota, Missouri, Ohio and Oregon in letting the corporate lackey republicans and the reactionary democrats know that they do not have the last word in politics anymore! I'll be going back to Kentucky and Mississippi over the next month and, along with Matt Bell and Rita Malloy, our candidates in those states, I'll do my best to help keep our victories coming.

"As for our opposition, tonight you said 'no' to all their money, mudslinging and shady salesmanship. You showed them with your votes that you don't want their stagnation- that you're not happy with the way things are, that you believe our nation can be better and that you will take positive action to make it better, which you have done tonight! In one loud, clear voice you have made your clamor for reform heard, and believe me- your voice is resonating not only around the country, but around the world!

"You have taken part in the biggest voter turnout ever recorded in the history of your state elections, so again I say each and every one of you who participated in this exercise of democracy are the real winners tonight! Our party has charged the democrats and republicans with loitering in public office and here in Louisiana, as in many states over the last year few years, you voters have turned in a guilty verdict and sentenced them to expulsion from office!"

There was still more laughter and applause. *Damn- they sure are charged up tonight!* John thought amid a big smile of his own.

His confidence just kept on building...

"Our next step is clear. We need to keep building upon our successes. The same recipe that worked here tonight applies nationwide: we need every man and woman who is of voting age to register between now and next summer, and then vote in the elections next year. We have the momentum; two of the three major political parties in our nation are on the run and we, the newest major party, need to keep them on the run.

"With our victory here, you have borne witness to the fact- yes, the fact- that your voice does make a difference and you must make it heard. When you put all of them together, the resulting shout is loud enough not only to shake the establishment, but also to make their rickety, decaying house come crashing down!

"Thanks to all of you and the voters everywhere who have ushered in the era of the Progressives, I take even more pride in being an American than I ever have! We have a lot of work to do in our country and with this vote you've acknowledged that you understand that and you're willing to chip in and do your part. You've taken a crucial step toward making your nation a much better place. Remember: the biggest enemy we face is apathy, which the democrats, republicans and the 1% of our population with too much money in their hands have thrived on in the past.

"Well, that's not the case anymore! We will do what needs to be done. A new standard has been declared: we do not accept politicians who sell out to special interests and the wealthy, reneg on their campaign promises and just sit on their butts and do nothing when elected! We are not a passing fad; we're here to stay! Our opponents are afraid now- believe it! As for the media, they don't know what hit 'em! They'll be running around in circles and talking to themselves for weeks!" More laughter, then another huge round of applause followed.

"All right, I think you've had enough of my mouth for one night. You have some celebrating to do, but be safe and don't make the police work too hard tonight as a result. Good night, everyone; enjoy this historic moment!

"Once more, here's your next Governor..."

John took care to be as quiet as he could when he walked into the bedroom of their suite. Sure enough, they were asleep.

He took a moment just to watch them, appreciating the picture of serenity and beauty as mother and daughter dozed, peaceful as they could be.

He left the door open a little so he'd have just enough light, crept over to the chair to get his pajamas, then turned and made his way to the bathroom to change.

"Congratulations, Baby."

Kim's voice was just above a whisper, but it was enough to stop him in his tracks. He turned and saw her smiling. She definitely had the sleepy face on, too, with the half-lidded eyes.

He smiled back, walked over to her and kissed her. "The same words that came to mind when I found out you were pregnant are coming to mind again: we did it."

"We sure did. Rachel and I drifted off not long after you finished; I think she's the soundest sleeper I've ever seen! I wanted to wait up for you but I couldn't quite make it."

"Trust me, I understand completely. I'm about ready to sleep for a week! At the very least, I'm glad we won't be taking off from here until the afternoon, which gives us a good ten-plus hours. On that note, I'll be right back."

Changing into his pajamas, climbing into the king-sized bed very slowly so he wouldn't disturb Rachel, bidding Kim good night and watching her quickly rejoin their daughter in slumber, then falling asleep himself took less than five minutes of those ten-plus hours...

* * *

310

...however, in his home outside Philadelphia, which wasn't far from where his office building was situated, Philip Raines was nowhere near sleep. The result in Louisiana brought very bad tidings, to say the least, for him and everyone in the same boat with him.

Not only had the damage been done- the situation probably would get worse.

"Fifty-four percent..."

That kept playing over and over in his head. The near-term ramifications were that the two remaining Governors' races in Kentucky and Mississippi undoubtedly would be affected by the outcome of this one, and it now seemed quite possible the Progressives could pull off the hat trick for this year.

Worst of all was what the easy victory by the outsiders boded for next year: Stratton, the heart and soul of the party, clearly had the momentum now. Unless he stumbled somehow, which wasn't likely since he was focused and a seasoned veteran of political campaigns although not even forty years old, he stood a good chance of doing the unthinkable in thirteen months...

...thirteen. An unlucky number.

"Maybe I should shoot that son of a bitch myself..."

As appealing a thought as that was, he phoned one of the two men he'd hired for that purpose. Given his displeasure with the lack of progress, it was time to turn up the heat.

Chapter 15

December 15

"...and that same tidal wave rolled up through Kentucky. So, in response to your question, there's no doubt in my mind that our victory in Louisiana paved the way for what we achieved last month, and also for what I'm very confident we will achieve on November 2nd, 2004. As for Kentucky, you want to talk about a nail-biting bonanza of an election? I'm happy to say mine finally have grown back to pre-recount length.

"We only won the Governor's race there by 238 votes after two recounts just to be sure, but we did win it. That was another reason why I keep saying every vote counts. Matt was outstanding and so was Rita in Mississippi. I'll repeat what I said on election night: she gave a valiant effort and there's absolutely no shame in finishing second- not when she fought as hard as she did and managed to edge out her democratic competitor for her place.

"I feel the same way about Rita Malloy as I do about Marc Andrews and Matt Bell; I couldn't be more proud that they're on my side. Overall, the best-case scenario I came up with regarding those gubernatorial elections was exactly what came to pass. For that reason and my wife's pregnancy you can expect to see this smile on my face for quite some time."

John was addressing a large group of reporters outside the main auditorium of the University of Missouri in Kansas City where his latest forum held that morning had just concluded. The attendance was so high that some people had to watch on closed circuit TV from overflow rooms set up in anticipation of the huge turnout. He'd decided to do some more campaigning after the conclusion of the Governors' races while Kim and Rachel went back home. Once this press conference concluded, he'd be on his way to rejoin them.

"I also want to let you all know that today's forum marks a temporary transition point in my schedule, which I'm scaling back for a bit. Kim, Rachel and I will be spending the final couple months before Kim's due date and probably the first couple months after she delivers at home. I'll still do some forums during that time, but they'll be fairly close to home so I can get right back just in case I need to. This pregnancy is extremely important to us,

312

needless to say; we've worked awfully hard to get to where we are, and-…I could have done a better job expressing that, couldn't I?" He said, covering his face as the reporters laughed. "In all seriousness, I'm sure every parent out there along with those who want to be parents can understand where I'm coming from. As for now, I'll take a few more questions."

"First of all, Sir, I hope everything goes well for you, your wife and your children. My question, Mister Governor, is how will the capture of Saddam Hussein factor in on the election? Do you think this will make the President tougher to dislodge?"

"Frankly, I doubt Hussein's capture will have much of any impact on the election- not when you factor in all the jobs we're losing here, many of which our businesses are shipping overseas. Not when the middle and lower classes still are getting rooked at every turn. Not when we have at least ten million illegal aliens here- and counting, since our border guards are overwhelmed. Not when the wealthy get tax breaks, and executives' salaries are ridiculous and still rising while that of their workers is declining. Not while actors and athletes make millions upon millions of dollars for doing nothing while those in the critical positions wither on the vine. Not while our healthcare and educational systems are substandard, to put them in the best possible light. Not when we're still totally dependent upon foreign oil. We're hurtling down the wrong course and we need to reverse this President's abysmal domestic programs as soon as we possibly can.

"He keeps telling us about how he's fighting the terrorists. That needs to be done but you can't let your own nation fall apart in the process. It's been my position all along that we need to take care of ourselves first. That's common sense, which I mean to bring back into our domestic policies."

"You do believe it's good we captured him, though, right?"

"Is it a good thing Hussein is in custody? In some ways, yes, in some ways, no. At any rate, that's what should have happened in '91. The President at the time screwed up badly by stopping when an easy and total victory was in his grasp. That's one of the half-measures you hear me railing against so often.

"By simply doing what he should have done and had every justification to do during the first Gulf War, all of this could have been avoided. We had the coalition then, we knew he was a bad guy who had no business running a soup line let alone a nation, yet the President stopped, which I never will understand. The excuses

313

given made no sense then and they make even less sense now. Plus, look how many more people suffered and died as a result. Simply put, the President had a golden opportunity and he blew it. Now, we have the same people in charge trying to clean up the mess they made 13 years ago.

"You must not take half steps; if you do, then you haven't solved the problem. It's still there and inevitably it will come back and bite you- case in point, Iraq. Time and time again throughout history we've seen that's the case. Either do the job right or don't do it at all. It doesn't get any plainer than that.

"However, I want to bring up what I see as the main issue here, and again we can go back to '91, after Gulf War 1. Why did the Iraqis not finish the job that we started? Think about it; Hussein's army was all but destroyed, he was in hiding and at his weakest. The people there had the perfect opportunity to overthrow him, yet only a small faction of the Shiites rebelled. Why did *everyone* not rebel? They knew perfectly well what he was and what he'd done, yet most of them did nothing when the time came to act. Simply put, they lacked the will to do what was necessary, and what our military made possible for them.

"Since that was the task the current administration took upon itself, truthfully I wish there was a way we could make them pay for it directly. They're all wealthy oil people, right? That's where they made their money, so why not make them give it all back? Boy, how I'd love to do it that way since, try as they might to take your attention away from it, the fact is that their reasons for taking us into that war were deeply flawed and they knew it.

"Primarily, this is about oil. We know that in spite of their efforts to convince us that it isn't. Their shortsightedness in keeping us locked into gasoline and their need to keep the energy company profits up certainly play a part in this administration's foreign policy. Also, we were deceived and misled by a President who wanted to try to atone for the misstep his father made by not taking Hussein out when he so easily could have in '91. Or, maybe he wanted to 'one-up' his father.

"Speaking of 'father-son' relationships we could put the Iraq scenario in that light. Look at us as the parent and Iraq as the child. If you coddle the child too much, always come when it cries, always simply give it what it wants- or worse, what you think it needs-, ultimately you're not helping the child at all. The child comes to expect everything to be handed to it and thus will not appreciate anything and will not be inclined to find its identity, strike out on its own and fight for what it wants.

"Also, if you force your beliefs on the child- continuously browbeat it to do only what you want it to do- the child's own will is repressed and perhaps destroyed altogether. You ruin the kid; it becomes nothing more than an extension of you and unable to stand on its own. If we were to stay over there in force and continue to subliminally dictate terms to the Iraqi people under the guise of helping them, we would drastically hinder- if not destroy- their ability to find their own identity. We need to let them ferret out the insurgents, take control and move forward as a nation, or as three nations, if that's what they want to become."

"*Three* nations? What do you mean by that, Sir?"

"The national boundaries in the Middle East are artificial and arbitrary, drawn up by outsiders after World War I. Perhaps the officials of the whole region should sit down and hammer out new boundaries that better reflect what they want, without anyone else's meddling. Would make sense, right?

"Look, the bottom line is, in addition to the loss of more American soldiers, our continued presence in Iraq is causing mayhem and death for the people there. They want us out and I don't blame them. It's their country and it's time they mold it into what they want it to be.

"We keep hearing crap like, 'when will the Iraqis be ready to take control?' Who are we to make that determination? That's not our decision; it's up to them. They are a sovereign nation. They need to step up and plot their own course, and we need to get out of their way and let them. Besides, nation building is not our responsibility. You already know my feelings on that subject.

"To answer your question directly, based upon several recent reports I've heard from you in the media, I want to add that we've found the funding for Iraq's reconstruction- in all those billions of dollars ol' Saddam kept stashed away. $40 billion, which by far is enough to rebuild the country and make it better than it ever was.

"Among other things, that'll get their oil production up to 100% again- and probably pretty quickly. We don't need to send a penny more; their former dictator, in a huge twist of irony, has supplied all they'll need. That money must be confiscated and turned over to the Iraqi treasury, where it belongs, anyway. Let them employ and pay their own people to do that job instead of having American taxpayers pay the bill for companies from here, which didn't even have to bid for their contracts, the excessive amounts they charge.

"Ok, gang, I'm afraid that's all I have time for now. We have to be on our way and figure out where we'll stop for the night, if we do. Thanks for your well wishes and I hope you all have a great holiday season. See you soon!"

* * *

"Hello?"

They were rolling toward home that evening when John's phone rang, waking him from a nap.

"John? It's me."

The tone of Kim's voice had the effect of ice water dousing him. He sat up straight. "Honey, what's happened? Are you all right? The twins?"

"Yes, we're fine, but-"

"Is Rachel Ok?"

"She's fine, too, Baby. Things couldn't be better between us. The reason I'm calling...it's Jenny. She was attacked at her apartment late this afternoon. I don't know the details, but needless to say she's awfully upset. I'm on my way to get her and take her home with me; Herb's driving me there now. How long until you get back?"

"Probably not until tomorrow morning."

"Ok, we'll see you when you get here. We're almost at her place, so I'd better go…"

Ben was frozen, sick with worry.

He stared at the screen, watching the repeat of the breaking news report. Even though the image of the door to Jenny's apartment with the five bullet holes in it had disappeared minutes ago, it still was terribly lucid in his mind.

He knew.

There was no other explanation. Somehow, Raines not only had found out that Ben had a daughter- he'd also found out where she lived. Who else would want to get to Jenny like that? To kill her, or to put one hell of a scare into her, and thus send a message to him?

316

The only other explanation was, the so-called rival he'd hired to join in on the hit on John Stratton had found out. Regardless, it still was Raines' doing.

If they know that much, they probably know my real name and where I live. I have to assume that I'm totally compromised.

The more he thought about it, the more the panic wore off and a sense of urgency took over. He had to act, and fast.

He gathered together what he needed and was out the door. The first thing he had to do was check his car for any bombs; he could leave nothing to chance. After a thorough scan, he found none. He put his things into the back seat and started the engine.

While it warmed up, one thing kept running through his mind:

I'll kill you. This might be the last thing I ever do, but I will kill you...

However, there was something he had to take care of first.

"Tell me what happened, Jenny."

John and the team had decided to drive through the night, alternating behind the wheel. John himself pitched in and they made it back as Kim, who'd just completed a pretty vigorous workout despite being seven months pregnant, prepared breakfast.

John sat with Jenny and he saw her hand trembling as she reached for her glass of orange juice. Her eyes were somewhat glazed and bloodshot. It was clear she'd barely slept.

"I'd just put my uniform on and was warming up a little. It was our last home game and Monday night games always are a big deal, so I was gearing up for it when there was a knock on my door. I wasn't expecting anyone, and since it was just about dark, I was a little leery, thank God. I looked out the peephole and saw a guy holding a bouquet of flowers.

"I was about to open the door, but I watched him for a moment and noticed he was acting kind of weird. He kept looking back and forth, like he was nervous and checking to make sure nobody was around. I asked what he wanted and he said he had flowers for me and he needed me to sign for them. I asked if he could leave them for me because I wasn't dressed and he said no, I needed to sign for them. I've gotten flowers before and one of the delivery guys even said they usually didn't require a signature, so I asked again if he could please leave them and...he just blew up.

He started screaming at me and beating on the door, calling me a typical slut and prick tease. I was shocked- I mean, I have no idea who this guy is! Then my neighbor came out to see what was going on and he-…he shot him."

John put his arm around her, seeing she needed that, and waited for her to go on.

"I dove away from the door just as he started firing into it. There were five bullet holes in my door! I guess he took off running afterwards, and that was it."

"Your instincts served you well, Jenny- not only by causing you to dive away from the door, but most importantly by not opening it in the first place."

"I guess they did."

"No guesswork about it." He smiled at her, and she managed to return it in spite of the after effects of what had gone down. "Well, apparently they still haven't caught him yet. I hope they do soon, but until that happens, I agree with Kim: you need to stay here with us."

"Thanks, you guys. I sure won't argue. I'm definitely looking forward to the New Year; this one can't end quickly enough."

"I can see how you'd feel that way, but remember: it could have been worse- a *lot* worse. Have you heard from your Dad?"

"No, and I've been worried about him. I haven't been able to reach him since he came to my place on my birthday back in June and spent the day with me."

"That is really weird…"

"That's what I said," Kim added. "We still don't know how he knew all he did the day before he talked with Jenny, when all the festivities in May happened. I-…well, good morning, Sleepyhead!"

Rachel had just joined them. The way she rubbed her eyes combined with the bit of a frown had prompted the last word in Kim's greeting. However, her frown was gone quickly. "Good morning, Mommy. Hi, Daddy- welcome home."

"Hi there, Sweetheart. It's good to see you again," John replied, then he turned to Kim when Rachel addressed her once more.

"What's wrong, Mommy?"

Kim immediately had stopped what she was doing and turned to the child. A first had just happened, and for her it was a big one. To make it even better, Rachel had said that most anticipated word again. Apparently, things between them were even better than Kim thought.

John knew exactly what was on her mind, recalling their conversation as he rubbed her down with her lotion the night they got the call to fly to New York to be with Rachel and her mother. He watched as Kim, smiling broadly and eyes brimming, went to her, knelt in front of her and hugged her. "Nothing. I'm fine."

"Then why are you crying?"

"Because you called me 'Mommy'."

"I'm sorry, I won't do it anymore if-"

Kim pulled back and touched her face. "No, Honey, please don't think it's upsetting me. You've just made me so happy by doing that and I hope you always will. I just-...well, sometimes I cry when I'm really happy, like I am now."

"I thought you only cried if you were sad."

"Not if you're like I am. Some things affect me so much that I can't help myself."

"You won't cry if I tell a joke, will you?"

Kim cracked up. "No, I promise I won't do that! I see your Daddy's sense of humor is rubbing off on you already! Ok, you little stinker- breakfast is almost ready."

"Come sit with us, Rachel," John said, reaching out for her. She walked over and held her hands out toward him, and he lifted her up into his lap.

"What's your name?" she asked, looking at their guest.

"I'm your Aunt Jenny. It's very nice to meet you, Rachel."

"You're pretty, just like Mommy. Are you her sister?"

"Why, thank you! Your Mommy and I do look a lot alike; people say that all the time. We're not sisters, but we're very close. We've known each other for a long time and I've known your Daddy even longer."

"Aunt Jenny will be staying here with us for a while. She-" John's sentence was interrupted by a big yawn. "Excuse me. She's looking for a new place to live."

"You really look wiped, Baby," Kim noted as she glanced at him. "I can't imagine you'll be up very long."

"You've got that right. I might sleep through much of today as well as all through the night. In fact, I doubt I'll last much past breakfast. I suppose the world can do without me for a day or two so I can recuperate..."

It had gone surprisingly quickly.

Better still was the result.

As the dark stain beneath where he lay grew steadily bigger from the six holes in his body, Ben reflected upon what would be the shortest day of his life. Never had he accomplished so much, and never would he again.

He'd decided that it had to happen today; it was the only opportunity he'd have had since everyone would have know by the next day. Even if he'd survived, which he didn't consider as remotely possible when he put his plan together, there was no way he could have lived a life that even approached normalcy. He'd have had to walk away from everything- no way could he have subjected Jenny to the fallout that was sure to come. There was no guarantee they would leave her alone even if he was killed, but on the other hand, he couldn't do nothing. He couldn't have let them get away with attacking his daughter.

Ben had decided upon the direct approach, right into the mouth of the beast. He figured it was what his chief enemy would least suspect.

From the outset he knew this was a suicidal mission, but even so there was no question that it was far better to go out swinging, like he was, than to try to hide and be hunted down.

All that had troubled him were the repercussions it would have on Jenny, but again, it already was too late in that regard. Given the way it had gone down, along with the rest of the world she would know very soon what he'd done. She'd probably have to stay with John and Kim for some time before she'd be safe enough…

Without thinking much about it he walked into the office building of Tizer Pharmaceuticals, signed in and went right up the elevator to Philip Raines' outer office at the top floor.

When the door opened, he had his hand on his ten-millimeter automatic, expecting company.

His first surprise of the day was the sole member of his welcoming committee: Raines' exceptionally beautiful, buxom and very personable- although somewhat bubble-headed and quite vain- private secretary/hostess of four years, Ginger Reynolds. She looked as though she was the product of a sexual fantasy and, as always, was dressed for the part in her tight blouse, miniskirt, nylons and high heels. That was her uniform, as dictated by her boss. Of course, it was apparent she had no problem with that stipulation and he in turn was generous with her salary. She always wore the same alluring scent, too. Raines had told him this wasn't her only job; she had a nighttime gig in which her looks also served her very well.

She flashed the smile that was terribly seductive without her even intending for it to be, which, coupled with her other physical assets, was what got her hired. At no time when Ben had visited the office did he ever see the young woman working.

Ginger announced Ben's presence to Raines, who had her send him right in. There wasn't even a hint of alarm in his voice.

Ben smelled something besides the secretary's perfume; he smelled a trap as he followed the voluptuous, taller-than-average, twenty-something redhead into the spacious office…

…and surprise number two. Raines sat behind his desk and there was one other man in the office, standing by the window. Ben waited for Ginger to close the door behind her.

He didn't acknowledge Raines' greeting; he stared at the other man instead. There was something about him…

…it only was a matter of seconds before Ben knew who he was. It was in his eyes.

What happened next was right out of the old west, with a twist. The man reached for his gun but Ben already had his hand on his. Even with the silencer he managed to draw first and fire. Once more, his proficiency with firearms paid off. He snapped off three shots, all of which hit the younger man in his chest and dropped him. At that point, his competition was no more.

Then, he caught a movement in his peripheral vision: Raines.

Ben turned and fired twice more. Again, the bullets found their mark- square in the middle of his chest, knocking him out of his chair and making him drop the gun he'd pulled.

Just like that it was done.

He went over to Raines, who was gasping for air.

"Why?" the once-powerful man asked.

"You know why. You crossed the line and now you're paying for it along with your second-hand g-man over there, who I bet you sent to take care of your latest project." He glanced at the open drawer from which Raines probably had produced his gun. Inside it Ben saw some papers and a couple small notebooks. While keeping his pistol trained on Raines, he looked through the materials and found some interesting reading. "Here's some evidence that you aren't the only one who wants John Stratton dead. I'm sure he'll find this very enlightening."

"What-...what are you doing?!" he wheezed and coughed between words. "I hired...you to kill him and you're going to give him-" He clutched at his chest and fell back to the floor.

"You've got it. You're getting what your goon tried to do to my daughter," Ben said, taking the materials and depositing them into a cardboard express mail envelope.

"Your daughter? What-...what are you talking-" Those were his last words. Raines' head lolled a bit to the left until his cheek rested on the floor, and the darkness consumed him.

Ben dismissed Raines' attempted denial. "You never were much of a straight shooter, were you? Just wasn't your style," Ben mused out loud as he addressed the packet to John and took it out to Ginger, making sure to close the door behind him.

She was oblivious as to what had happened inside the office, since the only shots fired were from his pistol with the mounted silencer. Her radio surely drowned out any noise made.

Ginger was otherwise engaged, anyway; she fussed over a snag in her nylons. Her incredible legs were crossed and she worked on the imperfection in the material that was situated on her thigh. Her lower lip was turned down, as he noticed when she turned to him.

"I can't believe I did this; I just bought these pantyhose! I brushed against the edge of my desk when I walked over to get some water and looked what happened!" she fretted.

He moved closer and looked. "It's hardly noticeable, really, especially considering where that little snag is. If I may say so, as sexy as your legs are, I can't imagine anyone will even see it," he observed, with a wink.

"Thank you; you certainly may say so!" Her smile was dazzling.

"Actually, I believe I should be thanking you." With a coy giggle, she blushed and lowered her head. *I guess this girl can't help being sexy, even when she's being modest. I know someone else like you; you'd be tough competition even for Kimberly...*

He wrested control over his thoughts away from her when necessity re-emerged. "Uh, Ginger, would you do me a huge favor and run this to the mail room? It needs to go out right away."

"Sure!" She eagerly accepted the envelope and provided him with another visual feast as she rhythmically sashayed over to the elevator and pressed the button.

She has the walk down, too…damn…

"May I bring you a drink when I come back?"

"No, that's all right, but thank you, anyway." Another thought hit him all of a sudden; he didn't want her to be the one who found her boss. "Actually, why don't we step out for an early lunch? I'll, um, clear it with Mr. Raines."

"I'd love to! It's almost that time, anyway. Be right back." She still was smiling at him when the doors closed.

Ben raised his brows and gave a low whistle. The girl was something- that was for sure. Her nice and cheerful manner made her even more appealing.

Unfortunately, the next sight he saw fell at the opposite end of the pleasure spectrum.

The doors of the second elevator opened, and those who came out of it made a drastic change to his lunch plans.

At that moment it hit him that he'd allowed himself to drift, thinking the operation was over and contemplating what he'd considered unthinkable at the outset: survival. He'd forgotten all about the cameras Raines had in his office, which were monitored by his security personnel.

Even so, they'd taken some time to respond…

That thought was whisked away when three armed men rushed out, guns drawn.

Ben instinctively reached for his and instantly realized his second mistake as many bullets tore into him: he'd left his pistol on Raines' desk upon coming out here to give Ginger the envelope. There had been no need for him to bring the gun- so he thought. Raines was all but dead and every last bit of his hired gun's blood probably had run out of his body by now.

As Ben crumpled onto the floor, he knew it wouldn't be long before he joined them.

Two of the three men rushed into the office while the third kept his gun on Ben. "Don't you move! Don't you fuckin' move!!" The guy hollered such phrases several times.

If he'd been capable, Ben would have laughed at the sheer idiocy of those remarks. With six bullets in him he couldn't raise his arm to scratch his head let alone do something to hurt or kill this budding Einstein. Satisfaction, however, came when one of the men from inside the office yelled out, "he's dead!! Mister Raines is dead!! Get the cops on the line!!" Ben figured that was the case, anyway, but confirmation was a good thing.

If not safe altogether, at least Jenny was saf*er*, anyway…

The bell rang, signaling the return of the first elevator. Ginger emerged from it, turned pale, screamed and fainted, collapsing into the arms of the gunman.

Sorry, Ginger- didn't want you to see this…

While the physically huge but mentally tiny bodyguard, now without a charge, fondled the gorgeous receptionist under the guise of tending to her, Ben's thoughts turned inward.

Amid his lingering bafflement over the ease with which he'd disposed of Raines and his hired gun, Ben reflected on everything and the complex question that came along with it.

When all was said and done, who was he? What was he?

No one ever really knew- least of all, Ben himself. It could be said that what Weldon did to him destroyed what he could have been, which in some ways was the case. However, that didn't excuse how Ben ran away and hid- not in his own eyes. All he knew was that he was very adept at killing, regardless of whether he did it from a range of eight hundred yards or point blank…

…that's not true. There's another thing I am, which I was very good at for a while and happy being: Jenny's father. Even though there was quite a spell when I was far from the best one for her, that doesn't take away from the fact that I am her father and we did have our good times early on in her life. Plus, a few months ago there was that talk I've waited for so many years to have with her…

That thought led him to the one thing he wasn't able to do on this, his last day, which wasn't for lack of time. He knew if he'd called Jenny there was a good possibility he either wouldn't have been able to go through with all he had to do, or his instincts might have been hindered by the heavy emotions that call would have brought on.

As much as it hurt that he never would hear her voice again, he had to believe it was for the best that he didn't. Now he was certain he'd helped make her safer by getting both the man who'd come close to killing her and the one who'd given the order in spite of his denial.

324

That thought and his fond recollection of the last time he saw his beloved daughter, which best of all was on her birthday, were the last Benjamin Jacobson would have.

He'd answered his own question: when all was said and done, he was Jennifer Jacobson's father, and that was good enough for him.

That was the reason for the half-smile on his face that made the investigating officer, who arrived on the scene just after the assailant died, curious.

* * *

"...John!! Baby, wake up- you have to see this!"

As he said he would, he'd slept through much of the day before while the girls just hung out, and he slept the whole night and still was dozing heavily when Kim roused him.

He finally woke up and looked at the clock, still quite groggy. "Wha' time's it?"

"It's ten-thirty. Come on- get dressed and come downstairs! Hurry!"

"Ok, Ok. What's wrong?" he asked, getting out of bed and reaching for his sweats.

"Two packages came, and-...you have to see them. I still can't believe what's in 'em; it's all about the murder yesterday, and-"

"Murder?!" Now he was awake and moving at full speed.

"Philip Raines was shot and killed in his office; it's been all over the news," she said as she descended the stairs.

He stopped while following her down. "Philip Raines?! The head of-"

"Tizer Pharmaceuticals. Yes, that's him. He was killed mid-morning, right in the full swing of business hours. Here- let me turn on the TV." She clicked it on and the top cable news channel came up.

Sure enough, there was the story.

"I'll be damned...where are the packages that came?"

"Right here," she gestured to the papers, notebooks, audio and videotapes on the table in front of where she sat. "Read this letter first," she said, handing it to him.

He put his reading glasses on and started...

John:

It's time for me to come clean with you. I'd much rather have done it in person, but if you're reading this letter, chances are that's no longer possible.

I was hired to kill you. I'm sure you remember the bomb incident at the Channel 11 studio very well. To my eternal shame I have to say I probably would have killed you if you'd shown up that day, but I'm glad you didn't. Your father and I were friends once, and it would have been a horrible tragedy if I'd killed his son. I had to detonate the bombs to make sure they wouldn't trace them back to me when the stagehands found them.

I also have to confess, I was the one who shot at your kitchen window that same night, but no- I <u>was</u> <u>not</u> shooting at Kimberly. I wouldn't hurt her if my life depended upon it- not after all she's done for Jenny. Danielle Searles was my target. If you look at where the bullet struck, you'll see that it was right where she stood- not where Kimberly was. You should take some comfort knowing that the bulletproof glass you have in that window stopped a slug from a very high-powered rifle.

As for who I did shoot at, there's a lot of history- all bad. I could have handled things a lot better with her father than I did, which was why she ended up trying to kill me once and probably would have if succeeded if she'd gotten another opportunity. I should have just left Ray alone; I never should have gone to his place that last night. I was drunk and at a very low point and needed to unload. Ray always was quiet- he wouldn't let you know how he felt. I didn't know how far gone he was or else I'd never have laid everything on him that I did...

Danielle blamed me for his death. Although ultimately it was his decision, I didn't help any. After he shot himself, I went to ground, more or less. I went back to my old ways to make a living. I was a good sniper and there's always work available in that field. I took on the alias of 'Ray' as a reminder of what happened to my friend and what probably was coming for me. As for Danielle, the night your brother, Henry and I split off from you two and your team, I found out who manipulated her. Jack Weldon, the puppet master himself. He really did a job on her- turned her into a remorseless killer. She ended up killing Harry Lawson and probably didn't blink an eye doing it.

I was turning to ice just like she did until something happened that changed my perspective where you're concerned. My job was to kill you or try to scare you out of the race. It was partially personal, given our history, but that night in May, when you got Jenny away from that rapist and kidnapper she was seeing and made him pay with his life for all he'd done- that was the turning point. You looked out for my daughter. You did right by her, and so you did right by me. I actually had you in my sights when you, Tom and your bodyguard walked up the steps to Jenny's apartment.

John shivered when he read that part; he'd never had the slightest inkling that he was being watched that night, let alone being watched through the scope of a sniper rifle.

I was all set to pull the trigger, but then I thought about what that would do to my little girl- to see you gunned down right in front of her, so I held back.

It's the best decision I could have made, especially given the huge favor you did for her- and for me- when you killed Hedges. I hope you'll do me the further favor of looking out for her like you said you would as you rode home afterwards; you two are all the family she has left. She needs you and Kimberly now, and she'll need you even more, I'm afraid, given what will have gone down as indicated by the contents of this package and what you'll see on the news related to it all. As for when I killed Danielle, I figured I owed you one and I wanted to help nail the one who tried to kill your wife- more so on account of how good she's always been, and not just for Jenny. At that point I also decided that your death would not come by my hand, since that would devastate your wife.

When I found out Weldon was behind the attempts on Kimberly, that really made me want to help you both. Killing Jack was my primary objective, but not for its own sake, given that additional tidbit. Even though Jack caused a lot of trouble in my life, I wasn't worth too much in those days, anyway. I can't blame it all on him. All the same, I wasn't about to let him kill Kimberly. She's like another daughter to me. Her safety was paramount and I'm glad she came out all right. I'm also very happy that you two are about to have twins. It's good to know that there are at least three kids in this world who will have top-notch parents.

In case you're wondering, which I'm sure you are, I knew what I did because I planted a bug in your car the night you killed

Hedges. I did that while you, Tom, Jenny and your bodyguards were inside her apartment.

There are five other packets like this one in the mail. One each will go to The Baltimore Sun, The Washington Post, The Philadelphia Inquirer and The New York Times, and the last one will go to the federal prosecutor in Philadelphia. Each packet except the one you have has copies of audio and video tapes made of my conversations with Philip Raines, owner and CEO of Tizer Pharmaceuticals. He's the one who ordered the hit on you. In the video he says it clearly. Your packet contains all the originals.

If you haven't heard from me by now, that means I didn't make it. If that's the case, please look after my Jenny. Inside you'll find a separate letter addressed to her.

Goodbye, Mister President. I wish you, Kimberly and your children all the happiness in the world, and I'm truly sorry for what I entered into with Raines.

Ben Jacobson

An open-mouthed John had just finished reading when the news flash came.

"We have a stunning new development to report in the murder of pharmaceutical executive Philip Raines yesterday. Apparently, in a bizarre twist, Raines was killed by the same man he'd hired to kill the Progressive Presidential candidate, John K. Stratton. Not only that- based upon evidence the contracted killer sent in to several newspapers, other corporate executives had knowledge of the planned murder of former Governor Stratton and there were several references to Baltimore on November 1st of next year: the day before Election Day. The meaning of those references at this point is unknown, but according to U.S. Attorney Gloria Jefferson, a full-scale investigation is being launched to find the answer.

"Raines' killer was identified as Benjamin Jacobson, a former military sniper and gun shop owner who also served as a Deputy Sheriff under the father of the man he was hired to kill. Then, Mister Jacobson also ran against John Stratton in that fateful

Governor's race in 1994. A lot of history between the two men-that's for sure.

"One question that emerged from all this was, what could have caused Jacobson to turn against Raines? Videotape taken from one of the closed-circuit cameras Raines had monitoring his office revealed the entirety of the fatal confrontation, and a possible explanation. The gunman said to Raines, 'you're getting what your goon tried to do to my daughter', which in all probability was in reference to the attack in Silver Spring, Maryland a couple days ago on Jennifer Jacobson, his only child.

"However, police arrested Miss Jacobson's assailant last night. It turns out he's a flower deliveryman named Bart Groves, who'd made a delivery to Miss Jacobson's apartment earlier this year. Apparently, Groves had some sort of breakdown after asking another young woman out on a date and being rejected. For some reason, Miss Jacobson became the target of his anger.

"Evidently, Groves became obsessed with her as well, as a number of photographs of Miss Jacobson, along with a calendar she made after becoming second runner-up in the Miss Celestial pageant three years ago, were found in his room in Baltimore. Groves has confessed to the attempted murders of Jennifer and her neighbor, who still is in critical condition from his wound. If that's the reason Raines was killed, it seems he was killed by mistake.

"Meanwhile, from all over the country the popular sentiment arising from the assassination plot against Governor Stratton is one of uproar from the implications of all that was revealed. Maryland's ex-Governor is being hailed as the champion of the middle and lower classes, and this uncovered conspiracy against him is seen by many as an attempt by the wealthy to block progression toward a more just and fair society. They see former Governor Stratton as the vehicle to that end and obviously are incensed by the intentions of the owner of a large company, along with other CEOs who might or might not have similar intentions. I'm sure everyone will be paying close attention to this story as more becomes known. Now, back to the main studio..."

It had taken a while, but Jenny finally managed to calm herself as John and Kim sat with her on their backyard dock overlooking Kent Narrows.

"I want you to know this doesn't change how I feel about you, Jenny. I can see you feel guilt about all this, but you shouldn't. You didn't know- you couldn't possibly *have* known because to his credit your father shielded you from it. My Dad did the same with my brothers and me when he killed all those criminals, so we have something in common there."

"Right. Your father killed criminals and mine killed anyone for the right price."

"We don't know what he did or who he killed; chances are we never will. I definitely know how that feels. I never thought we'd learn the truth about my Dad, and also to your Dad's credit, he helped bring it all to light. Remember, too, that he saved Kim's life by killing Danielle Searles. He did some bad things, yes, but he did some good as well. Since there's so much we don't and probably won't know, let's try to concentrate on the positives."

Jenny turned to him. "Even though he tried to kill you, you'd do that?"

He nodded. "It probably seems pretty strange, but look how it all turned out. I certainly won't complain about the results; our Guardian Angel is alive and well."

Kim added, "it sure *is* strange- everything that's happened. This has to have been the weirdest drive for the White House there ever was. Talk about taking the road less traveled…how many twists and turns have we come across?"

"I've lost count." He was glad they'd managed to get a giggle out of Jenny. "You did say this before, though; it wouldn't make sense to dwell on the bad things that have happened, considering where we are."

"I did, didn't I?"

"Mm-hmm, and you're right." He turned to Jenny and touched her tear-stained face. "You're still welcome here, Jenny. You've been through the wringer and you need all the support you can get. Kim and I will help you any way we can. There's no time limit as to how long you can stay and there's no pressure whatsoever. Ok?"

She hugged him, and then Kim. "Thank you- both of you have been wonderful. I'll never forget all you've done for me. I don't want to be dead weight around here, though. You need to start taking it easy, Kim, so I'll help keep things in order around here while you do that. I'll help with Rachel, too."

"I'd appreciate that. You're right, too- I should cut back."

330

When Jenny fell silent and gazed out over the water, with a little head gesture Kim signaled to John that they should leave her alone. They stood and walked back into the house.

Both noticed a concerned Herb, who was watching Jenny.

"You think there might be something more to these guys, then?" Tom inquired as he looked over the list John had given him. It was that of the names extracted from the little notebook Raines had kept: the one Ben Jacobson had taken from his desk after shooting the executive.

"I don't know, but at this point I'm not taking any chances. Keep this between us, too, just in case. There's a good chance no one knows Mr. Jacobson sent this little journal to me, so it could prove to be our ace in the hole. If the others on this list were in on that hit on me, or if that note about November 1 indicated another one they've planned, they're worried enough and they could have people watching us. I don't want anyone to know we have this.

"If you would, Tom, do what digging you can without involving anyone else and see if there's anything on these people that we don't know about. For all we know they could be part of one of those secret societies that I hate so much…"

Chapter 16

February 1, 2004, 9:53 PM

"...so, when will Mister Stratton start facing reality? What he proposes can't possibly work. His youth and inexperience sure are showing."

John shook his head and laughed as he observed President Black's comment on the Sunday morning talk show. He'd just started a live interview on the evening of that same day with one of the regular anchors on a popular news program.

The grinning anchor said, "care to elaborate on that reply?"

"Certainly. Is that the best he can do? Talk about my age? And how *I'm* not facing reality? That's funny. My question is, when will *he* stop being arrogant and start telling the truth, if he even knows what that is? I'm surprised his nose isn't a mile long by now. A lot of his state of the union address sounded like a reject from 'Night at the Improv'. His writers must come from Fantasyland or a newly added state called Denial; they've created a bizarro world and made him king of it.

"The reality he fails or refuses to see is, our economy only is strong if you're wealthy already or you're a corporate executive benefiting from all the cheap foreign labor they exploit. Even then it's a fragile situation because it's all on paper. One good push and the whole system will fall apart. Unfortunately he has many people thinking like he does, meaning conventionally, which in this case is something no one should do. At the moment we're inside the confines of a broken system. If you look from within its barriers and use the blinders they put on you, you'll never come up with a solution.

"I cannot believe he's so irresponsible, uncaring or blind that he actually believes what he advocates with this disastrous free trade policy is good for America. Well, sorry, Mister Black, but you and Senator Green are wrong again; it's good for every other country *but* America. He says I advocate tired policies? There's another poor attempt at comic relief; it's just as ineffective as his policies. However, in nine months he and his party will come tumbling down just like Humpty Dumpty after his great fall because the people are fed up with him.

"He and his cronies still babble on about how they see me as a defeatist because I want to pull our people out of Iraq. They say that I would 'cut and run', or let them 'chase us out', in the gibberish of Black and his party, and that of their so-called rivals, the democrats. They all sound like one broken record, don't they? One of 'em comes up with a cute slogan and the rest repeat it at every opportunity, like mindless robots. They just don't get the point, either. Nobody chases us out of anywhere; I want our people out because we don't belong there."

"The President and several of his cabinet members have gone so far to say that your approach is irresponsible, not to mention the coward's way out. How do you respond?"

John shook his head again as he smiled. "They really should take this act on the road, I tell you. The coward's way out, huh? Well, let's talk about cowardice.

"Mister Black identified Iraq as part of his so-called 'axis of evil', along with North Korea and Iran. He left the Chinese government, one of the consistently biggest violators of human rights, out the equation. He also skipped over Saudi Arabia, another bastion of tyranny. So, from the get-go, his 'axis of evil' conveniently leaves out some of the grossest human rights abusers: China, because it's a very strong nation, and Saudi Arabia because, well, they give us oil. Same reason why our governments past were so friendly to the old regimes in Iran and Iraq.

"That leaves us with North Korea, Iran and Iraq. Which one should Mister Black and his red-blooded administration make an example of? Well, North Korea has a pretty strong military, and they would fight, so even though they pose the biggest threat of the three, the Black team rules them out right away. Iran? Hmmm- there's a possibility. Not as strong a military, but they could put up a fight, too, so they're better left alone.

"Then, we come to Iraq. Our military all but wiped theirs out in '91, and they never recovered. The Iraqi army was one in name only. Most of their soldiers no doubt remembered the whipping they took, and really wouldn't have been inclined to stand and fight because they knew the same thing would happen.

"Well, that's exactly what *did* happen; the result was a foregone conclusion, which I'd bet is one of the main reasons why Black and his people chose Iraq. It's like Muhammad Ali in his prime picking a fight with Forrest Gump.

"Given those circumstances, you tell me how it's anything but cowardice to pick on the weakest of your enemies. Contrary to what some believe, through his actions Mister Black has shown that he has no guts at all. He's a bully who doesn't fight unless the odds are in his favor- decisively so.

"Also, contrary to their denials, what the Black administration proposes in Iraq is Vietnam all over again: no exit strategy, a constantly precarious situation for our troops and a populace that does not want us there. If allowed to go on, this will tear our country apart, just like Vietnam did. By the time I take office we'll have been in Iraq for nearly two years when we never should have been there in the first place. We certainly shouldn't be rebuilding them, either, especially not the way it's being done, with all these sweetheart deals being tossed around. That's another topic, though.

"Armies should have but one purpose: to kick butt and leave. None of this rebuilding, which constantly is where we run into trouble. I don't want any more of our soldiers dying for nothing and I don't want to waste another single tax dollar there while the Iraqis demonstrate over and over that they want us out. As I've said on numerous occasions, it's their country; they need to take control of it. If they don't- if they choose to live in chaos, or a repressive theocracy-, that's their problem, not ours."

"I can't imagine that's their choice. Look at all the insurgents over there- obviously that's a determined segment, albeit a minority."

"*Is* it a minority? Does the administration know that for fact, or are they just telling us that and hoping we'll believe 'em? Even if that's the case, they need to deal with that segment if they disagree with the opinion! Again, they are a sovereign nation- they need to start acting like one and stop expecting others to do their dirty work.

"Our forefathers threw off the yoke of tyranny because they wanted to be free. They wanted freedom and they were willing to fight for it- even to die for it if they had to. If the Iraqis want it but aren't willing to take positive action including stamping out these insurgents, then maybe they don't deserve it or maybe they just don't want it. I'll say this until I'm blue in the face: it's their decision to make. It will do no good whatsoever for us to stay there and prop up some phony government- the longer we're there, the more they'll hate us and rebel against anything we create or support. The situation is chaotic enough and our continued presence is making it worse for everyone there. Mister Black is trying to build a nation in the Islamic world fashioned after our own. It's a project based on arrogance. The democrats do not offer a way out, either, so you'd get no different by voting for them.

"Look, animosity toward us in the Arab world is alive and well. That will continue to be the case if we keep trying to tell them how to run their countries, as we've been doing in Iraq and as we did in Iran until 1979, not to mention a host of other nations. My position stays the same. Once I'm elected, by February 28th, 2005 all our troops will have been withdrawn and we will concentrate on securing our borders and defending our own nation against terrorism. Anyone capable of rising above blind party rhetoric can see that this President has failed in both cases- two more failures to add to his list of 'em."

"I'm sure you've seen the polls indicating the majority of Americans believe the President was right in invading Iraq."

"No. What I've seen are polls taken from a very small segment of our society that shows the majority of that small segment, for whatever reason, believes the administration's propaganda. As you know, Walt, it's so easy for polls and statistics to be manipulated; this administration does the same thing when they all go on about how wonderful the economy is when only the wealthy are doing well.

"You know how polls are conducted. We have 300,000,000 people in this country. Of those, 1000 to 2000 are questioned, and how do we know the same people aren't chosen every time? They say the people are chosen at random, which may or may not be the case. In political polls, I doubt that *is* the case. Even if they are chosen at random, there are so many differentiating factors between people. You cannot gauge the mood of the majority of Americans by polling them; it simply can't be done, no matter how 'scientific' they claim the polls are. The only one that matters is the election, when the people make their voices heard. Only indecisive fools and manipulators pay attention to other polls."

"And politicians."

"Not all of 'em."

"Well, how would you gauge the mood of voters?"

"I wouldn't, and I don't. Instead of doing what polls tell me is popular, I simply will do what I believe is right and not try to snow the people or take every side of every issue.

"To finish the answer I owe you, I don't believe for one minute that the majority of Americans buys into the myth that we need to stay in Iraq. Republicans and democrats seem to believe that, but I'm willing to bet the presidency that the majority of Americans do not. The powers-that-be just can't seem to grasp that it's up to those Middle Eastern nations to get their collective act together. We cannot and must not impose our will upon them just because they have resources our business people want, which won't be necessary, anyway, once we switch to ethanol and biodiesel. If those nations descend into chaos because they're not willing to get smart, pull together and move forward as a culture, that's their own fault. Either way, it is up to them- *not* us."

"What if we took your approach, then they banded together and came after us?"

"That would be their undoing. Let me be perfectly clear about this: if our military was to return to the Middle East because of any acts of aggression toward us, we'd be far from a liberating and rebuilding force. We need to hold those governments complicit in acts of terrorism accountable for those acts along with the individuals that commit them. Upon our return the gloves would be off; it would be total war. We wouldn't just be there to defeat the enemy- we'd be there to destroy them completely along with their ability to wage war for decades to come.

"For the sake of the people I hope their leadership is not that stupid. I intend to give them the opportunity to turn themselves around and I hope they make the most of it. All the same, I intend for us to keep an eye on them while we shore up our borders, intelligence capabilities and national defenses.

"Along those lines, I also want to say that we need a fundamental change in our Middle East approach. We have far too many soldiers and are wasting far too many resources on defending oil fields and pipelines while getting cozy with governments we should be standing against. Case in point: Saudi Arabia, where a repressive monarchy is being aggrandized and supported by our government. Our currently elected officials just won't see or don't care that you can't be a legitimate champion of human rights when you support tyrants, especially in the name of greed. It's absolute hypocrisy, and it's dead wrong.

"You can see why such a large percentage of the citizenry of the Middle East hates us. They've been victimized by the policies of our government, just like we have. That's been the way for decades, again with the democrats and republicans sharing responsibility for that and for increasing our dependence on foreign oil instead of weaning us off it.

"However, under my administration, those practices are history. What's right is right, and as we embrace ethanol and biodiesel while trying to perfect even better fuels, we also will cut ties with repressive governments- including the current one in Saudi Arabia. The will of the people there must reign supreme. They must be allowed to make their own choice- just like the people of Iraq- without the interference of anyone else."

"And if they go the way of Iran?"

"Then they go the way of Iran. If that's what the people want, that's what they should have. It's their choice."

"Speaking of Iran, you caused quite a stir when you said the American people have points in common with the revolutionaries in that nation who took control of that country exactly twenty-five years ago today. The conservative groups still give you plenty of grief about that."

"Ok. I also want to clear that matter up once and for all, since those running against me keep distorting it. I *do not* support and never have supported the form of government- that being the ultra-conservative and equally repressive theocratic regime- that took control of Iran after the shah was run out of there. As much as I'm against such governments that are based on religion, it's absolutely ridiculous for anyone to accuse me of supporting one. If anything, they were just as bad as- if not worse than- the one they replaced, with all the mass executions and suppression. For the thousandth time, I never have and never will support religious fanaticism as a way of governing; it's one of the worst forms there can be, if not *the* worst.

"I also disagree vehemently with some of the methods they employed during their revolt- in particular, one in 1978 in which they set fire to a theater and killed over 400 people, then blamed it on the government. That was a cowardly, reprehensible act, so while I agree in spirit with their uprising against the shah, I do not approve of the methods they used or the leadership they installed. If the best way to bring about change- that of Mahatma Gandhi and our own Martin Luther King, Jr.- don't work, our revolution showed the way to do it.

"That said, in one way we do have common ground with the revolutionaries- at least, those Americans in the working class do.

It stands to reason that the conservatives would criticize and distort my position, especially those who profited from the oil they exploited Iran for and used the shah in order to get. They jump on me because I point out the irresponsible acts of past administrations both democratic and republican that primarily were based upon greed. Installation and support of the shah in Iran by the Eisenhower administration was a case in point. Such actions of overthrowing legitimate governments in other countries and backing brutal dictators that replaced them are the hallmarks of our government during the latter half of last century. You sure don't hear much said about that, though, do you?

"We, the American people, so often have paid the price for the sins of our government. We reaped what they sowed. In American History books we use to teach our students, all you see are the positive actions our government has taken. The writers and editors of our history conveniently minimize or leave out the gross injustices, such as CIA Director Allen Dulles' part in the Mossadegh overthrow in Iran in 1953. Eisenhower knew about that and he did nothing. As a result, a country that just might have become a democracy on its own ended up going the other way.

"He may have been an able General, but Ike wasn't much of a President. He warned us about the dangers of the rising military-industrial complex, yet he didn't lift a finger to stop it. You would think if our leader felt so strongly about such a threat he'd have taken action against it, or at least tried to take action, but in effect he just looked the other way. Then, almost as an afterthought, in his final speech he warns us about that insidious complex, which gained power during his eight years in office.

"He also stood by and did nothing about Dulles' inexcusable, intrusive action, which contributed heavily to the Iranian Revolution in 1978 and the consequences of it. Dulles wrought plenty of havoc elsewhere in the world as well, in a similar manner. You want to talk about a terrorist? He was one of history's worst.

"Back to Iran, as for our people being taken at the embassy in Tehran in '79 and held for all the time they were, both the democrats and republicans are at fault. Our oil magnates took Iranian oil and made plenty of money for themselves- with the blessing of our government. The Iranian people suffered under a regent that only was too happy to make himself excessively wealthy while the majority of his people existed in poverty. When

President Carter granted asylum to the shah, the enemy of the Iranian people, that was the last straw. His action showed them who our government really supported, and shortly thereafter our embassy in Tehran was seized.

"People saw the President as such a good, moral man, who talked up human rights when all along he supported a Saddam Hussein-like character that repressed his own people brutally through an organization called SAVAK, his secret police. No wonder the Iranians hated us. As for President Carter and his conduct, that's a double standard if I ever saw one; you have to wonder if he knew about what a tyrannical slave master the shah was and- like his predecessors and successors- turned a blind eye, or was he just that clueless? Either way, he got what he deserved in the 1980 election- kicked out of office.

"Unfortunately, in a clear example of voting between the lesser of two evils, we went right from him to Reagan- the greater evil-, who proved the adage that those who refuse to learn from history are condemned to repeat it. Instead of realizing, a la Iran, that it's bad foreign policy to inflict your way upon other nations- in particular when your reasons are based on greed-, the Reagan administration went right ahead and made the same mistake the Eisenhower administration made.

"They weren't ignorant about it. Again, they let greed and intrusiveness guide their foreign policy decisions. They wanted another Middle Eastern oil-producing nation for their wealthy corporate allies to pillage, since they no longer could do that in Iran. So, they aided Saddam Hussein in his rise to power and provided money and arms to him because they were ticked off that the Iranians would deny American energy companies their cheap oil. Plus, a third-world nation had shoved it in the US government's face for helping make life so much worse for them.

"I mean, the nerve of them, wanting to rid themselves of the tyrant the American government helped install- how dare they, right? The Reaganites were all too happy to help Hussein when he waged war against the Iranians, and didn't care a bit when Hussein gassed them and the Kurds. It was another case of our government helping create a monster.

"You cannot point the finger of guilt at Hussein alone for all he did without also leveling it at Reagan and the rest of his bunch, many of whom are running things now. They provided the dictator with the armaments he used to wage war. Without their help,

Hussein was a paper tiger. Deep down, they all knew their complicity, although in typical fashion none of them ever took responsibility for that. They probably just didn't care, and it's clear they still don't.

"Of course, ol' Saddam was making the oil magnates richer and providing good business for US arms dealers, so why would Reagan and his gang care? 'The Gipper' always did side with big business over the people, anyway, so I guess it was no surprise."

"Clearly, you have more than one issue with Mr. Reagan."

"Clearly. In addition to propping up Saddam Hussein, another tyrant running an oil-producing country, Mr. Reagan quadrupled our national debt during his tenure. I don't buy the rationale he and his gang of stuffed shirts used to justify his massive deficits: that by way of his reckless defense spending he beat the Soviets. Their fall was inevitable. When Stalin took over after Lenin died, he caused more damage to that nation than anyone- maybe even more than Hitler. Thirty years of Stalin crippled them, and Afghanistan did them in. If our government continues with the irresponsible example Reagan set- that being the ridiculous notion that deficits don't matter- our fall also is inevitable.

"The worst damage he caused was how he lulled so many into a false sense of security, making them believe everything was all right while he 'vanquished the evil empire'. The problem was, another evil empire arose here at home, also by way of his policies. For starters, his administration and the lapdogs known as the democrats who controlled Congress at the time made the mess of our healthcare system that we need to clean up. Reagan's way turned healthcare into a profit-based industry, which it should not be. That's why average people can't afford it; the HMOs are in charge, and they only worry about making money.

"Reagan basically gave license to the wealthy to help themselves to even more while many of them broke or skirted every rule of fair play in the process. The republicans diverted our attention away from all the wrongs those wealthy business owners and bankers were committing by focusing us on the Russians. There was no counterbalance for their avarice. Their all-consuming greed.

"That greed affects everyone who works for them, too: you can't seem to give the executives enough of your time, or your effort. It's never enough for them, and for what? So they can squeeze you for all you have and toss you aside when they're done with you. There's no such thing as job security anymore- there's no loyalty. No pension is safe, either, unless you're one of those executives. Mind you, I'm not saying all of them are tyrants, but a lot of 'em are, in addition to being liars and cheats. A bunch of our own Saddam Husseins, also propped up by our government. What really gets me is how not even the worst of the lot were punished as they should have been, which continues today. They can rob us blind with near impunity.

"That started in earnest in the '80s with the Lincoln Savings and Loan disaster, which was made possible by the Reagan policy of banking deregulation. The head of that racket never was punished; his conviction was overturned on a technicality, which was yet another example of legality defeating justice. Worse, he was aided and abetted by a few serving Senators, one of whom had the gall to run for President last time around. Today, in the new millennium, among others we have the latest example: Enron. The government just keeps delaying and delaying the bringing of charges, hoping the people will forget about it and they won't have to prosecute their benefactors, and masters. That's the pattern.

"The way things are, even if brought to trial I doubt any of those executives will get much more than a slap on the wrist and a mild fine, which won't amount to anywhere near what they stole. Plus, I doubt it'll be long before they find employment with another big company, whose executives also want to pillage our nation and are only too happy to bring on those with experience in that. As far as I'm concerned, that's tacit approval of their misdeeds and encouragement for those who would follow their poor example. If you're a white-collar criminal, crime does pay.

"That's been the situation for a long time, particularly over the last two decades, and it's one of our legacies from the Reagan era- part of the trend of further widening the gap between the haves and have-nots, even when the haves are criminals. He consistently chose the side of the wealthy against the working people. Reminds you of what's going on now, doesn't it?"

"Your last comment is reflective of the many shots being fired between you and the President. Are you afraid that all this might backfire on you?"

"I can't see how it would. As for me, I'm not just firing blindly like he is. He has no plan and no clue, and he knows it, which is why he's trying to make everyone running against him look bad. I see what's wrong and, once elected, I will fix it. I don't spew empty rhetoric and employ fear mongering; I actually want to fix things.

"He also knows I speak the truth about the amoral policies past and present- so do all his flunkies. They're just too arrogant to admit it. Then again, why would they complain since most of them benefit from those policies? I was taught that evildoers must be punished, especially those who willfully commit crimes, and you can rest assured that under my administration that's exactly what will happen. Who knows, maybe that's why my campaign has raised such hell among the ranks of the parties in power?

"So, I'm sure the jabs from the competition will continue, and whoever thinks I'll sit back and let them snipe at me without responding had better think again. If they're going to dish it out, like they have been and will continue to do, they'd better be ready to take it. We have two wealthy, out-of-touch elitists- him and Senator Green- who want to keep our great nation in the same degenerative state it's in now, if not make it worse, and keep us bogged down in Iraq. I think we've had enough of their way."

"Is there anything you *do* agree with the President on?"

"Actually, there are a couple things. I support the part of the Patriot Act that's used in the pursuit of terrorists here in America, in that it calls for sharing of intelligence among the agencies responsible for nailing them. It makes no sense to me how, before that, the FBI and CIA were so territorial and involved in gamesmanship- trying to 'one-up' each other instead of doing their collective duty.

"Also, it's utterly asinine when you hear talk about the priority some people place on the civil rights of those who would commit acts of terror against this country or support in any way those that do. Same thing with the way civil rights activists cry 'racial profiling' when those of Arabic descent are investigated. Hello?! What do they think racial makeup is of the vast majority of terrorists chanting 'death to America' and attacking us?!

"The bottom line here is, if you ally yourself with al qaeda and other such organizations that seek to kill as many innocent people as they can to that end, you forfeit any civil rights you otherwise would have. Without question, our national security supercedes their civil rights. We need to hunt these vermin down and eradicate them; to that end the Patriot Act can be a plus.

"I also agree with Mister Black in that the UN never should be allowed to dictate how we use our military or protect ourselves in any way. No such organization should have any say whatsoever in how we conduct our affairs; that's for us to decide."

"Opinions like that undermine the strength of the UN, especially when they come from heads of state."

"True, but organizations like the UN do what they can to undermine the strength of individual nations. Think about it: who's the strongest nation on the planet? We are, of course. In a representative organization like the UN, everyone has a say. Now, take the less powerful nations, which means everyone besides us. They see us as the power, so they'll do what they can to weaken us in any way they can. If all nations in the world shared our views and our direction, I wouldn't have nearly as much problem with elevating the status of those other nations, even if it meant giving up some of our power.

"The unfortunate reality is, plenty of them do not. Their vision is backward and they bear antipathy, jealousy or both toward us. Given the actions of this administration and past administrations, some of those feelings are not unjustified, but be that as it may the fact remains that our first responsibility is to ourselves.

"Our credibility among the other nations in the world has been damaged significantly by our current President. As it stands, it would take years of effort on the diplomatic front, not to mention probably billions, if not trillions, of dollars to undo the damage he's done by way of Iraq. Even so, we don't know if that would work. In all probability, nations that traditionally have sided with us will continue to do so after Mister Black has exited the White House; perhaps they'll be even more amenable to us then. Our enemies probably will continue to be our enemies.

"We have a decision to make: do we go about the task of building other nations and continuing to pursue failed policies like so-called free trade, or do we concentrate on fixing our own nation? Solving our problems?"

"Pretty daunting task there, isn't it?"

"You can say that again; we need major improvement in just about every area. Look at our national debt; thanks to the current administration, $2 trillion has been added to it, as if it wasn't big enough already. Besides the huge burden it puts on us, what kind of example does that set for the average citizen? 'The government doesn't live within its own means, so why should I?' *That* is the example.

"The last three republican administrations have been responsible for turning our debt from an already bad $1 trillion- courtesy of Lyndon Johnson and his Vietnam debacle- into a $7.5 trillion nightmare. Even so, all is well according to the republicans and their current front man. The Reagan principle still applies: deficits don't matter. Mister Black couldn't care less and apparently he doesn't mind making it worse. Same logic- or lack thereof- applies to his turkey of a plan for Medicaid overhaul, which he also pushed the responsibility of paying for onto the next generation.

"His fellow republican in California had a similar 'solution'- if you can call it that- for the state debt there that was caused by the '01 energy crisis, which the energy companies including Enron took full advantage of. They did that while both the Black administration and the Federal Energy Regulatory Commission sat on their hands and did nothing to stop that case of theft on a huge scale. Instead of holding those crooks in the energy companies accountable and allowing California to halt payments pending an investigation, nothing was done. Mister Black's friends made out like the bandits they are, and Governor David took the fall in that sham of a recall election. I bet the situation would have turned out differently had it been a republican governor in charge at the time of the crisis. No doubt he'd have gotten plenty of support from the White House in that case.

"So, in comes the republican replacement and his superficial movie star bluster that way too many people fell for. All the democrats out there just rolled right over for his bond idea, too, just like they did in the '80s for Reagan and his bad ideas. Real party leadership at work, huh? They're just as irresponsible as their supposed adversaries. What will the result be? Once California's bill comes due, there won't be any money to pay for it the way things are going now, so another republican will try to push *that* off on a future generation, I'm sure. Apparently, that's what many of them do and it's another reason why actors never should govern."

"Ouch! The President calls you an economic isolationist and one who would reverse our recovery. How do you respond?"

"Recovery?! *What* recovery?! I'm surprised he even wants to open that can of worms, as sorry as his record is. He has the audacity to say the economy's strong. Every time he says that there should be the little drum roll in the background, like when a comedian tells a joke. This isn't April Fool's Day and we're not buying it.

"Tell the millions of Americans who've lost their jobs under his tenure and haven't gotten them back or have had to settle for lower-paying and less fulfilling positions how strong the economy is. Those jobs won't come back under his administration, either, and Senator Green's plan is no better. Ask those whose wages are lower while executives and Congress give themselves raises how strong the economy is. The feudal lords continue to get stronger while the serfs get weaker.

"Then, in perhaps his most senseless move, Mister Black calls for an amnesty for illegal aliens, which I couldn't be more against. Contrary to his denials that's exactly what it is, and again, it shows how out of touch he is. We're losing jobs by the boatload and he's encouraging illegal immigration so more aliens can come here and take more jobs away from our citizens! He kowtows to the Mexican President- just lets him send as many of his people here as he wants so the guy can avoid his responsibility to them.

"The democrats are worse; they don't seem to want any restrictions whatsoever on immigration. What they advocate with that would be more disastrous for us and burden our economy even further than the President's measure.

"Am I an isolationist? No. I believe in revamping trade policies to make them more favorable to us and equitable for all. I also believe in getting the jobs we lost back here and keeping them here. I've already outlined the measures I'd take to make that happen, along with the other initiatives that will create millions of new jobs.

"Regarding the economy, as I've said for months, I think we're big enough. What we need to do is consolidate and move toward a more efficient and equitable economy. We need to close the huge gap between salaries of executives and workers, do away with the so-called golden parachutes and take other steps to insure that workers share in the successes of the companies employing them. That would increase their productivity and their desire to help make our nation stronger and better. We need to go back to the days where companies were an integral part of the communities around them instead of a stranger lurking around and leeching money.

"Once we've righted the ship we can set our sights on growth again, but not explosive growth like we saw in the '80s. I'm talking slower, steadier progress that won't backfire on us when the pendulum swings the other way, like it always does when you get too big too quickly."

"What is your take on the President's desire to privatize Social Security?"

"Terrible idea, which is par for the course for his administration. That's part of the big picture he wants to bring about. He talks about individual investments on the whole taking the place of government benefits or pensions from companies. I don't know how he can say that with a straight face. How is anyone in the working class supposed to be able to invest when the best they can manage is to scrape by on the diminishing wages they earn in the face of the steady increase of the cost of living? All the while their fatcat bosses keep making more. Sure, those who make six-figure salaries or better would benefit from such a system, but upwards of 95% of Americans would suffer.

"Along with the administration before him, Mister Black has allowed American companies to ship jobs overseas, or to be bought out by foreign companies. Pensions that were promised to employees are disappearing. Company executives are reneging on their promises, aided to that end by all these mergers and the buying and selling of corporations without care or consideration of how the action will adversely affect the employees, and no one is doing anything about it. Every decision in this field that is made anymore benefits only the executives and upper management. The worker is left out in the cold time and time again.

"This latest stab at the working Americans cannot be allowed to come to pass. We have to put a stop to Mister Black and his people, who are nothing more than lobbyists for the wealthy."

"How's your campaign funding coming along?"

"I have about $10 million in the coffer. You and anyone else are welcome to examine the records pertaining to where it came from; you'll find all of it was from private donations of up to $100 each and they're still filtering in. 'How will I use it' probably is your next question?" The anchor nodded and John went on. "I'm in the process of augmenting my staff a little. I'll use the funds to pay my people and for travel expenses we'll incur. My family is helping tremendously by volunteering time when they can but they can't do that full-time; we're not a wealthy clan and everyone's time is at a premium. That fact makes me appreciate what they do all the more."

"I don't mean to interrupt, but speaking of your family, I understand your brother will be promoted effective April 1st."

"Yes, indeed- his second promotion in four years. I love seeing good and able people being rewarded for what they do. We called him 'Major Tom' for a while until he started throwing things at us. Apparently he got that from plenty of others besides his family.

"Getting back to my funding, as promised, I will not advertise on TV. I know my opponents will, so I'll take this opportunity to say I hope they'll have the guts and integrity to confront me personally about any issues they have with me or my campaign and not resort to behind-the-back attacks by way of TV ads. It's laughable how they make those attacks and then pass them off on some poor flunky of theirs who they claim got carried away. Using such attack ads is the way of the coward. Once I'm elected, you can kiss those ads goodbye along with the other ways those parties throw their money around.

"The same goes for the attacks their cronies in Congress or other branches of government have conducted against me on their behalf. The most yellow-bellied thing you can do is use someone else or some other medium to level criticism because you don't want to stain your own reputation. That's how Mister Black and his republican machine work. In fact, if they don't have the stones to come at me personally by way of debates, forums or otherwise, they should just do us all a favor and drop out of the race. I'm sure our people want a President with the courage of his convictions as opposed to one who ducks challenges rather than facing them."

"Have you chosen a running mate yet?"

"No, not yet."

"Any lingering effects stemming from the conspiracy against you? Have any new threats come up? The investigation by Miss Jefferson seems to have stalled."

"Apparently so; it doesn't seem likely she and her team will uncover anything new. I really didn't expect she would, since all we had was Raines' written words against the testimony of his powerful friends. There's no documentation or tapes of their meetings; she has nothing solid on them. Are they guilty? Who knows? At this point, I'm not concerned. I still get my share of death threats; they come with the territory, I suppose.

"As for lingering effects, I'd say no. A big part of why they don't get to me so much is all the encouragement I'm getting from my family along with the throngs of well-wishers and believers in the cause. Those cowards who send their threats had better come to accept that I'm here to stay. I will not stop. Ever. I won't be bought off and I won't be scared off. I know what needs to be done and I will do it."

"Have you picked out any names for your babies? I suppose I also should ask if you know yet whether they're boys or girls?"

"We have, and we do. We finally let our obstetrician tell us we're having a boy and a girl, so we didn't waste much time picking out names for them and going through the process of elimination. We decided on-" He stopped when he saw Herb signaling frantically to him. "Excuse me." He stood and went over to him quickly.

When Herb told him the news, he made apologies to the interviewer and rushed out.

10:48 PM

John charged into the room where Kim waited with her mother for the doctor to arrive. He took his wife into his arms. "What's wrong, Kitten? What happened?"

"I don't know- I don't know what it is, but I'm afraid something *is* wrong. Doctor Sharif should be here any minute. She told me to stay calm, but-"

"I agree. It won't help if you're upset; just take it easy."

"I'll try. I was taking a nap when I started to have this awful dream. Something was wrong with our son; he couldn't breathe and I tried to help him, but I-...anyway, I woke up crying, but thankfully, Mom was with me. I'm glad you came along," Kim said as she squeezed her hand.

Diane kissed her cheek. "I wouldn't have missed it. Now that you're here, John, I'm going to the lobby to get something to drink. Can I bring either of you something?"

Both shook their heads 'no' and thanked her.

"Ok. I'll be back in a few."

After she left, Kim clung to him as tightly as she could. "Baby, I'm so afraid. I can't help it. This is what I've wanted most since I was fourteen. We've done all we could and I was so upset when I started to think it might not happen, and now that we're so close..."

At that moment Doctor Sharif walked in, accompanied by an orderly. "Hello, Mister and Mrs. Stratton. Kimberly, let's get you into the room so we can get started."

"I'll wait here for Mom, Honey, then we'll be in if we're allowed. Just hang in there; you'll be fine..."

11:24 PM

John looked up as the doctor came out.

She didn't wait for him to ask. "We're taking your wife into the operating room for an emergency Caesarian section. The umbilical cord is wrapped around your son's neck; obviously, this could cause problems if we let it go. He appears to be all right at this point but I don't want to take any chances and neither does Kimberly. We're prepping her now, so I have to get back in there. I'll let you know when you can see her but it will be a couple hours, maybe more."

All John could do was nod in response...

...and start pacing as Doctor Sharif disappeared back into the operating room.

"How is she, John? Any word yet?"

John turned to Tom as he, Donna and Leslie appeared in the waiting room. After he and Diane greeted each of them and apprised them of all that was known, which wasn't a whole lot, the women broke off and chatted amongst themselves. Donna and Leslie did their best to help keep Diane's worry level as low as possible.

John pulled Tom aside and they moved to a relatively isolated part of the waiting area. When he knew they were out of range of anyone else, he raised the topic that was becoming more of a concern for him. "Have you found something about them?"

"Frankly, it's what I haven't found that worries me."

"What do you mean?"

"This goes back to when you told me how you wondered if all those guys were part of some secret society. I have a strong feeling they are. Many powerful people belong to such organizations- maybe most of 'em do, and I'd bet my next paycheck that everyone on Raines' list falls into that category.

They sure fit the mold of the sort of people you'd expect to find on the rolls of The Society of the Axe, if not running it."

"The most prestigious organization that doesn't exist. It makes sense; I doubt they'd be part of any bush league castoffs."

"Exactly. Needless to say, there's nothing in their files to that effect and we won't find anything to that effect using conventional methods. The next question arising from that would be, if they are part of such a society, is their bent against you reflective of that whole organization? *Do* these guys run it? If so, who's to say they don't have a big pool of members to draw from who wouldn't think twice about killing you because their leaders say you need to go? Again, I can't prove any of this, but I have a strong suspicion. Also, if that's the case, chances are they have lots of well-placed members in just about every important segment of the regular society.

"All that aside, there are lots of similarities among these guys that do show up in their files: all are Ivy League educated, close in age, part of the same social circles, and most of 'em are related by blood or marriage. Tradition, continuation of family businesses- the whole nine yards. Archetypal neoconservatives who sure as hell wouldn't want to see you become President."

"Yeah. We've already seen one example of how far they'd go to keep me out of office. It's probably more a question of when their next attempt will be than if there will be one," he mused as he looked around just in time to see the women approaching them.

The subject was closed for now, which the brothers didn't mind in the least.

4:18 AM, February 2

"Mister Stratton?"

Diane finally had persuaded John to lie down at around 3:30 and he'd just fallen asleep when the doctor re-emerged.

He practically jumped up when the doctor touched his shoulder, then looked at the clock. "What's going on, Doc? Is everything all right?"

"I would say things look pretty good."

"May I see them?"

350

"Certainly. Your wife should be coming out of the anesthesia by now. I'll walk you to her room. You may come, too, Ma'am," she said, gesturing toward Diane.

A very excited Diane took John's arm and they moved toward the door.

"I'm sorry, the rest of you will have to wait for a little while until Mrs. Stratton is a little stronger, or you can go in once her husband and mother come out. I appreciate your patience." With that, she led John and Diane toward Kim's room.

"When was the delivery?"

"2:18. The delivery itself went very well; I saw no complications for your wife. She's a very healthy young woman, which certainly helped to that end. Your daughter weighs six pounds, ten ounces and seems perfectly fine. She's in the room with your wife and a nurse is keeping watch over both of them.

"No damage was done to your son as a result of the umbilical cord being around his neck; it wasn't wrapped tightly enough to be a real factor. All the same, Kimberly's maternal instincts served very well. In fact, they might have saved your son's life. Given what we found with the cord, letting the pregnancy go full term obviously was not an option. We could not risk the last month. Your son's birth weight was four pounds, fourteen ounces."

"That's pretty small," Diane noted.

"Yes, it is, and we'll probably want to keep him here until his weight reaches six pounds, at least. Dr. Tanaka is checking him over now; she shouldn't be much longer."

When they walked into the room, the attending nurse brought one of the two newest additions to the Stratton family over to John. "Mister Governor, I'd like to introduce you to a young lady who I bet would love to meet you."

John gently took his daughter from the nurse, smiling proudly at her as he did. He sat in the chair right next to Kim. The infant stirred a little, but fell right back to sleep as her father greeted her by kissing her on her forehead.

"So, you and your wife settled on a name for her and your son? I was watching your TV interview and just when you were about to say what they were, you had to come here."

Never taking his eyes off his child, John replied, "funny how that turned out, wasn't it? This little lady's name is Heather Alexis and her brother is John Kenneth, Jr. I wasn't leaning toward

351

making him a junior at first, but I'm glad Kim talked me into continuing the family tradition that way. She was right; that does have a nice ring to it."

They all looked up as Dr. Tanaka walked into the room. "I think someone's talking about you," she said, leaning in close to the tiny baby she cradled. His hand touched her lip and he smiled.

"Well, look at that; just a couple hours old and already he's a flirt!" Diane said.

"He has good taste, too, just like his Old Man!" John replied merrily as his newborn son joined his sister in their father's arms. "He looks pretty chipper. Anything out of the ordinary, Doc?"

"Of course, I am a bit worried about how small he is, but otherwise, no. Since your wife will be with us for a few days while she recovers from the C-section, we'll keep an eye on him, too. I'm sorry, but I will need to take him back to infant ICU soon."

"No apology necessary, and I understand you'll keep him here until he's 6 pounds, right?" She nodded. "That sounds good."

It wasn't long before the twins grew restless and began to fidget around. "I bet they're getting hungry," Diane observed as she looked over John's shoulder.

"Could be." He looked over as Kim began to stir. "Looks like Mommy's waking up, you two. Let's say 'hello'." He carefully stood with his precious cargo in his arms. "How do you feel?" he asked as he prepared to hand the twins to her.

Not even the lingering effects of the anesthesia could dull Kim's joy when she saw her children for the first time. "I'm fine, Baby; I doubt I could be better. And how are you two?" she asked, sitting up to receive them.

"So far, so-" The twins began to cry as their peace was disturbed and probably, John surmised, for another reason as well. "Correction: I'd say you're right, Mom. They probably *are* hungry."

"Well, if that's the case," Kim said as she opened her shirt, "you little ones have come to the right place…"

After the twins had fed for some time and were at the point of being sated, Kim glanced toward John and noticed that he'd

352

fallen asleep. She turned and looked up at Diane, who'd moved over and was standing right next to her.

"It was well worth the wait, wasn't it?"

Even though Kim's answer was obvious in the way she glowed, she voiced it anyway. "It sure was. I know how happy you are, too. In the span of a few months you've gone from zero to three in the grandchildren department."

"You said it!" Diane replied amid a chuckle. She then kissed her daughter's cheek and brushed a few strands of hair away from her forehead. "I'll go let everyone in on the wonderful news; I'm sure they're all out there pacing. Will you be all right by yourself for a moment? Have you shaken out the cobwebs yet?"

"Mm-hmm. We'll be fine."

She nodded in acknowledgement. As she looked at her family minus Rachel, she voiced the thought that came to her, which was very appropriate. "You and John certainly have weathered enough storms; you deserve all the happiness you have." She covered John with a blanket and went to step out. "I'll be right back."

Kim smiled after her, but just as Diane was stepping through the door, she said, "Mommy?"

Diane stopped short and looked back at her daughter, a little surprised but very pleasantly so. "You haven't called me that for some time." However, seeing her daughter's expression and knowing her as well as she did, it was pretty clear what she meant to convey.

"I know. I just-…" She knew if she uttered one more word she'd lose it and just start crying, which she did her best to hold back.

Diane sat with her. "I'll never forget the first time you called me that- when you talked me into buying you the green evening gown for your first date with John. And, of course, let's not forget those shoes with the ridiculously high heels. I still can't believe I agreed to that- more so, how easy I made it for you!" That made Kim laugh. "You always did know how to get your way, even when you didn't try very hard!"

"But I didn't abuse that too much, at least."

"Oh, didn't you?" Diane retorted, with a grin.

Kim's mouth fell open. "*Mom*! I wasn't *that* bad!"

When Diane raised a brow at her reply, Kim smiled sheepishly. "Well…then again, I did have my moments, didn't I?"

"Yes, you did, young lady! All I have to say is, just wait until Rachel and Heather are teenagers!" she retorted merrily.

"Do you hear your Grandmom talking about you like that?" Kim said in mock indignation as she leaned in close to Heather.

Her daughter always had the knack of making Diane laugh, which she'd done yet again. However, the next thought she had made the moment of levity a rather brief one, although that thought was as far from unpleasant as one could be. It came to her as she watched her infant grandchildren, but more so as she observed Kim.

As she'd done on so many occasions, Diane reflected once more upon how much her life had changed when Kim, then fourteen, mixed up and fragile, agreed to come live with her. In every way, that change had been for the better. Although over the years she'd made that perfectly clear to her daughter, in this situation she couldn't help but reiterate it in another way.

"You know what, though? You'll come to cherish those moments with your daughters every bit as much as I have ours. I'm just as grateful for them as I am for every other minute we've shared."

That statement immediately pushed the levity aside for Kim as well, and stirred her emotions up once more. This time she couldn't hold them back, and all she could manage to say in between was 'thank you'.

Diane dabbed at Kim's eyes as she wept. "Easy now, it's all right. And, thank *you*, Sweetheart. It's only because of you that I have a family again, including the most wonderful daughter I ever could have hoped for."

Kim's tears of gratitude flowed for some time before she was able to say what she had to say. "Because of you I'm still free, and alive..."

She could see that her mother was taken aback, and she certainly understood why. For obvious reasons she'd been hesitant, but now Kim wanted to share with her everything she'd learned during that eventful month of May 2003. She wanted make perfectly clear the depth of the love and appreciation she had for the woman who helped her in every way possible, and who was nothing less than her savior.

This seemed to an appropriate time.

"What do you mean?"

"Go ahead and let everyone know we're all right first, Mom. When you come back, I'll tell you everything. It's quite a story, so I hope your chair is a comfortable one."

"It is, and I'll be right back."

When Diane left the room, Kim gave her complete attention back to the twins. All was as well as could be.

Chapter 17

After they looked in on their sleeping children, Kim led John back to their bedroom where she revealed the surprise she had for him underneath the long cape. It fell to the floor along with his chin. "I knew you'd approve," she said with a naughty grin.

"Like there was any doubt! I had a feeling this was what you had in store for me. Of course, you were merciless with your teasing!"

"*Moi?*" she replied, touching her chest and batting her lashes.

"Yes, you!" John said, grinning back as he moved over to her, eased her back onto the bed and joined her. After kissing her, he pulled back a little to enjoy the view.

He was infinitely pleased- and excited- to see her in her Tigress outfit, which was her uniform at the cocktail lounge where she'd worked in the late '80s. Even today, much to their mutual amazement, the billboard depicting Kim in that sexy outfit and lying on her side in front of the huge Bengal tiger adorned the strip in Las Vegas. From the tiger-striped bodysuit that still fit her like a glove that was a bit too tight to the similarly patterned high heels with the sexy ankle straps, this outfit was a winner every time.

"You sure caused a stir at the party, not to mention in the neighborhood where we went trick-or-treating, even though you had the cape over this! For a while I wondered if someone might try to drop a net over you and hit you with a tranquilizer dart. It's no wonder Rachel got so much candy!"

Kim giggled. "Oh, it wasn't just because of me! She's so sweet, and wasn't she adorable in her Fairy Godmother costume?"

"She sure was. She really had a blast tonight- or should I say *last* night? It's past twelve already. Time really does fly...anyway, she seems to be doing fine now, especially with school. That's been good for her, coming into contact with other kids."

"Definitely. In addition to being smart as she is, she's adjusting so well, which is very encouraging. Our little ones had fun tonight, too. They were smiling and laughing the whole time."

"Yes, indeed, it was quite a night..." Even as he talked, John's hand was drawn magnetically to Kim's body and he happily indulged himself with her curves. "Those cameras just wouldn't leave you alone, would they?"

"To say the least! I think I was photographed with everyone at the party! I have to say, though, along with our first night of trick-or-treating with our children, the best part for me was the look on your face a few minutes ago when I let my cape fall."

"I can't imagine a better Halloween surprise you could have given me, which in very short order I'll show my appreciation for. That explains why you asked Dawn to help you, and then kicked me out of here." He just gazed at his breathtaking wife as he continued to caress her, taking yet another moment simply to appreciate her. Aided by her flashy nylons, his hand glided easily along her legs. "We sure have come a long way since the first time I saw you in this outfit, haven't we? Very happily married with three terrific kids…you even got past all the stress that the doctor said was hindering your pregnancy."

"You helped me do it, John- don't forget that. Things couldn't be better right now, could they? Not only did we come through with Johnny and Heather, we're also right at the threshold of becoming the next President and First Lady."

"Yeah…"

She frowned a little when she saw his expression. "Baby? What's wrong?"

"This is it. I'm not a novelty anymore; it's for real this time."

"You're nervous…"

"I guess I am, a little. In the back of my mind, I knew 2000 would turn out like it did. As we discussed the next day, I was more concerned with showing well than with winning, which I really didn't see happening. I wanted to be on the map and I accomplished that, but now… the moment, it's-…it's here, it's happening," he said as he turned over, lay on his back and looked at the ceiling. "I want to do so much… sometimes I wonder if it's *too* much. I only know that I'll do my best; that you can count on. I just hope it's enough and that enough people believe in me."

Kim faced him and propped herself up. "It will be, and so many people *do* believe in you. I believe in you, too; I always have. In fact, I have a feeling you'll end up accomplishing even more than you hope to once you're elected- and you *will* be elected tomorrow."

John gazed at her, his tenderness crystal clear. "I love you- for that and everything else. You're always so optimistic…"

"It's much more than optimism, John. I believe what I said."

"What makes you so certain?"

"I've already seen all the evidence I need to, and not just what you did as Governor."

"Really? What do you mean?"

"You have the ability to pick up on impulses and exploit them, but in the best way. You also have vision and a clear sense of purpose; you see what's needed and you do all you can to make it happen. You've done that with me so many times during our relationship and you've made me so happy, especially because I know that's what you're ultimate goal is by doing what you do.

"You know, I think you're something of a healer, too. You've helped make me a better person on every level because you've helped show me all the good I have and you do all you can to help bring it out. That's why I believe you'll be a great President- possibly the greatest ever- because I have no doubt you'll do for the country what you did for me.

"You feel it, too; you know you'll be elected, which is why you're so nervous."

He nodded. "It's strange, in a way..." He fell silent for a moment. "I'm thinking about the kids, too. There will be some firsts that I might not see, and..."

"There's more to that, isn't there?" He didn't respond and she contemplated what it could be. It didn't take long before the answer became clear to her. "This is about what happened to your father..."

He nodded and turned away again. "I lost him so early in life and I can't stand to even think about-...what if that happens to me?" Given what Tom suspected about the list of industrialists and heirs in cahoots with Raines, which John hadn't mentioned to Kim or anyone, it was becoming clear that he and his family were nowhere near out of danger. That probably would apply regardless of the outcome of tomorrow's election. "What if one of those conspirators ends up taking me from you and our kids before-"

"Don't, John- please don't think about that too much. If you do, even if that doesn't end up happening it will just eat away at you if you let it. You can't dwell on your fears. I can relate to what you're feeling; as you know, I lost my father when I was born and the last thing I want is for our children to lose you, but there's a little adage your Dad told you that couldn't be more appropriate now. You remember it well, I'm sure."

When it came to him, he was taken back to the day on the old rowboat when his father, Tom and he were experiencing one of their days of being skunked while fishing next to the support pilings of the Chesapeake Bay Bridge. "Never let fear make your choices for you, no matter what you end up doing. Giving your all in the right pursuit is what matters."

"He was right. This *is* the right pursuit and you are the right man for it. I wish we could be together all the time, too, but the country needs you, just like Rachel, Heather, Johnny and I need you. We just have to share you with a couple hundred million people- that's all." That made him smile.

"There will be plenty of firsts you *will* see, though, and like you also told me four years ago, you only can serve eight years at most. After that, you can stay home and take on phase two of raising our children. They might need a break from me by then!" Kim was glad to see him chuckle, but that light moment passed quickly.

"I want you to think about this, too. As a result of what you'll accomplish while you're President, along with millions of others for years to come, those three beautiful children asleep upstairs will have a much better and stronger nation to grow up in than you and I did. Best of all, they'll have their Daddy to thank for that."

His smile broadened and his eyes began to glisten. "Well, you've done it, Kitten. I'm totally speechless."

"Wow, maybe we should mark this moment with- ...mmmm..."

He'd moved back on top of her and silenced her with a kiss. "What I meant was, words couldn't possibly express what I want to tell you now..."

10:04 PM, November 1

"This is where it counts. This is where in past elections people have lost faith and fallen back on the 'safe bet'- that being perceived security over necessary change. Feeling apprehension in such situations is natural; the right way generally is the hard way, especially when you're taking a new, uncharted course. In one respect, though, it might feel a bit easier because you know their way isn't working, so what do you have to lose by trying my way?

359

"In those elections past we had little hope because we saw the same candidates over and over from the democrats and the republicans. Their message never changed and it *won't* change; all that does is the face of the messenger. We thought, 'what choice do we have'? Worst of all, because there's so much bickering and gamesmanship between those parties, nothing of any importance gets done. All they do is blame each other endlessly for our stagnation.

"Then, you have to wonder how much of that is genuine philosophical differences. The more smoke the parties create with their so-called feud, the more they obscure the issues and keep themselves in the spotlight, which I believe is their real objective. They don't want other parties to come into prominence because that undermines their influence. They seem to be so concerned with holding onto power that they're not doing their job- not that they hold the reins as much as the corporate sponsors that fund them. That's been the case for far too long. Then, they have the audacity to openly discourage other party candidates from running while they keep telling you they're your saviors- you *have* to go with them, which you do not.

"Now you have a real choice- a genuine alternative that finally will get us moving in the right direction. Don't take what you might think is the safe bet. It isn't the safe bet at all and it's the worst thing you can do. We all know we need change- badly. The economy is far from strong; don't believe the propaganda to the contrary, because you know that's exactly what it is.

"We can't go on like we are. My fellow Progressives and I realize that just like everyone else who lives in the real world. The difference between us and the other parties is, we will bring about that change whereas they only will give you lip service, then forget about it once the election is over or compromise it away while our nation continues to erode. That is the cycle of futility and hopelessness we will destroy.

"John Forbes Nash's improvement to Adam Smith's theory applies very well to what I'm spelling out- that being, you do what's best for yourself *and* the group. This 'every man for himself and everyone else be damned' mentality that unfortunately is so pervasive in our society does not work and will not work. The capitalism we've been subjected to for so long is nothing more than modern feudalism, and it gets worse each year.

"We have to do what's good for everyone- look at our country as a whole and understand that if we're going to pull through the hard times we're in, we must come together. We must work toward the collective goal of making life better for all of us and not be so greedy in our expectations of how much we can have for ourselves. If we can do that we'll all benefit and prosper from our combined effort.

"So, once again, we find ourselves at a crossroads. Domestically, we have a chance to correct decades of wrongs perpetrated upon our people by the corporations, special interest groups and political parties, all of which have the same voice. Yes, that voice is loud, but remember: if you- the so-called average Americans- join together, your combined voice will drown theirs out. They may have a lot of money, but they have very few votes when compared to yours.

"You can throw the lot of them out, which you've already done in three Governor's Mansions, seven Senate seats, twenty-two congressional districts and scores of state districts over the past few years. I can feel in my bones that we will make even larger gains this time around- larger than anyone expects.

"A lot of people are saying what I propose can't work, and guess who they are? Those who have the most to lose, meaning the long-entrenched, stagnant political parties and the rich. Well, I say it can work and an awful lot of you throughout our nation seem to agree. Yes, we will have some hard days ahead of us, but once we pull together, bear down and do what needs to be done without letting the short-term difficulties we'll face stop us, we will see a much better society.

"I don't know about you, but I can't stand knowing that at least 20% of our population has no health coverage and a lot more have inadequate coverage. That is unacceptable to me. Plus, so many millions of children are getting substandard education and thus will be hindered in their chances of making the best of themselves. *That* is unacceptable to me. All the while, a tiny, gluttonous segment of our population is helping itself to the vast majority of our national wealth and not leaving enough for the rest of us. That, people, is the root of so many problems we face, and that is absolutely unacceptable to me.

"The days of cheap gasoline are over and, with China and India becoming the next super-consumers, those days will not come back. Now is our chance to break free of that dependence once and for all. Cheap foreign goods also have undermined our economy, but with your help we can rid ourselves of them along with their slimy peddlers.

"We can improve the situation of the middle class so you all don't face the impossible conditions you face now. We can make sure that, at the very least, people will make enough money to get by. The healthcare and educational systems we build will make all of us proud. It will be difficult to create the new way, but we must do it, we can do it and we will do it. We need to go back to the basics and rebuild our nation in every way. Our wheel does need to be reinvented for the good of us all. A Herculean task, perhaps, but one we can accomplish if we pull together and see it through. This is a labor of love, once done, will benefit everyone.

"The best way to make it happen is to burn our bridges and start anew. Any construction worker or craftsman will tell you that it's much easier- and better- to tear down the old and start anew than it is to try the patchwork technique. We need to agree that once we set this in motion there will be no turning back. The only direction for us to move will be forward, which will be the best possible motivation.

"As for the Iraq debacle, think of all the soldiers we've lost there and those who are maimed and disabled- all over Mister Black's vendetta, and oil. They and the rest of our soldiers deserve much better leadership than they have. The death tolls on both sides would continue to mount if this President was to maintain his delusional and deceitful course of action.

"This dogmatic, stubborn President simply will not see that we're not wanted there. He even says he sees it as our national duty to do the same thing to other countries around the world- to go where we're not wanted and impose our will upon other nations, which is a new form of imperialism. Senator Green wants to keep us bogged down there as well, so he is not an alternative to Mister Black. I stick to my vow to end our second Vietnam as soon as I take office and to be much more sensible about how I use the military. I also won't tie their hands when they're in a hostile area, nor will I expect them to rebuild another nation."

John took a slight pause before going on. "A lot of people have asked me about my religious persuasion, to which I answer I really don't have one other than believing there is some sort of Supreme Being. There are those questions we can't answer- the big ones no one can explain. Someone has to know, right?

"That's about the gist of it for me, but I know how important a part of life religion is for many people. To that I say you have every right to believe whatever you choose to believe, as long as you respect the rights of others to do the same.

"However, when answering that question about my religious persuasion, I also add that as important as religion may be, there is something that matters even more- *much* more. Love for your family and your country, and the desire to do all you can to make it as good a place to live as we all can make it. In short, taking pride in your home- your neighborhood. There are many different religions practiced here but there is only one America, which is where we live- which is *our* neighborhood.

"It is our liberty that allows us to practice whatever religion we want, to be outspoken in our beliefs- even if those beliefs might be unpopular-, and to pursue the lives we want to lead. We must never forget that. We must do all we can to uphold and perpetuate that liberty, which is the legacy of those who went before us and made the sacrifices they made to bestow upon us that most cherished gift.

"Liberty is the bond we share- the glue that holds all of us together. It's what sets us apart from every other nation and is far more important than any religion. In addition to that most vital one, our pillars are courage, industriousness, vision, enlightenment and tolerance. Those are the principles upon which this great nation was founded. Those principles are the essence of what America once was, and can be again.

"Unfortunately we seem to have lost our way over the last several decades. That's because we've lost faith in our leadership, which has failed us. It's been the norm to expect politicians to sell out and make promises they have no intention or desire to keep, which in itself is a sad statement. More importantly, as a result of the poor leadership we've had, we lost faith in our ability to make a difference- to make a positive change. So many of us have come to believe our voices don't matter, but I'm here to tell you they *do* matter. Look at what's happened in so many states already- how your fellow citizens banded together, kicked the dead weight out of office and started the new era.

"You see by those examples that it can be done on every level, but in order for us to make it happen, every voice must be heard. Another thing the liberty we have allows us to do is what we need to do in order to bring about the changes that are so necessary. That ability is within our reach, if we can consolidate our forces.

"The other parties don't believe we can come together and effect positive change. They don't want us to, either; that goes against their game of divide and conquer. On the other hand, my party and I are convinced that as a nation we can unite, and we will! We believe that you, the citizens with whom the true power lies, share in our conviction.

"We Progressives don't offer up little scraps from the table for each ethnic group in an effort to divide you or buy your vote. We offer every American- meaning every Native-American, every Caucasian-American, every African-American, every Hispanic-American, every Asian-American, every Polynesian-American and every Arab-American- a place at the table, which every hard-working citizen deserves. The common element in every one of those ethnicities is 'American', and that's what my party places the emphasis on.

"Our ultimate vision for this country is that of a United States of America that is truly united, in which our people work together to achieve that vital goal and every goal we set. By now I believe the majority of you see that if we don't work as a team, our house will crumble. We're counting upon each and every one of you, for without your help we cannot succeed.

"So, here we are. Tomorrow all will be decided. The future- and quite possibly the survival- of your nation is in your hands. Remember, you have the power. It doesn't belong to the media, the corporations, the lawyers, the wealthy, any special interest group or any political party. It belongs to you, so go home and get plenty of sleep, then get out to those polls tomorrow, vote for change by voting Progressive and take your country back!"

"There you have it; that was John K. Stratton's televised address to the mass of supporters gathered here inside Baltimore's Convention Center. It was ten years ago that Mr. Stratton did what was described by some as drawing the sword from the stone. He capitalized on the lack of confidence Maryland's voting populace had with the major parties' gubernatorial candidates and drew votes away from both of them while leading a very effective campaign of getting those who were eligible to register and vote.

"The majority of those who did vote here in Maryland on November 4th, 1994 made him, at age thirty, the youngest Governor ever elected in this nation's history and Maryland's first Independent. The man went on to shake things up here in the Old Line State, improving the educational system, simplifying the tax code and reforming the election process here in a way that caused no small amount of friction between the young Governor and the established political parties. But the end result? Governor Stratton's system worked, and it worked very well.

"Now, at age forty, he stands on the verge of making history again- this time as the youngest President ever. His attempt four years ago fell short for a number of reasons. I'm sure most of us remember the personal trials that he, his wife Kimberly and the rest of the Strattons went through that year as well as the constant criticism, ridicule or dismissiveness he endured from most politicos because of his stance and his youth.

"However, he caused a major ground swell among the people. The then-36-year-old candidate garnered twenty-one percent of the popular vote, proving himself a formidable opponent and- as he promised he would be- here he is once more, poised to take the helm of this country. His basic stance on the issues has not changed, but this time around he's refined his platform and given us the nuts and bolts of how he would bring his vision for America to pass. In addition, he's far from alone in his quest. He stands at the head of a rising political army.

"The maturation of this charismatic young man has been astounding. In the past four years he's gone from doing an impression of Atlas, carrying all the weight on his own shoulders, to one of Paul Revere, rallying the whole nation to his cause. He's also inspired plenty of like-minded citizens to run for office under the banner of the party he formed so recently. His choice of a running mate also has resonated well among Americans. Mr. Morrison has proven to be a very passionate voice for reform as well, and was the clear winner in the vice-presidential debate. He was every bit as effective as Governor Stratton was in the presidential matches.

"And how about what turned out to be one of the biggest surprises- not to mention one of the best moves- of all: the Governor's donation of the rest of his campaign money for the purpose of installing more voting stations where needed? What better way could there be for a candidate to show the people that he really wants them to vote? We sure didn't see any such gestures from the other parties, despite the fact that their collective war chest exceeds his by far.

"In terms of success, over the past two election seasons we've seen a level of it that, other than Governor Stratton and the Progressives, few of us truly expected. Not even the assassination attempts could knock him off course. Speaking of which, apparently, after nearly a year, U.S. Attorney Gloria Jefferson's investigation into the Raines conspiracy as yet has produced no tangible evidence of additional conspirators. However, security here is very tight, given the reference to this day before Election Day in Baltimore from Raines' notebook. If we see a Stratton victory, the candidate has said that the investigation most definitely will continue until the answers are found.

"Back to the election, as those in Maryland were in '94, the democratic and republican candidates in this imminent presidential election are quite vulnerable. The democrats keep searching for their identity and the republicans increasingly are becoming labeled throughout the country as the party of the wealthy and thus reviled by what seems to be a large portion of the populace.

"In the context of the polls we've conducted, they're even more vulnerable than we suspected they would be. Although Mister Stratton says he doesn't pay any mind to polls, I can't imagine he's displeased by what he sees in them! The current President's numbers have slumped consistently. That is due in part to what seems to be the feelings of many that his domestic policies have been a total failure and, as Mister Stratton has pointed out repeatedly, would lead our nation to disaster.

"Not helping Mister Black is that many view him as totally out of touch with them and their plight. The latest example of that is his lack of a plan to relieve the oil crisis we're in and his lack of preventive action to offset its result. Senator Green, the democratic candidate, also is viewed by many as an out-of-touch elitist and one who, as an entrenched member of the current establishment, would not bring about the changes we need.

"On the other hand, Governor Stratton has provided very viable answers to many of our woes, including the oil situation. I'm talking, of course, about his commitment to immediate implementation of the transition to ethanol and biodiesel as our fuels, which even some of his staunchest critics are acknowledging is a good plan. In light of the current oil prices, the main argument against ethanol- that of overall cost- no longer seems valid, and there's no argument at all against biodiesel. However, there's rampant speculation that should he be elected, we could see a big drop in the stock market, given how many of his reforms could adversely affect big business- at least, in the short term.

"As for where the voting public stands, even the latest conservative-backed poll shows a virtual dead heat between Mister Black and Governor Stratton, which does not bode well for the incumbent at all! Ever since last fall, when Marcus Andrews and Matthew Bell- respectively, the Progressive Governors of Louisiana and Kentucky- were elected, former Governor Stratton has gained momentum steadily as we've approached the moment of truth, which almost is at hand.

"Mister Stratton's rising influence played a crucial role in both those elections last year. That sentiment was backed up strongly by both new Governors who, along with their wives and children, are here in Baltimore with the rest of the Progressive contingent now serving in office to show solidarity with their leader.

"It's funny how in the spring of '95 during his first legislative session the newly-elected Governor was called 'The Young Lion' as a joke by one of the ranking legislators in Maryland's General Assembly. That happened during the time when Governor Stratton, looked upon as an unwelcome outsider, had so much trouble dealing with the Assembly. Not a lot of people outside Maryland know that's how the moniker came to be.

"Very funny indeed, given how things are shaping up. Mister Stratton really bared his claws and fangs and went after the political establishment in his home state back in '95, which he's doing on the national scale now. From all indications, he's very close to dealing it a crippling blow- perhaps even a fatal one. I'd say 'The Young Lion' is a very fitting title for him, only this time no one is laughing about it- especially after the debates.

"Tune in to our station tomorrow for live coverage of what has all the makings of the most exciting presidential election our country has ever seen. Back to you, Nick."

367

10:36 PM, Election Day

"...and so, at this point, we have President Black with 232 electoral votes and leading Governor Stratton, who has 194.

"Senator Green, with 27 votes, already has conceded defeat. He's only won his home state of Massachusetts along with Connecticut, Rhode Island and Maine. Even if he were to take vote-rich California, which in all probability will not happen, an overall victory for Senator Green is an impossibility. The question is, will those electoral votes he has hurt Governor Stratton? And if so, to what degree will they hurt him? It would be a very strange case of turnabout if the democratic candidate cost him victory.

"Senator Green's plight is indicative of the democratic party in general, which is seeing defeat everywhere. Even that party's members in Congress whose seats were thought to be secure have been ousted, some by surprisingly wide margins. The republicans are seeing their share of losses as well, but not on the scale of the democrats, who by all indications are coming apart at the seams. Apparently it's the Progressives- not the democrats- who are seen as the genuine alternative to the republicans and wealthy corporate America. When the American people said they wanted change, Barbara, they weren't kidding!"

"No doubt about that, but I still wonder if the harsh rebuke Governor Stratton recently laid on the hierarchy of the catholic church after being asked about their feelings on his and Senator Green's positions on abortion was a difference-maker for voters. The Governor countered that the church hierarchy, after decades of covering up its clergy's sexual abuse of young boys and failing to hold its own accountable for those heinous sins, has no moral high ground from which to judge anyone. He went on to point out how history clearly has illuminated catholicism's rigidity, greed, intolerance and cost to humanity over the centuries in terms of overpopulation, bloodshed and destruction of civilizations. Although his statements outraged many, many others agreed with him, so it's hard to say what the overall effect will be."

"That was one provocative statement, to put it lightly! So far, I have to say that it doesn't seem to have hurt him much, if at all, given how the evening has shaped up so far. We have totals of all states from the Mountain Time Zone east and only are waiting on those from Nevada, Oregon, Washington, Alaska, Hawaii, and the biggest prize of all: California."

"That's about the size of it, Dave. President Black has enough to win if he takes California. The republican Governor of the state has been campaigning hard for him. In spite of his efforts, however, the most up-to-the-minute results show Mister Stratton with a lead, although there still are plenty of districts that have yet to report. This much is for certain: neither candidate can take a majority of the electoral votes without capturing California, so this election is by no means decided. That might continue to be the case for hours to come since there still are so many votes to count in the Golden State. I hope everyone has plenty of coffee or hot cocoa; we could have a long night ahead of us."

Kim turned the sound down. She looked over at John, who was taking a brief nap in hope that, along with a couple ibuprofens, would rid him of a slight headache.

I can't believe you can sleep now, she thought, smiling. She went into the bathroom, closed the door and got ready for her shower.

11:30 PM

Kim emerged from the bathroom to find John awake and watching the election coverage. "Feeling better?"

"Much better, thanks. I'm glad you're always prepared for such aggravations as sudden headaches," he put his arm around her as she sat next to him.

"You really do need to break yourself of that bad habit of not drinking enough water; I bet that's what caused the one you just had, not to mention several others."

"I know. I forget sometimes."

"I'll just have to keep reminding you, then." She kissed him and started to brush her hair as they turned to the TV and listened.

"Looks like more results are coming in…"

"Welcome back, folks. We have postings from Nevada and we can project President Black as the winner there. Senator Green drew enough votes away from Governor Stratton to give that state, by a plurality margin of only 1526 votes, to the President. The result in Nevada has been the same in the vast majority of states he's won. In very few instances has the President won a state outright, which speaks volumes about how far his popularity and the public's confidence in his ability to govern have fallen.

"We should have the final count from Washington soon, but we won't have the official word about California for some time, since so many districts have yet to report. Then, there's the recount factor. Given the number of close calls we've seen, don't be surprised if one or more states decide to go that route.

"As it stands, we have President Black with 237 electoral votes and needing 33 more to clinch reelection. Governor Stratton still is at 194 and needs 76 to win, which means he almost has to win out.

"Regarding the popular vote, Governor Stratton has had the lead for the past two hours. According to the latest numbers and in spite of the last setback, he still has it, although barely. He leads the President by two percentage points, even though the President leads him by 43 electoral votes, one of his biggest leads of the night in that category.

"That disparity gives those who want to do away with the Electoral College- Governor Stratton among them- some justification for their position. It would be very ironic indeed if President Black was to repeat what happened in 2000, when he lost the popular vote but won in the Electoral College.

"Even so, he still must take California, so in turn there certainly is hope for Governor Stratton, whose organic fuel proposal seems to be resonating strongly there. The findings of a 2001 study by the California Energy Commission on the subject basically corroborate the Governor's views on ethanol.

"His running mate, Golden State native Clayton Morrison, is a leader in the biomass-to-ethanol industry there and owns several successful plants, which he conceived and funded himself. A 44-year-old former Marine officer and decorated Desert Storm veteran, Mister Morrison certainly has strengthened the Progressive presidential ticket, and he could end up being the difference-maker in his home state. His experience in the first Iraq war, among other things, opened his eyes to the need to break our oil dependence. For years he has been an outspoken proponent of that, which brought him into contact with Mr. Stratton, who's put into motion the plan to do it. Californians seem to be embracing the idea, which could spell trouble for the President. He-...

"Well, here's a swing in the other direction! Washington goes to Governor Stratton, who now is up to 205 electoral votes.

370

He still must prevail in most of the remaining states in order to secure enough electoral votes to win the election, but Washington with its eleven is a very nice prize itself."

"That it is, and-…hold on, we also have results from-…it looks like we can project Governor Stratton as the winner in Oregon as well! He sweeps the Pacific Northwest and now has 212 electoral votes! He's closed the gap to 25 in that part of the race. So, the plot thickens…

"You know, Barbara, I'm very impressed by how well the Governor and his party did in Texas, the President's home state. Who'd have thought the Progressives would take six congressional seats there and that Mister Stratton would garner nearly forty percent of the vote?! He was very strong in the Farm Belt and the Midwestern states in general, undoubtedly in large part because of his ethanol and biodiesel proposals.

"I'm sure I sound like a broken record by now, but again I have to point out that what impresses me most about this election is the huge voter turnout, which by all indications has benefited Governor Stratton far more than any other presidential candidate. We haven't seen any less than a 75% voter turnout in any state; the national average so far is almost *eighty-three percent*, which truly is astounding! It surpasses by far any turnout in history! He really has brought 'em out in droves; for that alone he should be commended! Those who, for whatever reason, chose not to vote in past elections are making all the difference in this one.

"As far as I'm concerned he's surpassed all expectations, no matter what happens in the presidential election. The Progressives have retained all their seats in Congress. In the House, with a number of California's districts reporting, so far they've made a net gain of 166 more, bringing their total to *188* Representatives who will report for the next session of Congress! It's absolutely unbelievable! Already this marks the biggest and most drastic shift in power ever in that body and it's possible the Progressives could end up gaining a majority there!

"Add to that 18 Senators so far, bringing their total in the upper house to 27. That includes two serving Senators who officially have aligned themselves with the Progressives. We're also hearing noises from some Representatives and officeholders on the state level indicating that they might follow suit.

"As for now, keep your eyes on those last three states. It looks like nail-biting time again!"

"For you guys, maybe," John said as he muted the TV's sound and sat with Kim again. "It'll be a while yet before all those votes are counted." He kissed her and smiled when she turned to him.

When he started to undo her robe, she stopped him. "Apparently you're not worried about California."

"Nope. Not there, Alaska or Hawaii. I bet you we'll take all three. Come on, Kitten, we have a little time yet," he said as he reached for the flap of her robe again.

She was glad she'd worn the robe that covered her almost completely. Opting for warm and comfortable over sexy and barely there looked like a good move.

"That's enough, you!" she scolded as she slapped his hand away. Nonetheless she gave him a little peck before she stood. "Let's hold that thought before we get carried away, Ok? We have to leave for Baltimore soon, so I'd better get dressed."

"Need some help?" He said in a flirtatious tone.

"Given your sudden friskiness and the look in your eyes, I don't think that's a good idea. We do want to get up there sometime tonight, after all!"

"I suppose you're right," he replied with a tinge of disappointment in his voice, which disappeared when he went to his alternative plan. "I'll look in on the kids again, then hang out with Mom and Jenny until you're ready."

Kim checked in the mirror to make sure the back-seams in her silk stockings were straight. Considering the mood he was in there was no doubt in her mind that if John saw her in this first layer, which was for his eyes only and a present for him later that night, she'd never finish dressing.

Not that that's an unpleasant thought, she mused amid a lustful grin. Satisfied with the look of her stockings, she was about to start on the next layer that would hide the sexy one from everyone else. This definitely was a departure from her preparations for John's conference in 2000, during which they clashed with that reporter.

Up until a couple years ago she wouldn't have thought twice about showing off her legs, but recently, as a leading presidential contender's wife- and as a mother-, she'd decided it was prudent to tone down her style of dress. The day had come after all...

372

...even so, this would take some getting used to, and she hoped that it would help further diminish the voices of her critics. John didn't need the aggravation from them, and neither did she...

Suddenly, from the corner of her eye she caught a movement. She turned and saw something she didn't expect, but probably should have. The silk blouse she'd laid out on the bed was moving, and in the next instant was yanked off the bed and out of view. She walked around to investigate and heard a guttural, rather unsettling snarl...

...she slowly moved forward and gasped when she saw-

"Jezebel!! Why, you- *oh*!! I do *not* need this tonight! You'd better *give* me that blouse, you little weirdo- *right now*!!" Her chastisement was met with more snarling by the small black cat. Her ears were pointed straight back, her eyes were as big as golf balls and her mouth was full of fine silk as she ran for cover, tripping herself continuously while dragging the garment along behind her. "Give me that- don't you *dare* go under that bed!!! You get your furry ass over here and you'd *better* knock off that growling!! Why can you not be more normal, like Simba?! When I get my hands on you...*come here*!!!"

The next sound she heard made her aware that she and Jezebel weren't the only ones in the room. She looked out from under the bed and saw John, who'd just fallen onto the floor, doubled over and laughing so hard that no sound was coming from him. Tears were streaming down his face.

Right when she was about to demand to know just what in the hell it was that he found so funny, it struck her what he walked in on. There was his wife, partially under their bed, dressed in her black thong, bra, stockings, garter belt and super-high-heeled pumps, ass sticking up in the air as she cussed out her blouse-thieving cat. In no time at all, she was laughing, too, almost as hard as he was, but Jezebel still clung fiercely to her blouse and wasn't about to give it up.

"It looks like I'll have to redo my mascara, thanks to this fruitcake under our bed! I thought the tie of yours that she partially devoured last year was the end of it, but apparently she *hasn't* gotten past her silk fetish- at least, not yet. Is she my cat, or what?" She smiled at John as he moved over to where she was.

"So, you see the reward I had in store for you later after the dust settled. I'll have to get another blouse, needless to-...wait a minute: why are you still in your sweatpants and t-...and now just

373

your sweatpants…" Her mouth fell open when he shed them too, and his smile made his intention clear. "But…Baby, we'll be late!"

"So, we'll be late. You know, although it doesn't get as much mention as other types, laughter makes for some pretty good foreplay- don't you think?"

"*John*!! We have to go in a few minutes; they're expecting us! This is only the biggest night of our lives!"

"I disagree with you there." It only took a moment for her to catch on. When she did, her expression conveyed the happiness his statement by design had brought her.

That was all it took to steer her in the right direction.

"I'm sure you meant to say tonight is *one* of the most important nights of our lives. That I agree with, and it's all the more reason why we should be relaxed, right? I can't think of a better way to get to that state than this. You're already dressed for it, anyway, which I guess I should thank Jezebel for. Look at you," he marveled as he moved his hand down along her hip to her legs and began to stroke them. "You are living, breathing proof that being a good person and living a good life pays off.

"I think whoever the Supreme Being is knew that was the course you'd take and rewarded you with beauty outside that's a physical manifestation of what you are inside. I can't stop looking at you, touching you…for the past twenty-two years your spell over me has been unbreakable, and it will be for many years to come. Seeing you now…physically, you've changed so little since that day by my locker, particularly your skin. I can't help wondering if, to me, you'll always look the same."

"Maybe," she replied, smiling tenderly. "After all those years you still make me blush!" She lay back and sighed as his attention to her legs escalated from caressing to fondling.

Apparently, John didn't mind in the least that they would be a little late. *Can't say I do, either…*

"In addition to the rest of your amazing body, you've kept my favorite pair of stocking stuffers in such great shape that I feel compelled to show my appreciation at every opportunity- especially since you have these dynamite gams all dressed up for me. Now, how am I supposed to resist?"

Kim gave in completely as he kissed her again. There was no sense in arguing- not that she had any desire to, anyway.

"You're not," she replied, grinning wickedly as her other response quickly followed…

...later, as they reached the outskirts of Baltimore, the news anchor disrupted a conversation between a couple pundits as John and Kim watched on the TV they'd had installed in their car.

"...and so, Alaska with its three electoral votes goes to the President- again by a threadbare plurality-, bringing him up to 240 total, even though its Senate seat went to the Progressives.

"Hawaii is at the other extreme from the standpoint of climate, and the same goes with the way the vote of the state's populace was cast. The Aloha State's four votes go decisively to Governor Stratton, bringing his total to 216, and it's my understanding that the results from California are imminent. Mister Stratton has gained momentum as the totals from the rural areas have poured in and-...wait- here they are...

"First, we have the tallies of the last of the congressional races. How about this? In addition to the Senate seat up for grabs in the Golden State, the Progressives have won 14 more House seats from there, which brings their total to 202. That means the Progressives have become the majority party in the House of Representatives! However, they don't have an outright majority, which they are 16 seats shy of. As it stands they have 29 seats in the Senate and 10 Governor's mansions. Now, we only need to-...

"He's done it!! All the districts have reported and the result: California, with 55 electoral votes, goes to Governor Stratton! Ladies and gentlemen, there's a new Sheriff in town! As Dave pointed out, the difference-makers in this election were those voters who normally don't vote. California was a little above the national average in its turnout with 86%, which nearly doubles their average in each of the past ten elections! As for the final count, in the end it wasn't even as close as we thought it would be; Mister Stratton took the Golden State by nearly two million votes!

"So, ten years after the incredible upset he pulled off to capture the Governorship of his home state, he's pulled off another, the likes of which we have never seen! John Kenneth Stratton has garnered 44% of the popular vote and 271 electoral votes, enough to make him President-elect of the United States!

"I tell you, folks- elections just don't get any more riveting than this one has been! Good night, everyone, and thanks for staying with us. For those of you in the Central and Eastern Time Zones, make that 'good morning'."

San Jose, California

"...I don't see what difference it'll make, Pete. Without funding, we can't move much beyond where we are now. We have all the elements identified. We could finish this and make it work- I'm sure of it! We're ready for our next round of tests, which should be the last round of them we need, but the facilities we have aren't sufficient anymore. I think the higher-ups are catching on to us, anyway.

"So, here we are. We can't even think about approaching anyone in the private sector. Same goes for the Black administration; he can't see past the Bible, anyway, so I seriously doubt he or his people would be friendly. The guy has no vision- no plan for the future. He won't even get us off gasoline, for Christ's sake! All he wants to do is keep us in Iraq, which will take even more resources away. It would have been nice if Stratton had gotten in."

"He did get in," Pete said as he hung up the phone, just having received the news from a buddy who would be a part of the incoming administration. "This sure could change things..."

Brad Barlow turned to his friend since college and longtime partner in the project they'd undertaken years ago. "Huh?"

"That was Brett on the phone. Apparently, you counted our boy out too soon; he just kicked Black's ass out of the White House. As of January 20th he'll have to find another job, although I'm sure some stuffed shirt friend of his'll be too happy to give him some bullshit position where he does nothing and makes millions each year. Then again, he'll probably use more of the money he inherited from Daddy and Granpappy to buy another business he can fuck up, which is what he does best. That's how it works for those people- the 'good ol' boy' network. They think they're gods just because they were lucky enough to be born into money. What a joke. Well, at least *we'll* be rid of him!

"I have a feeling the new kid in town will look favorably upon our project; he indicated as much with the remark he made last year his forum. I couldn't believe it when he said that!"

Brad turned the TV back on and watched as the man and his wife walked up to the podium. "This is good news," he said as the President-elect began to speak. "I believe you're right; he'll be a very good friend to us. Better yet, we have a connection inside..."

Pete still had a concern and despite Brad's growing irritation, he had to voice it. "Look, Brad, are you sure we don't need to-"

"-be concerned about the discovery? For the thousandth time, no. Neither the police nor the FBI would have the first clue about where to *start* looking- if they've even figured out what happened, which I guarantee you they haven't. Nobody in the rest of the scientific community has an explanation, for crying out loud! No one ever has seen anything like what we did. There's no precedent. Nothing can be traced to us, anyway, but we do need better facilities and equipment now, and we have to maintain total secrecy. That's the part I'm most concerned about. Overall, we've done a good job of it so far. It's getting tougher, though; I'll grant you that."

"Yeah. We don't need any more incidents like we had with Mrs. Winters. I guess you're right about this one being a fluke. All the same, we don't need a repeat."

"I know. We have to be extra careful from here on out, and we will be. What we and humankind stand to gain from this is far too important to be lost because of a stupid mistake. Mrs. Winters was too far gone. It's looking more and more like there's a point beyond which our method doesn't work, since that's happened three times now with the same result. We have to shift our focus to younger people."

"Agreed." Pete turned back to the TV. It wasn't long before he became engrossed, and not so much from the speech.

Brad saw the same thing. "Are you thinking what I think you're thinking?" Pete glanced up, and Brad saw his answer. "It would be nice, wouldn't it?"

"That it would."

At that moment, Brad saw another answer. "It also would give us all the funding we could ever need, I bet- at least, over the next eight years, which probably would be enough to get us over the bridge..."

A big smile slowly spread across Pete's face as he got the point. "It might...it just might, at that."

"All right, then. In the meantime we have a lot to do. We have to be sure it'll work first..."

November 25, Thanksgiving Day

"...in every way, the election just couldn't have gone better-right, Baby?" Kim raised her voice a little with the last part of what she said to get John's attention as she saw him trying again.

"Huh? Oh, yeah, no doubt about that. We really-"

"Now, surely you didn't think your little sneak raid would be successful, did you?"

"Sneak raid? I wasn't-"

"Yes, sneak raid- trying to sleaze your way by us like you are, thinking you're just going to help yourself while everyone else is patiently waiting. Well, you'd just better turn around, Mister, and go somewhere else for the time being! Out!" Kim admonished as she shooed him from the kitchen, which was off limits to him and the other men in attendance.

"Ok, Ok- I'm gone!" Everyone laughed as the President-elect was chased out of there by his broom-wielding wife.

The Stratton clan, gathered together for the holiday and having spent the night at John and Kim's, was deeply involved in preparation for the delectable Thanksgiving feast- at least, one faction was. Starting the night before all the women had pitched in, and now they were in the final phase. Given the multitude of tantalizing aromas, it was a good thing the first course was almost ready.

It had been a beautiful and rather blustery day in Kent Narrows- very fitting for the time of year, and for the day. While the women did their thing, the children did everything ranging from playing with Simba and Jezebel to feeding some ducks to napping. The men went a few rounds at horseshoes and darts before they relaxed in front of the TV.

All in all, the gathering of the family couldn't have gone better in any way. The hostess and host were infinitely pleased with the way the post-celebratory period of the election victory was transitioning into the holiday season. They were happier still to have the opportunity to get the whole family- including Jenny-together for the best part of this particular holiday...

...but there was something on John's mind, and he decided he couldn't wait until after dinner to present it to Tom, like he'd planned. He walked over to his brother, who was chatting with his neighbor and friend Bruce, and with Leslie's new boyfriend, who they all liked.

378

"Tom, come on down to the dock with me for a bit. There's something I need to ask you…"

Once they reached the dock, John didn't waste a second. "I want you to be the Director of the FBI."

Tom looked away for a moment. Even though John was sure he saw the uncertainty he expected, he wasn't about to let it go. "This job was made for you, Brother- think about it. I know you're the right man for it. In a little over twenty years you've gone from patrolman to Major, and you've done that on your own merits. You've headed departments on the city and state levels; no one questions your bravery, dedication, integrity or ability.

"You can do this, too; you could become the best Director the FBI's ever seen. Who knows- maybe you'll end up being the best justification of all for getting that piece of shit Hoover's name off the building. Plus, with you at the helm I know I'll sleep better at night, which I admit is one reason why I want you in that position. Besides Kim and Herb, there's no one in this world I trust more than you. I know how you despise nepotism, but that's not what this is about- at least, not to me. Of course, there will be plenty who think otherwise. Along with taking that position I'm going to ask you to endure some such name-calling, but once everyone comes to know what I know- that you are the man for the job- all that will stop."

John moved over and stood directly in front of him, making his brother look him in the eye. "I need you, Tom; I need you to do this. It's not just because you're my brother…on the other hand, it *is* because you're my brother. Still, it's up to you. What do you say?" He was surprised to see a grin on Tom's face…or was it a smirk?

"I had a feeling you'd approach me about that." His eyes briefly went out of focus as the thought came to him. "Head of the agency Dad devoted so much of his life to- the very agency that came after him for discovering what morally vacant shitheads we had running the show. A nice piece of irony, eh?"

"You could say that. So, you'll do it?"

He nodded. "I'll do it, and thank you, John."

John hugged him, and clapped him on the back. "Good. Now I know my back will be covered. You have total power over that bureau, so you'll probably want to clean house, which is exactly

379

what I'll do on January 20th. Herb's staying on, too; he's already accepted his new title as head of presidential security. The rest of my current team also will be incorporated into the Secret Service and stay close to me. I don't give a damn who doesn't like it- that's how it will be."

He pulled away from Tom and looked out over the water. "Even more people in high places want me dead now that I've won. You know that as well as I do, with all the investigating you did. Those maggots on Raines' list are at the top of that list, and they'll keep after me. They know what's coming and I think they've gotten the message that I will not stop until the job is done. There is no middle ground and there never will be. For that reason, I'm a little-..."

He didn't say it- not that he had to, as Tom knew exactly what he was feeling. "I know. Then, we have the market going south, which won't help. All this talk about a crash when you take over...a lot of analysts are saying it could happen."

"*Could* happen? No, I'd say it's a safe bet that it *will* happen. That could be a good thing, though."

After the moment it took for him to fully digest that statement, an incredulous Tom asked, "how do you figure?"

"Well, in the event of a crash we'd get to rebuild, and do it the right way- wipe the slate clean, so to speak. I already have that scenario in mind and a few of us are wargaming it now. A fresh start in many respects would be good for this country. Look at it this way: limits on wealth would be much easier to bring about. Necessity would dictate them; everyone would have tighten the belt. We'd all have to pitch in, learn to be more responsible and less indulgent.

"It's not always a plus when a company's stock goes up, anyway. Nowadays it often means the company has axed several thousand workers. Good for the shareholders, maybe, but bad for the thousands of workers who've lost their jobs.

"And, as I've said before, you notice how even in those situations the executives don't take pay cuts when the company's having hard times. Even worse is when they give themselves raises after cutting staff. I mean, they have their winter palaces in Hawaii and the Caribbean, their summer estates in Maine, their yachts and their fleets of gas-guzzling cars to keep up, all the while stashing hordes of money away and thus taking it out of the economy, right? Well, they'd better enjoy their excesses while they can, because changes, they are a'comin'.

"They have to stop seeing themselves as better than everyone else and entitled to anything they want without any limit; they need to be made to see how detrimental that mentality is. We won't go to the opposite extreme, mind you. The comfort zone we've found in terms of income and personal wealth should work for the vast majority of us. Financial independence and a comfortable life still will be attainable for those who earn them.

"The only ones that'll be ticked off are the extremely greedy and those who expect things to be handed to 'em. Then again, who gives a damn about their opinion? If they don't like the new way, they're free to leave. They sure don't seem to give a damn about anyone else's besides their own…

"…so, yes- a crash might be a *very* good thing."

"Might get us thinking more in terms of 'we' than 'I'."

"You've got it," John said with a smile. "Spoken like a convert to the 'dark side'!"

Tom grinned back. "I guess that's right. If it comes to that, we'll be in for one hell of a ride…then again, we already *are* in for a hell of a ride. Herb has quite a task ahead."

"That he does." He turned very serious. "Make no mistake, Tom: my ultimate goal is to bring an end to capitalism as we know it. This whole system is headed for a huge crash anyway unless we can undercut it and soften the landing by already having another system ready to go. There's been no consistent sense of restraint or responsibility for a long time. It's safe to say there will be a pretty big drop even if we do get our way, but we can make for a smoother transition. If we were to keep going like we are, inevitably that would lead to a free fall.

"None of the jokers in charge would have clue one as to what to do about it, or they'd just argue endlessly over what to do. They're either ignoring reality or they just don't know what to do other than watch as we move ever closer to the edge of the abyss, courtesy of the regime that came to power in the '80s. Their way was a losing proposition from the outset; people just have no idea of the scale on which the Reagan gang fucked us.

"Well, now it's our turn to fuck them and their allies- take back everything they were given plus interest, and we will if we take Congress in '06. Our first two years will be the real test. If at minimum we can weather them, we have a good chance of achieving our goal. A lot of the big players and their companies will go down, which is what they deserve and what needs to happen. I'm pretty sure they realize what's coming, now that I'm President and not just a hopeful, and since my tune hasn't changed and won't. So, either I'll destroy them or they'll kill me. They won't accept my plan since by necessity their system- their way of life- will be eradicated. They'll come after me every way they can. That prospect is starting to make a good night of sleep even harder to come by than before.

"It's more for Kim and our children- and for our whole family- than for myself that I worry. Then, on the personal level, I don't want to end up as someone who tried to change things but got cut down before he could. That's happened too many times."

He turned away and reflected on something for a long moment. When he spoke again, he gave at least a partial answer to a question he knew Tom wanted to ask him for some time but never did. Given all he just laid on his brother, John figured he owed him that.

"You wonder, I take it, if all that went down between Dad, Mister Jack and the others had an effect on me. It did, and it does; how much is hard to tell, but...what's done is done. I've been elected and I'm not giving that up, no matter what the two most influential men in our lives did, which so few of us know and never will tell anyone else about. I have a job to do, and in under two months I'll take an oath to do that job to the best of my ability. To quote my favorite Frost poem, I have promises to keep. I *will* keep 'em.

"We have to play the hand we've been dealt, although I'll say this much: the trump card sure was a kicker."

John turned back to his brother, and just like that, the matter was closed.

At least, it was for the time being.

"An awful lot is at stake, but now that you and Herb will be keeping watch, I feel much better. As for your new position, in a minute I bet everyone will be as happy as I am when we tell 'em.

"Well, what do you say we go eat? I don't know about you, but I sure am hungry..."

Chapter 18

December 19

"...so, as I see it, the best way we can improve our national security and our intelligence is to keep the CIA as the primary intel-gathering agency, but change its policies to make it more practical and less secular. We can use the provisions of the Patriot Act that call for intel sharing as our justification. I think that's enough. The way I propose calls for the CIA to conduct daily briefings attended by liaison officers from my bureau, NSA, DIA, INS, Customs and a board of law enforcement officers that will represent those of the entire United States of America as broken down by regions. Those officials in turn will disseminate the information to the state and local departments. Between all these agencies, we have all the bases covered, so I don't see why you couldn't make your move."

John smiled. "I like it, Tom. Sounds like the justification we've been looking for. In effect, what we're proposing is to make the system work like it should have in the first place. In the process we can eliminate a redundant department as part of our streamlining campaign while we make those we have more efficient. This also will enable us to hire more federal officers, including border agents, with the money we'll save by eliminating the HSD. Last but not least, it makes another reason why I'm glad you took the job, Brother.

"All right, gang, we have some details to work out, so let's get on it. We go with the Director's plan. That's all for now."

As the meeting broke up, Tom and Clay hung back from the rest of the group. Herb closed the door behind them.

Clay posed the question. "When will you meet with Greg?"

"Tomorrow, after you guys take off. He'll be on his way in the morning. Since we're so much closer to him here, hopefully it won't be such a disruption."

"Did you have a chance to look over his file?"

"Yes, I did. Seems he's every bit as qualified as you both have said. All that remains to be seen is, will he go for it?"

"I see you're not happy about being here."

This was the last of John's stops on the international journey he'd taken, which had been a very productive one. Judging from the preliminary indications, the situation was looking good on that front. The next step was to make into reality the vision he presented. It went without saying that that would be the hard part. The more he thought about all he had to accomplish, which was all he could do right now, the greater the task seemed to be. John always had hated transitional periods and this one was no exception.

However, at least during this period he had Kim and the children, who proved to be the best possible diversions. They awaited him at the Prime Minister of Spain's home, where the soon-to-be First Family of the United States were very welcome guests. Once this impromptu but important meeting was over, John would be with them again. The next day they would head home for the Christmas holiday.

After an uncomfortable pause, Major General Gregory Swanson, commander of the First Marine Division, prepared to address the man who a couple months ago had unseated a Commander-in-Chief who was quite popular with the military.

There was plenty of uneasiness in the armed forces at large as to what the new man in charge would do. He'd already made it clear that the mission in Iraq was over, which by and large had caused friction. Many soldiers and leaders were using what had become the catch phrases, like 'cut and run' and 'chickening out'.

Greg himself hadn't used them, but on occasion he'd agreed in spirit. It caught him by surprise when he received the summons to meet with the President-elect while he was in the process of preparing his commanders for the withdrawal. Nothing was in the communique as to the nature of this meeting.

It's about time I found out, he thought as he replied the incoming President's statement. "To be frank, Sir, I'd much rather be with my troops."

"I understand."

"Do you?"

John frowned. "Come again?"

General Swanson's expression told John that he was hesitant about expanding upon the response he'd given, which was understandable since John soon would become his boss. Even so, John wanted to make something clear to this man, as he'd done in a couple similar situations. "General, if you have something on your mind I'd rather you tell me what it is, face-to-face. Let's set rank aside for the time being; right now we're two men with very important jobs to do."

"Fair enough, Sir. With all due respect, you've never served, so I don't see how you could understand that I don't like being here while my soldiers are in harm's way. That's not something you *could* understand unless you've been in uniform, and especially under fire."

"Point given; I won't argue that. You've been under fire quite a few times in different places, haven't you?"

"I've had my share of action, yes."

"I'll say," John replied as he looked over the file again. "In '72 as a private you were involved in one of the last battles in Vietnam. You earned the Silver Star with the 'V' device for valor and leadership when you took command of your rifle squad after your NCOs went down. From the looks of your dossier that set the tone for the rest of your career. You went on to become an officer the hard way- through Officer Candidate School- and have worked your way up to Major General over the course of a 32-year career. I take it part of reason you empathize so much with the plight of your soldiers is the fact that you came from their ranks?"

"Yes Sir, that's a big part of the equation."

"I'd think it haunts you sometimes, that added dimension. You know what they're feeling when you order them into battle."

"It does weigh on me- sometimes a lot- but it also helps keep me focused on what matters. Besides, it's my job. I owe it to the soldiers to use my best judgment when I send them out to do their job, which entails the highest sacrifice anyone can make. It's a job I love and hate, but it's the one I believe I was meant to do and also one I'll never take lightly."

"Your track record certainly confirms all of what you just said. Do you think it's a bit different for your peers who come from the academies, who weren't in the trenches like you were? Seems to me that could make them more detached."

"In many cases I'd say yes, but overall it comes more from the elitist viewpoint that plagues some of the insecure, narrow-minded, self-serving and arrogant among us. Such a state of mind for those who have it probably existed before they ever set foot in any academy. That said, if we could do away with the nepotism and favors for the rich brats when it comes to securing appointments, our military would be much better off."

"Our society in general would be much better off if we could eliminate all such preferential treatment for the currently privileged. So many people who otherwise would have made great leaders and innovators in their own right don't get their chance because they don't come from money and don't kiss ass or sell out. One of my fondest hopes is to make it so people from all backgrounds have an equal chance to get where they want to go based on their own merits, drive and accomplishments."

Greg nodded. "I'd like to see you succeed in that myself." Once more he hesitated before, in effect, asking the man to get to the point. "Sir, as yet you haven't told me why I'm here. This feels like... some sort of interview. I'd-"

"In a moment, General. I won't keep you much longer." John put the dossier down on the table and leaned back into the comfortable chair. "You and I have something in common, in one way. We're at war. The type of combat we're engaged in might be different, but my war still is a dangerous one, and potentially deadly. It's one of classes, and it could get ugly not long after I take office. The campaign was just the beginning.

"Another point in common we have is how we got to where we are, and the perspectives we have because of that. Being a product of the working class, I know their plight and I'm convinced that I have the way to make things better for them and for our nation as a whole. A big part of why I was elected President is because I can relate to them, whereas the other main candidates couldn't. In that respect I've come up through the ranks taking a similar path as yours. Things could get pretty rough on the home front, so it's of vital importance to me that I know our foreign situation is being monitored closely by people I can trust with that task."

The General nodded. "I think I see what's happening. I'm very flattered, Sir. You'd like my take on your choices for the Joint Chiefs of Staff, right? You haven't named 'em yet- at least, not that anyone knows."

"That's sort of why I wanted to meet you, but not exactly."

"Care to enlighten me, Sir?"

John held his stare for a moment, then smiled a little and stood. "General Swanson, I want you to head the Joint Chiefs. You have all the tools and you seem to know how to use them. You're a first-rate soldier and student of the art of war. As such, I also want you to hand-pick the other Chiefs and give me your list as soon as possible, along with recommendations you might have for the posts of Secretary of Defense, National Security Advisor and CIA Director."

Greg kept staring. His guarded, wary expression became one of outright disbelief. "Sir?"

"You heard me correctly. I want you to be the next Chairman of the Joint Chiefs of Staff. What do you say?"

"Uh...first of all, I appreciate your...confidence in me, but again, with all due respect, I'm only a two-star General. There are a number of three- and four-star flag officers ahead of me."

"While they might have more seniority, rank, command time and face time in DC than you have, none of those factors makes any of the others a better choice. I've looked over their files, spoken with them and with their peers about them. Many strike me as more politicians than leaders. I also get the distinct impression by way of their words and actions that they've long since lost any connection they might have had with the average soldier. I don't like that.

"Also, it appears that no one at the top of the chain is happy with my decision to leave Iraq, and many have criticized me pretty harshly. In so doing, they've ended their careers. I can live with dissent, but not disrespect. My decision about Iraq and the Middle East in general is final. Those who can't live with it are out as soon as I'm sworn in." John saw his discomfort clearly, and Tom had forewarned him as to the probable nature of that discomfort. "You're thinking about some animosity this could cause among your peers and those higher in rank if you take this job."

"Yes, Sir."

"Granted, that probably will happen and it's something you'd have to deal with. I believe without reservation that rank and time in grade do not- and never should- entitle anyone to anything. Ability, focus and smarts, but most importantly how well one performs under pressure, are what matter to me. The bottom line here is, you're the man I'm calling upon to do the job I know you can do very well."

"What makes you so sure of that, if I may ask?"

"In addition to your qualifications you come highly- and personally- recommended."

"By whom, Sir?"

"Among others, a couple acquaintances of yours, who also are combat veterans. One served under your command when he

387

got his first taste of combat. He told me about that firefight in Grenada, when your company was pinned down. He said he never saw a cooler customer than you. What impressed him most was how your decisions were well thought out, even though by necessity they were pretty hasty. You knew what to do and you stayed in control the whole time, even- and particularly- when things looked bad. He learned from your example and applied it in every position he's held ever since."

"There were close to two hundred men under my command then. You'll have to be a little more specific-..." He trailed off as it came to him. "You're talking about your brother."

"I am. Look, I don't have the luxury of knowing any of the top brass and I didn't want to make a choice blindly, or just by looking at a resume. Given the way my selection process works, I needed all the input I could get. Better yet, you had another stellar recommendation from another ex-Marine: Clay Morrison, the Vice President."

Greg's brow furrowed. "I've been wondering where I heard his name-...ah, the CE commander in the Gulf."

"CE?"

"Oh- sorry, Sir. Combat Engineers. He was well regarded; the high command didn't choose his company to breach the most dangerous part of the Iraqi lines for nothing. He sure knew his explosives. Good man there.

"Same goes for Tom. I actually got a chance to chat a little with him after I observed him leading his squad in action in Grenada. As brief as that encounter was, I do recall how much he impressed me. When he told me he was leaving the Corps once our deployment was over since his enlistment was up, I tried to persuade him to stay in. We do more than just look for a few good men; obviously, we try to keep 'em once we find 'em, but he'd made up his mind by then. He came across as very decisive and focused for such a young guy- one who makes the best of any situation he finds himself in, and a natural leader as well.

"I guess it was inevitable we'd lose Tom to a certain young lady he'd been steady with since high school. It was good to see him take the career path he did, though, and I'm not a bit surprised that he's where he is now."

"I couldn't agree more with your assessment of him, which is why I chose him to head the FBI, the fact that he's my brother notwithstanding. I trust Tom's judgment completely; if he says you'd be a good fit for Chairman of the Joint Chiefs, I'll take his word at face value."

"Even if, like a lot of my contemporaries, I don't necessarily agree with your decision to pull out of Iraq?"

"Even so. In this case, for every reason you give me why we should stay in Iraq, I can give you a better reason as to why we should go. The bottom line is, it's their nation. They need to take charge and make their own way, and we have to let them. I know you're far from the only military man who disagrees with me, but I believe time will prove me right. As for the personal dimension here, I don't sense the obstinate or 'yes-man' extremes in you that I see in many of your peers. As long as you can abide by my decision once I make it, which I believe you could, I think you'll make a good fit.

"As a corollary to that, chances are you'll find yourself in other situations when you don't agree with something I propose. In such cases, if you have one or more good reasons why you think I shouldn't take said course of action, I want to know that I can count on you to come to me and let me know how you feel and why you feel that way. That's extremely important to me, and there might well be times when I'll agree with you and go with what you recommend.

"What it boils down to is, I need the most intelligent, most capable leaders heading every venue where they can make a positive impact on policy and action. You are one such leader. You'll be the point man for military matters, most importantly that of molding our force into what we need it to be in order to deal with the threats we face."

With that, John moved right in front of the General. "I blindsided you with this, so I don't expect you to give me an answer right away. You have a lot to digest and I'm sure you'll want to discuss it with your wife. I'll need your answer in a week, though. Inauguration Day isn't far off. For now, I know you want to get back to your troops. I appreciate you taking time to see me."

John figured that would end the meeting, but it didn't.

"You haven't offered the position to anyone else, have you, Sir?" Greg asked in a tone that indicated his question was a rhetorical one. He already knew John's answer before he gave it.

"No."

"That's what I thought," the career Marine replied as he nodded, then stood. No further internal deliberation was required.

"I have a good feeling about this. I've been around enough to know that when much is uncertain, which is the situation of the world right now, sometimes all you have to go on is gut instinct."

He looked the next Commander-in-Chief square in the eye and extended his hand. "Mister President, I thank you for your confidence in me and I accept the position. No consultation with the wife will be necessary, as she voted for you and was glad to see you win. She wants us all out of Iraq as badly as you do, so she'll be ecstatic that I'm part of your administration."

John laughed as they shook hands firmly. "I'll be happy to thank your wife in person for her vote. I get the feeling you and she have some rather spirited political debates."

"We do indeed, Sir, we do indeed. Well, if you'll give me a few days I'll have the other Joint Chiefs picked out. I'll also have the list of my recommendations for nominees for the other posts."

"Thanks, and congratulations, Mister Chairman. I'm glad to have you aboard. Oh- one thing, which is my only pet peeve here: try to avoid choosing anyone who says 'I serve at the pleasure of the President.' Those generals are just like the politicians; one of 'em came up with a line and many use it now. I never would hire anyone who tried to feed me horseshit like that. Bottom line is, you want the job or you don't. More importantly, have the balls to tell me 'yes' or 'no' instead of handing me such a ridiculous line.

"Pardon the rant, General, but that crap got old quickly. That doesn't apply to you at all; you didn't use the line and your case was different, given your current rank. All things considered, I already have enough evidence that you are the best choice. One, you think things out before deciding. That's a very important quality. Small unit commanders can make quick decisions, and obviously have to in certain situations, but those with the responsibility on larger scales have to put more thought into it. This was a very big decision you just made. You considered it while feeling me out, and I'm sure your choices for the Joint Chiefs will be just as good.

"My second reason is, I can tell this is a job you want, in spite of your misgivings about wrinkling some egos. I have no doubt you'll get past such non-issues quickly and focus on the job.

"For now, you and your soldiers enjoy Christmas and New Year's as best you can. Be safe, and I'll see you soon."

January 4, 2005

"James, how have you and your Mom been? How did the holidays treat you?"

Even though a fair amount of time had elapsed since the last time he'd heard this voice, James Richardson recognized it immediately. "Gov- sorry, I mean, Mister President!"

John laughed. "Not quite, but in a matter of days, I will be. I'm sorry it's been awhile since I last called. Needless to say, it's been a hectic period in more ways than one."

"I know, Sir. You and your wife have been in the news almost constantly for the past couple years. To answer your question, Mom and I have been very good. She's enjoying her work and I'm in the middle of my sophomore year at Maryland; classes start in a couple weeks. Thanks again for your help with that scholarship."

"You're welcome. I knew you'd be a good investment- so did the rest of the panel. I understand you made the Dean's List again. Way to go!"

"I appreciate that, Sir. Hey, I wanted to let you know, I decided on a major. I remember you asked me about that last time we talked when I wasn't sure."

"I'm glad to hear you have. What was your decision?"

"Aerodynamics and jet propulsion, both with space applications. It's a fascinating field; your passion for advances in space travel and desire to see the next generation of shuttles or interplanetary craft sure are contagious! After my 'A' in Calculus 3, out of curiosity I decided to take a couple basic courses related to the field- physics and mechanical drawing- and they really put the hook in me. I decided a taste wasn't nearly enough, so off I went. This summer I'm also taking a course in design of such craft, and another in the principles of rocketry- both at MIT."

A big smile spread across John's face. "No kidding- MIT?!"

"Yes, Sir- the one and only Massachusetts Institute of Technology. I contacted a professor there about a program he's heading there. He liked my enthusiasm and requested my transcripts, which apparently also impressed him. A couple of my professors wrote to him on my behalf, and there's a possibility I might be transferring there this fall. It depends upon how well I do this semester, and in those two classes I'll be taking this summer."

"That is fantastic news! I think you'll do very well in that field, my friend. I want you to keep me posted on your progress, and I'll make sure you can stay in contact with me. In fact, I'd also like to have you and your Mom over for dinner before your semester starts and before I move to the White House."

"I'd like that, too, Sir- so would Mom."

"Great! Check your calendar and let me know when is good for both of you- or, will it be reservations for three? Any girlfriends in the picture yet?"

"No time for one right now. I'm gearing up for classes; this has been a busy school year so far and obviously there's no letup in sight, but that's all right. Sure beats the crap out of where I was five years ago," he said, thinking back to the night of April 14th, 2000.

Back then, at age 16, he was a prospective member of the gang that at the time was the scourge of east Baltimore. On that fateful night came the moment of his initiation, which was the pivotal moment in his life. He had a pistol pointed at the forehead of a man who the leader of the gang, James' friend Anthony, had just shot in the chest.

It was up to James to finish the man off with the gang's signature of three bullets fired into the victim's head.

The man in question was Douglas Stratton, then-Governor John Stratton's younger brother.

The moment came, and went. There was no way James could have brought himself to pull the trigger. Then, when he lowered his gun, he'd turned to see Anthony, who he'd thought was his friend, levelling a handgun at him. The only thing that had saved James' life that night was Anthony's gun jamming.

The next night, James went to the police and told them all he knew about the gang, not caring what the consequences would be. He followed through in court as well. His testimony against them destroyed the surviving gang members- those who were not in the dead-end alley that became a killing zone the same night James first went to the police.

Even though James did not shoot Douglas Stratton, the man died of the gunshot wounds from Anthony's weapon- the same one that spared his life only a moment later. The younger Stratton's death weighed very heavily on James for some time. Sleep was hard to come by, even after Tom and John Stratton showed up at his home and helped get him on the road to recovery.

It had been a rocky road, but a very worthwhile one.

"It sure does. I'm proud of you, James; you really turned things around."

"So have you, by all indications. You're in a much better place five years later, too. How are your wife and children?"

"They're fine, and you're right; I am in a much better place, thanks to them. My personal life couldn't be better, which is why I'll remind you on occasion to take some time out from your schedule for yourself. Get out, meet people, unwind, date- you need that, too."

"I will, Mister President, when I get to where I need to be."

"Fair enough. Give me a ring or drop an e-mail when you decide on our dinner night."

"You've got it. One more thing..."

"What's that?"

"The way you've believed in me, and the opportunities I'm getting because you and your family have stood by me...I'll never forget this, Sir- any of it."

"We're glad to do it. You also should remember that opportunities themselves are only part of the picture. What's most important is what you do with them. I know you realize that and you're well on your way to a successful future. You might even change your mind at some point, and that's all right, too. Find your passion- what makes you happy and what you can't be without- and that will make all the difference in your life...

"Well, I guess we'd better hang up before we get too sappy, eh?"

"That sounds like a plan, Sir," James replied as he laughed. "I'll see you soon!"

"See ya, James."

After he pressed the 'end' button on his phone, John turned his attention back to Kim, who just was starting into her routine on the rink in conjunction with the beginning of the musical score she'd chosen.

Almost immediately, Kim, her skates, the ice and the music became one captivating entity.

John leaned against the rail and watched, completely transfixed...

* * *

"If anything, you seem to keep getting better at this, Kitten. You were terrific out there!"

In addition to his wonderment over her ability, which came through clearly in the amazing show she'd just put on, John couldn't help but love the view. Kim's skating outfits were as sexy as they were functional; the leopard-print bodysuit and black fishnet tights combination she had on was no exception. By nature, conservative simply was not her way, despite her public efforts to hide that. In all aspects Kim was a marriage of beauty, style and substance, which was abundantly clear when she was on the ice.

She'd decided to focus on figure skating again, and try to recapture her form of old. It had been in the back of her mind for some time, ever since she nailed the double jump early in '03 while she and John were on the campaign trail in Boston. Her love for it hadn't gone away in the slightest and probably never would, and her regular and thorough workout regimen quickly had her back in top condition only a few months after the twins were born.

In sum, all the pieces were in place. Skating was far less dangerous an outlet than detective work or other such endeavors, and thus was cause for relief for John. Even so, it still was very exciting and challenging for her.

It was a bridge to a part of her past that held unlimited promise until her sudden loss of confidence and inability to adjust to the marked changes to her body just a few months after she'd won the state championship at age twelve. This was a way to prove to herself that she could regain her form and possibly even improve upon it. Figure skating was one venue through which she was free to let her essence- her entire being- come out.

The probability that very soon John would experience another such venue seemed pretty high as she closed in on him.

Kim's smile was wide and dazzling as she skated off the rink, then practically jumped into her husband's arms when she reached him. She channeled her excitement into the kiss she gave him. "It sure seems that way! I haven't felt this confident in years; I'm hitting the double jumps almost every time!! Isn't this wild?!"

"Definitely, and it's always great to see you so stoked!"

"Same goes for you, Tiger." She embraced him and pressed against him. "I could feel you watching me, enjoying the show as much as you did. Knowing that made me do even better, with the jumps and everything.

"As well as I perform when you're not watching, I seem to be at my best when you are, but...I think it's more than just you watching me that does it. I'm sure you know what I mean. I love that feeling, Baby. I love how much you want me, and I love making you want me even more..." she kissed him again, and very hungrily.

John had to sit down, as Kim's intensity was taking him right up to where she was, and fast. He had to take a deep breath as they slowly ended their steamy kiss.

"You are," John said as he grinned, "one naughty girl, Mrs. Stratton, teasing me like this and stirring me up when we're in a place where I can't do anything about it. Seems like I just might have to punish you again, doesn't it?"

"Oh, you must! I was so blatant with my teasing, and I'm not even close to finished! I do need to be punished. Our ride home should give you plenty of time to think of something appropriate."

"Like I need a lot of time for that!"

Kim laughed, but at the same time the tremor ran down her spine- still a regular occurrence when she knew she was 'in for it'.

If anything, those occurrences were becoming even more frequent, which was cause for yet more happiness for her since her hunger was on the rise.

That trend certainly was evident to John. Any doubts he might have harbored about a woman's sex drive increasing during her thirties had been washed away some time ago.

Even so, he noticed that she was starting to drift again. Sex wasn't the only thing occupying her thoughts...

"What's on your mind, Honey?" She looked up at him, then shifted and turned away. That told John plenty. "I've noticed that look on your face a few times now, and each time I've seen it after you've finished a skating session...you really have missed it, haven't you?"

She sighed. "I guess it's no surprise that from time to time I still wonder what might have happened if I'd have stuck with it- how far I'd have gone...

"...Baby, you know how happy I am with our life together. Just because I'm-"

"I know- I never would think you weren't. It's easy to tell when you're happy; that's pretty much a constant state for you."

"It sure is," she replied, kissing him again as she did.

"From a purely selfish standpoint, I have to say I'm glad you stopped skating when you did, at least competitively. Who's to say that, if you did stick with it, you might have moved away after junior high and we might never have met?"

"You're absolutely right; *that* would have been a tragedy. Ten gold medals wouldn't have made up for all we have...

"So what if I didn't get my shot at the Olympics? I still love skating, and aside from my occasional nostalgia flashes I'm so glad I'm doing it again. It's one way for me to express this confidence I have. I honestly can say that I never have felt so much of it, and in every way- every facet of life. Oh, John, I love where we are. I also love where we're going, I love our children, I love our family...I love everything about our life, and I'm so grateful that I was able to help us get to this point."

With that, she climbed into his lap. "And, there's no one else I'd rather show my appreciation to..."

January 19

"...and so, tomorrow we will see the official changing of the guard as John Kenneth Stratton becomes our 44th President. So far there are no surprises; he's made clear his directive to draw down our military presence in the Middle East. His subsequent directive for those bases that will remain to in effect become dual-purpose military and relief force bases is resonating very well around the world, in light of the natural disasters we've seen.

"Then, he got specific. From the outset of his campaign he consistently has held to his position that no nation has a right to invade another sovereign nation unless said nation is a clear threat to others, or in the case of genocide. That particularly applies, said Mister Stratton, when the invader simply doesn't like the current regime and wants to impose its own form of government. The people of any nation must decide that for themselves, take charge of their own destiny and be accountable for it.

"With those words he officially will end our occupation of Iraq and give the people and the new government they elected control of their nation. Likewise, all US construction projects there will be cancelled. Mister Stratton also is pressing for return of all of Saddam Hussein's assets held throughout the world into the hands of the Iraqis to finish the job of reconstruction there.

"In one of his boldest gestures of all, he is taking his case for biodiesel and ethanol to the world. Just yesterday was the conclusion of his meeting with the leaders of Ukraine, Brazil, Australia, South Africa, the European Union and many other key nations with vast amounts of farmland. The general reaction to the President's commitment to alternative fuels is very positive.

"Their primary topics of discussion were the increases in the planting of the fuel yielding crops, and also in the necessary refineries for production. Our head of state expressed clearly his hope that such a new partnership among nations will provide a new direction for the world that everyone will benefit from. Follow-up meetings between the incoming Secretaries of State, Interior, Agriculture and Commerce and their counterparts in those other nations already have been scheduled to iron out the details, including production goals and pricing.

"One reason world leaders in general are so happy with this development is because of the experts' claims that the supply of oil is predicted to be perhaps twenty years away from decline. In light of that, said one of them today, obviously it is in everyone's best interest to actively explore, and then to implement, the options we have. It seems to be the overall consensus that Mister Stratton's moves, if turned into policy, will go a long way to make up for the outgoing administration's lack of commitment to progress and the environment.

"Needless to say, the oil business at large is not so happy with this development, and most executives are calling the Stratton initiative 'very premature and flawed'. Mister Stratton promptly dismissed such criticism as the voices of an embittered, regressive-minded few expressing sour grapes over being excluded from any involvement in this new venture.

"He cited the fact that internal combustion engines were invented before the advent of gasoline as their fuel, which in his words never should have happened in the first place. His disdain for the oil companies and the way they've conducted business over the years came through loud and clear. It will be interesting indeed to see what becomes of those companies in the near future.

"Our incoming President laid out a big picture net gain our nation alone stands to see in the neighborhood of half a trillion dollars annually between the new biodiesel/ethanol industry and the elimination of crop subsidies. And that, as he stated, is from a totally domestic standpoint. If we become an exporter as well, we

397

stand to reap even more benefits, as does the environment of the entire planet.

"Hand-in-hand with that venture comes the very ambitious plan to upgrade our mass transit system. Mister Stratton points to the bullet trains in Japan and the maglev trains in China as systems we should move toward in regards to travel between cities and regions. He also hopes to see all major cities upgrade their systems to the point where most if not all commuters have it as a viable option. He cited the city of Boston as a good example of how it should be done here.

"The incoming Secretaries of Education and Health will lay out the proposals they in turn will submit to Congress as bills for the overhaul and reformation of their respective areas of responsibility. As has been the case with all the other major areas, we don't expect any deviation from the proposals the President-elect laid out during his campaign.

"Finally, we expect to hear a major announcement from the new administration regarding the Intelligence community and the Homeland Security Department in light of the findings of the 9/11 Commission. There is much speculation that the Homeland Security Department could be dissolved.

"There is no doubt that our next President is eager to hit the ground running. He already has not only our nation, but the whole world, abuzz with the promise of what's to come.

"Now, we go live to what will be Mr. Stratton's final press conference as President-elect..."

"...so, instead of accepting dysfunctional or outright broken institutions because that's the way it's been done for so long, we will tear those institutions down and build new ones. Better yet, we'll get them right this time. We will be receptive to new ideas and willing to give them a try as opposed to the old way of being distrustful of them because the powers that be fear losing their power. Merit, not money and connections, will pave one's way to success. The wealthy few no longer are calling the shots.

"Ok, I'll take your questions. You're first, Hal."

"Sir, there's a lot of talk about nepotism in your appointment of your brother as Director of the FBI. How do you respond?"

"I'm glad you brought that up. My response to all that crap is simple. Tom is about doing the job and doing it well- period. He's not egotistical, doesn't need the glory, doesn't care about it. He expects results and he gets 'em, and people have nothing but respect for him. They work hard for him, too. He's exactly the breed of leader we need in every important post there is. Tom has devoted his life to law enforcement and I can't think of anyone who's better qualified to lead the FBI. Those who have a problem with me appointing him will have to live with it. By the way, I hope you all will join me in wishing Tom a Happy Birthday."

"You also are getting a lot of negative press about the military brass you basically are forcing to retire."

"Another simple matter. They clearly had sided with the outgoing administration. Soldiers are supposed to put their personal feelings aside and accomplish the mission given to them, which those generals could not do. I've received many accounts of how they went so far as to subtly lean on those in their commands to vote against me. That was the final straw. Since they couldn't let their prejudice go, I'm letting them go, and that's that. Eve?"

"What is your word on trade with China, Sir?"

"It shouldn't come as a surprise that my word on trade with China is that there will be no more trade with China. They're very stubborn and selfish, and have no interest in playing fair, so we're through with them until they change their ways. The days of us turning a blind eye for reasons of political expedience are over.

"Also," John went on as he produced the cover sheet of the NAFTA document and ripped it into several pieces, "this disaster of a trade agreement is history. We will meet with Canadian officials to hammer out a more reasonable policy. As for Mexico, until the government there gets its act together, as we'll do with China we'll do with them: cut trade. You're up, Bernie."

"Sticking with the Far East, Sir, what is your timetable for starting the withdrawal of our troops from South Korea?"

"Right away. On Thursday General Swanson will hold a press briefing about that along with our withdrawal from Iraq."

The next correspondent piped up. "Sir, you were very critical yesterday of how the airline situation has been handled, or mishandled, as you put it. You really would consider a federal takeover of the airlines that have filed for bankruptcy?"

"Not only would I consider it- along with the incoming FAA Chairman I'm looking into how to make it happen. The airline industry on the whole has hemorrhaged money for the past three years to the tune of billions of dollars, and now the pensions of everyone except the executives are in jeopardy. I'm not going to sit by and let the pilots, flight attendants, mechanics and everyone else lose all their money while the executives and upper management make out like bandits; it's just not going to happen. They clearly have performed abysmally, so they'll get what they deserve for the lousy job they've done. They'll get nothing.

"This is an extension of our plan to eliminate corporate subsidies; if lots of taxpayer money has gone into failing businesses, the way I see it the American people in effect have become the new owners of those businesses. As their elected representatives, we in office become the new board of directors.

"So, yes, I'm sure there's a way we can take those failing airlines over. I plan to find the way and exercise that option as soon as I can. The same could happen with our TV stations and airwaves. They're supposed to be the property of the people- not a few corporations that only want what they approve to be broadcasted. That covert censorship doesn't work for me, and I'm sure it also doesn't work for the vast majority of the people. Abe?"

"The republicans still claim that there isn't nearly enough money in our system to bring about the reforms you and your party campaigned on. What do you say to them, Sir?"

"If that's the case, then we might need to change the monetary system."

The reporter was caught off guard. "Are you serious?"

"Absolutely. If something's broken, you fix it. If it's antiquated, you replace it. I'm sure there's a better system than the one we have now, and I would be ecstatic if we came up with it and implemented it during my administration. Just another challenge we'll gladly take on, if need be. We are the Progressives, after all," he said, grinning. "It's your turn, Wendy."

"Among other things, can we take that to mean your administration will move forward with stem cell research?"

"Yes. We're looking into all avenues of that, as we want to get back on the edge of technology in every major area. During this session you can expect to see a bill to that effect being presented to Congress for a vote."

"The religious leaders undoubtedly will be even more critical of you than they already have been."

"When it comes to progress, they usually are. Religion and those who propagate and adhere to it so dogmatically are counterproductive, and seek to keep power in their own hands.

400

"They automatically dismiss as wrong or condemn as evil anything contrary to their beliefs. Case in point is my proposal to counter the problem of welfare babies by mandating birth control for anyone on governmental assistance. A sensible solution, yet the religious community sees it as wrong. That's how they operate, and that's why we need to do what we can to minimize the influence of religion- perhaps even wean ourselves off it like we will end our dependence upon foreign oil. We really don't need religion- at least, we don't need it to be so pervasive. Furthermore, any leader who allows religion or its purveyors to influence his or her line of thought is no leader at all, as far as I'm concerned.

"Let me expand upon that, as my next point is related. For some time there has been a very disturbing trend in this nation, in part because of the heavy presence of religion. The trend I'm referring to is political correctness. I've brought this up in a few of my forums, and I think it's time we made a concerted effort to steer ourselves away from it.

"I see no good coming from a mindset that castigates a person for expressing a viewpoint contrary to that of the mainstream. I can't imagine anyone would want a culture where everyone thinks, acts and talks alike. Differences and animosities will not go away if you ignore them and put on your happy face. It is infinitely better to get them out in the open and deal with them instead of burying them and letting them germinate into antipathy or outright hatred. Live and let live. Just because someone may not see eye-to-eye with you does not mean that person is wrong or should be cut down.

"As a nation I want us to get to where we're comfortable with saying what we mean and standing by it, even if one's opinion is not in line with what most may believe. We must move toward acknowledging differences and resolving them, or at least accepting that there are points you cannot agree upon while still respecting another's right to his or her opinion.

"Through those differences, and the discourse and debate that come from them, we gain knowledge, understanding and ultimately advancement as a people, which beat the heck out of ignorance, inflexibility and intolerance."

John decided to end the conference on that note. "Sorry, gang, but that's all for now. I have to start getting ready for a big event taking place tomorrow in DC that Kim told me about- an inauguration, or something..."

401